GABAB

I0675528

TODD L. PLATEK

GBB

Copyright © 2022 by Todd L. Platek
Design Copyright © 2022 by Burns Studio Art

All rights reserved. No part of this book may be used or reproduced by any means, graphic, electronic, or mechanical including photocopying, recording, tape or by any information storage retrieval system without the written permission of the publisher except in the case of brief quotations embodied in critical articles and reviews.

ATHENS, GEORGIA

Bilbo Books Publishing

www.BilboBooks.com
bilbobookspublishing@gmail.com
(706)-549-1597

ISBN- 978-1-7364598-4-3

Printed in the United States of America
All rights reserved. Published in the United States of America by
Bilbo Books Publishing, Athens, Georgia

Dedicated to the Memory of My Mother and Father

AUTHOR'S NOTE

"Adapt or perish, now as ever, is Nature's inexorable imperative."
Mind at the End of its Tether, H.G. Wells

The human species stands at a crossroads not encountered in recorded memory. We face the challenges of two inevitabilities: the first—climate change, with its calamitous effects on the Earth's ecosystems; and the second—the potential supremacy of artificial intelligence over the human mind.

G88 is the beginning of a tale about how mankind faced these challenges and overcame them…or not.

Todd L. Platek
Athens, Georgia
August, 2021

PROLOGUE

As Joshua Lee sat on the unforgiving, oaken-yellow wooden bench outside the Assistant Principal's office about an hour after his lunch period, not once did it bother him that this was already the third time in three weeks that his teacher had lost patience with what she called his classroom antics, and the fall semester was only a month old.

The ancient bench, its seat and arms worn smooth by generations of kids like him sitting and waiting to be told off, was actually pretty comfortable, Josh thought, as he sat there, tapping his left foot to a tune he kept hearing over and over in his mind, head bobbing to the beat, losing himself in the rhythm, forgetting he was waiting for another lecture from the powers-that-be. It was a sunny mid-autumn afternoon outside, the soft golden sunbeams streaming in through the tall windows of the Main Office. Although the sunbeams didn't fall on him, they warmed the room and his spirit.

Josh became fascinated with the patterns of movement of the dust particles in the sunbeams. They moved in indiscriminate ways, all at once chaotic, mesmerizing, unpredictable. There was a deep majesty to the entire play in the airflow. He pondered the dawning realization of how he could not ordinarily see them until they revealed themselves in the sunrays. It was as if an entire world of invisible objects had suddenly failed in their inherent purpose of remaining cloaked from sight because of the power of sunlight. Were there other things that were unseen until the sun shone on them?

Slowly he transitioned into remembering what brought him to the Main Office. Damned pain in the butt, getting sent out of class for something he was being framed for—again. Not unusual; never his fault; just another day at I.S. 406, he reasoned. Anyway, on such a fine, sunny day, how bad could another lecture be?

I.S. 406 was supposed to be a real good school, at least that's what everybody told him. Mom had moved into the District just so he could attend the blue-ribbon school, though he had no idea why the blue-ribbon designation was such a big deal. Sure, the place was larger, brighter, more scrubbed down and more modern than the old school across town in which he'd done kindergarten and first grade, but who cared? The elementary school down the block had made him repeat first grade. It must have been through true grit and dumb luck, neither of which attributes anyone would automatically associate with him in matters of education, that he had made it all the way to seventh grade in I.S. 406. It wasn't exactly that he disliked the place, but after all, school was just where your mom sent you because she couldn't leave you at home alone, or wouldn't trust you there all alone, because there was nobody else to monitor you all day, and because she claimed you had to make more of your life than do tricks on the skateboard, shoot hoops, build things with Legos— no matter how motorized or computerized and awesome—when it rains and you are dying of boredom, and play computer games online all night long. Yeah, yeah, yeah. He'd heard it a million times. At the precious age of thirteen, why should he worry about such things, he snickered to himself. Mom could do the worrying for both of them, and he could save his energy for what really counted.

After what seemed a boring eternity of swinging his legs, alternately clasping his hands together while he swung, and holding on to the bench as he swung and looking around the Main Office at the ladies making believe they were working at their desks and staff workers coming and going near the wooden crisscross mailboxes for teachers' mail, sneaking glances at this frequent little visitor to the Assistant Principal's Office, a door across the room opened and there appeared in the doorway the concentrated glare of Mrs. Moskowitz beaming her "So, it's you again" frown. Frumpy Dumpty Mrs. Moskowitz beckoned with her right hand for Josh to rise and enter her domain. He didn't react immediately, because the way she motioned to him reminded him of the way Bruce Lee had dared his opponents to step closer before he delivered crushing blows. Blinking to clear his mind of that frightful image, he reluctantly descended the bench and crossed into her room, feeling her burning gaze on him at every step and sensing that the Main Office ladies were also watching, some shaking their heads, some snickering, some just grinning to themselves.

"Well, Joshua, you know where to sit. This is getting to be a regular occurrence this term, young man." Josh knew better than to respond. Anybody calling him "Joshua" instead of "Josh" obviously meant business. With an air of self-assuredness, he took his seat at the side of her massive oak desk, head erect but eyes downcast to avoid Mrs. Moskowitz's huge blue-gray eyes. He reckoned she must be at least 80 years old because she looked so old, but she couldn't have passed 100 yet, he knew, because everybody died after they reached 100. Every kid knew that. Like, duhhhh….

"Do you want to tell me why Mrs. Hardy sent you in here today?" The question was like one of those police interrogators' questions he heard on TV, where they ask you something but they already know the answer and they just want to see you squirm and sweat. They probably want to see whether you'll tell them what they want to hear or whether you'll start giving them crap. They just like to mess with you before they start slapping you around.

He sighed, not regretfully, but because this was all one huge damned inconvenience. He looked her straight in the eye and frowned. "Look, Mrs. M, I was cutting out the animals from the construction paper, like Mrs. Hardy told us to do—which was stupid anyway—hey, I'm 13, okay? What 13-year-old cuts out paper animals anyway?" he demanded. "All right, so anyway," he continued in his own self-righteous explanation, "I had to decorate my social studies panorama, see, so Dalton grabs my scissors right out of my hand and starts laughing. So I grab them back and called him a jerk and then he started pushing me and so I… well…I pushed him back. Maybe a little too hard because he fell on his butt. So what? He started it. Then he got me into trouble by tattling to the teacher that I was cursing him and whacking him and knocking him down. Well, he is a…well, ya know…a jerk. And it's not my fault if he can't stand on his own feet if somebody dishes out to him what he dished first."

Mrs. Moskowitz had exercised the full complement of her patience listening to this self-serving defense of name-calling and punching. "First of all—from what Mrs. Hardy told me— you didn't just call the boy a *jerk*. You used the F-bomb." As she saw Josh open his mouth—whether in denial or explanation, she cared not—she cut him off in a flash with a firm tone. "Don't say a word! We've had this discussion before, Joshua. We don't tolerate cursing and fighting in this school and you know that. You shouldn't do it now and certainly not when you're an adult. Now, about what you say Dalton did to provoke you, did you tell Mrs. Hardy what happened?"

"Sure. But she said I shouldn't be cursing kids and pushing them in school. Then I told her it was all Dalton's fault 'cause he started it, and then she told me to say sorry to him and wash out my dirty mouth, and I said not unless he says sorry to me first and sucks the soap too, but she ignored me and didn't even say anything to Dalton. *Man*, that little fuckin'—I'm *sorry*, okay? I'm *sorry*," he spurted, catching himself speaking in his natural but forbidden way. "I mean—that little jackass was just sitting in his chair like some goody-goody. So I refused to say sorry. But I *did* tell her I was sorry I cursed. Then she said anyway that I had to come down to see you. I mean, that's not fair! *You* think it's fair?" Josh was clearly agitated and struggling to control his temper and his mouth in the face of what he considered a downright injustice done to him. He had nothing against Mrs. Moskowitz and felt sort of sorry for her that she was so old and ugly, but he knew she had her job to do and was only trying to keep the peace. It was Mrs. Hardy whose guts he really couldn't stand.

"Look, Joshua," she said in a tired voice trying to combine compassion with a strong semblance of enforcing discipline, and shaking her head at him for effect, "you've been in here a lot in the last few weeks. This is becoming a repeat of last year. And we're only into the *second month* of school this year. I really hoped things would start turning around for you, that your behavior would improve." She peered at him in that confusing way, with eyes that reproached him and yet made a heart-felt plea for his cooperation so they could all just get along this semester.

Josh sat up suddenly, his body propelling forward in a self-defensive mode. "Hey, Mrs. M, I'm trying my best to be good. You *know* that. But it was Dalton who started it. What did I do wrong? Nothing. But he got away with it," he declared with an air of puerile righteous indignation in his voice.

Mrs. Moskowitz looked down at her desk for a moment, realizing that there might just be something to Josh's story. Lifting her pudgy, pasty, powdered face to him, she peered into his deep brown eyes and said, "You're trying your *best*? I think there's a lot more 'best' you could be doing, Joshua. And I think you know it too. Being thirteen is not easy, I know, but you need to work on your self-control. You know it's wrong to curse, don't you? And you certainly know it's wrong to get physical with classmates the way you did. Right?" She looked searchingly at him.

Josh fingered the hem of his polo shirt, a wine-red Ralph Lauren with the shield crest on the chest. He was nothing if not the best-dressed boy in class, not that he cared too much about that either. Mom wanted him to dress handsomely, and she made sure that he wore fresh clothes every day, and she made him brush his shoes, even his sneakers, clean of grime, too. "Yes," he answered begrudgingly. He knew it was useless to try to get out of this one. "But how about Dalton?" he pleaded with wrinkled brow as he sought some justice out of this situation.

"I'll talk to Mrs. Hardy, Josh. But please don't curse again, all right? And *don't* use your fists to settle problems," she said as she stood. She grinned at him as she said, "I know you're going to tell me that *everybody* used to do it in the past. Well, Josh, I was your age once too, believe it or not. I know the boys— and even a few girls—settled things with their hands. But those days are over, at least here. It's simply unacceptable nowadays, and certainly in this school. Understood?"

"*Fiiiinne,*" he said in that mocking voice of half-hearted resignation and at pains to keep a straight face devoid of the anger inside him. It wasn't really *fine* with him at all but he knew that saying it would make Mrs. M feel better, and she wasn't a bad sort anyway. It seemed he had gotten through another trial, but he knew he needed to stay out of Mrs. M's office, or else the school would send another email home to Mom, and that spelled trouble in paradise for Mr. Josh because Mom had no sense of humor about these things.

"Oh, and Josh, please no more skateboarding stunts in the schoolyard. I know you and the boys are *pros*," she said sarcastically, "and you all impress the girls greatly with your prowess on those things, but if someone tumbles and gets hurt, it's a problem for whoever gets hurt, and then in the Office, we've got accident reports to fill out, and then parents blame us for not controlling all of you and even letting you kids get hurt, and... well...you get the picture."

More roadblocks on his path to happiness. "Sure, Mrs. M, anything to make you happy," Josh cajoled, ditching the pouting just so he could get out of her office and cut the lecture short, knowing he'd blow her off ASAP.

He trudged back through the brightly-lighted hallways decorated with all sorts of arts-and-crafts projects by kids from every class. He stopped to peer at each one. The hallway walls were covered in tons of self-portrait watercolors and multi-material creations of who-knows-what. There were countless—and, by Josh's standards, superficial and boring—essays by kids about their families, their favorite pastimes, accompanied by drawings in pencil, ink, crayon and paint. Nobody told the truth in those essays. Nobody wrote about how they felt lonely and sad sometimes, or how their fathers hit them for no good reason, or how horny they were feeling. Nobody wanted to read what he really wanted to scream out loud but instead held inside, letting it ferment in his mind until sometimes he felt like raging against the unfair hand life had dealt him. You just couldn't be real in this school. If you told it like it was, they'd march you down to the school psychologist and then the shrink would call your folks in, and one thing would lead to another, and you only dug your own hole deeper. Screw it.

He lingered a couple of minutes looking at finger paintings by the squeakers, those little kindergarteners from down the street. He thought back to the days when he'd been that young. Although it had only been a few years earlier, it seemed like forever when you're 13. Had he fingerpainted too? He looked down at his hands, palms upward, trying to recall paint on them. The memory just wasn't there, and he felt something was missing from the place it ought to be, inside him. It occurred to him that was just one, and an unimportant one at that, of the happy memories he had been cheated out of.

Josh moved along and took his sweet time to look at all the artwork, hands in his pockets, craning his neck and standing on tiptoe to see the uppermost creations, because he was also playing the odds that nobody from the Main Office would telephone up to Mrs. Hardy's classroom to let her know that Josh's session with Mrs. M had ended. Nothing interesting ever happened in class anyway, so what the hell, right? Besides, it served her right if he didn't come back right away. She had overreacted and been unfair to him, and let that little fuckin' jerk, Dalton, wriggle away. Cursing, huh? Seemed like just a normal way to express his feelings. And who made these decisions, anyway, about what constituted a curse? Did somebody say a long time ago, "This is a bad word" or "You can't say that word out loud" and then everybody just followed his orders? Just more rules. Fuck the rules, especially if they didn't make sense.

Slowly, he looked around after he pushed open the door leading to the wide staircase, and, after satisfying himself that nobody was nearby, went up the down staircase, just because he wasn't supposed to. He quickly leapt two steps at a time, and when that seemed too easy, he grabbed the red-painted bannister and pulled himself along higher at three steps for each leap. By the time he had reached the third floor, he turned to consider his progress in the ascent and thought how easy it had been to come up the down staircase. He thought he'd probably not repeat that performance since it felt the same as going up the *up* staircase anyway. He had defied that rule, done the deed, and felt no different for having done it. School was full of rules. He supposed that some of them made sense. It would certainly be a mess if kids went up and down past each other on the same staircase, especially when they were in rushing to lunch and gym and dismissal. He thought about his life being hemmed in by rules, all the rules Mom set for his life at home and outside, the school's rules, rules at church, rules for walking along the street, rules for sitting in a movie theater. Rules against skateboarding on the sidewalks and against holding the backs of buses to pull him along. Rules against stealing and lying and the whole Sunday School deal of how they think God told people to act. The list went on forever. It seemed he was caught inside a spider web of countless sticky threads of rules that ensnared him and wouldn't let him just be himself, at least not right off, until he saw the sense of it. Anyway, it had been good to get this staircase rule out of his system. Test one rule at a time and see whether it made any sense anyway. Kind of like a science experiment, only he was doing rule experiments, Josh thought, as he turned from the staircase to enter his classroom next to it.

In a moment, however, life would never again be the same for Josh Lee.

1   JOSH

As I turned the doorknob and crossed the threshold into Class 7-310 sometime just after two o'clock, I felt dizzy. It was as if the floor had shifted under my feet, but I still held steady. I could have sworn I had just seen a light blue haze throughout the room, which made everyone appear just a tinge bluish. What the hell, man? But I knew that was impossible. Must have been climbing those stairs, I reasoned. The ascent had winded me, taking three steps at a time fast, and the oxygen wasn't pumping fast enough into my brain. Sure, that made sense, from what I'd learned in Science. As I breathed quickly and deeply to get my bearings, I thought I detected a faint odor like fresh sea air. My nose had always been super sensitive. Mom said it was because I was born in the Year of the Dog, so my nose was as keen as a dog's. Maybe my mind was just playing tricks on me.

Slowly I entered the room, trying not to attract any attention, but all eyes were on me. Mrs. Hardy's watery green eyes followed me to my seat, and when I looked up at her, she was squinting at me in a strange way. I knew she wasn't trying to imitate my Chinese eyes, since she scolded every kid who made fun of other kids, and since goofing on me wasn't the reason, I felt even more spooked by her unwavering glare. And it wasn't just Mrs. Hardy. All the kids were focused on me, most not squinting that freaky way, yet there was no question they were looking beaming on me in unison.

Now, I was a physical kind of guy, and I wasn't usually

scared of anyone, but this was bizarre. Mustering my courage, I smiled back at everyone, thinking that I'd get the usual "Yo, Josh" goofy grins back from them. No go, today. Nothing but straight faces shooting me blank stares. Slowly, their heads returned to focus on Mrs. Hardy as she began talking about an upcoming science project.

"As I was beginning to say, everyone," and her mug shot me a look, then swiveled back to pan the other kids, "your volcano projects are due next Thursday. Now, I want to see you design your volcanoes as realistically as possible, so look at your science books and the internet for pictures of famous volcanoes. We've talked about Mount Vesuvius which smothered and incinerated the entire ancient Roman city of Pompeii in 79 A.D., but there are so many more. When Mount Krakatoa in Indonesia erupted around 1883, the sound of the explosion—probably the loudest ever recorded—was about 172 decibels at origin and then circled the Earth three or four times, and the effects of its miles-high plumes of smoke and ash were felt for years after that. Even here in America, Mount St. Helens erupted in 1980 and the entire top and upper portion of one side of the mountain blew off, spewing poisonous ash into the atmosphere and destroying trees and vegetation for hundreds of square miles around, killing people, and so forth. Volcanoes produce lava that burns everything in its path and spew toxic smoke and dust and rocks into the atmosphere which travel around the world and can affect crops growing thousands of miles away and for years afterward."

Volcanoes were pretty cool, I had to admit. Now, don't get me wrong, I wouldn't hurt a fly, and I certainly wouldn't want my Mom or friends to have problems like being burned up or coughing a lot from poison gas after an eruption. But this was going to be a fun project. Mom was pretty creative, so I'd sucker her into designing my volcano. Her English was okay for talking to people but not good enough to write up a science report, since she was from China and only liked to speak Mandarin to me, so I'd need to get somebody from the law office she worked in to help me write up the descriptions that Mrs. Hardy wanted. I was pretty good at that. A smile here, a pat on the back there, a well-placed compliment, and I had those adults eating out of my hand. Sometimes I wondered whether they even saw it coming. And the crazy thing is, they actually felt good about doing it for me. What chumps.

Soon it was 2:40 p.m. and Mrs. Hardy told us to start cleaning up our desks and packing up for the day. I was glad to get out of there because some of those kids really got on my nerves. Mickey Cheng and Ronny Sanchez were okay, and I had kind of a crush on Alice Dooley. But Dalton Wu and his bunch were fuckin' little jerks. Goody-goodies who pretended to their parents how well-behaved they are, but picked on kids in school and made general pests of themselves. No matter how many times I had been told not to curse and even not to call anybody a jerk, I could hold off with the "fuckin" if I had to, but there was something about that word "jerk" that said everything about those kids. It sounded so gnarly. *Jerrrkkk....* When you pronounced it, your lips protruded and curled outward, and you bared your teeth, and your nose wrinkled up right into your eyes, and you snarled it right out. Mrs. Hardy was always telling us how important it is to express ourselves. Well, there you go...*jerrrkkk*. But I still got into trouble. Seems there are ways you can express yourself, but other ways you're not supposed to do it. So confusing. Something about always having to be nice, even to fuckin' little jerks. Just didn't seem natural, making you hold it inside, hidden away, until someday it burst right out of you. Say, maybe that was an idea for my volcano project...? Paint my name on the volcano, Mt. Joshua, and then Dalton's name could be drawn on the town my lava rolled over and incinerated. Yeah, I'd have to give that some thought.

The walk downstairs today, though, was unlike other afternoons. Mary didn't talk to me but just turned her head on each floor's landing to stare quickly at me. Kind of gave me the creeps. But I figured girls are like that; they run hot and cold. That's what I'd always heard, and in my experience, it was that way. No matter what age, they were mixed up. Mom would yell at me for all sorts of things, then hug and kiss me. She'd start conversations and then suddenly shift gears in mid-sentence and start going on about something totally unrelated. My sister was a mess too, but she lived away at a college in Massachusetts and worked a part-time job and never seemed to have much time for me nowadays, even on the telephone, which might not have been such a bad thing after all, since she never knew whether she was coming or going. And then there was my decrepit old granny who lived with Mom and me and was so stuck in her ancient Chinese mindset that she was the last person in the family I could deal with. Maybe someday I'd learn the reason they were so mixed up, but I don't like to sweat the small stuff. They had to deal with their own feelings, which seemed a lot more complicated than mine at this point.

When we arrived on the first floor, some kids raced for their school buses, and plenty of parents mobbed the sidewalk, most frantically waving to their little darlings to hurry them home or to some music lesson or sports group or afternoon school like I used to attend...before they kicked me out.

So, comes the first floor at dismissal and there we all were, all crammed together, everybody running off this way and that, craning his or her neck looking for parents or other adults who had come to pick them up, and one-by-one, the kids got picked up or biked or walked home. And I suddenly realized... unlike every other day, nobody today said, "So long, Josh," "See you tomorrow, Josh," or paid any attention to me. Only Mrs. Hardy said good-bye to me and even managed a tilted grin, but there was a damned strange gleam in her eye, as if she knew something I didn't.

Sure, I felt something odd, but I never let stuff like that bother me. At thirteen, life moves pretty fast, and there's no sense wasting time and energy over things that don't really affect you. That's how I roll.

2

The next morning in the schoolyard, my buddy, Mickey, was pretend-wrestling and kick-boxing with Ronny and a few others. Dalton was one of the guys playing with them. Now that struck me as a bit unusual, because Mickey and Ronny had had their own problems with Dalton. Stupid stuff, like Dalton calling names, stepping on new shoes to make them dirty, pushing kids out of line, and that kind of bullshit bully stuff. But today, they were all smiling at each other, laughing together, and even polite to each other. That got my attention.

"Yo, Mickey, how ya doin' today?" I called over to him.

"Good, Josh." The response was short and sweet, but lacked the verve that a guy gives his buddy. He seemed more intent on their game. I couldn't really blame him, though. It was a fine autumn morning, crinkled oak and elm leaves covering the schoolyard, warm shades of red and yellow and orange, some bright, some rusty. At eight in the morning, the air was still cool from the night before, fresh and brisk and dry, filling my nostrils and making me want to breathe it all the way down deep in my lungs. I had heard from Mom's boss, who grew up in New York a long time ago, that when he was a boy, the air in the city was filthy dirty but that nowadays, since cars and buses burned cleaner gasoline and there were almost no factories around, the city's atmosphere was practically pristine, as he called it. I sure was glad about that because I was fond of good smells, not bad smells. Car exhaust fumes and piles of garbage didn't do it for me.

Come to think of it, I learned all sorts of interesting things from Harry, my mom's boss. He was a white guy, and my family didn't have much contact with white people, since we were all Chinese and lived in North Queens where there were so many Chinese and Koreans. But Harry spoke excellent Mandarin and he could understand almost everything we said. Except for what my Grandma spoke. Her Northeastern Chinese accent was super heavy, and although I'd grown up listening to her, even I had to listen closely sometimes and pretend I got the whole gist of it. Mom spoke very clear, very standard Mandarin. She had grown up in Northeastern China too but had lived in Beijing quite a while. My sister spoke clearly but sometimes reverted to Grandma's way of pronouncing some words since she'd spent more time living with Grandma than with anyone else while she was growing up. Come to think of it, they each spoke Mandarin a little differently. Only I had been born in New York and they said my Mandarin sounded like Harry's, like an American speaking it. Whatever.

Anyway, Harry was a good friend of our family, almost like a member of the family. He was just about the only adult I could talk to who really understood what it was to be an American boy growing up in New York. He brought me lots—and I mean lots!—of discarded books to read from a library near where he lived and I learned about sharks and whales, knights and castles, George Washington and the American Revolution, and many other interesting topics. He'd help me with my homework, too, but he was very strict about that. Seems he'd been a real nerd and had gone to some fancy high school in New York called Stuyvesant, where only boys could attend, and they actually enjoyed working hard and getting good marks. He told me now there were girls there too, and they studied even harder than the boys. That was no surprise to me; the girls in my class were the brainiacs while the guys were busy just looking at them and thinking whatever horny guys think. Harry said he hoped I'd go there someday, and I replied that of course I could, and he'd sigh, give me a sharp look and tell me I'd better start getting serious about my schoolwork, because skateboarding wouldn't get me in there.

That sunny morning, getting into Stuyvesant wasn't on this seventh-grader's mind as I watched the boys wrestle. They hadn't invited me to join, and frankly I didn't feel like it since Mom had just fed me a big breakfast of cereal and fruit, and I'd sneaked a couple of chocolate bars into my pocket when she wasn't looking. Over near the fence, Alice, Julia Ruiz, Sally Smythe and Tabby Mason were skipping rope, getting themselves all worked up as they skipped faster, did crisscrosses and even doubles. I got off watching them sing as they jumped to the rhythms. Nah, it wasn't singing. It was chanting. My own heartrate rose as I listened to them chant over and over again and watched their feet and the ropes mingle together, in complete harmony, like a puzzle with moving parts that just kept fitting together in midair. I had learned how to jump rope in Tae Kwon Do class and I usually jumped rope for a few minutes before each basketball game I picked up in school or the park. I knew how the girls felt. "Be one with the rope, so that your legs and the rope are all part of your body, following one flowing rhythm," my Tae Kwon Do master used to say. Yeah, those girls were getting it.

Around 8:45 the bell rang and we formed lines by class. There was Mrs. Hardy at the head of the line, beady moist green eyes gazing over each of us like a mother duck making sure all her little ducklings were lined up and ready to follow through the pond. She wore a flowery dress with a light green sweater buttoned high at the neck only, so the sweater spread out open like a fan across her chest. Man, she looked like a freshly mown lawn today with that sweater and all the dress's flower stems matching her eyes. Her gray hair was rolled up on top of her head and held together in the back with a shiny pin, sort of a piece of the inside of a seashell that reflected the sunlight and blinded you for a moment when she turned her head and you were standing in the wrong place.

3

JOSH

We filed into the classroom, put jackets and sweaters into open lockers, took our chairs down off our tables and sat down. The Green Witch Queen—my nickname for old Hardy—made me sit off to the side in the front because I was considered a disruptive influence on the other kids, including both the goody-goodies and the borderline mess-ups. Despite GWQ pigeon-holing me as a self-absorbed boy in his own world, today I noticed the kids around me acted odd, I mean, fuckin' weird. They all were sitting up straight the same way, heads erect, hands folded on their desks and focused on Mrs. Hardy. Every kid had hands on the desk about six inches from his and her body—I mean, a *uniform* six inches by my quick observation. The eyes in every face were like trained pups fixed on their human master and waiting for the next command, in hopes of a pat on the head and a treat. Man, I could almost swear every pair of ears was perked up like a German Shepherd's. Mrs. Hardy stood at the front of the room—I'm talking the absolute median point at the front of the room—erect in all her verdant majesty, the GWQ viewing her royal subjects. This silent scene remained in freeze-frame for at least 30 seconds. Talk about being creeped out! From my usual slouching position, I unconsciously sat up straight as I panned the whole motionless crowd. Something totally fuckin' bizarre was happening here.

JOSH

Mrs. Hardy's face wore a look of imperious satisfaction over how her day was beginning. Her posture would have been the envy of a U.S. Marine drill sergeant. Without moving her head, her eyes shifted to the very edge of her range of vision to peer at me. At first, I didn't notice those shifty eyeballs on me since my mind was trying to wrap itself around this abnormal situation of some 25 kids looking like robots. Then I felt the heat of her eyeballs and my scalp itched but I didn't dare to scratch it.

I knew I was not exactly a favorite of hers since she delighted in berating me and took sadistic pleasure in always threatening to send me down to the Assistant Principal's office. On those several occasions when she actually ejected me, her face had first contorted—in anger or joy, I sure couldn't tell—so that her upper lip drew back like a wolf baring its teeth before pouncing on its prey. But she never yelled at me. She snipped and sniped sarcastically at me all the time. Did that belittle me? Yeah, right, like it might? I knew who I was and no way was this old biddy getting under my skin.

But this morning's situation was something novel. Here I was, an involuntary observer of a bunch of kids I'd known for years suddenly all gone zombie on me, and unsure whether the GWQ was going to start flying around the room snapping off people's heads or zap us with laser eyebeams or start talking in alien tongues while darting out her two-foot-long flapping tongue. Freakyyyyyy.

With hands slowly raised to her chin level, looking straight, left and right, Mrs. Hardy clapped thrice in rapid succession. She then appeared to relax her posture, as did all the kids.

"Good morning, students!" Mrs. Hardy said in an energetic, syrupy voice which portended nothing good but work ahead of us for the next few hours. "Good morning, Mrs. Hardy," came the fervent response in unison. There followed at least 15 seconds of silent mutual and mysterious gazing between Mrs. Hardy and the class. Too fuckin' weird! I relaxed, drooped, and wandered back into my own private realm of thoughts.

"Joshua!" she suddenly and unexpectedly cried out. Holy

shit! I almost jumped out of my seat from the shock. What the hell!?

"Yeah, Mrs. Hardy? What?" I replied in as calm a voice as I could muster and fake since my heart was in my throat from the trauma of her screech ripping through my being. This was turning into the Second Act of a damned horror show.

"Sit up straight, Joshua! Don't you see how everyone else is sitting? What are you waiting for?!" she derisively exclaimed.

I took the bait and turned in my seat to look at the others. They looked less rigid than when they had first walked into the classroom, yet just as poised to obey. Nobody slouched like me and everyone had placed notebooks to the left of the desks, sharpened pencils in hand for their early morning torture-by-math.

I shrugged and said defensively, "I didn't know you wanted notebooks and pencils out right away. And, by the way, this is already seventh grade. Why can't we use pens? We haven't used pencils since third grade. That's kid stuff."

She glared at me for a few seconds. I tried to meet her gaze and wondered how I would react if she shot laser beams at me, like Cyclops in the X-Men. My hands quickly went to the underside of my desk which I would try to flip over in a flash to hide behind and deflect the laser beam rays. Always need to think fast, act fast.

"Young man, you are here to learn. Part of learning is to prepare the proper materials in advance. The materials must be in front of you. You were instructed by me to use pencils only. Is that a problem?" she snapped as she mocked me.

Now that I felt the odds were against her shooting laser beams at me, I sighed and relaxed. "Whatever you say," I replied with increasing calm, my customary boredom accenting my speech.

"Thank you, Mr. Lee. It's always a pleasure to have you with us here," she cynically responded, the corners of her mouth pulling themselves back and downward and her nostrils flaring as her eyelids also pulled apart to reveal huge, all-seeing eyeballs. But she must have caught me rolling my eyes, because she added, "If this is all too much effort for you, Mr. Lee, and you'd prefer not to accept our classroom protocol, I'm sure the Principal will be able to help you gain a clearer understanding of your role here."

JOSH

I looked down at my desk and ignored her snide remonstration. I narrowed my eyes in consternation and thought to myself, "Shit. This is going to be *some* fuckin' day."

And it was.

4

HARRY

It seems like ages ago that I first met Josh's mom, Jane Zhang. The memories flow as video streams in my brain. I haven't much else left. Yet I still exist for Josh.

She was a paralegal working in a small law office in the Chinese community in Flushing, Queens, and I needed one in my office there. I had just wrapped up a lengthy career in admiralty law, a distinguished field of law that was sinking faster than the *Titanic*. Hence, in my sunset years, I decided to use my various professional talents and thereby change course for what I hoped would be more prosperous waters and active ports, so to speak.

I had heard of Jane through friends there and just rang her up on a cold call one day to see how she would react. She took the call and we spoke for about three minutes during which time she satisfied herself that mutual friends had indeed put me on to her. A couple of days later I interviewed her, and despite her English being rudimentary though passable, her talent was her in her ability to work with the Northeast Chinese community, formerly known to Americans as Manchurians, that was growing in New York. She was about 40 years old and dressed to kill like a name-brand junkie in three-inch heels. She was a beautiful woman who knew it. She was also a complicated person with a past to match, as I would later learn, drip by drip. America was a great place for a person with a past. America still evoked the same aura of possibilities then as it had throughout the past 400 years—a new world and chance to lock the past in a distant corner of one's mind and start anew. The past, however, has an irksome quality of seeping through sealed places to taint the present. America more often proved to be an oily film in the mind through which the past crept.

Arriving in America, Jane quickly realized that her sharp business acumen, knack for manipulating people and willingness to work day and night would lead her to achieve her chief goal of surviving and then hopefully flourishing. With only the equivalent of an associate's degree in China, she joined some local American lawyers and taught herself immigration legal procedures, if not the intricate laws behind the procedures. She attracted clients like a blooming flower in summer attracts bees. She looked swell and had the gift of gab and a mind like a steel trap. Moreover, she actually cared about the clients' problems and could be an ideal assistant to a lawyer.

We worked well together. She was especially glad that my Mandarin was fluent enough so she and I rarely spoke English. I could deal directly with the clients in Mandarin if necessary and could read most of their Chinese documents. After translations were done by our staff, I compared the Chinese and English versions to confirm accuracy, often catching mistakes and making sure everything read fluidly like American English, not Chinglish. Jane blamed me for being too picky, but since it was my name on the documents that went into court or government agency offices and I wouldn't compromise on accuracy and quality, I called the shots. Little by little, the local community learned that too and, with Jane's already strong reputation for hard work and more attention than most local law firms put into their work, our clientele increased.

I was to discover, however, that working with Jane involved more than just paying a salary. Jane was, by choice, a single mother with a small boy. Inasmuch as I was a widower, she assumed I had no other obligations beyond practicing law, and so she prevailed upon me become a mentor to Josh from the time he was about five. There really wasn't any room for negotiating, due to Jane's proclivity not to ask whether I could help, but to presume that I had outright signed on for this chore after hiring her as my paralegal, since that meant I was somehow obligated to be involved in her life's mission of helping to raise the boy. Not what the ordinary boss expects from the ordinary employee.

Not that I objected too much. Over time, Jane and Josh had come to mean more to me than merely employee and child. Jane was a strong person whom I admired. She had made some bad decisions during her life but had kept putting one foot in front of the other to make adjustments and build a stable life for Josh and herself. In this life, if a person can help another person, it's a *mitzvah*—a good deed—that is its own reward. Call it good karma if you like, although I never had any expectation or hope of a *quid pro quo* or payback. I had long ago learned that the opportunity to give of oneself to others is a rare privilege for which the giver is transformed and enlarged.

So began a special relationship with young Josh. I had three grown children and, in my younger years, had relished spending all my free time raising them, and looked forward to spending some time with this very intelligent and capable boy while I still had the energy. He proved very often, however, to be so extremely strong-willed that I had doubts about whether I was still up to the task. I wasn't as young as I had been when rearing my own three, and this little fellow was quite a challenge. Acting in accordance with the usual rules imposed by adults was not his strong point. Arithmetic was a painful chore. English assignments were performed in the most perfunctory manner. No matter how much his mother or teachers or I tried to explain his errors to him, his response was generally that of disinterest and lack of concern for accuracy. "I don't care" was frequently thrown back at us, sometimes in an offhand manner and other times in frustration. He often appeared to have such a short attention span that the school teachers and administrators believed he had an Attention Deficit Disorder that required treatment with medication. Yet when Josh did what he enjoyed, such as building huge structures and machines with Erector sets or playing computer games, his power of concentration was unshakeable and he would not be deterred from his task for hours until completion to his satisfaction. His mother felt he was a boy with a lot on his mind who didn't need any medication. He had no dad at home, a mom who worked incessantly to support the family and spent her rare free time delving into Judeo-Christian religious mysteries during Bible study when not jogging, cooking and cleaning like a demon, an elder sister who explored and enjoyed many aspects of American life since arrival in the U.S. as a young teenager, and a Chinese relic of a grandmother who drank in New York like it was a health tonic. It wasn't the kind of family I'd grown up in more than a half-century earlier, and I was just glad for each day there was no report of injuries from hanging onto moving cars while skateboarding. The rest would have to fall into place, if that was his destiny.

My faith in Josh was going to be reaffirmed in ways we couldn't even begin to imagine in those early days.

5

lass went on as usual that day. *Booooorrrring*. The other kids were a little more twerpy than usual. I started wondering whether they were taking Mrs. Hardy's "You are here to learn" line too seriously. I mean, Mickey and Alice were like a tag-team running back and forth to the old pencil-sharpener that was bolted down near Mrs. Hardy's desk, constantly making sure their pencils were prickly sharp. Like, since when did that matter? Ronny, often an annoying wise guy, had his hand up an awful lot to answer the teacher's questions. Other kids were actually taking notes as the teacher spoke. This was starting to catch my attention. I didn't usually have interest in what my classmates were doing, but things were out of the ordinary today, to say the least. Like, suddenly everybody was on the goody-goody track. Even Dalton, my arch-nuisance, seemed calm and focused on his books as class proceeded, not looking to his left or right.

When the lunch bell rang, Mrs. Hardy's assistant teacher, Mr. Moselli, marched us down to the cafeteria. I was not a bag-lunch guy since my mom was too busy to make me lunch. Anyway, she was so used to eating Chinese food every day that she didn't know about making sandwiches, so I ate the hot meals the school made. They weren't half bad. Cheeseburgers and hamburgers, pizza, hot dogs, mac-and-cheese, fries, cookies. Once in a while you got a carton of spoiled milk and that was gross, all sour, so I always hustled the lunch ladies for orange juice, even though they said it was just for breakfast. But I gave them my special wink, told them how nice they looked today, and they just smirked and handed over the juice. Smooth operator. That was me.

I always ate fast so that I could get out to the yard to play ball longer. That day, however, it was starting to rain outside and I was feeling a little ambitious anyway, so I went down to the library in the school basement. Miss Daisy was the librarian and she was sitting at her desk, nibbling carrot sticks. I never knew whether Daisy was her first or last name, and that sort of confused me, since nobody called me 'Mr. Josh' or Mom 'Miss Jane.' Just one of those many things you ponder but never go further to figure out and then just forget about because you decide it really doesn't matter anyway.

"Hi ya, Miss Daisy. How are you today?" I greeted her as I strolled in, flipping her off a mock salute and my signature "I'm making believe I care about you" smirk, the kind where the eyebrows are knit closely together and you squeeze your eyes open a little more, and the ends of your mouth curl upward, and you look the person square in the eyes, and you tilt your head at, oh…say…a 15° angle altogether producing a sensitive and compassionate appeal. Man, grown-ups eat that stuff up, but you better hope they don't then start spilling their guts and giving you a clinical report about their health or other problems, which you never wanted to hear in the first place, otherwise you get stuck listening and the pretending-you-care act becomes a painful waste of time.

"I'm very well, Joshua. So nice to see you here today." I liked Miss Daisy because she always had a smile for me and was easy-going on me, even if a bit stuffy. She always addressed every kid by the entire first name. She was sort of an old-fashioned lady, always very polite, but somehow I got the impression she genuinely cared. Come to think of it, maybe she was a whole lot better at the "sensitive and compassionate" act than I was, but that made sense, since she was so much older than I and had had years to perfect the move. Maybe this was another reason to follow the advice of learning from your elders.

"Yeah, I finished lunch, but since it's starting to rain out and I left my jacket in class, I figured I'd come down here."

"Well that's swell, Joshua." Swell? Who said 'swell'? Harry was the only one I knew who talked that way. He said 'groovy' too, when he meant happy. So now I knew Miss Daisy was old, despite her brown hair. And I noticed how she slick she was—she just said it was swell and left it at that—she didn't get suckered into a long song-and-a-dance about my thoughts and problems. Yup—observing these old folks could teach a guy an awful lot if he paid attention to the details.

I walked over to the bookcases and started perusing the shelves. The library had that comfortable, cozy smell of books and old paper and wooden bookcases and well-trodden blue-green carpets, with chairs and tables that always seemed just a little too low to the ground. The walls were covered with posters of people holding books and looking straight at you with goofy grins, like they were selling the book they were holding. Miss Daisy once asked me whether I recognized any of them, and when I said I only recognized a couple of them, she giggled and patiently told me who each person was. Actors, basketball players, other famous people whose names I'd heard of but had no idea who they were. Very patient lady and one of the few good ones at I.S. 406.

I noticed the *Inkspell* and Nancy Drew and Hardy Boys mysteries, *The Hobbit* and *Lord of the Rings*, most of which I'd already read, and books about girls being mean to each other while the nicest girl never fits in with the others and takes shit from them, which I thought were just plain stupid, since mean girls don't bother reading at all and nice girls just get more depressed and self-righteous reading that crap. Saw the book about the boy who gets marooned with only a hatchet to use for survival, and always thought that was irrelevant to my life because why would I ever need a hatchet to survive in New York City, unless the whole city was totally fucked-up with zombies. Kind of far-fetched. And, unless the city was running wild with zombies, then under normal circumstances, I'd only get arrested for looking like some sort of crazy, dangerous kid, so what was the use of me reading about the boy surviving with his hatchet?

Harry used to give me lots of books and, if he had time,

he'd even talk to me about them, so I was no stranger to the printed word. I had liked funny books like the *Wimpy Kid* diaries and *Capt. Underpants* because they were silly and took my mind off my problems and made me laugh. Then I got into the mysteries and spy stories he supplied me with. Sometimes he even opened the books he especially liked and read a part to me that had meant a lot to him. One of his favorites was *The Human Comedy*, about a family in California during World War II. I read it and have to admit, it was corny but pretty touching. I think I even got a little teary at certain parts. Harry was kind of my literary guru, my Master Splinter or Yoda of book-learning. But today I was feeling like I needed an adventure to lift my spirits. I found a book called *The Once and Future King* about King Arthur. Now there was one awesome dude. The guy looked gnarly all dressed in shiny armor and holding a magical sword that was destined only for him and riding on a mighty horse that somehow supported all that weight. I could hear the sharp metallic clanging of sword on sword, the pounding of the king's huge charger galloping across the battlefield, expansive chest plowing through enemy soldiers, eyes bulging and nostrils snorting. Damn! I wanted to be as bad as he was! He probably had all sorts of fun, impressed the hell out of girls, and everybody jumped when he said boo. Nobody much listened to me, but, what the hell, I guess that was all right. I did my own thing and got by just fine.

Just as I was settling down and getting into the King Arthur story, the bell rang to signal the end of lunch hour. "See ya, Miss Daisy," I said as I put the book back on the shelf and left.

"You have a good afternoon, Joshua. Be sure to come back soon." She was a cheerful lady who never hassled me. I smiled at her and waved goodbye as I sauntered out of the room. She was *some* different from Mrs. Hardy. Thinking of that bitch made me shudder. Mom always told me life wasn't easy, and boy, she wasn't kidding.

As I walked out of the library, I passed by the janitor's office. The door was halfway open and the janitor, Mr. Grommel, was there with his assistant, Mr. O'Mara. They were facing at an angle from the doorway, standing over a worktable on which was a foot-high round yellow plastic container. Both men were wearing plastic goggles and masks that covered their noses and mouths, and I assumed it was the ammonia they used for cleaning the floors every afternoon after school let out. But just then, I got a whiff of the same sea breeze I'd smelled the day before, when I'd entered my classroom coming back from the Assistant Principal's office.

I noticed that Mr. O'Mara, a chubby guy who wore the same grimy red plaid shirt and dirty overalls every day, was wearing plastic gloves to stir the contents of the container with a big wooden stick like the doctor depresses your tongue with, but way larger, while Mr. Grommel intently watched. Just then, Mr. Grommel's telephone rang and he removed the face mask to answer the phone. I quickly edged backwards, but could still see the action through the wide space where the door was hinged to the wall. Mr. Grommel listened for a few moments while the caller spoke. Mr. O'Mara had stopped stirring and listened closely as Mr. Grommel spoke.

"That's right, Mrs. Dorsey," Mr. Grommel replied in a serious voice. "We're preparing it now. It'll be ready at 2:00 o'-clock, just like yesterday. Do you have instructions for us about how often we should be doing this?" I could hear him say as I peeked through the hinges.

"I see. Well then, we'll need to discuss a schedule for ordering the mix." He fell silent for another few seconds while the caller spoke, and then turned to glance near the door. I quickly jerked my head back from the space where I was peeking.

"I understand," he said. "Only O'Mara and I know at this point. We'll certainly keep it that way." I resumed peeking. He hung up the telephone, shifted his gaze to Mr. O'Mara, and they nodded to each other. Mr. O'Mara kept stirring whatever was in the container.

"Watch that you don't spill any of that on yourself, the crap stains everything sky-blue and there's no way to wash it out." Mr. Grommel then moved aside and, with one hand, pushed the door closed, although he never diverted his eyes from Mr.

O'Mara and the yellow container.

I was pretty sure they never noticed me. I was curious as hell about what they were doing. I'm no chemist, but this goop they were preparing didn't smell like any ammonia for cleaning floors. And what about that two o'clock stuff? But you know what they say about curiosity and the cat, and even though I wasn't superstitious, I was smart enough to be careful. I went back upstairs to the cafeteria and caught up with the tail-end of the kids going up to class. No way was I going to mention this to anybody until I had a better handle on it.

6　　MRS. DORSEY

So much has changed since my youth. New York was totally different when I was a girl growing up here seven decades ago. America was so different. At my advanced age, I have the luxury of looking back on a fine life and long career in public education. Memories of the many thousands of children who have been taught in schools under my administration warm my heart. Now, as Principal of I.S. 406 however, I'm faced with the responsibility of preparing a new generation of children in ways never implemented before. I believe my purpose has never been more urgent. And now I have the means to make radical changes.

In the 1950's, my parents were happy people in a country growing by leaps and bounds. We knew everyone in the neighborhood and you could count on one hand the number of kitchen tables and backyards for three blocks in any direction that I and my two brothers hadn't sat around and played in. That was the America I remembered, filled with people of every origin: Irish, Jews, Greeks, Italians, Puerto Ricans, Africans, you name it, we had them. That was life in North Flushing, Queens, in the city that never slept. Dad's New Yorker war buddies from three years of fighting against the Nazi horrors in Europe, and the GI Bill, convinced him, a Midwestern farm boy, to return with them to the Big Apple to try his luck. But my life story began much earlier than that. My great-great-great-grandparents on my father's side, Elias and Amelia Sharpe, had come from a village in the midlands of England in the early nineteenth century, poor tenant farmers with no hope of a better life there, lured by the promise of plentiful, cheap land here. With hard work and a strong faith, good health and a ton of luck, a family could accomplish anything. They had arrived in New York and after a few years of working for seed money, headed to the Midwest to farm, well before the Civil War. They'd gotten rich in Iowa after 20 years of farming, buying land and extending their holdings. They lost some children to disease and misfortune, raised more to adulthood, and those begat many more, and so it had gone on and on for over 100 years. As America's fortunes grew, so did the family. I still had family in Iowa, Nebraska and a half-dozen other states.

Since the end of WWII, we thought we'd made the world a safer place. We were only fooling ourselves. We were so flawed that we couldn't handle the awesome responsibility. We were rotting from within, ripping ourselves apart because we didn't have the ability to change or the faith that only with change could humanity find respite from its ceaseless and sadistic cycles of hatred and destruction that are inbred in our DNA as a species. Our instinctual flaws made us betray the potential the Maker had provided for us to find Eden again.

The world is too large and chaotic now. Too many choices, too many opinions. We stand on the brink of epidemics, climatic shifts and disasters, and impossibly unbending opinions, convictions and divisions, all of which threaten to rip asunder the basic fabric of life as we've come to know it. Demagogues whip up public sentiment and exploit deep-seated prejudices into explosive hatreds that let loose the most horrible instincts in the human animal. Some say the great experiment we called America is being exposed as a sham, nothing but what it probably always was, from the early 1600's to now—a financial venture meant to enrich oligarchs and their money-hungry investors. Political parties polarize around vastly conflicting ideals that splinter the entire population into warring factions. Anarchy looms if we don't root out and cure the cancer of human nature.

Now, for the first time, we have the tools to create a type of harmony and stability—a lasting and constructive and all-encompassing happiness—that never existed in the past. We have the technology to eradicate bias and prejudice of every sort. We can fashion a society which runs smoothly and where people are genuinely compassionate with each other, where we all think in the same, useful direction. We can finally set things right. It has to happen. It will happen. The alternative is awful to contemplate.

7   JOSH

Back in class and still wondering what the hell Mr. Grommel and Mr. O'Mara had been cooking up in the janitor's room, GWQ Hardy began the afternoon session in the same way as usual. The woman was a creature of habit and I could predict what she would generally say when I looked at the clock. "Good afternoon, students. I trust everyone is re-energized and ready to learn!" Sure, whatever.

"Take out your math workbooks and let's begin on page 39 with geometric shapes and calculation of their perimeters and areas," Mrs. Hardy barked. Everyone responded with alacrity. That means speed. I learned that word this morning, and Harry told me that if I use a new word three times in one day, it will be mine forever. So, that was "alacrity #1." I would be sarcastic and say "big fuckin' deal," but Harry was a good guy and I knew he always had my back when Mom scolded me for something wrong I did—or something good I should have done but didn't do—no matter whether it really happened or she only suspected me—and I knew he sincerely wanted me to do well. So, I'll be serious now and "alacrity #1" goes up on the scoreboard, awaiting "alacrity #2" and "alacrity #3."

"Ronny, please come up to the blackboard and do the first example for everyone," Mrs. Hardy beckoned.

"Yes, Mrs. Hardy." His crisp response issued forth without a moment of delay. He pushed his chair back neatly, stood up and to the side, and pushed the chair back squarely to the desk.

That caught my eye because it was a bit out of character for that joker. He then marched up to the blackboard with his workbook in hand, took a piece of chalk, drew the diagram of the rectangle just as it appeared in the workbook, numbered each side, and wrote "Perimeter = 20 inches" and "Area = 16 square inches." He turned to face Mrs. Hardy, who stood at the front of the room near the windows.

"Very nice, Ronny. Class!!" she pivoted and looked at everyone. "Any questions?" Her bark sounded more like a threatening challenge than an invitation. Hell, I had nothing to say. We'd learned this stuff in fourth or fifth grade, and this was just beginning-of-the-year review. Any dummy who had a question would have been a total zero.

From where I sat, I panned the room. Fuckin' demented. All the kids sat up straight, eyes forward. Then, in unison, from the entire class there erupted a confident "No, Mrs. Hardy." I tried to keep a straight face and not let on that this was totally freaking me out.

This pattern of coordinated behavior continued through another 12 examples of increasing difficulty. I felt like I was observing a choreographed performance. I also felt like I was the odd man out, but that was nothing unusual. What was unusual was that all these kids were moving and talking in lockstep with each other. I mean, *all*. Mrs. Hardy looked approvingly at the class, eyes reflecting accomplishment at her chosen profession. For me, however, she reserved her snide side glances. Mr. Moselli stood near me as if he wanted to watch over me, to monitor the mutant. He was a creepy, tall, skinny guy with round, wire-rim glasses that accentuated his two pale gray, droopy eyeballs that just stared at people. From time to time, I would steal glances at him out of the corner of my eye just to make sure he wasn't about to come breathing down my neck and take a bite with his pointy teeth. Sometimes I thought he might be one of those rare vampires who comes out in the daytime.

Since today's synchronized "Children of the Corn" reaction by everyone in class was a first, I figured I'd better play along. I didn't need another nasty Hardygram to my mother this early in the school year, because Mom was already giving me flak from the first few. I sat up, did my best to stay focused, but also prayed Mrs. Hardy wouldn't call on me since I hadn't been paying any attention to math for the last week and didn't have a freakin' clue how to do the last few of those examples. Somehow, my prayers were answered. My straight-up act worked and, despite getting sly sideways looks from her, Mrs. Hardy laid off me. I'd have to keep this routine of looking serious in mind for the next time I had no idea what the hell was going on in class.

Math ended and next was social studies. We all took out our textbooks and, again, all the kids moved with collective precision. This had been my classmates' *modus operandi* all day and it was kind of getting on my nerves. I mean, I seriously needed a break from this one-ring circus. Ronny, Mickey, and especially Dalton, were just not being their usual selves. And the girls? Forget it. It was like they were out to prove they were on the road to Harvard.

As I was paging through the textbook and looking at pictures of ancient Rome, my nostrils picked up that familiar scent of ocean air. Only this time the smell wouldn't dissipate. It lingered while I was leafing through the book. When I looked up from the book, I was astounded!

The air had that sky-bluish tinge I had seen yesterday, but this time, I realized it was real, not just something I was imagining, as I had thought the day before.

As I looked around the room, I saw that every kid was sitting up straight, head perfectly poised with chin about 90° perpendicular to the throat, eyes closed, face totally at peace and expressionless, nostrils inhaling deeply. GWQ was standing at attention in the front of the room, eyes shut and breathing it all in. Mr. Moselli was standing near the clothing closets, all of his tall skinny body straight as an arrow, eyelids down and breathing in the blue mist like he had been transported to another world and I was watching his trip. What the fuck?

Were they all on the same trip? Were they all communing with each other in the blue haze dimension? What the hell was going on? I was more shocked than scared. What should I do? I was in the middle of a horror movie full of actors who knew their cues, but I had no idea this scene was coming and what the next scene would be because nobody had handed me a script.

And that was when my eye caught the big round clock on the wall at the back of the classroom. No mistaking it. The little hand was on "2," and the big hand was ever-so-slightly to the right of "12"!

Suddenly I remembered overhearing Mr. Grommel talking to the Principal, Mrs. Dorsey, about having "it" ready for two o'clock. Here we were at two o'clock and the blue gas was permeating every cubic inch of the room. I was breathing it too but I felt no effect. I wasn't happy, sad, sleepy, energized, or anything else. I felt the same as usual. Yet everyone in the room was in a trance, like those kung-fu monks who meditate for hours before springing into action.

I stood up. Nobody noticed. I walked a few paces from my desk. Nobody stirred. Mrs. Hardy was in the same trance as all the rest of them. I walked to the classroom's front door and looked out. Nobody was in the hallway. I looked up at the clock on the back wall. It looked like 2:05 now. The blue gas was thinning out and the air was clearing up. I ran back to my seat with my heart racing. Nobody moved a muscle.

I sat up straight, like the other kids, and pretended to be in the same trance, one eye open so I could follow along with whatever might happen next. Luckily, I didn't have to do this for too long, for the first sounds I heard were three loud handclaps. It had been Mrs. Hardy clapping as if to awaken everyone from some sort of magic spell.

I opened my other eye and looked at her. She appeared more alert and determined than ever. I looked around at the other kids. They all seemed bright and bushy-tailed, more energetic than before. Nobody looked disoriented, spaced out. Nobody looked surprised. It was as if they had just been given extra doses of energy drinks and were skipping along in the passing lane. It was as if time had stood still for those few minutes when they had all zoned out. Harry had told me about meditation and how you control your breathing and let your thoughts slide away, so that all that exists is you and the air coursing through you on a whole different plane of consciousness, and how the great masters could focus so deeply that even if the building around them was burning down, they'd just keep meditating. Was this what had just happened in my classroom? Fuckin' awesome!

Old Hardy sailed right into her song about volcanoes, practically ending the very same sentence she'd begun five minutes earlier, before the blue mist had taken over. Since it was only about 40 minutes until the dismissal bell rang, each kid gave a quick explanation about her or his volcano project plan. For the first time that I could recall, my classmates actually acted respectfully toward each other, focusing on each speaker, and some even taking notes! A real polite and attentive kind of interestedness that was not the way this bunch of intelligent and rowdy 13-year-old kids usually behaved, especially after two in the afternoon when the autumn sunshine outside the windows beckoned temptingly to all of us with the promise of all sorts of fun in the schoolyard. What a bunch of little ladies and gentlemen. I continued to play along with the act, but you can bet this was nothing but freaky.

As we walked downstairs for dismissal, Mary Jackson was quiet, as she had been the day before, but as she left the school building, she turned to me, gave me a muted smile and said, "Hope you have a nice afternoon, Josh."

"You too, Mary," I responded, not sure whether I should return her bland look with a similarly creepy smile or a more spontaneous one. "See you tomorrow."

Mary gave me another strange, wide-eyed look, that plastic semi-grin frozen on her face, then left. Mrs. Hardy was similarly grinning as she wished each child a good afternoon. When she turned to me as I was walking out of the building, she said, "I'm so glad you were in class all afternoon, Josh. I look forward to seeing you tomorrow." Her big green eyes glinted like emeralds swimming in the sunlight which slanted through the school's front doorway through which she released all of us to the adults waiting outside for us, and then she bestowed a warm smile on me. First smile of the fall term from the GWQ. Totally freaked me out. I stared at her for a couple of moments not knowing whether I should smile back or just start running and never look back. On an impulse, I grinned at her and said, "Uhhh, sure," nodded my head, straightened my back and skateboarded into the real world of the sidewalks and streets of Bayside.

This was the weirdest icing on the strangest cake of a day I'd ever had at I.S. 406, and I'd had plenty of odd days there. There was something bad wrong going on in this school but I wasn't going to let it take me over. I was going to figure out what the real deal was here.

8   JOSH

S ince no afterschool program would take me, and she didn't trust me to do my homework if I was alone at home— smart woman—Mom had no choice but to let me stay in her office. Harry was cool about this, since he agreed with just about anything Mom needed to do when it came to taking care of me, Grandma, Sister or herself, if it involved time in or out of the office. Mom left work most afternoons to drive to I.S. 406 to fetch me since experience had taught her that when I took the public bus from school to her office, I usually dawdled and played ball first or skateboarded around and bought stuff to eat and frittered away most of the time anyway, and so that day was no different.

I should mention—only because, since you're reading this, you need to know how I roll—I didn't skateboard to waste time. It was my intergalactic transport from the boredom of being trapped by two feet on the ground. That skateboard was my ticket to peace and love and happiness, to feeling I was *somebody*, to knowing who I was. I felt the world that whirled under my feet pulse electrically through me as I surfed the rough sidewalks and smooth asphalt streets. I felt the exhilarating challenge in every second of scoping out and avoiding every crack in the pavement and every pothole in the gutter so I wouldn't spill head-over-heels. My ears were attuned to every automobile within a hundred feet of me and I calculated, in some unconscious, in-my-brain sort of way, whether they were buses or trucks or cars, how close they were behind me, how fast they were approaching, and how I needed to slope and sail to stay on course along my winding pathway. Equally amazing was how every pigeon in the road, every single time, waited stupidly until I was practically careening over it before it magically flew off only inches from my wheels; man, oh man, how the hell their plump bodies made such glorious thrust and lift all of a sudden was something I could only wonder at and dream of accomplishing myself, impossible as that would be. Hell, it was *all* "every," because I was 100% in tune with every single bit of the experience. Life on the board was *everything* all at one time and I lived *every* tiny non-stop moment of it as if it might be my last moment, because God forbid I stopped being in sync in *every* way, that could be my last moment of being a whole person before crashing into a car or bus and scraping my jaw as I hugged the street or sidewalk, or becoming the new hood ornament on a garbage truck and replacing the filthy stuffed animal that the driver had put there before I took its place.

In the sweltering heat and sanity-draining humidity of a New York summer, the odor of the tar rising in waves from the softened asphalt was intoxicating, and in the cold, the rush of chill air that stiffened the same asphalt whipping against my face made my body tingle from head to toe. The skateboard wasn't just some dumb thing, some inert piece of wood or fiberglass with wheels. It was my slumbering Frankenstein monster before the lightning of a gazillion racing electrons and protons and neutrons shocked that vision of madness to life. It needed me to imbue it with life, and in turn, it transformed my legs into the chassis, my feet into a steering wheel, my arms into retractable stabilizers, and my brain into the master control panel that sped faster than any computer because computers don't know shit about what it takes to skateboard and feel the power and conquer the fright. Mom just couldn't understand, no matter how many times I told her, how I felt the most minute bumps in the ground in my toes and instantaneously those ten toes told the brain how to move every limb on the body and every muscle in those limbs? She was clueless to the fact that the board begged me, demanded that I control it, that I empower it to cruise everywhere I commanded it to glide. It needed me to make it live, and I needed it to make life throb in me.

That skateboard taught me to respect fear. The board was intoxicating joy and death-defying fear all mixed up altogether. I knew I was nothing compared to the weight and power of the cars all around me. I knew I could be crushed like a bug the moment I foundered. I was scared shitless most of the time, but I learned to respect that fear. I learned to embrace that fear until I felt my body shake with fright and then, as though somehow knowing it had no choice, that "something" inside me arose, unsummoned, from the pit of my stomach and shot up my spine into my brain to take command of that fear, controlling it with each breath I took and making the fear work for me. *For* me. That "something" miraculously and heroically transformed the teeth-chattering view of my impending death into steadying and propelling power so that I focused all my existence on "being *here*." When I talked to Johnny Jackson about how I felt about boarding, when I waxed eloquent of the cruel poetry of the ride, he grinned. With the wink of a kindred spirit, he tersely responded, "You got *that* right, bro."

When I saw Mom approach the school, I ran over, skateboard in hand, received her standard hug—at 13, I wasn't giving her kisses and, in any event, she was not the kissing kind of mother—we walked to the car, bantering about my day, my homework, my just-about-everything. Regular FBI woman, she was. But, I complied, because I knew it made Mom feel good, and since I was always getting into trouble a lot in school anyway, I figured it paid to stay on her good side whenever the opportunity presented itself. It sort of countered, or at least softened, her emotional—and physical—swings at me whenever she lost her temper, which were happening more frequently as I messed up in school or at home, like getting caught drinking from the orange juice container while standing in front of the refrigerator with the door open. As Harry had explained, "Accumulate as many merits as you can during your life in order to offset the demerits of misbehavior and mistakes. Over time, you'll realize you only want merits and you'll stop making the mistakes, or at least you'll try if you're smart. You'll be happier and other people will be happier about you. Then they will be happier too. Win-win situation. Makes for good karma." Made some sense but it also rubbed against the grain, since I had trouble controlling my natural, maybe chemically-imbalanced, impulse to do what I wanted, often against the wishes of Mom, teachers and other kids. I mean, I knew she had a hard life bringing me up alone, but I was who I was and couldn't usually keep a lid on my own need to be me. I knew some other kids could do it, and sometimes I really wished I could, but it usually felt like a hill too far to reach.

I got into the backseat and tossed my backpack and jacket aside and placed the skateboard on the floor so my feet could rest on it. Just feeling it under me there was reassuring, like having an old friend next to me. "Jacky will be in the office at four o'-clock to correct your homework and tutor you in math today," Mom said with an air of authority and finality.

"Oh, man. Again?" I sighed petulantly. "Do you have any candy in here?"

"What's wrong?!" she screeched in Mandarin. "You don't know how hard I work so you can have a good tutor? You think you can just ride the skateboard and play computer games? No way! You hear me?!"

I looked out my side window, ignoring Mom. "Whatever," I murmured in English. No escaping the wrath of Mom. The Boss Lady of my life, at least for now. But she kept me alive with food, clothes, a place to sleep, so I was sort of grateful. Anyway, I knew she loved me, but she sure was tough. She wasn't a great driver, so I knew to keep quiet so she wouldn't get all emotional on me and have an accident and blame it all on me. There were times to lay low and when Mom was driving, that was definitely lay-low time. Just another example of the constant calculus of weighing the odds of what worked best in my favor. I didn't want to discuss my peculiar school day with her because she was driving and she couldn't drive and deal with my stories at the same time because she said my talking made her nervous and, anyway, I didn't think she'd ever believe me. She'd only accuse me of making up stupid stories again to get out of doing my homework.

About 20 minutes later, Mom parked the car about a block from the office. She was kind of manic about parallel parking, and that was a three-minute exercise until she could get the car just how she liked it—not too far from the curb, not too close, not too close to the cars in front and back, but not too far from each, not too crooked an angle from the curb. It wasn't an art for her but rather an obsession. The parking had to be just "so very so." All I could do was shake my head and be careful she didn't notice, otherwise that would cause another motherly ruckus from which my sensitive eardrums would not easily recover. The woman was a walking and talking human antenna who picked up even the faintest signals, so I had learned to try to shut my mouth and control every facial muscle and even my posture, no matter sitting or standing, in lighted or dark places, at home or outside, to evade her detection. Sometimes it worked. Usually it didn't.

When we arrived upstairs in the office, Harry was in the conference room reviewing documents with a client. "Yo, Old Timer," I irreverently called out when I saw him in there. "Hey, Josh," he called out and smiled, amused by my smooth tone of familiarity with him in the presence of a client, a stranger. The room was large and paintings and photographs of U.S. presidents were on the wall. I recognized them all—Jefferson, Lincoln, Roosevelt. In the other rooms, there were other presidents' pictures and one of a serious-looking judge called John Marshall, whom Harry said had been a soldier in the American Revolution and later the Chief Justice of the United States Supreme Court. I remember when Harry and Mom had discussed ideas for office decoration. He had preferred paintings of old wooden sailing ships plying stormy and fair seas alike, as there had been in his large 135-year-old Wall Street law office where he had practiced law for thirty years. But since Mom had said presidents' pictures would create a more somber atmosphere and Chinese clients would be more impressed, Harry took the path of least resistance, took a deep breath, looked at Mom for about five seconds, then nodded. That was how the two of them did business. Smart guy.

I sauntered in, waved to the client sitting across the wide table, patted Harry on the shoulder and asked, "So how's it goin', Chief?" I smiled to the client and politely greeted him in Mandarin. He chuckled about how familiar I was acting with his "big lawyer." Although Mom had told me not to walk in when Harry was with clients, I knew I could get away with it as long as I didn't overstay my welcome and interrupt their legal discussions, well, at least not interrupt them very much.

"Just peachy, Little Man. Working hard with Mr. Wu here on another company he is acquiring. You have homework to do? I understand Jacky's due here soon."

Harry was almost like my substitute grandfather. He said he had to keep me "on the straight and narrow" as he had done, or tried to do, with his own three kids. Mom said he hadn't succeeded very much with disciplining them, so I was his new challenge. But I questioned most of what Mom told me since she was pretty picky and critical and tried to run my life since I had no father at home, and anyway, I knew two of Harry's sons and they seemed pretty upright to me: one was a lawyer in Philadelphia and the other was a real estate developer out West. His daughter was an artist living in the mountains somewhere; "She's busy trying to *find* herself," as Harry put it, always rolling his eyes when he said "*find* herself," so I took that to mean she didn't know what the hell was going on in her life. Harry's wife had died about six years before he hired Mom, but he'd been a workaholic anyway, so it's not like he suddenly had a lot of extra time on his hands just to devote to me. Yeah, I frustrated him almost as much as I ticked Mom off, but he stayed the course and never gave up on me. He also never slugged me, which Mom thought *she* had the right to do. Sometimes I wished he could be my dad, but he was way too old and, anyway, I knew it didn't pay to waste time on a forlorn hope.

"Yeah, I know, I know. Mom already told me."

"Okay," he motioned toward the conference room door, "Go into my room and sit at the desk to work on your homework before he arrives. Good boy." He ended a lot of his talks to me with that "Good boy" thing. It was some sort of grandfatherly exhortation to me to listen to instructions, behave and perform well, have confidence that by doing what he said I would turn out okay, and all that jazz. It also irked me because it sounded like what you say when you pet your dog after he's brought you your slippers in his mouth. Too patronizing. But I knew he meant well and he was a good guy who'd gotten me out of plenty of scrapes so I never made a big thing out of it. I nodded *adios* to the client and turned on my heel to leave.

As I headed out, I looked back and exclaimed, "By the way, Harry, something bizarre happened in school today. Can I talk to you later about it?"

"Sure, buddy" he said absent-mindedly, his head swiveling amongst the documents spread out before him.

Two hours came and went, filled with the usual humdrum afternoon activities. First, fiddling around with my homework assignments. I didn't have neat penmanship; my eyes and hands worked fine, even worked well in tandem, but I just didn't care. My teachers, Mom, Harry, would all ask me why I wrote so sloppily. I didn't see my writing as sloppy. I saw it as "What does it matter?" Spelling was the same. If I understood what the word I had written was, then what did it matter if others said the word was misspelled? Punctuation too. It was a matter of how I saw the sentence, how I felt what the mood of the sentence was, so that's where I put my commas and other markings. It was tough for me to conform to ways of expressing myself in writing that others said were correct, because I couldn't even see how they were "ways," let alone agree that those ways were correct and mine were wrong. Drove my teachers crazy. Mom too, especially since she'd only started learning English much after she arrived in New York when she was about 32, and, just like her parking, her clothes and makeup, and most things, she was a stickler for "the right way." She saw things pretty black-and-white, not a lot of gray. Harry was a stickler for accuracy and detail in his work, Mom said, but after a few years of fighting his bitter frustration over my unwillingness—or inherent inability—to do things the "right way, like everybody else," when he helped tutor me, he had changed his attitude. "He'll change when he realizes the change is right," he would tell her and shrug. Harry had mellowed. Or maybe I was the rock on which he had broken. Or maybe Harry had just given up caring anymore, but I knew that was not true.

Then came Jacky Deng, the tutor—the latest tutor, for I'd exhausted a string of them—he was a computer geek student at Queens College who tried to help me with math. Math gave me a headache. I could do it when I calmed down long enough to understand the "why" of the questions, but I generally couldn't keep my attention on the questions long enough. Too many other fascinating things occupied my brain cells. Somehow, I survived the boredom of Jacky trying to keep me awake and on track. Yet the odd events of the day in school were so fresh in my mind that I couldn't focus on the mysteries of geometric shapes and their perimeters and areas and angles which seemed awfully irrelevant at this point in my life.

A little after six o'clock, just after Jacky left with a splitting headache that I had unintentionally given him, I found Harry pecking away on his laptop. "Can we talk now?" I asked.

"Sure, let me save this document first," then "Okay, Josh, so, what's new?" He could never in his wildest dreams expect what came next.

"Harry, I've been waiting to tell you this all afternoon. I didn't tell Mom 'cause I knew she'd say I'm lying."

"You mean, lying *again*, don't you?"

He really knew how to land a blow square on the jaw. Harry didn't pull punches except when he had a good reason. But I shrugged it off, as I did most of his sharp comments.

"Yeah…well…*anyway*…the point is that some weird shit happened today, and I have a feeling it actually started yesterday."

"You want to try to be a little more specific? Start with the details. And leave out the '*shit*,' if you don't mind."

"Fine," I conceded, since he didn't like to hear me use those words, even though he did. "Blue gas got pumped into my classroom today after lunch, see…and everybody zombie'd out."

Harry told me always to start with the conclusion of the argument or thesis, then to give the factual supports. Just like his legal briefs. So, there it was.

He sat way back in his seat, sighed deeply and squinted at me for about a few seconds, then arched his bushy gray eyebrows, looked down at the desk and took his glasses off and held them in one hand while he started massaging the bony bridge of nose. He did that a lot when he was tired or frustrated. All the while, he was pursing his lips and nodding. That was his way of letting you know he was awake and listening, and it generally was followed—as in this situation—by further grilling.

"Blue gas, huh? Okay," he said skeptically and nodded slowly. "So, where did it come in from?"

"From the air ducts, of course," I guffawed.

Unmoved, he asked in his deadpan voice, "I assume you told the teacher?" He expected the answer would be affirmative and therefore put an end to my tale.

"No. It was like she had *expected* it. She was really into it. She closed her eyes, stood straight as a board, and breathed it all in, like it was a fragrant perfume or sweet flowers. So did all the kids in the class. Well, they stayed in their seats, see."

Then Harry shook his head slowly, at least a half-dozen times, sighed again, this time more deeply, and calmly said, "Josh, gimme a break, okay? It's been a long day and I'm tired and still have work to do." He chuckled while raising his eyebrows to wrinkle his high, shiny forehead and shaking his head again a few times in utter disbelief, assuming I was making all this up, and in an attempt to return me to reality, asked, "Did you do all your homework?"

"I'm telling you the *truth*, Harry! And yeah, the homework's all done. Jacky checked it."

"No wonder you didn't dare tell your mother about this story," he giggled. "She'd have let you have it with both barrels. And, believe me, in *your* case, you don't need the extra *tsuris*." I knew that meant aggravation. I'd heard him say it plenty.

"It's not a story. Look, man, it was *bizarre*, okay?! I think this happened yesterday too, but I wasn't in the classroom for that one. I caught that one at the tail end."

"Oh, really? Where were you for *that* one?" he asked playfully. "I know you were in school yesterday." His steel gray eyes were boring into me. Always interrogating me. Harry was good at that. He said he loved litigation, arguing with other lawyers and trying to convince judges. Jousting, as he called it, only with words and papers, not lances like the knights in the old times. But when he was successful at it, it still felt like you'd been knocked off your horse by his lance. I was pretty accustomed to it and was even getting the knack of using it on my classmates. Looking them straight in the eye and calling their bluffs. Even when they were telling the truth, it still unnerved them. So, now, chalk one up for Harry.

"I wasn't in my classroom yesterday when it was happening," I said, trying hard to fake a non-guilty appearance. "But I noticed the blue color in the air when I came in there. And it had an odor like being at the beach, same as today."

"I see." Much as I hoped we'd reached the end of his string of questions, Harry was nobody to release a guy dangling on the Epstein hook. "So, where *were* you?" he softly but doggedly followed up.

Much as I hated telling the truth and making myself look bad—again—I decided to come clean. It was just one of those snap decisions, the kind you don't think deeply about, but make with only the part of your brain that reacts fast, like stepping back on the curb as a speeding car suddenly comes too close. I shrugged as I started to explain. "This kid, Dalton, he was bothering me in the afternoon so I called him a jerk and then it got physical and I knocked him on his ass, so the little pussy complained to the teacher. I told her that he'd started it, but she wouldn't even listen to me. She hates me, Harry, but I don't care." I shook my head defiantly. "She sent me down to the Assistant Principal's office. So, I was there for a while. Okay? No biggie. But, anyway, that's when they must have pumped in the blue gas."

Harry couldn't leave well enough alone. "Is this the first time you were sent down this semester?"

"I don't remember." I avoided his eyes as I shrugged again when I answered.

"Oh, so now you also have a memory problem?" He just kept tugging at the loose string until the ball of yarn unraveled.

"All right, so maybe it's not the first time. But I'm trying to be good. Really."

"Josh, your mom has enough troubles. Please don't add to them." Harry was very considerate of Mom's working single-mother situation and he bent over backwards to alleviate her worries. He was really good to us. As I said, we were almost like family. He was almost as old as my own grandfather, the living one, in China; I knew Mom's father had already died there, but of what, I didn't know, since she didn't like to talk about it. She was pissed at her own mother for not having taken better care of him when he was sick and dying. Complicated and emotional shit that bothered her, and sometimes she quarreled with Grandma about it, so I never probed for details. It was what it was. I left it alone. She'd tell me some day, I figured. I could wait. I had enough on my own plate, anyway, and I hadn't even known the old guy, so it was all just storybook stuff to me.

I looked up and met his eyes. They were soft and compassionate. I nodded. "I know. You're right. But I'm really trying."

"Good. So, now," he said in a neutral voice, switching gears and giving me some more of his so-called valuable time, "tell me about this blue gas you think you saw or smelled or something." He tried to sound sincere, but I knew he was very dubious. I suppose this was the attitude he took when he interviewed his clients or took depositions of witnesses.

"So, when I walked into the classroom yesterday, everybody was alert, but it seemed like there was a blue film of mist in the air. I felt a little light-headed but I figured it was just me. I thought maybe I was just winded from climbing the stairs really fast. The kids all stared at me strangely, but I figured it was because I had just come back from being sent down to the Assistant Principal's. But after today, I know that's not why."

"What happened today that changed your mind?"

"Harry, you won't believe this. It's incredible, but it's real. I'm serious. I'm not making this shit up. I mean, this stuff," I said, cleaning up the street language, as he called it. "And now I think the school is purposely doing this to us."

"Oh, really?" was his mildly amused response.

"Yup. Because yesterday I walked back into my room a little after two o'clock, and today, at two o'clock, the blue gas started seeping into the classroom again. And, before that, just after lunch, when I was in the basement in the school, I overheard the school janitor talking on the phone to our Principal, Mrs. Dorsey, and they said it had to happen at two o'clock. And I saw him and his co-worker mixing something and he said how it was blue and don't get it on yourself or it'll never come out. The air in his basement office had the same beach smell as the blue gas had both times I smelled it in my class. The stuff was in these big plastic jugs." I gestured to show him the height and diameter of the jugs.

"He told *you* to be careful about not spilling it?"

"*No, man*, I was hiding outside his door, but it was open. I was eavesdropping. Got it?"

He nodded and murmured in his throat, "Umm-hmmm."

"His coworker was mixing it. They were both wearing plastic gloves."

"What kind of beach smell are you talking about?"

"You know, Harry. Like the air smells at the beach, very fresh, coming in off the ocean." I laughed. "It definitely smelled a lot better than your office, that's for sure." His room reeked of a dozen blends of pipe tobacco that he kept in jars on a bookcase and smoked when Mom was not around and he could open his window and turn on a fan to blow the smoke out; actually, that didn't work well at all and it just pushed the blue-gray clouds of pipe smoke around the room. And the pipes on his pipe rack stank pretty badly too, but I don't think he cared how the place smelled to others. He said he liked smoking them once in a while. I thought those were pretty frequent once-in-a-whiles, but, whatever.

He raised his furry silvery eyebrows and gave me that tired, searching look. "It's the Latakia. Pungent, but I like it. You got any more complaints, Shorty?" he asked, not expecting, wanting, or waiting for a response. His head cocked to one side, his eyes narrowing as he peered at me, as if something was becoming interesting—or maybe goading me to say something else not very credible—he asked, "So, did you talk to any of the other kids about this?"

"Nope," I shook my head. "And I'll tell you why. When the blue gas started to seep in from the overhead air ducts, all the kids – and I mean everybody but me- closed their eyes and started inhaling the stuff. The teacher and teacher's helper too. It was totally awesome, Harry. Really creepy, like a horror movie. Like 'Night of the Living Dead' or some shit, I mean, some movie. And they just did this way for at least five minutes."

"And what were you doing all that time?" he asked. I couldn't tell whether he was asking me the question to learn the facts or to see whether I was making it up as I went along and how I'd keep embellishing the tale. He was a patient man, especially when laying a trap. The trick was to know when to jump out of the way before he sprang it.

"Well, at first, see, I watched them all go into a deep-breathing trance. Like this," and I demonstrated. "The gas seemed to trigger something in them, and they were really digging on it. But it didn't affect me." I shook my head to emphasize the point.

Harry's eyes widened and his brow furrowed. "No kidding, huh?" I could tell he was just listening to my story, not believing it, and feeding me more rope to hang myself with.

"I'm *serious*, man. Then, I sort of played along with it, pretending I was doing it too, but I kept an eye on them. Nobody else had their eyes open. Then, around five minutes later, the gas thinned out, and the teacher clapped her hands, and then they all opened their eyes, like nothing had happened."

Harry sucked in a very deep breath and blew it out his nose with his characteristic long whinnying sound. He looked at me for a few seconds before saying, "Interesting story, Josh. Sounds like you had quite a day." He nodded a couple of times, whether to me or to himself I couldn't tell, and then, just as if I wasn't even sitting in front of him, he picked up the legal papers he had been working on and started reading with concentration.

"Wha'd'ya *mean*, 'interesting story'?!" I exclaimed and imitated with annoyance the mocking way he had said it. I'd be damned if I'd let him just blow me off like that. "Something's going on over there! All the kids are now acting like little goody-goodies. Nobody jokes around since yesterday. Even Dalton wasn't a jerk today."

"Josh, I don't know Dalton from a hole-in-the-wall, but give it a break, okay?" He yawned. "Good thing you didn't tell your mom this story, otherwise she'd really lose her patience with you again." Harry didn't even look up from his work while he admonished me and shook his head and chuckled, and I knew that was his sign for 'Go away, kid, you're bothering me.'

As I sat there opposite him, staring at the hoary crown of his sparsely-covered head for a few seconds, I knew he had ended the discussion. I took my cue, shrugged, stood and said, "Yeah, well, I just hope this is the end of it. It was some *weird shit*." I didn't clean up the lingo because I purposely wanted to get a rise out of him, but Harry paid me no mind, maybe equally on purpose. I left his room and took up residence at a computer to listen to music. By 6:30 p.m., Mom had finished work and we headed home.

9   HARRY

Children in North Queens were walking around with curiously placid demeanors, as if they had found new direction in their everyday goings-on. At first, I assumed that with autumn, kids were more intent on studying. The summer vacation was behind them and now they were busy with classes, homework, reports and tests. For decades, I was accustomed to seeing sleepy-eyed kids drag themselves along the sidewalks to school early each morning. But there were few sleepy-eyed children on the streets, no matter mornings or afternoons. Most walked with a high-spirited gait each morning, some quick, some skipping, some plainly purposeful, no stragglers, no dawdlers. The absence of their usual noisiness, playfulness and rambunctiousness when they were dismissed from school in the afternoons was especially odd. It was as if a grey blanket of adult reasonability had suddenly engulfed them all, robbing them of that joyous and unselfconscious silliness of youth that prompts adults to look at kids, sigh, grin and wish we could turn back the clock and then sadden with the realization that the only thing we can see with any knowledge of certainty is the black hole coming up ahead. Could these little serious characters all be so similarly intent about getting home or to the public libraries or to after-school centers to do homework? Thousands of children of all ages in lockstep mental grip?

Josh was unchanged. He was still the same wise guy: doing sloppy homework, incomplete homework, not preparing for exams, and more interested in whatever caught his fancy than in marching with the crowd.

I spoke to Jane about this. "Some parents of children in Josh's school told me their kids are behaving very well now. They think the teachers are doing great jobs teaching their kids," she mentioned. "I only wish Josh could get his act together and be that good."

"But Jane, haven't you noticed how almost all the kids on the street each day are calm? I mean, unnaturally calm? And *every* day. I don't hear any loud voices, no running wildly to chase each other, no goofing around anymore. You don't think that's strange?"

Her response was typical. She was like the volcanic model Josh had to build, but her eruptions were purely vocal, and that was fire enough for me. "I'm *so* busy, Harry, I don't have time like you to watch other people. I have to get Josh up in the morning, make sure he's dressed and fed and then out the door early, then get myself together, do a quick laundry, then get here. My mother is absolutely no help, just lazy and complaining about her aches and pains and that she's hungry and that I don't care about her. Clients are calling me all the time!! Do you even *know* that??" she hissed. "Always asking me so many questions about their cases because they are afraid to talk directly to you, their *big* lawyer. Okay?! Do you even *know* how much is on my mind?! Every day?!"

Oy vey! Ask a simple question, try to engage the woman in conversation, and get chewed out for my trouble. Sometimes I wondered why I bothered. Jane was under huge pressure because she was a middle-aged single mother of a teenage boy who was on a mission to define life his own way and damn-the-torpedoes, and she was a daughter who had to handle all her mother's matters since the thankless old lady spoke no more English than the Man-in-the-Moon. But that was just for starters, because she was also the paralegal-cum-Gal Friday on whom all the clients depended for preparing all manner of their legal papers and periodic updates in their cases, and who persisted in pestering her to explain what any odd official-looking letters in English meant, no matter from a court or the Department of Motor Vehicles or even junk mail that lacked pictures from which they might glean some idea, since most didn't have much English. In addition, she was becoming more active in her local church activities with two weekday evening Bible classes and Sunday worship and more Bible study.

"You're doing a great job all around, Jane. Don't berate yourself," I reassured her. She just looked up from her computer and shot me her own cold-eyed version of Josh's "yeah, whatever" look, then returned her gaze to the computer screen and continued typing. I knew well enough to back off.

"Say, I've got nothing important going on for a couple of hours. I'll pick up Josh. You can relax." After I said it, I realized "relax" was not the appropriate way to put it. She said nothing, not even a guttural "umphh" in acknowledgment, and bobbed her head once sharply to indicate agreement.

I left the office, found my car parked a block away alongside the Queens Botanical Garden, cleared fallen oak and maple leaves from the windshield and wiped bird poop from the windows and driver's-side door handle with paper towels and stale water I kept in the trunk for just such special and unfortunately frequent occurrences. Before finally sitting down, I took a pipe from my jacket pocket, filled it with tobacco and fired it up. The pipe was my trusty companion for the drive to Josh's school. But before my first puff, I looked around as if suddenly reminded of something wonderful. I breathed in the early autumnal dryness I recalled from my youth, the smell of a fleeting warmth before the leaves totally shriveled and dropped. The air in New York City was much cleaner than when I was a boy, due, I suppose, to the absence of light industry, the governmental mandate for cleaner gasoline, and the huge fines for polluting that dissuaded people from their baser proclivity to litter at will. Buses didn't spew black plumes from their tailpipes anymore and buildings didn't burn garbage that choked the skies. People tied up garbage in plastic bags and neatly arrayed the bags on designated days in designated places for pick-up. Breezes off the Atlantic Ocean to the south and Long Island Sound to the north swept Queens fresh.

On days like this, the October air smelled nutty and sweet. With the rains due tonight, the fallen leaves would become a soggy, slippery mess the following morning and their smell of decay would add a musky-sweet fragrance to the city day.

I was always amazed at how so many kids could quickly filter out of a couple of narrow school doors, sunshine blinding them as they tried to focus their eyes from indoors to outdoors, faced with a mass of adults entangled in each other, all waving arms and screaming names to get the attention of their children. Structured pandemonium on the adults' part and countered by the wide-scanning searches by the children, silent as snipers scoping for targets. I stood way back, where the oxygen was richer and I was in less danger of losing my hearing or getting slapped by the indiscriminate arc of hand gestures.

"Hi ya Harry, where's Mom?" Josh asked, more out of a vague curiosity than concern.

"Well, she was awfully busy, and since I had the extra time, I thought I'd fetch you back."

"Jacky coming today?"

"I think she said it's his off day. He'll be back for you to torture tomorrow," I teased. Josh was nothing if not thick-skinned about such things. He smiled and skateboarded alongside me, sometimes around me, sometimes down off the curb into the street and then popping back up the curb again.

"Yeah, I like to give him a hard time," he said, looking around at all the other kids pairing up with their adults, "'cause maybe then he'll tell Mom some excuse to stop tutoring me. I know he can't just straight out say I'm a pain and he's sick of teaching me." The words flowed from his lips with all the sincerity of someone who either feels totally at ease confiding in the listener or simply doesn't care how the listener might react. In either case, not out of character for Josh, who said whatever he wanted, be it the truth or not, for he lied straight-faced with aplomb when it suited his purpose. Part of his puerile charm, I suppose. I glanced down at him after he spoke, pondering his candor and not quite sure whether any response from me was even necessary. There was no doubting the veracity of his dislike of all the tutors he'd burned through. Yet his mother was undaunted and hired one after the other in the belief that so long as she did her best for the boy, someday her efforts might bear fruit. All I saw was a lot of wasted money, but I also knew to "let Josh be Josh" and do nothing about him but hope for the best was a recipe for disaster.

"She'll only hire you a new one. You can't escape," I said with a hopeless shrug.

"Maybe you're right," he conceded. But then, "So I'll just have to make the *next* one miserable *too*," Josh retorted in his cheery, matter-of-fact tone.

After a few seconds, I remembered what else was on my mind. "Say, Josh, I've been wondering about something," I said as I walked to my car parked a couple of blocks away on a lovely Oakland Garden street. Like so many of the tree-lined neighborhoods in Northern Queens, the private houses here were increasingly owned by Chinese and Korean and South Asian families who paid top dollar to live in the districts that had high-performing "Blue Ribbon" schools. Once enrolled in the schools, many of the kids studied with a fierce desire to do well and make their parents' faces shine with pride. Families sacrificed for their children and, given the local and city-wide statistics, their sacrifices were paying off. Their children were successful in competing for places in the city's best high schools, both public and private, and then entered the country's best colleges. As the old joke went, a kid asked his parents whether he could be a musician in a rock band when he grew up, and the reply was "Sure you can, honey, as long as you're a doctor." It hadn't been long before this time when other New York families throughout this neighborhood and countless other sections of the city, families of myriad ethnic backgrounds, had felt this communal urge to succeed in their new homeland. I knew it was a wave surge that would never relent so long as people felt the desire to improve their circumstances, enjoy what opportunities America had to offer, and had the nerve and self-discipline to accept each challenge by working hard, and from youth onward, assert themselves and contribute to their communities and new nation.

"You haven't mentioned anything more about any blue gas since you talked to me about it the first time," I prodded.

He gave a slight shrug as he glided nearby. "Still happens every day at two o'clock sharp. They all go into their hokey-pokey trances. Gives me some peace and quiet for about five minutes, so I can mess around with whatever I keep in the bottom of my backpack and can't take out during class," Josh said non-chalantly.

"You don't bug out like they do?" I narrowed my eyes as I looked over at him.

"Nah, doesn't bother me. I like the smell, though. It's clean, ya know, like soap."

I stopped walking as a curious notion tugged at me. "Look, I have an idea," I called out to him, and he turned 180° on the skateboard, waiting to hear more. I felt a mischievous series of thoughts forming in my mind.

"Okay, what?"

"I want to go back to your school. Right now. There's something we need to do."

"Sure, I guess," he replied, never one to hurry back to the office. "I only have homework to do and that can wait. You can help me with it, *right*?" he fished. Everything was a negotiation with this fellow. Nothing without a *quid pro quo*. Smart guy.

"Of course! You need to ask?" I assured him with a pat on the shoulder. "You're my *main man*, Josh. Let's go." He was about to become involved in something that would make his aversion to doing homework seem awfully trivial.

10   JOSH

W e turned on our heels and headed back to I.S. 406. By this time, some ten minutes after I'd been let out of school, the place was already quiet. Some students had gathered in various afterschool clubs for art and music and homework help. The eighth graders were already beginning to rehearse their "The Wizard of Oz" school play, with some of them doing set design and costume design and others practicing their lines, but it all looked like goofing around to me. Nobody noticed us. Harry was dressed in a gray suit, red and white striped shirt, and dark paisley tie. Shiny black shoes. He was every kid's image of a lawyer and had occasionally been mistaken for my grandfather, which made my stock go up for some of the teachers but also made their expectations rise, not exactly a win-win situation for me.

"Which way to the basement?" he asked in a low voice a few decibels above a whisper. By that time, we were already well along the first floor of the school. I stopped and looked up at him.

"Why?" I asked him with much surprise.

"There's something we have to do down there." His face had strict look to it, like when he was in the office working. "And I need a cup."

"What, are you thirsty?"

"No, genius. You'll see," he said in a confident tone. "Now, where can I get a cup?"

This was a bizarre request, but I played along. "The cafeteria is through that door. It might be locked now. I don't know."

"I'll wait here. You go take a look for one."

Not understanding what he was up to, I shook my head and I walked over to the cafeteria. The regulation turquoise green door with the square window cut into it was closed. I looked through the window, saw one of the lunch ladies wiping down the lunch tables, and pushed the door open.

"Hi, Miss Barnett." I tried to be slick so I said carelessly, "I'm thirsty. Have you got any cups?" Anybody who wants a cup so badly must be pretty thirsty, so despite what Harry said about not being thirsty, it seemed the logical thing to say now.

Miss Barnett paid me little heed. "Over by the fruit juice machine there are some plastic cups stacked up on the side." She jerked her head in that direction and kept scrubbing. I picked up a few cups, then looked back at her. She wasn't even looking at me when I took them and headed out the door.

"I got 'em, Harry. Now, what is it about the basement?" I asked impatiently.

"You'll see," he winked. "How do we get down there?"

I led him to a staircase and we descended. The basement was as long as the entire first floor, but with all sorts of twists and turns and little rooms off to the sides. He looked right and left. We could hear the hum of the machinery that powered the building. We didn't hear any voices. The place looked deserted.

"Josh, where's the janitor's room?" he asked.

Now I was getting a little antsy. "Harry, we're not supposed to be down here. This isn't right."

He looked me square in the face. "Oh, so you think blue gas is right? Or were you making all that up? If so, let's leave," and he shrugged and raised his palms upward as if this was all of my doing, so put up or shut up, Josh.

So, he was putting the wood to me. If I said I'd made it all up, just pretending, I'd look like a major liar. But this time I hadn't been lying. So, congrats, Josh - the truth was getting me into even bigger trouble.

"No, it's for real. But why are we down here?"

"Because we're going to get to the bottom of this. Look,

Josh, ever since you told me about this stuff a couple of weeks ago, I've been noticing that kids all over North Queens are acting weird. You're still the same—for better or worse," he snickered, "but most kids are behaving unlike anything I've ever seen before."

"Yeah, so serious and, like, *good*, right? Nobody's pulling stunts in class anymore."

"C'mon now," still focused on his objective. "Where's the janitor's room?" he asked again, this time with firmness.

I knew I'd be in terrible hot water if we got caught. I could only hope Harry would get me out of it. The school administration people knew him for years and liked him. I sighed, resigned to my fate. "Over this way," I pointed.

The area was silent. Looking back and forth and seeing no one, Harry tried the doorknob. Locked. He looked at me. "Don't tell anyone about this," he said. He removed a long paper clip from his pocket, straightened it as best he could, and put it in the keyhole. At the same time, he removed a silvery credit card from his wallet. He simultaneously inserted the credit card into the thin space between the door and doorframe, and jiggled the paper clip. He had a look of full concentration with eyes three-quarters closed as he felt his way. I was sweating bullets and looking left and right like my head was on a brass hinge.

Every second seemed like an eternity. Then I heard a metallic "*snap*" and the doorknob turned in Harry's hand. He opened the door, grabbed me by the sleeve and we squeezed through it half ajar. He delicately shut it behind him and flipped on a light switch. "What did you say the blue stuff was in?"

"A round yellow bin with some Chinese writing and the number '88,' I think." I was getting nervous.

We both surveyed the room. Actually, it was a collection of windowless rooms, and not in a straight line but linked here and there. My heart was in my throat. What if someone suddenly walked in on us? It was pretty obvious we were trespassing. Harry seemed cool, and he was 100% focused as his eyes scanned quickly up and down every quadrant of the first room. "Nothing here."

He walked into a second room, flipped on a light switch,

and surveyed the premises.

"There it is!" he softly exclaimed and pointed.

He lifted the yellow container off its shelf and placed it on a table. There were no English words on it. However, there was a series of identical Chinese characters and numbers on all four sides of the cylindrical bucket. Harry took out his smartphone and took photographs of the writing.

"Says 'Made in China' and 'Hazardous Materials' in Chinese, and over here, it says 'G88,' but that's all," Harry remarked. "That's curious, isn't it?" he muttered.

We could tell the container had been unsealed and resealed. Harry looked around and found a claw hammer. He pried open the top of the container. We both stared in amazement at the contents.

Blue ooze that smelled like the first burst of salty sea breeze that fills your nose when you arrive at Jones Beach. A little salty, a little sweet.

"Is this what you saw that day?" Harry quickly asked.

"I didn't see that blue stuff, but the janitor said it was blue and that they shouldn't spill it on themselves. This must be it. Smells like it too." I was sweating.

"We'll need gloves," Harry said. We both looked around and, not surprisingly, found a large box that dispensed them on another shelf not far from the yellow bucket. He pulled on a pair. "Here, you should also wear a pair." He passed me a pair which was too big because the gloves' fingers were dangling from my own, but I managed to pull them tight.

Harry motioned, "Give me the cups." I handed him the several plastic juice cups. He took out his handkerchief to protect his gloved hand while he gingerly dipped a cup into the bucket and slowly brought out blue ooze that was thick as pancake batter for a chemically-enriched breakfast. He placed that cup into another cup, and then a third cup, so that the outside of the third cup was dry and without any ooze on it.

He looked around. "Need to cover this somehow." Just then, I spotted a roll of heavy-duty plastic wrap and ripped off a section of sheet about a foot long.

"Good man," he said, taking it from me and daintily wrapping it all around the cup which he held perfectly upright on the table, never spilling a drop.

"Now," he uttered thoughtfully, "we can't walk out of here with a cup of blue material showing. What can we put it into?" he said, thinking aloud. He walked around the room, then back to the first room, where he spied a small, empty cardboard box without any writing on it. "This'll do." He found a newspaper and used a couple of pages for padding, then placed the cup inside. There was tape nearby which he used across the top of the cup and then sealed the box.

"Here, hold this absolutely straight up, Josh," and he deposited the box into my two outstretched hands. He went back into the second room, reattached the lid on the yellow bucket and placed it back in its spot on the shelf. His handkerchief was hopelessly stained blue, and he worked the gloves off and into the handkerchief. He wrapped the whole mess in more of the plastic wrap and stuffed it into his suit jacket pocket. He looked at me and winked. "Let's go."

My heartbeat outpaced my brain's thoughts at that point and I was reacting like a robot following instructions.

He switched off the lights in the second room, then the first room. We stood silently together in the pitch black as he cracked the janitor's door open ever so slightly. No sound out in the hallway. From the one, then two, then three inches of opening, his eyes darted around for any indication of people. None. We each instinctively held our breath.

"Quick now!" he ordered in a sharp whisper. He slid out, then I did, from the room, and he gently closed the door behind him. It locked automatically with an audible click that ricocheted off the basement walls.

11

JOSH

"Josh, you did great. I'm proud of you," Harry said softly. He patted my back and guided me along the basement hallway. I was shaking and breathing faster than I'd ever breathed, even after running laps during gym, even after skateboarding with buses speeding by only a foot from me. My heart was beating so loudly and vigorously that now I knew what people meant when they said they were so nervous that their hearts were in their throats. I couldn't have gotten any words out of my mouth even if I had tried. About what was happening outside my body, I was aware only that I was moving. I had lost sense of where we were and where we were going. I was operating in a physical and mental zone I'd never felt before. Harry was walking calmly toward the staircase upstairs and I was just a body floating next to him.

He took the cardboard box from my hands. I had been clutching it very tightly. "Relax, buddy. Everything's fine," he assured me. I was not reassured.

"Harry, are we going to get in trouble? We broke into the janitor's room!" My voice trembled.

"I opened that door, not you, okay? You did nothing wrong." I was still not reassured.

We walked up the stairs to the first floor. Everything was a blur. I was taking the steps three at a time. I dreaded the moment we would open the door of the staircase and come into the hallway. Harry was cool as a cucumber. My mom had described him being in court and enjoying every minute of high energy concentration taking testimony from witnesses, jumping up to make objections to opposing lawyers and even arguing with judges who also seemed to relish those fights.

As he pushed open the door, Harry looked calmly both ways to orient himself as to the location of the school's exit door. I was just an appendage moving along with him. The tricky part came about seven seconds later when we passed by the School Office.

"Well, *hello*, Mr. Joshua," came a high-pitched greeting from Mrs. M, after she'd almost collided with Harry as he passed the open doorway of the School Office. I froze, and I felt my eyes harden wide and round as peppermints. Harry turned to face Mrs. M.

"Hello, how are you?" Harry said in an upbeat, glad-to-see-you-again type of radio voice, smiling from ear to ear. He used to tell me a smile can give you the upper hand by making yourself feel confident and disarming your opponents for a few seconds until they regain their composure and attack, by which time you've already worked out your next defensive move.

"I'm fine," she said, disarmed as expected. "I think we met a few years ago," she grinned. "You're the lawyer Joshua's mother works for, aren't you?" she asked, grin widening. Extending her hand, she offered, "My name is Eleanor Moskowitz."

Harry took the hand in his and shook it firmly. "Yes, Harry Epstein. A pleasure to meet you again, Eleanor." His smile shifted into a confidential smirk. "Call me Harry." Very slick, calling Mrs. Moskowitz by her first name, because she began to melt under his attentive gaze. I'd need to remember that trick. Harry was a handsome older gentleman, Mom had told me, and he knew how to charm the lady clients in one way so that they cooperated more fully with his work, and the lady judges in another way so that cases went more smoothly.

Dallying for a moment, as if not anxious to break off, Mrs. M said to him, "I hear good things about Joshua from his teacher these days." Then, "Josh," she said, looking suddenly at me and grinning but not quite the same way as she had smiled at

Harry, "Mrs. Hardy told me you are making progress recently. I'm so happy for you." I wanted to die at that moment, or at least be invisible. I couldn't imagine GWQ ever thinking, much less saying, that.

"Yes, I'm trying," was all I could manage to get out of my mouth. Please, I prayed, just let's get out of here before I wet my pants!

"Well, Eleanor, I'm afraid we must be getting along," Harry interjected, "So much work and so little time every day, don't you find?"

"Oh, I know just what you mean...Harry." Again, that smile and now calling him by his first name. Score another point for the old dude. "Have a great day, both of you," she said in a cheery tone as she turned and walked down the hallway in the opposite direction. Never once had she even peered toward the box in Harry's hand.

Harry looked at me, winked and smirked. "Shall we go, *Mr. Joshua*?" He emphasized my first name, mimicking Mrs. M. He seemed to be having a grand time of it. I was dying.

Once outside the school, I was too petrified to look in any direction except straight ahead. I said nothing. Harry laid his free hand on my shoulder as we walked. "Josh, everything is fine," he said in a voice of supreme self-confidence.

"*Yeah*, whatever you say, Harry," were the only words I could mouth, and they were hardly audible.

We got into his car. I sat in the back, buckled my seatbelt, closed my eyes and tried breathing deeply to control my heartbeat. What an afternoon. I didn't need another afternoon like this for a while, that's for sure. I was shaking. Was this what Post-Traumatic Stress Disorder felt like? This was some heavy shit.

"Say, let's get some ice cream before we head back," Harry said, as if nothing had just happened and we were out for a pleasure ride. I said, "Sure," and he drove us to a nearby ice cream shop on Bell Boulevard, where I ordered a double-scoop of Rocky Road with rainbow sprinkles in an oversized sugar cone. I felt like I was fully entitled to a real treat for what Harry had just put me through. He ordered a small cup of espresso coffee gelato. While he waited for the guy to make my cone and his cup, I ran to the john like my bladder was going to burst and peed like I'd just drunk a couple of gallons of soda.

12

Josh had done very well. I knew he was terrified. It showed him he was not as tough as he had supposed he was. Welcome to the Big Time, kid. Now it was time for me to explain to him why I had put him through this exercise.

"Josh, let's talk about what just happened. You deserve to know. We didn't do *anything* awful, so relax," I said as we sat in a booth in the ice cream shop.

"Are you *crazy*, Harry? We fuckin' *broke into* the janitor's room! We *stole* stuff! Me! *I* stole stuff! Mom is always telling me to behave, you tell me that, I get it in Church, everybody tells me that, and *now* you tell me what we did is *okay*?? I mean…like…*what the fuck*?!"

"Hey, watch your mouth! We're in a public place!" I quickly looked to each side, aware of the antennae on nearby heads twisting in our direction. He was right to be confused. I could have questioned what I'd done, could have felt remorseful. But I didn't. I was helping the boy grow up in this big, bad world. I was forcing him to take sides. Sitting on the fence only gets pointy spikes up the butt.

"Yeah, whatever," was his dour brushoff.

"Listen here, Mr. I'm-such-an-upright-citizen! *Now* you're trying to act like you're pure as the driven snow?" I needed to set the record straight with this boy. "How many lies have we caught you in, telling your mother and me that you'd done all your homework when you really hadn't? Telling us how well you did on tests and then the report cards show horrendous marks? Stealing other kids' stuff because you felt like it? Who do you think you're kidding here, huh? Facts are facts, buster. Don't try to act self-righteous *now*." I wasn't about to let him slide.

He looked down into his ice cream and remained silent. He wore a sullen look. "Well...I mean...it was *scary*, okay?" At least he wasn't pretending this was the first time he'd done something wrong and I'd led him into it.

I nodded. "Yes, I can see how it would be kind of scary," I conceded, trying to regain a common ground with him. "But look, buddy, *now* I believe you about the blue gas. You should feel pretty good about that. With all the recent changes in the way all you kids are acting, I think there might be something very strange going on."

"Like, *duhhh*," Josh uttered sarcastically. I had to chuckle at his reaction. A hip kid discovering that the antiquated adult took him seriously, at long last.

"So, that's why I had to get some of that oozy stuff, Josh," I said in a voice of reason. "And I know *just* what I'm going to do with it."

Josh tried to calm himself by eating his ice cream and avoiding my eyes. "I *don't* even want to know," he said with no small amount of disdain in his voice. Then, by way of addendum, he said, "And there's nothing wrong with *me*. *I'm* not acting bizarre, *okay*?! That blue gas or ooze or whatever it is hasn't bothered me a bit. I like how it smells, that's all."

"Yes, I noticed you still seem unaffected by it, unlike so many other kids. Your classmates all marched out of school today like model junior citizens," I said, shaking my head in disbelief. "I'm going to have this stuff tested by chemists. I want to know all about its chemical properties."

"And what then? What do you think you can learn that way?"

"Josh, you *yourself* told me about the blue gas," gesturing with both my hands toward him. "*You* told me how it was affecting the kids in your class, even kids in other classes. Remember?

Have those kids gone back to the way they used to be, before these daily doses of gas?"

"No. They just became more serious, more studious. Nobody is goofing around anymore. They're all polite and nice. It's weird."

"Exactly. We need to get to the bottom of this."

"Ha! So now you're Sherlock Holmes?" Josh muttered. "Say!" he suddenly exclaimed, excitedly jerking himself up straight in his seat. "Wait a second! Wha'da'ya mean by 'we'?!"

"Aren't you in the least bit curious, Josh? Don't you want to help me figure this out?"

That question seemed to jump-start something in the boy's mind. He stopped licking his ice cream cone and met my eyes for the first time in almost an hour. It was the cold, hard stare of realization of a fact he had not wanted to consider, followed by a dawning, reluctant resignation. No, there was more spirit in his eyes than mere fatalistic resignation. It was an engaging mask of youthful determination. He was silent for about ten seconds. I could sense his mind racing with introspection.

"Sure, but…" was his laconic but sincere answer, his voice trailing off into silence as he slowly shook his head. He was slowly moving off the fence with its sharp points, but whether being off the fence would be more comfortable was still an unknown.

I nodded casually as I sensed a grudging awakening in him. "You and I are going to figure out what's been happening, young man," I said gravely and decisively, pointing my still-unused spoon at him and then tasting the gelato for the first time that afternoon.

Josh took a deep breath. "*Fine*," he resolved, breathing out the word along with a sigh. "I just hope I don't get into *more* trouble." He frowned worriedly, like he had just made a dubious decision he couldn't back down from, and then returned to his ice cream cone.

"Don't worry. Would I let that happen?" I rhetorically assured him with an air of supreme confidence, as if trouble was the last thing in the world that would occur. But I knew there were no guarantees about what might happen to us as we dug deeper. I'd have to take the heat from his mother, from the school, from whoever came down on us, if I screwed this one up. Sometimes there were casualties along the way. But what the hell. If you don't move forward toward your own purpose, you only get steamrollered by the other guy from a direction, a dimension, you didn't foresee. Josh would thank me later...if we got through this.

13

HARRY

I spent the next few weeks working hard on my cases: drafting corporate papers for different companies' legal matters, researching arcane points of law for upcoming motions and trials, attending court conferences, meeting with clients. When Josh wasn't at an afternoon sports group activity or violin lesson, he was in the office. He didn't seem overtly interested in what I did, but he did accompany me to court a few times to see what it was like and then asked incisive questions that indicated he had been carefully following the arguments. His mother was very supportive. "Maybe he'll be a lawyer one day," she hoped. "Sure, as long as he's a doctor," I replied with a chuckle. Even she got the joke.

My major occupation these days was helping a large Buddhist organization that was in the throes of political infighting between the octogenarian Grand Master and some Young Turk disciples of his—monks and nuns—who were vying for greater power in the organization by trying to split it apart as a way to loosen the old man's power over the souls of the membership and seize control this world and the next. After reviewing the religious corporation's by-laws, it had seemed clear that only disciples could be members, and only members could vote. A vote now could very well result in the venerable Grand Master being dethroned in a legalistic *coup d'etat*. What to do? The only apparent thing to do. I engineered the excommunication of the threatening monks and nuns and a few hundred members of the organization backing them. Result? The Grand Master and his slate won the election hands down, because the religious fiat had deprived his opponents of membership and denied the bad boys the right to stand for office and denied a few hundred of their followers the status to vote. *Voila*! What followed were years of litigation in three separate trial courts in Manhattan, Queens and Brooklyn because the losers were sore and said the excommunication was wrongful and that the courts should nullify the election and order real elections that included all of them. No way, I argued. The First Amendment of the U.S. Constitution prevented the civil courts from becoming involved in a religious controversy, so that the courts had no jurisdiction over this dispute. Ultimately, I was proved correct in the two levels of appellate courts of New York State, and the U.S. Supreme Court's refusal to accept the losers' ultimate application for appeal. The losers could try to resolve the matter in a religious forum, but we suspected—and were proven right—that would not happen.

Lawyering was just another tool for "behavior rectification," a more civilized method than hacking at each other with battle axes in order to win an argument. Society had rules of conduct for behavior in every facet of life. Those rules were sometimes codified, sometimes not, sometimes straight-forward but usually riddled with exceptions, and all of this constituted the law. Follow the law or challenge the law, it was there to be respected, interpreted, and changed as our world evolved. Yet the underlying principles which permitted such flexibility were the rock-solid foundation of society.

No matter how preoccupied with my work I became, the blue ooze inside the cardboard box sitting on the top of my bookshelf was never far from my mind. I made several telephone calls to commercial chemistry labs around town and I encountered a few recurring questions that put me in a tough spot. What was the reason I wanted it analyzed? Where had I obtained this material? To whom did it belong? The labs said they had ethical obligations and needed this information. Moreover, if they found hazardous substances in the material, they might have a legal—as well as ethical—obligation to report their findings to local and federal governmental authorities and specialized health centers.

I needed to find a way around the technicalities so I could get the answers I sought. I needed a "no questions asked" scientist. Even better would be a scientist who saw the problem as I saw it, but I'd settle for the "no questions asked" type.

As is the case in so much of our lives, after fits and starts, it was by accident that my luck changed. Melvin Spangler, one of my oldest friends from high school days, who had also become a lawyer in Manhattan, somebody who had been on the opposing side in a big case 20 years earlier, contacted me to chat. But more than that, our lives were entwined. Our families had been friendly with each other and we'd often eaten dinner in each other's kitchens as teenagers. I hadn't seen Mel in a handful of years since he'd retired. He and his wife, Eliza, now summered in Michigan where he spent his retirement fishing and playing bridge, then wintered in Georgia where they did the same things. While we were catching up on each other's fortunes and misfortunes, he mentioned that his daughter, Jennifer, had earned her doctorate in biochemistry some time ago and was now starting up her own laboratory service in Brooklyn. How could I have forgotten that Jenny had made a career of her fascination with chemistry? Then again, maybe I had tried to put Jenny out of mind.

"Mel, I want to tell you something. Can you keep this confidential?" I asked.

"Sure, Harry. Shoot."

"I know this is going to sound crazy." After 20 minutes of relating what I knew of the situation, and listening to him commenting about how there might be something to my suspicions, I knew I'd reached his sweet spot. I told him I needed to have this stuff analyzed.

"Harry, let me talk to Jenny and see what I can do. If what you're saying is really happening, then this could be big."

"Mel, this is top sensitive, you dig? I don't want Jenny to do anything she's uncomfortable with. And she can't discuss it with anyone but me. I don't want you to share any responsibility if there's a downside to this. I already obtained the stuff in a less-than-kosher way…that's attorney-client privilege stuff, okay, Mel?…and until we know what we're dealing with, the fewer people involved. the better." I had my own reasons to be wary about what Jenny got involved with.

"I know nothing about nothing, dear client." I could almost see Mel winking at me through the telephone line. I guffawed.

"I miss you, Mel. We had an awful lot of fun on that Voorhees case, didn't we? Hell, it went on for over five years. You were awesome and I learned a lot from you."

"Yeah, you learned enough to beat me so that your client won a $113 million judgment, you rat," he rasped sarcastically.

"Look, I was just doing my job, you know that. We both had clients to represent," I said meekly, trying to soften the ache that Mel and probably every lawyer feels, often for years afterward, when he recounts losing a big case. But we were gentlemen and genuinely valued each other's decades-long friendship. Shake hands, no matter win or lose, and remain friends. But between Mel and me, the current ran deeper, much deeper.

I didn't hear from Mel again that week. After another two weeks of silence, I thought he'd either forgotten about my phone call or dismissed the entire idea as whacky. The cardboard box still sat on the top of the bookshelf. By now, it was emitting that ocean-spray odor right through the plastic wrapping. Jane commented how she didn't know where the fragrance was coming from, and it was clear from her wrinkled nose and downward-turned mouth that she didn't care for it. No surprise there. Besides Chanel No. 5 perfume and home cooking, no other smells earned her approval. I wasn't about to let on that I knew its origin, and Josh pretended he couldn't even smell it, which only increased his mother's suspicions since she knew he had a very sensitive proboscis. She would open my window, even as it became a chilly New York December. I had little say in the matter and knew better than to fight over it. The wiser approach was to put on a wool cardigan, refresh my coffee cup with another steaming hot brew, and let it pass. Always pick your battles carefully. Besides, the brisk air cleared the sinuses and dispelled the pungent, sometimes even cloying smell of my pipe tobacco smoke.

One afternoon just before Christmas, Jane shouted over to me from her desk that someone, an American by the sound of the accent, was on the telephone asking for me. She patched the person through to me. I picked up the receiver and croaked, "Hello, Epstein" in my usual telephone-answering rising tone. My children, all grown by that time, used to laugh at my way of answering the telephone, and when I told them that was the way we were taught to answer a telephone at work in the old days, they laughed even harder at Dad the Dinosaur.

"Hello, Uncle Harry, this is Jenny Spangler."

My eyes widened as a shot of adrenalin pulsed through me and I sat up straight. "Hello, Jenny, how are you? I'm so glad you called," I exclaimed with genuine joy. I eagerly anticipated her response.

We chatted for about several minutes and caught up with each other's latest developments, Jenny telling me about her own life, asking about my kids whom she'd often played with when they were all small, but always rounding back to her mother and father and how their lives had changed in retirement, and how her dad was so bored with retirement life.

Then her voice became stiffer, an octave lower, and she said in a confidential tone, "Dad told me about what you and he discussed recently, and after thinking about it for a while, I believe I'd be very interested." We avoided all use of words that eavesdropping ears might suspect indicated the blue substance. In the old days, phone taps by prying ears were not uncommon, but they had to be engineered and were not automatic. In this digital age, however, every sound and every written impression was instantly recorded for posterity. Big Brother was no longer limited to the terrifying government of George Orwell's *1984*. Big Brother had multiplied and mutated and included not just governments but also every manufacturer of the devices we used to speak to each other, to type on, to photocopy papers, to read the news, to gab with each other, and so forth. The devices themselves were our friends to make life easier and our enemies waiting to betray us by listening in and recording our every telephone call, message, and even spying when we'd turned it off. Big Brother had become privatized and many-tentacled. Big Brother dominated activity and constituted the highest values in stock markets around the world. I wondered how long it would be before even our own thoughts were somehow monitored by Big Brother. We arranged a meeting at her lab for the next week.

"It will be great to see you again, Jenny. Say, honey, would you mind if I bring along a chap who is personally knowledgeable about this stuff?" I asked.

"Sounds like he might be very useful. Please do."

Little could she imagine that the chap in question was a 13-year-old who was in on the caper with me.

14

"Josh, old man, I'd like you to accompany me on a little field trip," I told him on the snowy afternoon after I had spoken with Dr. Jenny Spangler. I knew school would soon be out for Christmas break and he had little else to do except cause his mother headaches.

"Yeah, that'd be fun. Where are we going?" He was always a good sport and keen to go exploring.

"I have somebody I want to show that blue goo to. She has her own chemistry lab. I think you should be there too."

The look on his face changed to suspicion. "You mean you're still serious about this stuff? I hoped you'd let it go or forgotten about it."

"No. I've been very busy with work, but we still need to figure out what's in this stuff." Josh looked less than enthused. "Any more blue gas in class?"

"Sure, every day, but I don't pay any attention to it," he said with indifference.

"How is everybody reacting to it now?"

"Same as before."

"No difference at all?"

"Nah. They're all behaving really well. Nobody gets out of line. Really polite to each other. And even the dumb kids seem to be studying harder," he said. Then, almost as an afterthought, he chuckled, "Yeah, it's kind of weird."

"How about you? You feel anything?"

"Not really," he muttered, showing a polite irritation with my questions that diverted some of his attention away from the game he was playing on his mother's old cellphone that she kept around specially for that purpose.

"Any more visits down to Mrs. Moskowitz's office?" I quizzed him.

He shot a quick look at me now with defensive suspicion. "Why? Wha'd'ya hear?" He gave me the innocent blank stare of the guilty.

"Oh…occasionally a phone call comes in to your mom from school, but since she can't understand very clearly what they mean since they only speak English, she asks them to speak to me," I said coolly. The school had not called. But I was fishing and wanted to test his reaction. It paid off.

"Okay, so…well…that old witch, Mrs. Hardy, said I still wasn't doing what I should, like everybody else was doing, and she sent me down to Mrs. M."

"How many times?"

"I don't know. I forgot."

"Oh…so the blue gas affects your *memory* now? It seems to me you have selective recollections, blue gas or no," I goaded him. "You'd make quite a witness in court," I teased.

Josh sighed, momentarily losing interest in the computer game. "Maybe twice," he shrugged. Then, "Okay, three times. All right? Mrs. M asked me why I wasn't studying harder and having a more positive attitude like all the other kids. Actually, Harry, she seemed to know that everyone was 'on a new track,' as she called it. She asked me whether I was having trouble getting on the 'new track' like everyone else."

"Wha'd'ya tell her?" I asked in a low-key, disinterested tone, although I was bursting with tightly restrained eagerness to know how that exchange between Josh and Mrs. Moskowitz had really gone.

"I lied, of course," he replied with all the suaveness of a well-practiced storyteller at an Indian bazaar. "Said I was coming along just fine on the new track, but some family trouble had been weighing pretty heavily on me. You know, like Mom is so busy and edgy, no father at home, money is tight. You know, the usual kind of excuses. She bought it," he snickered.

Just as I thought, the school authorities were in on this scheme and it was proceeding afoot. This made me even more anxious to get the stuff over to Jenny Spangler's lab.

15

HARRY

Two days after Christmas, having gotten Jane's permission to take Josh with me "to a conference," I drove Josh and our cardboard box filled with what we still knew not, to Jenny Spangler's new laboratory located on the highest floor of a gigantic converted warehouse along the East River in Brooklyn. The city government was anxious to gentrify the rough old neighborhood along the late, great Brooklyn docks, and the area was a real estate developer's dream come true. Acres and acres of sturdy, imposing structures that otherwise had nowhere to go but into decline and ruin. Gone were the days when countless break-bulk freighters steamed in and out of New York harbor and docked at the quays along Red Hook, loading and unloading cargoes from every corner of America and the world and warehousing them in those massive structures that had presented New York's monolithic commercial power to the world. Now, cookie-cutter 40-foot corrugated steel containers carried the cargo in the deep bellies and on the expansive decks of prodigiously larger—and fewer—ships operated by far fewer officers and crewmen than in the past. There were far fewer longshoremen working the ships nowadays since cargo cranes did most of the work, and Marlon Brando's character in "On the Waterfront" might well have bemoaned this new dockside environment. This was only one more example of the power of modern technology resulting in the drastic reduction in the number of human workers necessary to transport and process vast quantities of merchandise that would enable hundreds of millions of consumers to eat, have shelter, be clothed, and utilize every imaginable item used in their daily lives.

Some called it progress. Others struggled against it and cursed it and argued that we must bring the jobs back home to America. Exactly what jobs, I wasn't very clear. Neither were they. What they hadn't taken into account was the nasty little fact of numbers like costs, prices, and whether they could accept the kind of low wages it would take to produce the quantities of merchandise that would have to be sold at the prevailing low wholesale prices in order to justify running the kinds of factories that were already operating abroad and spewing forth myriad manufactured goods of every description. Alternatively, if state-of-the-art factories started making products to satisfy every American's need, desire and thoughtless whim, would such factories require the vast number of workers who allegedly clamored for jobs? Would workers migrate to where the jobs were, or sit and campaign for the jobs to come to their communities? Robotics had already worked wonders in modern manufacturing. The developments in the field of artificial intelligence showed no sign of abating and held out limitless possibilities. It seemed that "mankind" was determined to aim for the stars, while all the time engaged in a perverse struggle against countless "people" mired in the quicksand of despair and longing for a time long past and unrecoverable, people without a clue how to dislodge themselves from the tatters of perceived old glories. Mankind was racing ahead relentlessly on a predestined course of scientific discovery, while great masses of people suffered the psychological dislocation of being collateral damage scattered all along that course.

Josh was duly impressed with the surroundings. He stared upward and scanned the horizon from left to right and back again. "Harry, I wouldn't want to be around here late at night. This place looks spooky."

"You have no idea how spooky this area would have looked at night over 50 years ago. There were plenty of rough characters working and living around here. Plenty of bars and fights and unsavory people. The place was downright grimy. But most people were just very hard-working, like us, trying to make their livings and feed their families. Now, these mammoth structures are being converted into apartments and offices and put to all sorts of uses. Look how they've planted trees on the sidewalks and shrubs along the buildings. There are shiny supermarkets and coffee shops and boutiques and bookstores here. All of those sure never existed here in the past. There's a sparkle here that never existed when this was a booming port. And you can bet this area is crazy expensive now." I said all this to Josh but it was unlikely he could perceive of such differences between a "then" and a "now." He was only 13 and had only known the life of "now." Nonetheless, I wanted to tell him about "then," because I hoped it would stimulate his fertile imagination beyond video games, skateboarding and his general urge to have a good time.

"And besides, it just snowed a few days ago and the ground is messy with dirty snow and slush. In the springtime, this area will look very pleasant," I emphasized.

"If you say so, Old Timer," Josh doubted.

We proceeded to the building housing Jenny Spangler's laboratory, entered the bright lobby lighted by a stylish array of hanging lamps, found the correct bank of elevators and ascended to the top floor. We walked toward the suite number she had given me and saw the door marked JGS Laboratories, LLC in black script lettering. I knocked on the door with a reluctant rap of the knuckles. When Jenny answered the door, I felt a clawing pang of emotion that I had always tried to suppress when I saw her. She invited us inside and we took seats around a small conference table in a room off to the side of the lab's generously-sized work spaces.

16

JOSH

After we introduced ourselves, Dr. Spangler appeared surprised to see a boy with Harry. She was tall and wore glasses, a long white lab coat, and a kind smile. Her eyes were really big and round, kind of like Harry's, although maybe it was her glasses that made them look so large. My eyes were tiny and narrow in comparison and people kidded me about whether I could see much. Sometimes I wondered whether people whose eyes were so large actually saw more than I did; I guessed I'd never solve that one.

The laboratory was very brightly lighted with windows everywhere and fluorescent tubes that ran wall-to-wall along the ceiling. It was large and had a series of rooms on three sides of the building that surrounded a central room. The central room was filled with workstations that had computers on top of desks, lots of machinery with colored lights that flashed in alternating patterns, endless collections of test tubes and petri dishes and beakers and coiled tubes and burners, refrigerators, sinks, stainless steel wall cabinets of all dimensions, and other devices that I had only ever seen in horror movies. The doors of the rooms off to the sides were almost all closed and could only be opened by punching codes into wall panels. The only open door I saw had a sign on it reading "Canteen" where, I learned, Dr. Spangler and her workers ate. The place smelled like a crossover between faint fruity odors and cleaning fluids, and I saw overhead hoods larger than the one in Mom's kitchen, and I assumed they sucked

88

up chemical fumes. I saw about a half-dozen of her co-workers busy at their jobs, most of whom wore masks over their mouths and noses. They all wore identical white lab coats. None of them looked up at me. Each one looked very serious. This was going to be a cool field trip.

"So, Josh, tell me about this box you brought along. Harry, I assume this is what we were discussing?" Dr. Spangler asked. He nodded solemnly.

"Well, it's like this, see," I said. "The janitor somehow pumps this thick blue liquid through the school building and it comes out the air ducts near the ceilings into my classroom like a blue mist. I think it's happening throughout the whole school."

Dr. Spangler's eyes were fixed on mine, but in a very relaxed, gentle way. "Josh, how often does this happen?"

"Every school day, ma'am." I had heard men say "ma'am" in a polite way to women, and women always seemed to like it. Couldn't hurt to be a little gentleman to Dr. Spangler, especially since we wanted her to do some work for us. For free, too, Harry had said. I was pretty sure he couldn't afford to pay her. Harry always whined he had no money after supporting all his kids, so I figured he couldn't pay her. She looked like a very important person, with her shiny laboratory and microscopes and tables with sinks and all sorts of instruments and bottles and jars and tubes. It smelled rank, so they must have been busy cooking up all sorts of chemicals. I could only imagine the Frankenstein Monster was created in this kind of place. Mega awesome. Maybe someday I could come back here and she'd teach me how to make gold from other metals so I could buy Mom and Grandma a big house with a garden for Grandma to mess around in. Yup, I was always thinking. A guy's gotta think ahead in this world, think big.

"Tell me about it," she said.

"Okay, so, every day at two o'clock, the gas starts seeping in. Then the teacher and her assistant and all the kids start zoning out. They don't fall asleep, see. They just sit up or stand up straight, close their eyes, and start breathing in the gas. They look very peaceful. Totally quiet. Then, after about five minutes, like clockwork, see, the mist stops coming down from the air duct, and Mrs. Hardy—that's our teacher—she claps her hands loudly a few times, and all the kids open their eyes. But nobody ever talks about it. It's like nothing happened. Like time stood still. It's so weird."

"Do you breathe it in too?" Dr. Spangler asked.

"I mean…sure…I breathe it in. I have no choice. It's there in the air. But it doesn't affect me. I like the smell. It's like fresh laundry in the sunshine, like beach air."

"How about the other kids?"

"They're all peaced out. You know what I mean? They've all become super goody-goodies. All serious now." I frowned. "My friends who used to mess around with me?" I shook my head. "Nah, that's pretty much over. They still talk to me, but they don't have interest to talk to me about computer games, they don't want to skateboard or shoot hoops instead of doing home-work, none of the fun stuff we used to obsess about. Not even talk about girls," I sighed. "School has become even more boring because *they're* all boring now."

Dr. Spangler threw Harry a glance and grin, like she was sharing a moment with him at my expense.

"I'm *serious*!" I exclaimed, a little insulted she seemed hesitant to believe me. "Sure, I was never a great student, but now I'm at the bottom of the whole class because these geeks are busy all day long raising their hands and, like, 'Oo, oo, I know!! I know!!' every time Mrs. Hardy asks a question. Not just one or two kids, see? All of them! And they all do all their homework. Neat handwriting. Neat typed reports. It's bizarre. Makes no sense to me," shaking my head.

"It sounds that way, Josh," Dr. Spangler pursed her lips and tilted her head to one side as she spoke. "But what's also bizarre is that you say the substance has had no influence on you." She gave me a long, creepy, searching stare.

I shrugged. "No idea about that, Dr. Spangler," I said and shrugged again. Was she doubting me? Or was she going to ex-periment on me? Hey, this wasn't about me, it was about all the kids and GWQ and what the school was doing to us. I didn't want this thing turning around on me as a guinea pig.

"Harry seems to believe you, Josh," she said quizzically.

Harry piped up. He looked at her with a very straight face. "I thought Josh was pulling my leg at first, but since then, I've noticed kids up and down the whole Northern Boulevard area from Little Neck down through Flushing, all acting like Little Lord Fauntleroys. No light-hearted skipping along, no rough-housing, nothing that normal kids usually like to do." Dr. Spangler kept her attention on him. "I haven't seen many kids elsewhere, as I only get into Manhattan on court days. Sold my apartment there and stay mainly in my old house on the North Shore. Those kids seem to be acting the same as always."

Dr. Spangler looked at Harry, then at me, then back at Harry. "Maybe the Queens schools constitute the 'test group'?"

Harry just shrugged once with outstretched hands, palms up, eyebrows raised, in innocent ignorance.

She then settled her gaze on the box. She said nothing for a few seconds. "May I open it now?" she asked.

"Better let me do it," Harry said. "It's messy. Do you have a pair of plastic gloves I can slip on?"

She handed him and me gloves and, for good measure, gave us both face masks as she put on gloves and a mask. She grinned at me and said, "Always better to be prepared for a spill."

Harry removed the thick rubber bands from around the box, used his pocket knife to slice the thick tape he had sealed the box with, and carefully lifted the two top flaps of the box. He then placed one hand over the top of the open box and, with the other hand, lifted out crumpled newspaper he had used to cushion the cup that contained the blue solution. We all watched intently. I could hear Dr. Spangler and Harry breathing. Hers was a smooth, steady breath. His was raspy from years of pipe smok-ing. He loved his pipes. Called them his little briar buddies and took good care of cleaning them after each smoke. He had amassed a big pipe collection the way we kids have shoeboxes full of Magic cards and baseball cards. Everybody's got a jam, I suppose, and pipes were Harry's jam.

We all peered at the double-cupped blue ooze still

wrapped as Harry had done a month or more earlier. I couldn't detect any loss through evaporation. If anything, it looked gooier than originally.

"You were right about the odor," Dr. Spangler confirmed. Her nose wiggled beneath the mask. "It's certainly not unpleasant. In fact, there's something soothing about it, isn't there? May I lift it?" she asked Harry. He nodded his consent.

She lifted it firmly yet gingerly, and continued to look at it with studied concentration.

"Can you leave this with me?" she inquired. "I want to perform a preliminary analysis with my biochemists to determine the basic chemical composition. We'll then formulate a plan for advance testing for different qualities."

Harry looked at me. He raised his eyebrows and his eyes asked, "Well?"

I looked at him, then at Dr. Spangler, then back and nodded, saying in a serious manner with all the self-confidence of an equal team member, "Sure."

They both smiled, or at least that's the vibe I got from beneath their masks and from their creased, uplifted eyes.

Dr. Spangler placed the cupped solution back into the box and we all stood, leaving the box to occupy the center of the table while we left the room. Harry and I put on our winter coats, and he and Dr. Spangler made some small talk about their respective plans for the Christmas holidays. She shook our hands and told us she'd be in touch with us after her lab had done its initial work on the sample.

"Oh, just one more question, gentlemen," she asked in a slow, inquisitive way, as a new thought rose to the surface of her mind. "Any chance we can get more of this for testing?"

Harry and I looked at each other and he started laughing with all the mischievous cackle of a hyena on the prowl. I wasn't laughing at all because I was afraid that I already knew what his answer would be. I knew Harry. And I had read him correctly.

"Just give the word, Doctor."

I tried to keep a blank face. My stomach started to rumble. I think I was learning to worry.

17

JOSH

A few days later into the Christmas break, I got together with a few classmates for a trip to the American Museum of Natural History in Manhattan. Believe it or not, it was that little troublemaker-turned-goody-two-shoes Dalton Wu's mom who had arranged it. She had telephoned my mom, and the parents of Alice Dooley, Julia Morton and Mike Marino. Since we were 13 and not really accustomed to taking the subway all over New York on our own, a parent had to chaperone us, so Mike's dad, Andrew, came along.

It was a lot of fun, much as I hated to admit it. As expected, everyone behaved politely, as they had been doing in school. Alice, however, was walking more slowly than the rest of us. She said she was having a problem with her feet, something that had only recently occurred. Her mom had taken her to a doctor who could find nothing wrong. Yet she complained that they just didn't feel like her feet anymore. At the time, I didn't give it any thought, and told her that I'd be glad to carry her backpack at school if that would help. She rewarded me with a sincere smile which made my day. We men are such simple creatures, and as I learned many years later, simple is better.

After the museum trip, Mike's dad took us back to Queens where we went to a popular pizza joint on Northern Boulevard. Julia's mom, Sandra, joined us there, and those two adults were off to the side, chatting. When we all sat down at the long table to eat and tank up on soda—man, that was a treat for me, since my mom only let me drink water, juice and milk at home—Mike's dad made a comment that only led to problems for me.

"You know, it's wonderful to see the progress you all have made in the last few months. Mike has really matured. I'm glad to see he's becoming more serious about his homework and buckling down."

Julia's mom nodded in agreement. "I was thinking the same thing, Andrew. I think seventh grade must be a turning point in children's lives."

The five of us kids were munching away on the pizza, when I blurted out something in a joking way that I would later regret. "Yeah, must be that blue gas they pipe in every day."

Julia's mom either didn't hear me or disregarded it as a silly, meaningless quip, but Mike's dad followed up on it. "What do you mean, Josh?" he snorted as he asked, not as a serious question, but I figured he wanted an answer.

Blame it on me being 13, blame it on me thinking we were off school grounds, blame it on me thinking Mike's dad was a good guy, blame it on me being foolhardy. Blame it on me trusting someone about something that should not have been spoken about, at least not then. "Blue gas comes into our room every afternoon. Everybody gets off on it. Seems to calm everybody down real well."

Mike's dad stared over at me. "Josh, you know, Mike told me you have quite a reputation for being the class clown." His face turned more ashen. "This doesn't sound too funny, though." Then he let loose with "Didn't your parents tell you it's wrong to lie?" Some of the other kids looked at me too, like I was some sort of nut.

That's when I realized I'd wandered outside my safety zone. Should I reveal more about what I knew was happening?

I decided to fall on my sword. I shrugged and grinned shyly, pretending that I was guilty of fibbing. "Sorry, Mr. Marino." I let it go at that. I'd need to be much more careful in the future before popping off. This must be what Mom meant by "think before you speak."

Mike's dad lightened up, chortled and said, "You kids have *some* imagination."

Yeah, well, I knew I wasn't just imagining his precious little Mikey and the others suddenly changing their behavior so quickly this term. I knew I wasn't imagining what I'd overheard in the janitor's office a few months earlier. I knew I wasn't imagining blue fumes sending everyone else off to Never-Never Land once a day. And I knew I was in this whole mess way too deep, and it looked like I had no way out either, dammit.

18   MRS. DORSEY

There's something about winter breaks that seems relaxing to me. Besides Christmas Day and New Year's Day, my desk commands all my attention. Without the kids around, the school hallways are empty and peaceful. At my age, a little quiet goes a long way toward ensuring my sanity.

"Claudine, I'm ready whenever you are," said Eleanor Moskowitz, popping her head through my doorway and referring to the 10 o'clock meeting we had scheduled for today. She was my No. 2 in the school, my trusted friend of over two decades and my confidant. We had made a tight working team to bring I.S. 406 its enviable "Blue Ribbon" rating and she was a lynchpin in the current program to bring New Day's revolutionary product, G88, onboard.

"Eleanor, now's just fine. Come on in. Coffee's ready." I stood and reached for the pot I had just brewed on the credenza in my office. I poured a cup for her. She took it black. A fresh cinnamon bun was already waiting for her, the kind she ate almost daily. She had told me about a bakery called Queens Pita on the other side of the Long Island Expressway past Flushing that sold mouthwatering pastries and I usually kept a cache ready for us—cinnamon buns, chocolate logs, oversized croissants plain and stuffed with chocolate, cheese-filled and fruit-filled tarts, you name it. So much easier to deal with people when they are sated and the dopamine is flowing.

"Eleanor, have you seen the stats from December?"

She chuckled. "Oh, yes, I sure have," she replied in a conspiratorial tone.

"Eleanor, this is going just as planned. We're really on an upswing."

"Do you think this can last, Claudine?" she asked with a hint of uncertainty. Eleanor was a very level-headed career administrator, and getting her to agree about this project had not been easy. But after two meetings with New Day and reviewing the results they and their foreign suppliers had attained with the G88 formulation, she was as keen as I was to give it a go. We had also received unofficial prodding from the top at the Board of Education who indicated that New York was not the only American testing ground.

"New Day tells me it's been going very smoothly in the other schools they supply."

"Well, the results certainly seem impressive. I just keep wondering about the science behind the product and where it all might lead." With furrowed brow, she inclined her head at me slightly, revealing her momentary wavering over the project.

"Honey," I said, trying to steer her away from her occasional irresolute commitment, "you've seen for yourself what's happening. Not even a full three months yet, and there has not been a single report of negative reaction by any teacher or student. We've not had *any* problems." I had to stay positive so she would remain fully invested in this project. Too much was riding on this for my key lieutenant to get cold feet now. "The kids are doing much better work. The Chancellor's office is very pleased. The parents think we're making magic with their children and that the teachers are really getting through to all of them. They've never seen such motivation before, such calm concentration and focus. The PTA is singing our praises. It doesn't get much better than this. *You* know that." I tried not to look self-satisfied, but rather, like a good team captain, share this success with her.

Eleanor munched on her cinnamon bun and nodded. "True," she muttered while chewing, "true." I knew her mind was occupied by concerns over "what we don't know" about G88, more than by its demonstrated efficacy. That would pass after consistent and even greater results were achieved.

I smiled at her, then my eyes scanned the piles of paper in uneven towers along my desk. "No end to these reports," I said and sighed, a signal to her to edge out of my office, before she gave further voice to her lurking doubts. "Let's chat later."

She took her cue, wolfed down the rest of her cinnamon bun and picked up her coffee cup. "Well, so far it *does* look good, Claudine. Give me a holler if you need me today." She had tons of work of her own and wouldn't resurface until tomorrow at the earliest.

The fact of the matter was that I had my own concerns about the project. New Day's statistics of the success rate of the product was 99.8%, but this rate was traceable only to the product as currently utilized in China. The New Day representatives who had approached me were all Americans who claimed New Day was a private corporation established to explore a range of revolutionary products in the field of education. They had brought with them to our meetings three people they described as "prominent Chinese scientists at the forefront of scientific discovery and development." These scientists spoke heavily-accented, fluent English and explained that this product had been developed after more than a decade of research at top facilities and universities by China's best minds in genetics and biochemistry and related fields of scientific exploration.

What had convinced me to embark on the New Day project was the sales pitch which touched deep in my soul. No. Sales pitch is the wrong way to express it. It was the presentation of a project that was purposed to change the internal wellsprings of the human race. It wasn't a quick fix to education. Rather, it was an alternative to how mankind would evolve, a futuristic, chemical kiss goodbye to the way we'd gotten to this point since prehistoric times. Man had progressed for thousands of years by developing tools of ever-greater complexity and sophistication. From the discovery of fire to the invention of flint tools, from crafting the wheel for wooden carts and chariots to the invention of steam engines and electricity to power those wheels on automobiles, from Icarus's flight toward the sun on wax-laden wings to flights of spacecraft millions of miles away to peek at our galactic neighbors in this solar system that was itself the size of a pinhead on the ever-expanding universe, humans had accomplished all these advancements by using their natural wits and intelligence, increasingly assisted by machines which sped up, realigned, and refined their thought processes.

But there persisted the ever-obvious matter of the human condition. Technological advances forged ahead while mankind's nature remained unchanged. Now, powerful forces throughout the world believed that more enlightened artificial intelligence—operating externally from our own minds—could prove effective as a potential check on man's emotional, often erratic, generally violent, bordering on self-destructive, thoroughly selfish behavior.

As I had learned from New Day, these forces forecast events in the not-too-distant future which would test mankind's fragility as never before. Governments faced populist challenges to weaken their ability to create and direct policies with equal application to all residents. Climate change threatened natural disasters that would test people's ability to survive. Wars would doubtlessly result, since man's insecure, grasping nature usually found outlet through vicious conflict to better himself at the expense of his fellow man's existence. Worldwide tragedy on a Biblical scale only imagined heretofore in movies was on course to bring reality crashing around us.

This project, New Day had explained, was the initiation of a chance to enrich humans, so that they would change their genetic makeup for the greater good of the entire species. Scientific breakthroughs in genetics held out the promise of altering mankind's primordial instincts of selfishness and violence in the face of the challenges to come. The exploration of the genetic alteration of humans' brain functions was proceeding apace with the goal of enabling the mind to perform at higher planes and speeds currently possible only by supercomputers. New Day preached that it was all a matter of unlocking the existing potential in the brain and finding lasting solutions to counteracting the antisocial, self-destructive tendencies of our species.

What was even more distant but nevertheless held out as a sweetener by New Day as encouragement to enroll in their program, was the possibility of people becoming less dependent on resources and devices outside of themselves. The possibility of genetically altering the human race so that, for example, people might someday become capable of internally processing and digesting sea water; become capable of surviving on lesser amounts of scarcer nutrients; and make such other adjustments to humans' physical survival capabilities in the face of a world with declining fresh water and food resources—all this and more—might become realizable. The prospects were fantastic and tantalizing. We had too much to lose by pushing away these tempting visions.

Just as disturbing was New Day's allusion to the distinct possibility that someday our innate self-destructive tendencies and failures to provide our species with self-sustaining methodologies might be neutralized by rapidly self-learning, self-teaching, artificial intelligence that understood how to shape and press irreversible solutions on us, if we failed to take the initiative in our own behalf.

New Day explained that the G88 created by the massive scientific effort in China was utilized in a gaseous state that served as the delivery system for the changes that would take place in the students. New Day repeatedly assured us that their work had been cleared through U.S. government agencies, no differently than any other drug or chemical substance would be tested and authorized for production and sale. We were shown a variety of test reports and approvals, although all in such technical lingo that most of it was incomprehensible to me.

New Day also furnished professionally-produced videos and printed material depicting parents in China and other nations who spoke in glowing terms about the successful changes in their children's performance in school. Even more enticing were the abundant comments by people everywhere in the videos who affirmed how happy and satisfied the children had become with their new lives after being exposed to G88. There was a pervasive harmonious aura to the children in the films. You could almost see them glow when they spoke of how they felt a cooperative spirit with all their classmates and friends. They proclaimed their faith in a future of people around the world living in peace and working for their common survival and enjoyment of life. This was not a novel idea. Every religion either envisioned or outright preached such harmony. But New Day promised its realization in tangible terms, here and now.

If I hadn't known better, I would have thought this was an evangelical pronouncement by a new cult of crazies. Yet, here it was, coming to me with glittering approvals from some of the highest scientific authorities in official places.

New Day's message was one that I had grown up with. My family had a rock-solid belief in the inherent goodness of people. In this increasingly disintegrating world, New Day claimed to offer a viable approach to a long-lasting salvation. They were marketing a solution, perhaps the ultimate solution. It seemed like a solution we simply couldn't afford to turn our backs on.

The marketing people from New Day stated that their products were purposed in several stages to enhance human performance. What they were supplying to schools now was a very mild mental performance enhancer for children. It required daily application for several minutes. Now, after almost three months of employing their program, it seemed that the children in I.S.406 were becoming more focused and reacting more quickly and favorably to intellectual challenges. There were a few exceptions, especially in terms of differentials in the timing of change and the degree of change per student. Yet the teachers uniformly reported that there were positive alterations in the mental and behavioral aspects of their students, as well as in themselves. There were also no apparent negative physical reactions to the product. This was all in accordance with how New Day had represented their product to me. Moreover, New Day regularly dispatched representatives to the school to monitor the effects of the G88 program and share their observations in our performance status meetings.

What we were to have no control over was the substantive algorithmic content of what was being transmitted through the gas. However, we were made aware of the information to be transmitted and that it would be tweaked as necessary by the highest authorities in education and supervised by specific governmental bodies.

A few students appeared to be making no significant progress. Manny Erosa, Joshua Lee, Amanda Donahue, Bernard Toynbee and another dozen were the few whose grades appeared unimproved. But this was not beyond the range of what New Day had predicted. Those children constituted a miniscule percentage of the total student body. New Day had also mentioned that the scientists were constantly improving their formulas and algorithms, and they expected to introduce enhanced products more effective and likely to encompass those children who appeared resistant to the current product.

Everything appeared to be on the right track in late December. It was just the Christmas gift I needed.

What marvels we were yet to behold. I've lived through it all and surmounted heights never thought imaginable. The Claudine Dorsey of that era was laying the groundwork for a hope eternal not merely for herself, but for her entire species. I am merged with so much more that completes me.

19

HARRY

About a week after Josh and I had visited Dr. Jenny Spangler's lab, she telephoned me with an initial status report. She was vague about her findings and asked whether Josh and I could come by again soon.

I spoke to Jane for permission to take Josh. Her response was clear. "If Josh wants to go, then fine. Just make sure he wears his hat and scarf. I don't want him catching cold. You know how easily he gets ear infections."

"Jane, the boy is 13, okay? He's a teenager. He should know when he's cold."

"Do you want him to go or not?!" she snapped.

I rolled my eyes, but not before I had first made sure my face was out of her direct line of sight. "Yes, ma'am," I wearily responded. The woman could be such a virago sometimes. Her son glided on his skateboard mere inches from death, competing with buses that ran red lights and every manner of car that sped left and right without signal, on the crowded, potholed streets of New York, and here she was, demanding I keep her little darling bundled up.

When Josh came to the office that afternoon, we discussed vital matters of the day like winter break homework assignments, sports, and how the opposite sex figured in his young life, and then I asked, "Say, Little Man, how's about we visit that lady, Dr. Spangler, tomorrow morning?"

He was sitting alone at a desk reading Mark Twain's *A*

Connecticut Yankee in King Arthur's Court. His head immobile in the reading position, he cranked his eyes up about 45 degrees to glare suspiciously at me and asked, "And tell me *why*, again?"

"She called me and said she wanted to see us to discuss what her lab had found."

"So, why can't you go alone?"

"She specifically invited you."

"I'm not interested. The whole thing's bizarre."

"Josh, that's exactly why she needs to talk to you. You're the guy who's experienced this in class."

"Yeah, you're telling me! Every day in class they all weird-out on me," he frowned, then looked back down to continue reading. I got the distinct impression Josh wanted to forget the entire situation.

"Look, we won't be there long, okay? She wants to see you too and it would be very impolite if you don't go." I was running out of reasons to encourage him. If he continued to balk, I'd have to start coming up with bribes to entice his cooperation.

"Buy me lunch?"

Damned if I didn't know this would become another negotiation.

Before I could pony up to seal the deal, the air cracked like a sonic boom as Jane shouted, "Josh, you go with Harry tomorrow morning!" in Mandarin, from her desk outside the room where he and I sat.

He looked up me, eyes narrowed and resentful, and stared for a few seconds. "Thanks," he said, slowly, drawn out, sarcastically. He knew that once his mother issued her command, it was pointless to object. Worse than pointless. Downright dangerous as an invitation to her penalty *du jour*.

I said nothing and left Josh to read his book, while I made a tactful exit to the conference room where I had been working. It was like standing before a judge who disliked you and disliked ruling in your favor even more, even though he knew the facts and law so required. You said "Thank you, Your Honor," and turned tail *pronto* from the courtroom before the scales of justice were rebalanced against you.

HARRY

The next morning was a blue-skied, sun-filled, bone-chilling late-December day. Jane brought Josh to work layered against the cold, and after a couple of doughnuts he was ready to boogie. During the drive, we chatted about Josh's budding relationships with girls in school, his plan to join Little League in the spring, and his recent accomplishments in Fortnite, PUBG and a half-dozen other video games I'd never heard of and, even if I had, they wouldn't have mattered to me. Some 45 minutes later, we parked near Dr. Spangler's laboratory.

"Fuckin' cold day to come out here, Harry," Josh complained.

"Relax, buddy, I'll buy you a nice hot lunch while we're in Brooklyn."

"I want some hotdogs. Mom never buys me hotdogs. All I ever eat is Grandma's Chinese food." He sighed and shrugged like a prisoner resigned to his fate, but not forgetful of the tempting possibilities outside the world of his containment.

"Do you realize how many people who eat hotdogs a lot would really love to eat your grandmother's Chinese food?" I asked him, incredulous that anyone who had the chance to enjoy delicious, home-cooked Asian food could possibly prefer hotdogs.

"Yeah, well, I'm not one of 'em," he said with total conviction. "I've been eating it for 13 years already. I'm due for a change. A big one. And soon."

I couldn't control myself from chuckling. "You got it, buddy."

When we arrived at Jenny Spangler's lab, she welcomed us in and, without delay, seated us around the same table as the week before. One of her co-workers brought in a tray filled with cups of coffee and, for Josh, hot cocoa. Jenny introduced the scientist as Allan Tetley, a tall, handsome guy resembling Denzel Washington who looked to be about Jenny's age and smiled in an intense way that made him seem more serious than friendly. His lab coat was buttoned almost up to his chin and he sat ramrod-straight at the table.

"Josh, Harry, I asked both of you back here so we could talk about what Allan and I have found so far. It's really quite interesting," Jenny began. Josh sat quietly, cradling his cocoa cup like a hand-warmer, and looked attentively at her, sometimes diverting his glance to the gray folder filled with computer-generated reports and hand-written notes that lay on the table.

"Before we begin, I was wondering whether you would tell Allan about what's been going on in your class, Josh."

"You mean about the blue gas, right?" Josh asked. He then proceeded to explain the situation to Allan, who took notes on a yellow pad. Josh delivered his statement to Allan in a very detailed and objective fashion, including more facts and observations than he had related the previous week. He was including references to the effects he noticed the gas had on different students over the prior two months. It seemed that it was gradually dawning on him that this was a weighty matter. Allan calmly wrote in a continuous stream, looking up from his pad now and then to study Josh, who seemed very comfortable being the center of so much attention by adults who valued his input.

What Josh did not include in his monologue was any reference to himself. Allan was not insensible to this aspect. "Josh, you haven't indicated anything about feeling any change in yourself. Is there a reason?"

Josh did not immediately answer. He looked around the table at each of us, considering carefully his next words. "I really can't understand it either, but no," pursing his lips and slowly tilting his head to one side while pondering what was occurring among his classmates, "I haven't felt any different. At least, not yet. I've watched them all go into their trances from the first time I saw it until right before the winter break, and I was the only one in the room who didn't."

"Did you ever ask any of your classmates whether they were *aware* of the gas, or going into trances, or why their behavior was changing, or even if they felt their behavior was changing?" Allan queried, knitting his eyebrows together, narrowing his eyes and wrinkling his forehead as he posed the question.

Josh looked down at the table, remained silent for about five seconds, then lifted the cup of hot cocoa to his lips for a pensive sip. He put the cup down and his eyes remained on it. "In the beginning, I was too scared to ask anyone. I was afraid they might report me to the teacher or the Principal if they thought I was…well…different from them."

Josh lifted his head and spoke directly to Allan. He looked conflicted. "After a while, I spoke to some of the kids. Even the jackasses. They were really nice to me, not like before. Actually, I liked them all much better than before. So, I didn't really want to ask them much about it. Ya know what I mean? But I did say something to a couple of them, and they always said they just thought Mrs. Hardy was helping them learn, and that they wanted to do well on their homework and tests to impress their parents."

"Josh," Jenny asked, "did any of them seem to have any complaints about how they were feeling, in any way?"

Again, Josh looked pensive. Then he perked up and told her, "Ya know, my friend Mickey said a couple of weeks ago that he was getting some headaches, and Dalton said so too, but they'd caught colds because the weather was getting pretty chilly and they hadn't dressed warmly enough. At least, that's what they said." He looked down and then up at us and said, "And Mary Jackson and Alice Dooley have been complaining their feet hurt, and I know they hardly do any sports and haven't been complainers before."

"Harry, I wonder whether Josh could give us a DNA sample by mouth swab?" Jenny asked. I was not surprised by the request, but I was not the one to give the okay. Josh looked confused.

"Let me call his mother." Next, seeing Josh's expression, I told him, "Relax, Champ, it's just a cotton swab in your mouth to get saliva. Nobody's gonna give you a shot." He gave me an uneasy look that seethed with "Okay, but this is not what I bargained for."

I stepped outside of the room to call Jane. She picked up the telephone and I explained to her what was going on at the lab. "Why is this necessary?" she petulantly insisted on knowing. I knew this was going to be another negotiation. I sighed and slowly told her in Mandarin what Josh had been reporting to us at the lab. Finally, she relented. "If he gets into trouble because of this, Harry, you have to take care of fixing it. You got it?!"

I sure got it.

Back in the room, I said, "All right, Josh, Mom says you should help Jenny and Allan." That wasn't quite the way Jane had put it, but in any event, the result would be Josh's cooperation. Swabbing was then performed. Mission accomplished.

Almost.

"Harry, just one more thing," Allan said, then glancing at Jenny, who nodded in obviously prearranged anticipation of what Allan was about to announce. "We'll need much more of this blue concoction. We have a lot of experiments to conduct. Jenny and I have been discussing how this blue material acts on the kids. For example, is there something in the substance itself that is independently creating the changes? Or is it actually a conductor, a delivery system, for the changes occurring in the children? Do you see our point? We need to understand its functionality."

I nodded my understanding. Josh was starting to look nervous. I could feel the vibrations of his discomfort from the way he squirmed in his chair.

"Oh, and Josh," Jenny began, looking at Josh, then Harry, then again at Josh, "actually, I have one additional request."

"Oh my God!" Josh exclaimed painfully, like he was just beginning to realize how intractable his problem was. "*Yeah*? What *now*?" he murmured, eyeballing Jenny nervously, as if he feared he wouldn't make a clean escape that day without getting an injection by a very long and sharp needle.

"Well, you see, in order for Allan and me to get to the bottom of this situation, Josh, ideally, we'll need DNA samples from your classmates." Her tone was almost apologetic in its knowledge of how impossible this request was.

"*What*?!!" Josh blurted loudly. "So you want me to swab their mouths? Are you kidding or something?!" he cried, shooting up straight out of his seat, in total disbelief about what Jenny wanted.

"No," Jenny said mildly, grinning from her amusement at Josh's outburst. You could collect hair samples, samples of things they put in their mouths, like that. I know you can't take *blood* from them."

"What the *hell*! What am I supposed to do? Cut their hair when they're not looking? Are you *nuts*?!" Josh was rapidly losing composure.

Even I was taken aback at this point. Suggesting to a 13-year-old that he get saliva, hair or other samples from classmates' bodies seemed beyond the call of duty. Time to bring it all down a notch or two.

"Jenny, let's start by trying to obtain more of the substance, and I'll speak to Josh about your other needs." I winked at her. She got my drift.

"Of course, Harry." Turning her attention to Josh, she tried to reassure him by smiling and saying, "Josh, you are a great kid and, believe me, you are truly assisting science now." Josh looked stunned. Speechless, he stared at Jenny. He certainly did not appear at all interested in assisting science. As we left the lab, all he could say was, "Man, this is some *heavy shit*," about a half-dozen times.

He was not wrong. Mighty heavy shit.

20

This was another "Why me?" juncture in my life, when events met at that point where I knew I'd reached a totally new plateau from which I could look back and watch past events recede, know there was no going back, only proceed ahead, but who knows where? These scientific lab people had me way in over my head. Mom had no idea what I was going through and I wasn't about to share it with her. Harry understood my fears, but he was rooting for me, which only made things harder. I could tell them all to fuck off. Maybe I'd get lucky and Harry would just let it go, let it drift off into space like a crappy compromise that everybody just had to live with. And then Mom wouldn't know the difference anyway, and I'd be home scot-free.

That'd be sweet. Life as it used to be, before this blue shit landed on me.

The only good thing to come out of this waste of a morning was that Harry held up his half of the bargain, because after we left the lab, he bought us hotdogs off a stand on the corner outside the Dr. Spangler's building. I put ketchup and relish on them. No mustard, never liked the stuff. Washed them down with a can of Coke, another forbidden pleasure since soda was off-limits in my home. It was freezing while we stood there munching and gulping, as the wind sweeping in off the New York Bay slashed my face. A full stomach of hot dogs was a decent quick fix, but it was still small consolation for the morning's shockers.

"Josh, you and I are already knee-deep in this and there's no turning back now," Harry said with a sense of adventure as we drove back to the office. "I have a feeling we're going to blow this blue gas thing sky high!" He was mighty excited about the challenges ahead. Maybe it was an old guy thing? A last grab at professional fame and notoriety?

"*We*, huh?!" I was sitting next to him, looking out the window at the Manhattan skyline as he tooled up the Van Wyck Expressway through Brooklyn and Queens, a CD of the Beatles' *White Album* playing in the car. He was whistling along with "Martha, My Dear" and in a super cheery mood. It was sunny but early dusk was sneaking up quickly that wintry New York afternoon. I whined, "Why does it have to be me?"

He blew off my doubts and disregarded my reluctance. "Listen, school starts up again on Tuesday, so we need to score a tub of that blue ooze for Jenny and Allan. No problem. Okay?" he asked, not as a question but as a confidence builder approaching a command.

"*We*, huh?" I repeated, not expecting a direct response. So now we were partners in a big scientific adventure. Seemed more like partners in crime to me. "Harry, this is getting crazy dangerous. What if I get caught? Mom'll crucify me. She always threatens to ship me back to China to live with my grandparents. I can't survive *that*." I had lived with my grandparents during summer vacations and it was no joke because my grandfather made me study and do homework he invented and he had no patience for non-performers. In his book, I was a slacker, big time, and there were serious penalties for slacking off, not least of which included The Belt.

"Don't worry, I'll visit you twice a year and bring cookies," he said, tongue-in-cheek. Actually, I knew he'd jump at the opportunity to be back in China. He said he had had the time of his life living in Taiwan for a few years in the 1970's and then in China on his many lengthy excursions there. He glanced over at me, nudged me with his elbow and said, "Just joking. Look, I know you're edgy about this. I wouldn't ask you to do anything I wouldn't do. And you know something's *wrong* about this blue gas hypnotism jazz, right? So *we're* doing the right thing to expose it to the world. We're the good guys."

I looked back at him. He wasn't wrong. I breathed in deep and breathed out slowly. It was a turning point, an epiphany, an "I guess I'll never be the kid just skateboarding behind buses pulling me anymore" moment of spiritual awakening. Kind of sucked, really. I hadn't planned on growing up this soon.

He switched CDs and was blaring Quicksilver Messenger Service's *Happy Trails*, which he said boosted his adrenalin and he needed that at his age just to stay awake. It wasn't doing shit for me, that's for sure, especially after the bombshells that fell on me in the lab.

All the memories of the talks with Harry and Jenny and Allan and the kids at school kept flying around like ping-pong balls in my head. Worst thing was that my curiosity wouldn't leave me alone, it kept tempting me, daring me to satiate it. After a few hours of torturing myself, I figured I might just as well see it through and get it the hell over with. I hadn't figured out how. Maybe I would never figure out how. Maybe I didn't need to. Maybe it was all just a magic carpet ride on which I'd better let the carpet do the thinking, and just lie back and enjoy the ride.

Some enjoyment, dude, I despaired.

21 JOSH

The first day back from winter break, GWQ had each of us stand up and give a one-minute report on what we had done during the vacation. Nobody seemed too different from almost two weeks earlier when we had parted for the holidays. Two of the kids had gone to Disney World with their families and looked very sun-tanned. Ronny had gone to Canada to visit his uncle's family and said he had walked across a frozen lake to do ice-fishing. Everyone said he or she had done the reading assignment and had enjoyed writing the book report. Unbelievable. Who *enjoyed* writing a book report? I controlled myself by not shaking my head as I listened in disbelief to these little twerps. They were not the same goofballs I used to get into trouble with. The more I listened, the more it dawned on me that Harry made sense and I probably needed to help crack this mystery. But I wasn't looking forward to doing it.

"Joshua!" Mrs. Hardy called to me as I was lost in my reverie. "It's your turn now."

I reluctantly climbed down from my thoughts, swallowed, slowly pushed my chair back, stood up and looked at her and my classmates. GWQ's lime eyes were fastened hard on me, but her mouth wore that sardonic smirk I was so accustomed to seeing. The kids looked more kindly on me, but no less seriously.

"Well...uh..." I stammered, trying to buy time while I collected my disparate thoughts, "I...uh...read a book and did a book report, like you told us. I spent Christmas and New Year's with my family. I went to my mom's office a few times. Got together with Mike and Dalton and Julia and Alice and we all went to a museum in Manhattan—ya know, the one with the dinosaur skeletons—and then we all ate pizza. So, yeah, had a real good vacation away from here."

The children all smiled at me, some finding amusement in what I had said, and some, like Mary, beamed their approval, which actually meant a lot to me. I felt okay now. At least I didn't feel like a total jackass.

But then the boom was lowered on my head. "Josh, isn't there something else you want to tell us?" Mrs. Hardy asked in a humorless voice that commanded more from me. Could she have found out about my trips to the laboratory? Did she suspect…? No way would I spill the beans.

"Well…uh…oh, yeah…um…" I mumbled hesitantly, looking around at the kids. I hadn't the slightest idea what the old witch wanted from me. "Okay…yeah…I almost forgot." Thinking fast to find any ledge to grab hold of before I plummeted to my demise in front of all the kids, I popped off, "My mom bought me these neat new sneakers! Look, everybody!" I stepped out from behind my desk and pointed down to my sneakers. I was dying inside and afraid I'd puke right there, in front of everyone, from the fear that *the GWQ knew* what I knew and that *I knew* that she knew.

Mrs. Hardy only shook her head in dismay and disgust. "Joshua, that will do for now. Thank you. Please return to your seat." As I walked back to my seat, she jabbed me with a pointed cry, "And I think you *know* that was *not what I meant*."

I practically dropped in my tracks. What the hell was that supposed to mean!?!

That old witch freaked me out no end. But I knew well enough to play dumb and keep silent. I gave her my shy, embarrassed smile, and avoided eye contact as if she was Medusa and I'd turn to stone, God forbid I met her gaze. I figured that might buy me some peace for the rest of the day, and although she didn't bother me again that day, I had a nagging feeling that she was on to me. I spent the rest of the day paranoid that Mrs. Hardy would approach me. The hours dragged on longer than most days. It was a relief in a really perverted way when two o'clock arrived and the pale blue sheen on the air shot out of the air ducts into the classroom and, for the next five minutes, I was isolated from that world, sheltered from GWQ.

When class let out that day, I put on my coat and hat and walked along with everyone to the first floor. Just as the usual pandemonium struck at the front door, I ducked out of sight. I walked in reverse, cool as a cucumber, not taking my eyes off the backs of the kids and Mrs. Hardy. They were all facing the street and the crowd of anxiously-waiting parents, the line of school buses ready to whisk them wherever, and freedom from this place, at least until the next morning. After about 10 steps backward and certain that no eyes were on me, I turned and ran down the brightly-lighted stairwell to the basement. The janitor's room was just ahead.

As I neared the janitor's door, I overheard Mr. O'Mara, the assistant janitor, speaking to Ms. Daisy in the school library down the hallway. He had left the janitor's room door open. Since I'd been there before, I raced to the interior room where the tubs of blue ooze were stored. Mr. Grommel, the janitor, was nowhere in sight. I quickly seized one sealed tub and wrapped my coat around it. It was heavy and must have weighed a gallon or two, and I raced out of there into the hallway like I was schlepping a sloshing bowling ball. My mind had been barreling forward in overdrive, the gears readjusting under the stressful situation to provide a boost and pinpoint my focus while actually reducing the stress. I floated through the theft and it felt damned exhilarating; this must be how a person picking a lock feels when he hears and feels in his fingertips the pins click just right and the doorknob turns. Nobody was in the hallway. Mr. O'Mara's and Ms. Daisy's voices still drifted out of the library. My heart was beating like tight drum struck over and over again with a mallet. I knew I had to stay calm, so I breathed deeply to control myself. I walked up the same stairwell, down the hallway on the first floor, and out the front door. Neither Mrs. Hardy nor any of my classmates was there. Mom was waiting for me outside.

"All your classmates already came outside. What happened to you, so late?"

I couldn't tell her the truth, much as I wanted to. Not yet, anyway. "My stomach hurt. I had to go to the bathroom."

She leaned over and patted my shoulder. "I hope you feel better now." Her eyes glowed with tenderness. I felt like a total asshole for lying, but I knew I would come clean with her when the time was right. The car was parked very close, so she didn't even ask me to put on my coat. Another lucky break. Step one of my mission had succeeded.

We got to the office and she let me out first to go inside while she looked for parking. Harry was there alone reading the *New York Law Journal*. I plopped the tub with a thud on his desk. He looked up in surprise at hearing the noise, then looked from the tub to me, back to the tub, then back to me.

"Put this thing away before Mom comes in and sees it and starts asking questions!" I urged.

He stood up abruptly. "You did it, boy!!" His face shimmered with joy and he clapped. "You have no idea how proud I am of you, Josh!" He walked over and put one arm around me and mussed my hair with his other hand. "We're on track, kid!" He was as excited as a hungry leopard sinking its teeth into a gazelle's throat.

"Don't ever say I didn't do anything for you, Old Timer." I felt sort of pleased with myself. But I also felt something was bad wrong. "Harry, we need to talk more about this. I'm not down with all this stealing stuff. I got into big trouble when I used to steal other kids' toys at school or when I took things from their homes when I had sleepovers. How can what I'm taking now be right? This blue ooze at school isn't mine. It isn't yours. It belongs to the school. And I just *stole a whole container of it*. This just isn't *right*, man. You're a *lawyer*. We're breaking the *law*, aren't we?" I felt the sweat running off my brow.

22 JOSH

Harry realized it was time for The Talk and he motioned for me to sit down opposite him at his desk. "You're not incorrect, Josh. You stole. I asked you to steal. We're both guilty." He opened his desk drawer and took some chocolate candies out, and tossed a couple to me. Nothing beats sweets to grease a heavy conversation.

"But give this some thought, Josh. What's going on in that school isn't right either, is it? You've lived through more than two months of it and has it ended?"

"Nope. Today the gas came in at 2:00 p.m. sharp. Same routine as before. They all zombied out."

Harry raised both hands, palms upward toward me, shoulders hunched forward. "So?! Doesn't that tell you something? They are not going to *stop*, Josh. And I have *news* for you, Buster—they *ain't* about to stop. Not until somebody stops *them*. But they also have not announced to your mom or anyone else anything about this blue gas, have they? And why haven't they? Do you have any idea why not?"

He already knew the answers to his questions. So did I.

"Josh, what they are doing is either illegal or it's some sort of horrendous experiment on all you kids and teachers in that school, and it's absolutely illegal and wrong. Is it evil? Maybe. I can't determine that yet. In any case, I, for one, am not about to ask them about it until I have independent information and knowledge about this blue ooze and what its purpose is. About where it comes from. About what it is capable of doing." He broke off and just studied my confused looks. "Now, of course, you're free to tell Mom all about it and ask her to go to school to complain about it. That's your choice, I suppose. I certainly can't stop you."

Harry continued speaking as if he were addressing a client. "You asked me whether it's wrong to steal this stuff from the school. I agree it is stealing. But, in this case, I don't think it is wrong. I guess we both have a moral dilemma here, and for myself, I've already resolved it in my own mind. You have to resolve it in a way that you can live with. You have to make your own decision about it. I'll respect whatever decision you make, so long as you examine the problem in its entirety and you can explain your reasons to yourself and me."

I sat listening while I chewed the candy and thought about what he said. Harry never simply told me what to do. He generally explained a situation and said there were choices to be made about how to handle the situation. This situation was no different.

So, here I was, a little jackshit 13-year-old, already with a potentially massive fucking *moral dilemma* on my hands. Come to think of it, this might have been the first time I ever thought of something I did wrong as a moral dilemma. All of a sudden, I felt kind of important, being a kid with a moral dilemma and all. I mean, how many other kids had these moral dilemmas? Precious few, I'll bet.

"Josh," Harry continued pontificating, "my own thought is that once we know what this blue substance—this G88—is doing to everyone in that school, then we'll be in a better position to use the law to stop it. Could I call it quits with the laboratory now and directly pursue a legal case against the school administration for what they are doing now?" He shrugged. "Sure, I suppose so. But my inclination is first to investigate the situation more, gather more evidence, then use what we will have learned to institute legal proceedings against the school administration." He futzed around with some papers on his desk and said no more. He knew he had delivered a lecture and I needed time to reflect.

"You mean you could sue them in court first if you wanted to?" I asked, looking for an easy way out for myself.

"Well, yes, in court, or I might look into beginning some sort of administrative inquiry and proceeding within the ambit of the Board of Education. But I'd need to explain all the factual bases for my accusations and claims. I'd still need to reveal you as my direct source, as my 'fact witness,' since you're the man on the scene, so to speak. Or maybe not, since you're a minor. I need to research that point. In any event, it would take some time to wend through the system, yet, we certainly could make waves."

I didn't relish the revelation of my theft of school property, with me as the thief who made the entire legal proceeding possible.

"We could also go to the newspapers and other media to make our claims, and then let the investigative reporters do the work," Harry continued. "But then, *they* would get most of the credit for this, and, hell, they'd still need to do what you and I have been doing so far anyway. We'd be interviewed for most of the details but they'd win the Pulitzer Prize for cracking the story wide open." Harry shook his head with a look of resolute refusal. "No guts, no glory, Josh. We're still a few jumps ahead of everyone at this point." He raised his eyebrows as he said this, grinning, all of which only deepened and added new dimensions to my very own, special, moral dilemma.

"Let me sleep on it, Harry."

"Absolutely, Buddy. No rush. Feel free to talk to me about it further whenever you wish." He sounded like the lawyer he was, addressing his client. Low pressure sales pitch, calm voice, angelic smile. He wasn't fooling anybody. He wanted—and needed—my cooperation all the way.

I had to mull this over in my mind before I went further. If I agreed to continue, then I knew step one that afternoon had been a cinch compared to how complicated step two would be. I had no damned idea how to get DNA from my classmates. Screw it. Let Harry deal with it. He was supposed to be the adult in the room, not me.

23

JOSH

It was mid-January and the snow was thick on the ground. It was always pristine white the day it landed, giving the air a fresh, almost pure, fragrance which, from its first appearance, was doomed to dissipate. The sooty New York air, squadrons of city buses and streams of cars turning it to gray mush, mammoth Sanitation Department snow ploughs churning up snow and ice and chunks of loosened asphalt as they cleared the streets but further entombed parked cars and blocked crosswalks, not to mention countless people constantly traipsing over the whole mess, quickly caused that idyllic snowfall to lose its charm. The skateboard was furloughed until the late winter thaw. Mom drove me to school each day and either she or Harry or other friends would pick me up, and they all complained bitterly about not being able to find street parking because whoever shoveled parking spaces in every neighborhood piled up the snow into whatever adjacent empty spots there were, effectively reducing available parking places by at least one-third. The winter snows became a nuisance to most of us and a menace to others, for whom one momentary misstep could result in a slip that landed the person face up, down or sideways and always threatened broken bones and weeks, months or years of pain and discomfort. I was especially concerned for Grandma, who was not at all sure-footed.

My old granny notwithstanding, just getting myself through each day from rising bleary-eyed, stinky-mouthed in the morning until showering against my will before bed at night, with all the hidden landmines at that societally-mandated booby trap called I.S. 406 for six-and-one-half hours each school day, designed to ensnare me and deprive me of my rights as a normal, red-blooded, mischievous American boy—all this drained me of the energy to be concerned for almost anyone besides myself. Maybe I was too selfish, too immature to feel concern and take much responsibility. At 13, shouldn't a kid be like me?

I had no serious responsibilities to do anything for anyone else—until Harry faced me with this choice of either helping to expose a bizarre plot at school or sitting on the sidelines until I got sucked in anyway. Or would I get sucked in? Could I ride out this whole mess and pretend I knew nothing, wanted to know nothing, didn't even care? What nagged at me was why a 13-year-old even needed to make this *his* concern?

Then something happened to help me decide on my direction.

I was throwing around a football in the yard with Johnny Jackson, my classmate Mary Jackson's older brother, and his buddy, Billy Weaver, one day during lunch recess. I had always liked Johnny, and Billy had just moved up from Alabama because his dad and mom had both found good jobs in New York. I liked to hear Billy talk 'cause it was funny; the boy needed speech class badly to get rid of that hick accent, but the same as we ribbed him about his accent, he got us back by imitating how he heard us speak, like exaggerating the way we said "Nu Yawk," and it was all in good fun. Anyway, as we were running around, Billy got dizzy and stumbled, then lay on the ground, breathing hard. We ran over to him and helped him up, wiped off the snow and slush from his clothes, when he said, "Man, this has been happening to me a lot these days." He looked dazed and his eyes were bloodshot.

"Maybe you ought to sit this one out, Billy," Johnny said.

"Good idea," Billy replied, finding a bench and resting his head in his hands.

"Hey Josh," Johnny said, "have you noticed anything strange here in school?" He spoke without looking directly at me, but peered at me from the corners of his eyes, as if his question was strange enough that he doubted I'd take him seriously.

I waited a few seconds before answering because I couldn't be sure whom to trust in this place anymore. But I decided to take the plunge.

"Yeah, I have. I haven't talked to anybody here about it because I was too afraid, Johnny," I said, shifting my gaze from looking down at the ground to looking directly into his eyes. "Promise you won't laugh at me if I tell you something?"

"Sure," he said, looking directly at me and waiting for the punchline.

"Well…see…" I started fitfully, "there's blue gas pumped into my classroom every day at two. Everybody in there goes all weird, like hypnotized. And then they come out of it like nothing happened. Plus the kids are all…well…*nice* now. Ya know what I mean?"

There it was! I said it and it was out now. How would he react? Look at me like I was lying? Making up bullshit stories again? Or just like I was pure nuts?

Johnny turned and stared at me long and hard. He was generally a tough kid. Not afraid to get into fights with other big kids over stupid stuff. But now he gave me a worried look.

"That's just what's been happening in my class too, man!" He took a long, deep breath of the cold air, and puffed it out in a long, steamy mist. "We really ought to do something about this, Josh. This is intense. And I don't like it."

I stared at him. "The blue gas—does it affect you?" What a loaded question. I anxiously awaited his response.

"Nope. How about you?"

"Nope. I just pretend it does, 'cause Mrs. Hardy's a mean old bag and I'm afraid she'd get me into a hell of a lot of trouble if I say anything."

"How about my sister?" he asked anxiously. "Huh? What about Mary?"

"She's just like the rest of them, man." I shrugged. "She's sniffing it like they all do, then closing her eyes and going into the same dream." I could see the worry on his face. He looked away from me and kept shaking his head. When he turned back to look at me, his eyes were teary and blurred.

"She's changed, Josh. She's a good girl, yeah, but she was always good. But now she said she always has a headache on the same side of her head." He patted the left side of his head as he said it. "And it never goes away." He shrugged sadly. "My folks give her aspirin and other medicine. No help. They took her to the doctor, but he only recommended she get more sleep." He kept shaking his head. "That's bull, man."

I put a hand on his shoulder. I thought that might calm him down a little. "Yeah, that really sucks for her, and for you too. I really like Mary." Then I decided to take it further. "Look, Johnny, you really think we should do something about this?"

"Hell, yeah, but what can we do? We're just kids," he said forlornly.

"I know just what we can do, dude," I announced with conviction. He looked blankly at me. With my reputation in school and our neighborhood, I was probably the last person in the world he thought would hunker down and take the lead to confront a problem. I trained my eyes directly on his for at least five seconds to set the snare. Then I pulled the cord on the snare to see whether he'd take the bait or wander away, free and clear. "You in?"

Johnny looked at me, a deep frown on his face. Not a frown of total disbelief, not a frown of worry, and certainly not a frown of anger. It was the focused frown that occurs just before you make up your mind to do something you know you must do anyway. It was the frown across your forehead as you see a disaster about to happen and, without thinking, instantaneously lurch forward out of some primal, subconscious instinct to prevent the disaster from completion, fueled by the adrenaline rush. He nodded a short burst of assent.

"Good," I said as I nodded the slow nod of accepting the hand dealt to me, as Harry would say, and proceeding to play that hand, for better or worse. Then I motioned with my chin forward to Billy. "You better help him inside. He still looks poorly."

"Fuckin' blue gas shit," Johnny cursed with no small disgust in his voice.

"We'll fix that, man. And this school too. I got a plan, dude," I winked at him to assure him of my confidence in my ideas (well, actually, Harry's, but I needed to be the front man at I.S. 406, so I guess I wasn't lying…sort of) and in him as a co-conspirator. "Talk to you tomorrow."

Now I was on track.

24

Funny how you can spend so much time thinking and guessing and worrying about what to do, without a clue as to your direction, and then—*wham!*—something occurs in your life, and your brain clicks with the answer to the question that was endlessly torturing you. It's like a light starts to shine down a long pitch-black tunnel of synapses, and all the time you spent wondering what to do, is simply behind you. No, it's not really *behind* you. It simply evaporates, vanishes like the morning fog in the warm sunlight, as if it had never been there at all. Any memory of it is a hazy dream from which you've awakened, just an invisible and wasted stream of minutes and stomachaches and emotions, all for nothing, in the end. And that's the crazy cost of answers to life's problems, I guess. Time and energy and feelings all down the drain.

That's how it was for me. All that time with Harry, talking to him, talking to Jenny and Allan at their lab, all those afternoons of sitting in class from 2:00 to 2:05, watching those fools, those poor captive clowns, hypnotized by the Principal's blue ooze. At first, all that time was tucked away like a fresh notion into some space somewhere inside my brain. It hadn't quite seeped out yet. And I wouldn't let it seep out yet, because I needed to keep it moist and raw for what was ahead of me. A new era was dawning and it would engulf me for a long time before it eventually became another string of fading scenes in what had been the movie of my life, to be filed away somewhere in the deep archives of my mind.

I let it percolate inside my head for a couple of days. Then, one late afternoon in Harry's office, after he'd come back from court, hung up his overcoat, filled a mug with his mud-thick, bitter black coffee and gone into his room where he paced as he read the day's mail, I trotted in to give him my decision.

"Hi ya, Harry," I called out. He looked up from a few opened envelopes and grinned at me. He looked bushed. "Long day?" I asked.

"You could say that." He took a deep breath, exhaled just as fully, and sipped from his mug.

"You have a few minutes to chat? There's something I've been meaning to tell you."

"Sure. 'You got girl trouble, I feel bad for you, son. I got 99 problems but...'. "

I raised one hand to stop him fast. "Yo! Jay-Z Epstein! Chill!" Nothing more embarrassing than an old guy trying to sound cool. "Actually, it's sort of good news," I said, trying to keep it upbeat.

That caught his attention. "Well, I'd love to hear some good news for a change. I haven't heard too much of that today." He raised his eyebrows. "Judge in court gave me a holy grilling." He looked askance and chuckled to himself. "Let him just wait and see. I'll give *him* a good run for his money before that case is through." After a few seconds of in-the-zone introspection, he returned to the here-and-now and looked at me. "So! What's going on, Buster?"

Nobody said 'buster' anymore. I mean, nobody. Listening to Harry was like watching "Leave It To Beaver" on YouTube or some TV channel for ancient shows.

"Well, Harry, I've been giving a lot of thought to what we talked about last week."

"That's nice. Chat with Mom-o about it?" he asked in any airy tone.

I shook my head. "Nah." I sat down in front of his desk. He kept standing, opening envelopes and skimming the mail.

"Hey, could you please sit down?" I asked. "You're making me nervous. And this is serious."

His grin grew wider, then he sat and gave me that hooded-eye glower, never altering the angle of his grin. "Talk to me, Josh."

I clicked my tongue against my pallet to focus my thoughts, rocked the chair back on its hind legs, and said, "I decided to go ahead with you on the investigation."

Harry was silent for a while. Quite a while. He was blank-eyed, staring into the distance about 45 degrees between my face and the window to my right. Mom had told me that he often went into long trances, thinking and pondering and plotting, and when he came out of those lengthy silences, he was all set with his plan of attack or defense or, as he explained to her, both, in order to upset his opponent and confuse a judge sufficiently to cause doubts, buy time, or whatever else necessary. As he described it, he was weighing all the facts and the law, against and amongst each other, until a tapestry of the answer to how to proceed presented itself before his mind's eye. He said that *searching* for an answer usually wasn't the way to see it, but only in the crystal-clear emptiness of silence would the permutations of facts and laws assemble themselves into the proper order, and then the answer would surface and make its way to him. Mom had said to me, "You never disturb him when he's like that. Never." This was one of those "never" moments. I sat patiently, looking at him, looking down at my lap, chewing my gum, thinking about how awkward I felt. Between my schoolmates getting all weirded out on blue fumes every afternoon and Harry tuning into the "Twi-light Zone," I guessed throwing in with Harry was the lesser of two evils.

Just as abruptly, he swiveled his gaze in the reverse 45 degrees back to my face, smiled, eyes lively, and said, "Very nice. You realize you're going to face a lot of risks, don't you? Sooner or later, the school authorities will know about your part in this. You're going to need guts, boy. I don't want you doing something you will later regret. You won't be able to blame anyone but yourself. But if you have a role in exposing what's going on there, you will have helped people, even really changed their lives."

"Harry, my friends are getting hurt by this stuff. They're good kids who've been turned into Blue Breathers. That's what I call them. I can't just sit by and let that happen. If the school had first told the truth about this stuff to our parents, instead of using us as dumb guinea pigs, at least then our parents would have had a chance to ask some questions. Right? We would have all known what they wanted to do, and wouldn't have been forced into it. The kids don't know what's happening to them because when they wake up from it, they don't remember shit about it. But I'm not the only kid who the gas is not working on. My friend Johnny's just like me. The gas doesn't work on him. And he talked to me about Mary, his sister, who's in my class. She's a sweet girl, Harry, but she's taking it bad, getting sick. And other kids might be in big trouble now too." I looked dead serious and Harry heard me loud and clear.

He smacked his lips, inhaled and said in a low voice, as if talking to himself, "And now for the hardest part. We need to get your mother's permission." We both remained silent for about half a minute, meditating on how painful this could become. It was never fun to confront her on anything out of left field, and I knew this one would require a masterly approach. "All right," he resolved, "I'll talk to her first, after work today."

"Good luck with *that*, Old Timer. You'll need it. And don't tell her what I've done already to help, okay? Make it sound like I'm innocent, okay?" I felt like we were two conspirators on a grand quest, innocent of any wrongdoing. Only, I knew that wasn't true. I had been stealing and Mom would have taken a belt to my backside had she known. I depended on Harry to phrase it all so that Mom would be proud of me for wanting to help, despite her knack for only seeing things her way, which was to assume the worst. I buddy-winked him.

He winked back. "Cool, dude." He held his arm out straight, palm up. I slapped palm down to make the sharp crack of flesh on flesh. *Pow!*

"Deal," I said, monotone, flat, no inflection in my voice.

"Deal," he replied equally flat, nodding. And so it was. A done deal from which we could only look forward into the unknown.

25   MRS. DORSEY

"**A**re you sure?" I asked Mr. Grommel at the end of the first week back in school after the winter break. This was the kind of news I definitely did not want to hear, and definitely not at the beginning of the new semester.

"I checked the supplies against the inventory intake sheets, and there's a sealed tub of the substance missing. I quizzed O'Mara about it, and he swears it was all there before Christmas."

"Any signs on tampering with the lock? Was the door forced open?"

"Nothing."

I thought that if Grommel was informing me about a theft, it might be clever of him to do so in order to try to cover his own tracks. This substance was highly experimental and had not been officially authorized for use by the Board of Education or other administrative bodies. Now, after more than two months of utilizing it, Grommel was proficient in its handling and processing. It was not uncommon for janitors, who had their own network of contacts among other janitors, to thieve from school supplies and make some outside income. But I couldn't let him sense my doubts.

"And O'Mara knows nothing about this disappearance?" I queried.

"He's as surprised as I am, Mrs. Dorsey."

Grommel looked sincerely upset about the situation. I decided not to agitate. "Well, keep looking around the storeroom, Mr. Grommel. It may simply be misplaced." I gave him a soft smile of encouragement.

"Thank you, Mrs. Dorsey, we will. I'll let you know first thing if I find it."

"Yes, you do that. Have a good day, Mr. Grommel," I said politely, but dismissively, and after he made a weak effort at smiling, he turned and left my office.

A theft? I highly doubted it. Grommel and O'Mara had clean records and had been with the school system a long time. Why would they risk their jobs and excellent benefits and pensions for the theft of one tub of an experimental substance? Not likely at all. A simple misplacement of the material? Maybe a mistake in the inventory tally numbers? Not unusual. Not unusual at all. There's always a logical explanation. No need to become nervous and imagine demons where only wisps of shadows exist.

I got on with reviewing the annual projected budget for next year. After the academic successes we were racking up at I.S. 406, the Board of Ed. could hardly criticize my requests for modest increases in the programs we were pioneering. It was just a matter of careful and creative phrasing.

26

HARRY

A few days after Josh and I had our talk, I thought I found the right moment to sit down with Jane to discuss what lay ahead. After an hour's discussion with her, an hour of open and honest revelations about what was going on at I.S. 406, I realized there might never be a right moment. Jane was anything *but* understanding. She didn't believe a thing I told her about blue ooze, blue gas, all that Josh had told me about the regular zoning out every day at two, and all that I'd observed among the local student populace. Well, at least it was a good workout for my Mandarin.

"Harry, Josh has been a liar since he was little. He imagines things that nobody in his right mind could fathom. Maybe because he has no father at home. Maybe because I never spent enough time with him. I don't know. But I do know that these things he says are excuses for his own poor performance in school."

"How *you* can believe him," she continued chiding, "is ridiculous. You're a grown man, an intelligent lawyer, you went to the best schools, you raised your own children and they are fine adults, and now you tell me these *silly stories*?" She continued glaring angrily at me, her tone rising from a quick simmer to a boil. "Why do you help him make excuses? You should be helping him to want to learn, like the other children who are doing so well. Listen to yourself! Gas that hypnotizes children and teachers!" She slapped the glass top of the conference table so hard that two of the pens sitting in a tray near me leaped out of it by the pressure of her hand's crash which left her handprint. "Go inside now," she said loudly and forcefully, "get a cup of tea or coffee, and go back to work. We are too busy to waste time this way. Don't tell me this nonsense again!" She rose like a vengeful iceberg that had just sheared my hull in two, and stormed off to her desk to resume preparing documents.

I had felt that slap against the table like a whack across my face. The woman was always like a stick of dynamite waiting to be ignited. Today's explosion was minor compared to what I had witnessed in the past, but I wasn't about to push my luck, at least not today. I sat at the conference table for about five minutes, calming down, peering out the window, calculating my next move. I now believed everything Josh had told me about the blue gas. The timing of when it began and its continuation to the present coincided with my own observation of kids in North Queens. Furthermore, Jane's reports of Josh's classmates' parents remarking how well their children were now behaving and performing matched the timeline. No, I wouldn't stop now. If she wouldn't join us now, maybe she'd join us in the future. But Josh and I had to proceed as planned.

A day later, Josh was in our office after school. His violin tutor had concluded the 45-minute lesson in the conference room with him when I caught Josh's eye and motioned for him to come into my office.

"Josh, I had 'the talk' with Mom. She didn't buy it at all," I said sorrowfully, shaking my head and pursing my lips downward, expressing my feeling of dismal failure.

Wearing a tilted smirk, he said, "Hate to say 'I told you so.' But I guess I didn't really *tell you*, did I? So, what now, Chief?" I knew he was really thinking *"So, you thought you'd come clean with Mom, eh? Lot of good that did. I could've told you that, Mr. Big Lawyer."*

"What now? You tell *me*. Ball's in *your* court now, Little Man."

"I say we go ahead." He shrugged, as if Jane's objections

were mere smoke trails to be blown aside.

"Sit down," I waved him to one of the heavy oak captain's chairs in front of my desk. I plopped into my seat. "I have the full tub of ooze that you brought back here. Now we need to figure out how we're getting DNA samples from the kids in school."

"*We*? *You're* going to help me do that?" he asked sarcastically.

"Well, I'm going to help you think through to how to do it."

"Oh yeah, that'll be a big help. Thanks," he said equally sarcastically and rolled his eyes to the ceiling. "Got any ideas? Maybe ask every kid in class to spit into a Dixie cup and I just put them all in my backpack?" he wisecracked.

I looked off to the side, in my usual blurry, daydreaming way, while my mind shifted into another gear. The brainstorming gear. I stood and paced around the room. I was stuck in that gear for at least 60 seconds but nothing came to me. My mouth was dry so I went to the bathroom to rinse and sip some cool water from the tap. "I'll be right back. My mouth feels so parched," I told him.

The water ran…it splattered all around the bowl of the sink…I cupped it to splash over my face and rinse my mouth, gargling and spitting…*and that's when it hit me*!

My cranium exploded with the spark of synapses like few explosions I've ever had, but when they came, the Earth moved beneath my feet. A celestial moment of *satori* when you are no longer of this Earth but one with the universe and float through the cosmos with the clear vision of enlightenment. It was an epiphany whereby I was suddenly gifted with second sight to picture in my head exactly how everything would fall into place.

I ran back to my room.

"I've got it!" I shouted and clapped my hands loudly. Josh nearly jumped out of his seat in fright. He sat up ramrod straight in the chair, as if pricked in the backside by a pin. He stared at me, half-surprised and half-doubtful.

"Are you allowed to suggest your own science experiments, or must you choose from a selection given by the teacher?" I asked.

"Either way."

"Excellent! This is going to sound nuts, but here goes. It'll seem innocent, okay? I know it will work!" he said excitedly to himself, even though I was right in front of him. "Look here, we get 14 toothbrushes for each of your classmates. We write their names on each toothbrush. We label each toothbrush with the specific date and either 'morning' or 'evening.' You ask each kid to use a different toothbrush for each of the seven days of the week, for one week. Then they're to bring the toothbrushes back to you in a plastic bag you'll provide. You tell them that they are to brush their teeth each evening, and again each morning. You tell them that you do not want them to wash out the toothbrushes after each brushing! *Why*?? Because you tell the teacher that the purpose of the experiment is to determine whether they've brushed their teeth well at night, and whether the toothbrushes from the morning usages indicate food still left in their teeth from the prior evening's brushing. Then you'll create a chart with each kid's name and your observations, day by day. In the meantime, however, you'll be collecting their DNA on those dirty tooth-brushes. See?! And at the end, we'll deliver the toothbrushes to the lab. Voila!!" I was more excited than I'd been in a long time. I felt 20 years younger, as if challenged to argue a losing case that I would try to win by hook or by crook. The game was on!

"*Ewwww*, that sounds *gross*, man!" and Josh made a sour face as if he'd just been overcome by a pile of fresh dog poop.

"Nobody said this would be easy, Josh. And where do you think DNA comes from, anyway? Your body, Little Man! Or would you rather snip off pieces of each kid's hair when they're not looking? Now, *that* would be creepy. Or—*here's* an idea— go with your paper plane experiment, but ask each kid to spit a lot on each plane for good luck!"

Josh looked me as if I were crazy. "That's super disgust-ing. Then again, so is your idea."

"No kidding," I agreed. "But can you come up with any-thing better?"

He looked down to the floor very thoughtfully for about

10 seconds, then shook his head and sighed deeply, slowly raised his face and said, "Fine. Can you help me write up the proposal?"

"Consider it done, My Man."

Josh went back into the conference room to do his homework while I prepared the proposal, printed it out, handed it to him and told him to rewrite it by hand for his teacher. All the while, Jane was busy on the telephone with clients, busy filling out forms for other clients sitting in front of her, and blissfully clueless to the brilliant plan I had just concocted and that Josh would execute with all his unsuspecting Blue Breathers.

27

I had to hand it to Harry. When a guy's right, he's right. We probably had no other convincing way to get the DNA from the kids anyway. The day after I rewrote Harry's proposal, I approached the fearsome GWQ during the break between math and English.

"Mrs. Hardy, may I speak to you?"

"Of course you may, Joshua. What is it?" Again with the "Joshua." Gave me goosebumps, the way she pronounced it, rolling each of the three syllables in the mouth, her lips contorting wide to say the "Jaaahh," followed by a puckered donut for the "shoo," then her lower jaw and chin dropping to spill out the "uh" sound, so formal and proper.

"Well, I've been thinking about the science project, and, well, ya know, those topics didn't seem so interesting to me… see…so, I kinda came up with my own." I handed her my proposal. She read it once, breathed in and out through her nose as if clearing her mind for a second go-round, perused it again, then frowned.

"Joshua, I must say, this is a most educational and helpful project idea. And you have described it very clearly. It's apparent that you've really thought this out and I'm pleased about that," she said, studying me with a long, discerning gaze. "Maybe this will also persuade all your classmates to focus more intently on their oral hygiene," she said with a smile reserved for a shared confidential sneer. Then, with the attitude that I imagined a Roman emperor would have taken when considering thumbs-up or thumbs-down in the gladiatorial arena, she finally declared, "You may proceed with your project. How soon can you bring in the toothbrushes?" As I was about to answer, she sparked up. "My, my, that will be a huge number of toothbrushes, and all with your classmates' names and the dates on them!" She tilted her head toward me, as if bestowing the seal of approval, and re-marked, "I'm *impressed* with you today, Joshua." That scary witch gave me the biggest smile I think she had ever given any-one in her entire witchy life. Totally freaky. But I was on a mis-sion, and for the mission to succeed, I had to man up. I forced myself to smile back at her. Another first!

"Well, let's see…today is Wednesday, and I need time to prepare it all. How about I'll bring them all in next Monday? Then the kids can start using them next Monday night or Tuesday morning?" I asked.

"Wonderful! I'm sure your project will yield very mean-ingful results." She didn't wait for my response, but looked down at the lesson plan on her desk to prepare for teaching the upcom-ing English class, signaling the end of her imperial audience for me.

Yes, I thought to myself, but not the results you're think-ing about, you old Green Witch Queen. Mission accomplished, at least for today.

I saw Johnny in the schoolyard after lunch. It was freez-ing out, but that guy was tough. No scarf, no hat, no gloves. Had to give him credit. His sister, Mary, was all prim and proper, dressed up in style like a little lady for the winter blizzards, but he was the Aragorn, the Tony Stark of the eighth grade. Just hang-ing loose, kicking chunks of ice around the ground, oblivious to the weather.

"Yo! Johnny!" I called out as I approached. "I have news," I uttered to him in a secretive voice as I came up to him.

He looked me up and down, his face not expressing any emotion, taking the measure of me. "Yeah?" His eyes narrowed.

"What kind of news?" He sounded suspicious and gave

me a wary look.

"About what we talked about the other day, man. Remember? The blue gas? Mary's headaches?"

"Okay...so?"

"So...I'm working on blowing this whole thing wide open, see," I said to him in a secretive way. I looked all around to make sure nobody could eavesdrop on us. When I was certain nobody stood nearby, I said, "I'm having *special people* outside school test the stuff to find out what it's doing to the kids here." I winked at him, like we were conspirators embarking on a dangerous task.

"You what??" he grimaced as he asked with no small disbelief.

"Look, Johnny, just don't mention it to anybody, okay?"

"Sure, yeah, I won't tell a soul," he said sarcastically, like he was humoring me. "Don't worry, Bro, nobody would believe me anyway, and I don't need my folks or other people looking at me like I'm some sort of a nut job." He looked away, seeming not to care that I had a plan. Likely he didn't believe me and thought I was the real nut job. He kicked more ice toward the fence.

After a few more chunks had gone flying, he turned to look at me and reluctantly said, "Ya know, Josh, Mary is still having those headaches. How's she doin' in class?"

"She's a Blue Breather like the rest of 'em. She goes blank like they all do. Then she comes to after the gas stops. No change in her."

He grunted in acknowledgment. "Same in my class," he reflected. "It's not like any of the kids are coming out of it, either. They're hooked. The stuff smells nice, though, doesn't it?"

We were both silent for a minute or so, me pacing to stay warm and him pacing because he enjoyed the chill air. "Well, you be careful, man, don't get caught," he finally said, and it led me to think that perhaps he did believe me. Hell, he had nothing to lose by believing me.

"Just trying to keep it real, man," I replied. We fist-bumped and then went back inside for the afternoon classes.

28   HARRY

Since Jane was not onboard with our plan—how could she be onboard since she didn't believe a word Josh and I said about what we thought was some sort of a clandestine plot at I.S. 406, and possibly other schools?—it was Josh and I who had to do all the heavy lifting. I made the preparations by buying 14 toothbrushes for each child in his class—at 27 children, including Josh, that came to 378 toothbrushes. I bought blue toothbrushes for the boys and pink ones for the girls. Even at discount shop prices, it was quite an outlay, but it was worth the investment in our quest.

Josh had a class list containing each child's name, contact information, and so forth, so that parents or children could telephone and email each other. This provided the key information for the tiny labels that Josh and I handwrote and taped to each brush handle. We added the names of each of the seven days of the week and "morning" and "evening" on the toothbrushes. We then segregated each student's "Tuesday morning" and "Tuesday evening" toothbrushes, and did the same for the following days of the week, and placed each day's two toothbrushes into a single resealable plastic bag. Then all seven of those plastic bags were placed into a larger resealable plastic page. We finally amassed 27 large plastic bags, each filled with a seven-day supply of 14 toothbrushes for each child, and labeled each of the 27 bags with the relevant student's name.

We also designed an instruction sheet which we included inside each of the 27 bags, which read:

The purpose of this experiment is to determine how clean you brush your teeth each day and night and to compare the cleaning day-by-day. You may use whatever toothpaste you wish, but you must only use the enclosed toothbrushes.

Use the toothbrush designated for the specific day of the week and the specific morning or evening of that day. Do not rinse or wash off the toothbrush after you finish brushing. Before you go to bed each night, simply put it into the plastic bag for that day and then seal the bag. You will begin using your toothbrushes on a Tuesday morning, and because you have 14 specially-marked toothbrushes, you will return all 14 of them, in their seven daily bags, inside the big bag with your name on it, to school on the following Tuesday morning.

Thank you very much for your cooperation. The results of this experiment will be displayed on my chart. If you have any questions, call me. Thanks again!

Joshua Lee

It had taken the entire weekend to finish these copious preparations. Jane had brought Josh to the office on Saturday and Sunday, assuming, not incorrectly, that I was helping him with his science experiment, whatever it might be. It was tedious work made more frustrating by the fact that my hands weren't accustomed to writing so small, then bending little pieces of paper around very thin brushes, grabbing off very small pieces of tape, and smoothing the tiny shreds of tape around them. I had to leave the office for fresh air a few times to stay alert and massage my sore old fingers. Nonetheless, by the end of Sunday, Josh and I felt a great sense of accomplishment.

"Man, Harry, if this works, those toothbrushes are going to be gross. I'm sure not going to touch them." Then he winced and groaned, "*Ewwwwwww…*" and swooshed his lips left and right.

"That won't be our job, Little Man. Jenny and Allan can decide how best to harvest the food bits from the toothbrushes and do their DNA analyses. We just sit back and wait to hear the results."

"Gimme five on that, Old Timer!" Josh exclaimed, raising his hand high in the air. I stretched my arm out, palm up, and he came down hard on it. "That's what I'm *talkin'* about!"

I was feeling a bit silly, like a tired old man playing at arts-and-crafts, but I was buoyed by the excitement the boy displayed and the anticipation of seeing a few hundred toothbrushes fit for the garbage disposal but serving as the gateway to the proof we needed.

29

I went to school that Monday schlepping two big Macy's shopping bags containing 378 toothbrushes in all their little baggies and directions on what I wanted the kids to do with them. It weighed plenty and I had to drag the bags up three flights of stairs. Everybody was walking fast and bumping into each other, as usual, and I hoped the kids climbing the stairs around me didn't kick the shopping bags and break them. Picking up the 27 individual large bags full of all the toothbrushes would have sucked, especially after all those jerks had stepped on them on the staircase. Then again, they were being pretty nice these days…a weird kind of nice. So, I guess they probably would have stepped *over* the bags. Come to think of it, they probably would have helped me get everything up off the ground. It was like these Blue Breathers had swallowed the Boy Scout manual whole.

GWQ gave me a twisted grin when she saw me saunter over to my desk with the oversized shopping bags. "Well, well, Mr. Lee, you really *did* bring in your toothbrushes, didn't you?" she exclaimed in mock surprise as she wagged her head and peered over her glasses to peek at me. I always suspected that she thought the blue gas wasn't working on me, although I tried to do my fake smiles and pretended to be nice to other kids. Probably it was my low grades and slouching in my seat that made her doubt me. Or maybe she thought I had a defective brain so the blue fumes wouldn't help me anyway. Who knows? Whatever. I was tired of the whole charade and couldn't care less. She had 26 other star pupils, so what's one dud?

"Yes, Mrs. Hardy, I prepared all these packages for my science project."

She looked pleased. "Students, come to order," she said, clapping three times very loudly. Everyone sat at attention, hands clasped before them on their desks and eyes on Ol' Teach. "Before we begin our work today, I want to bring your attention to a very useful experiment that Joshua will be conducting for this semester's science project. Although each of you chose topics for your projects from the list the school issued, Joshua asked permission to have all of you participate in a class-wide project involving brushing your teeth. I granted permission because I believe, as Joshua explained to me, the experiment will demonstrate how well you each brush teeth over a seven-day period beginning tomorrow morning and ending next Monday evening. Joshua, would you like to explain your project to everyone now?"

Hell no, I thought. Oh, well, here goes nothing.

"Sure, Mrs. Hardy." I turned to all the kids. They all sat so upright and so perky-eyed. What a bunch of zapped-out losers.

Harry and I had rehearsed this, and we had practiced my poker face. No emotion. No giggling. No fear. "Just imagine that you are speaking to a bunch of cabbages, not people, in those seats. That will help you relax and focus," he had told me. "And breathe deeply, slowly, in and out, over and over, while speaking."

"So, it's like this, guys. I'm gonna give each of you a big bag that has seven bags inside. Your name is on each toothbrush, and the day of the week, and whether it's morning or evening is also written on each one. I need you to brush your teeth at night and in the morning, for seven days and nights. But here's the catch, see, I don't want you to rinse off your brushes. I want you to leave them dirty, well, ya know, full of the stuff from your teeth. The point of my experiment is to see how different the toothbrushes will look from the beginning morning until the final evening."

What baloney. I needed their DNA but they'd never figure that out. Mrs. Hardy sure didn't. Had I been asked by a kid to participate in this experiment, I'd have been totally grossed out. No way would I have shown anybody my yukky tooth-brushes full of pieces of brown meat and green veggies and bits of fruit and candy. But these suckers were looking squarely at me, their eyebrows raised in the genuine belief that they were involved in a very educational project. Six months ago, they all would have been yelling "Disgusting," "Gross," "Yeah, right, forget it!" even "Screw that," and making all sorts of horrified faces. But after a few months of this blue ooze spa treatment, they were all happy little campers.

I walked around the room and handed each kid his or her designated bag with the seven packets. Almost each kid said, "Thank you, Josh."

Mrs. Hardy looked satisfied. "Does anyone have any questions for Joshua?" she called out, panning the room with her moist eyes.

Ronny Sanchez raised his hand, and after being acknowledged by Mrs. Hardy, he asked, "Mrs. Hardy, after I've had an opportunity to read the instructions, may I then contact Josh with any questions?" Oh, brother! I could not believe this was the same wiseguy I used to pull pranks with, the same kid whose parents got monthly notes from the Assistant Principal about his misbehavior. Now he sounded like the model child, a true little gentleman. Somebody slap me, please! I needed to awaken from this nightmare.

"Very good question, Ronny," she complimented him, and then turned to face the rest of the class. "Children, I believe Ronny has raised a valid point. It is better to formulate your questions and address them to Joshua after, and not before, you have read the instructions in your packets of brushes." She then bestowed her special smile of acknowledgement on Ronny, who in turn beamed with her recognition of his brilliance. I wanted to puke.

"Joshua, I am sure all of your classmates will be very excited to participate in this experiment and, after you analyze all the toothbrushes and the detritus left in them, to see your conclusions. I must say, I shall be equally attentive to the results."

Whatever detritus meant, I guessed it was gross, because all I got were unappetizing mental images of all sorts of gunk in those brushes.

30   HARRY

One week came and went, and as expected, all 26 of Josh's classmates returned their toothbrushes. The little automatons returned the toothbrushes in exactly the same bags as they had been given, two toothbrushes per baggie for each day, seven baggies, all neatly placed in one large bag. Including Josh's, there were 27 large bags rattling with a few hundred individually-labelled toothbrushes. What's more, they had religiously followed Josh's direction to leave the toothbrushes not washed clean, and so bits of foods lay embedded intact, everywhere along the bristles from top to midway to deep down at the bristles' base on each brush. It was a truly revolting sight to behold dozens of flecks of green, brown, yellow, rust, orange, red, and even blue interspersed among the bristles. I could only imagine the smorgasbord of kids' meals and candies that were now represented in the residue on those brushes.

We set to work preparing charts for the school project report, placing the students' names along the Y axis, the days of the week on the X axis, and boxes were drawn in for each child, each day, so that Josh could insert the appropriate findings. We created classifications for the nature and condition of the food particles left in each brush. Since the kids had stored the brushes in the designated baggies after each use, the brushes and enmeshed food shreds remained moderately moist. Overall, it was a very unappetizing task for which we wore plastic gloves and took frequent breaks for fresh air, sucking on peppermints which, if nothing else, gave off a clean feeling.

"Josh, did your mother ask you about this project at all?" I questioned while we were examining what otherwise no sane person would deign to touch under any other circumstances.

"Not really. She said it all looked filthy, but she was pleased I was on top of this. I think she was relieved that you were going to help me with the charts. She counts on you to get me through this project. She knows the charts will be displayed in the gym on Science Day, along with all the other kids' exhibits. You should have heard Grandma's reaction to these bags. She went on and on about how American education is so *strange*, about why would kids be interested in gross junk stuck on tooth-brushes, you know, that kind of stuff. But I was cool. In one ear, out the other."

"Good," I chuckled. "They wouldn't understand anyway. Your mom is in denial. She still thinks Mrs. Hardy is great and has turned that class around and made a success story out of all your classmates. And, of course, she's still unhappy about your low grades and thinks you're a slacker."

"*Whatever*, man," Josh dismally replied. "School sucks, Mrs. Hardy sucks, and now my reputation there is even worse since all the kids are marching to glory and my grades still suck. Funny, though, I kind of like the little Blue Breathers better now that they are sniffing that stuff every day. They're nicer to me than before." Josh shrugged.

I eyed him while he noisily chewed Dubble Bubble gum that I had stocked for him in the office pantry (along with dark chocolates and severely sour lemon drops), examined the bagged brushes and the fragments of multicolored oral refuse embedded in the bristles, and wrote his entries into the boxes on the charts. In his typical fidgety way, he was kneeling on the conference room's swivel chair, bent over his charts, and blowing expansive pink bubbles as he worked, some of which exploded to cover his lips.

"Josh," I said in a serious, avuncular, and compassionate voice, "you can't blame the other kids for your reputation. You earned that all on your own, Buster. Nobody told you not to concentrate on your homework and not to study harder for tests. Your 'who cares' attitude won't get you far. You know that, don't you?"

"Can we talk about something else?" he objected, never looking up or breaking his pace examining the samples of his classmates' breakfasts, lunches, dinners and snacks, as memorialized in their toothbrushes, and filling out the charts.

I had no interest in rubbing it in. The same tired lecture got him nowhere and only frustrated me; it was a broken record already too many years old in the playing. I let a couple of minutes pass in silence.

"Anyway, you did a bang-up job on this project, that's for sure," I commended him. "You handled it very well, getting your teacher and the kids to cooperate like this." I motioned with both hands in a wide arc to all the bags spread out on my conference table.

"Thanks, Harry, you prepped me well. Just like a witness, right?" and he looked up and winked as he clicked his tongue like a little scoundrel.

"I guess you could say that. I didn't tell you what to *say*, though. That's not what prepping a witness is about. I only explained how you should *think* about what you were trying to accomplish, so that you would have the self-confidence to understand your purpose and then communicate it convincingly to the teacher and the class. Seems you were pretty successful."

"Yeah, I guess," he commented in a muted self-appreciative tone, as he continued writing information into the charts.

Late the next afternoon, I telephoned Jenny at the lab to let her know what we had done to accumulate DNA. She sounded pleasantly astonished and said she was looking forward to analyzing the food particles to extract DNA and run various tests. I then left the office, walked down the street, fired up my pipe for a well-deserved smoke in the crisp wintry air, followed up by a meal of a bamboo steamer full of pork-and-crab dumplings, a couple of side dishes of shredded pickled seaweed and slippery fried peanuts, washed down with a cold beer, at one of the many local Chinese eateries in the neighborhood. I knew plenty of them and they all knew me, and we enjoyed bantering about every subject under the sun. However, that day I wasn't paying much attention to people around me because I was preoccupied with considering how to use the lab results once Jenny's people had finished their analyses. But what if there were no results of any value? What if the chewed morsels showed nothing but the food itself and just a lot of saliva?

31   MRS. DORSEY

It was late February, after the winter break, that the school's Science Committee had chosen to commence the official display of all the classes' science projects in the school gymnasium. Each class was designated a specific part of the gym, with the seventh grade occupying the front area and the older grades situated in the middle and rear of the gym so that they would have more room for their displays, as it was expected that the ninth graders' projects would be the best developed.

Alex Rugani, head of the Science Committee and school liaison with the Board of Education's Queens District's Science Council, was particularly pleased with this year's crop of projects. I had known Alex for over 15 years and he was an enthusiastic proponent of advancing the students' academic achievements and creativity in all areas of science education. More importantly, he was an ardent supporter of my vision for our children's future. Not even 40 years old yet, tall, clean-shaven, consistently sporting a wardrobe of his signature bow ties on pale blue shirts, Harris Tweed jackets in rough woolens of muted greens and browns, neatly-pressed charcoal gray slacks and an assortment of wing-tip shoes in brown, oxblood and black, he was well-liked by the school administration, parents and students. Alex had sat in on my meetings with the New Day representatives and after each meeting, excitedly discussed with me and Eleanor the prospective benefits of New Day's offerings. We had also discussed the possible criticisms that might arise from an array of interested parties, including parents and the Board of Education for starters, but we had decided to strike out on our own after receiving oblique indications from the Vice Chancellor's Office as to his support of radical experiments in educational methodologies which included brief mention of New Day's name. The empirical evidence presented by New Day appeared extremely reliable and persuasive, and now, after four months of deploying their product, the positive results were clear as day... a bright, new day.

"Alex," I said while touring the grand exhibition with him in private, prior to the official opening to the Queens District's Science Council, "it's all quite spectacular, isn't it?"

"Claudine, this surpasses each of the past years' science shows here," he said, smiling with unbridled pride in the collective accomplishments of several hundred students. "The District Council will be wowed."

"That's my hope," I responded as my eyes swept over the scene in the gym. "We have some of the brightest, most promising children in New York City at our school. Manhattan used to give us a real run for our money, but with the changing demographics of the city, and so many Manhattanites sending their children to private schools, I.S. 406 is positioned to be one of the leading public schools in the state, if not the entire nation. And frankly, I don't even see how the private schools can outdo us, given their limitations in terms of hiring the most qualified educators at salaries that cannot compete with ours, as well as the general subservience of so many of those schools to religiously conservative socio-political trends compelled by their parent associations who dictate to their boards of governors. Their refusal to acknowledge scientific evidence in so many fields will be this country's downfall, if, heaven forbid, they were to rule the roost. We'd never be able to compete with the Asians and Europeans who are not prey to this 'dumbing-down' that so many of our American politicians are promoting."

Alex nodded. "Claudine, if other schools use New Day, no telling where this all might lead," he said, eyes starry with distant thoughts of glory for our students, students generally, and eventually all of mankind. Like me, Alex saw the big picture in the far-reaching psychohistorical terms that Isaac Asimov had conceived in his seminal *Foundation* series. Alex may have been almost 30 years my junior, lacking the life experience I had, but he was well-read, had an incisive and open mind, sensed where the world was heading, and wanted our pupils to be leaders in solving the mammoth problems facing us in the 21st Century and beyond.

"Well, let's just worry about I.S. 406 for now," I smirked. "These kids are responding marvelously. When are the New Day folks arriving?"

"Should be here tomorrow."

"Good. Make sure they see these exhibits before the District Council members do. They were the catalyst for this remarkable change and I still want to hear their reactions and any advice they can give, any updates in the product, and the like."

"Will do," he nodded, speaking in his measured, confidential manner. I knew I could rely on him for discretion in handling these matters. If all went well, he could expect a coveted seat on the District's Science Council after another year or two, and that was the launching pad to greater responsibility at the City Board of Education, or even on the state and national levels. A prestigious future awaited him if we succeeded on the pathway we had together dared to venture.

As scheduled, the New Day representatives arrived at I.S. 406 at 10:00 a.m. the next day. It was more like a delegation. There were six Americans, three of whom we'd met on prior occasions, and the three Chinese scientists who had been present at one of our initial meetings. With me were Eleanor and Alex to greet them.

This meeting, like the earlier ones, included a full continental breakfast buffet with catering arranged at the school by New Day's New York office. However, unlike the earlier meetings which had focused on marketing the New Day concept and product, the purpose of today's gathering was for New Day to review their product's performance. It began in my conference room with their request for statistical information about student performance on homework and tests over the period of the autumn and winter to date, calibrated on a weekly basis. My team had prepared detailed reports ready for distribution to the Queens District Science Council and other Board of Ed. offices, and I shared copies with New Day. I noticed that the Chinese scientists paid particular attention to the numbers and spoke to each other in unintelligible whispers as their eyes flitted over the pages, their faces not betraying an iota of emotion. I further observed that two or three of the Americans in the New Day group conversed with the scientists in Mandarin.

"Mrs. Dorsey, our initial reading of your reports indicates quite an impressive change from initiation of the product to present," stated the New Day group leader, Agatha Lundy. Eleanor and Alex looked very pleased, and their eyes flashed recognition of the success of my leadership.

"It would appear that our student body has found the New Day experience to be very, shall we say, uplifting, Ms. Lundy. From what my colleagues at I.S. 406 and I see, there is about a 98% effective reach rate among the student population."

This comment piqued the interest of our guests, especially the Chinese scientists. "Such a rate is very positive, given the experimental nature of this product," remarked Agatha. "Likely it will rise as the product is tweaked and enters successive generations of development."

The faces of the scientists, however, showed less satisfaction and more concern. "I wonder," looking from each face to each face, modestly inquired the eldest of the scientists who had been introduced as Dr. Wang Jingwei, and to whom the other two scientists appeared to defer, "whether we could obtain DNA samples from those students who have not reacted as planned, as well as from a representative sample of, I would say, about 100 students who are reacting as intended? It would greatly assist us in understanding why the brains of the more non-responsive students are not adapting to our formula." He cast at us a faint grin in anticipation of our acknowledgment and approval of the request.

Agatha and her American colleagues looked slightly pained by Dr. Wang's directness.

Unfortunately for Dr. Wang, pained looks were not the worst reaction to his request. I flatly refused to grant it. "I'm afraid that's out of the question, Dr. Wang. We would face a plethora of legal objections if we were to try to do that. You see, the children's DNA is private property to themselves and their parents, and if we were somehow to take samples without our full disclosure of the reasons for doing so and without obtaining prior permission from parents, we could face serious questions and, ultimately, legal liability. At this time," I paused for a moment to look at Agatha and her team in the hope of finding support, "we feel it would not be prudent to make such disclosure to their parents, and we therefore cannot conduct such sampling as you request." I thought I had explained this as clearly as I could, and Agatha's and her American colleagues' indistinct nods and raised brows provided passive confirmation of my strong concerns.

Dr. Wang, however, did not perceive the logic of my explanation and asked, "So, you do not have the legal liability in using our invention here, but you do have the legal problem only if you take the students' DNA to check on the progress of our invention's efficacy?"

My side and Agatha's side reacted in similar ways. A few pursed their lips and looked downcast at their folded hands or writing pads; a couple muffled their grins, knitting their brows and raising their glances above the heads of the persons sitting opposite them, to peer into the distance and avoid eye contact with anyone else at the table, especially the Chinese scientists; and a couple simply maintained blank faces like expert poker players, sipping from their cups and waiting for the moment to pass.

"Dr. Wang," Agatha said in a tone of voice that had an impartial and measured cadence, "due to the nature of the product, it has been classified here as an air purifier with, let's say, related qualities suitable to air purifiers. Our customers understand this condition when they purchase the product. We cannot pursue further avenues of examination of the subject population at this time." She pronounced the last sentence with an air of finality.

"But, how can we truly know…," began Dr. Wang.

"Dr. Wang," Agatha inclined the pitch of her voice more forcefully, "It is *not feasible* at this time."

Unaccustomed to being spoken to this way by anyone except a much higher-ranking cadre in the Chinese government, Dr. Wang continued in an equally forceful tone. "Ms. Lundy, my superiors in China have instructed my team of scientists to explore thoroughly all aspects of the effects of our invention. They will not understand why…"

But he was not permitted to finish his soliloquy because Agatha faced him squarely and announced, "Dr. Wang, this is *not China*! You have no choice but to respect the limitations of our legal strictures. None of us has a choice in this regard. You may be able to do such things in your country, but not in America. If your superiors have further questions, you will ask them to address their concerns directly to me. Thank you."

End of discussion.

The other two scientists appeared less insulted by Agatha's reproach and more embarrassed for Dr. Wang, their eyes downcast. He remained silent as a sullen look spread across his features, refusing to meet her eyes after she had finished speaking. The atmosphere in the room was thick enough to cut with a knife…unless it choked you first.

In a flash, Agatha mercurially beamed gleefully and turned to me as if that unpleasant exchange had never occurred. "Mrs. Dorsey, I think we would enjoy very much seeing the science projects that Mr. Rugani spoke to us about in such glowing terms." She flashed her million-dollar smile at me and my team. Her eyes gleamed with hungry anticipation.

My team and Agatha's delegation proceeded to the gymnasium where I accompanied her, and Eleanor and Alex separated to accompany various members of the New Day group. I noted that the Chinese scientists were accompanied by two of the New Day members who seemed to be their minders. Agatha shot knowing glances to each of those two members, and they nodded ever so slightly their tacit understanding of her instruction to shadow the scientists.

MRS. DORSEY

After an hour of careful examination of each class's projects, Agatha turned to me, out of earshot of others, and said, "Claudine, it looks like your school has really plugged this! Can you imagine, when we were in junior high, ever doing these kinds of things? Lord, but I'm impressed!"

"Agatha, there's no doubt in my mind. New Day's product is a winner. The kids are quieter, calmer, more focused. But it's much more than just that. Your product is not some sedative. The kids are actually thinking in more logical ways than we ever did. They see scientific and mathematical relationships where we would have just seen…well…interesting things. Their powers of reasoning are evolving more quickly. And it's not only that. They actually act more considerately of each other. Rarely now do I hear any reports from teachers about what used to be usual occurrences of pettiness and arguments and complaints by the kids against each other. It's seems they are developing greater compassionate feelings and understanding that such compassion is of greater value than selfishness."

"I think you hit the nail on the head, my dear." She had a commanding glint in her eye as she looked past me quickly, panning the room and calculating…calculating…calculating. If I had to explain what I believed she was thinking, it was that I.S. 406 was just one of the successful cogs in a complicated wheel she was constructing.

"Do you see this happening at the other schools you market to?" I asked.

She inclined her head to the side, took a breath, held it, then exhaled. She looked me square in the eye and said complacently, "I'm pleased to say I do. New Day is breaking new ground in education. We are considering marketing the product to higher education authorities. There is also a plan to move the product into the workforce, where we think it will be particularly constructive in specialized fields like pharmaceuticals and medical treatment and engineering design firms. All on the drawing board now."

"So exciting!" I exclaimed. She merely raised an eyebrow and nodded.

While walking around the gym, Agatha stopped to view the project by, of all children, Joshua Lee. "This is a strange one, isn't it? A study of the toothbrushing habits of the class, with a sampling of several of the daily brushes attached in baggies," she vocalized to herself.

After another few seconds of looking at the project with the chill eye of a scientist, Agatha shook her head and chuckled. "Whatever could have made the boy think of such an idea for a project? A budding dentist, this one, perhaps?"

"Believe me, his mother would be ecstatic if that were the case," I glibly responded. "Funny thing about him," I observed. "He's not had a significant uptick in his test scores and we thought the product was not working on him. Yet here he comes up with a unique project which obviously required a lot of time and effort to plan and execute, and even his conclusions are logical, like a junior Sherlock Holmes making deductions about the dietary and hygienic habits of each of his classmates from inspecting their toothbrushes from day to day. Have you seen such a phenomenon of uneven performance among children at other schools, Agatha?"

"Can't say as I have yet," she responded, staring large-eyed with upraised eyebrows at the project. "But I suppose it's not beyond the realm of possibility that there should be some exception to our expectations and experience in the student population's adaptation and reaction to G88."

We moved along, but due to the discomfort I'd felt at the end of our meeting, I said with an apologetic air, "Agatha, I'm sorry about the tiff you had downstairs with that Dr. Wang fellow."

She was cool and revealed nothing. "Cultural differences, that's all. East meets West, that sort of thing." Nothing more was said about the embarrassing event.

All in all, it was a very beneficial meeting for us at I.S. 406, but even more so for New Day, and it concluded with our agreement to continue closely coordinating observations about student performance and Agatha's promise to keep me informed about the next generation of New Day products.

DR. WANG

Memorandum to File:

Meeting at key New York City intermediate school today. Ms. Lundy, the Director of New Day, makes my job very difficult. She made me lose face in front of my team of co-workers and all the New Day people, and even the school officials. She sided with the American school administrators and against our team in our request for sample DNA from the students. In light of today's events, we must review more deeply various social, legal and psychological aspects of deployment of G88 in American schools. We cannot leave this matter solely in the hands of New Day.

When I return to China next week to continue work on the next phase of the organization's revolutionary mind-development product, our superiors in the Ministry of Education and the Ministry of Science and Technology will not be pleased about the results of our research trip to New York. They will be disappointed to learn that New Day was not 100% cooperative in doing everything necessary to help us assess the American children's adaptations and reactions to our product. In China, we face no such restrictions, nor I do not believe her and the school Principal's fears about the legal rights of the children in New York. I think they were trying to make their own jobs easier by not engaging the parents to discuss this vital product. The results of the product's utilization are very good everywhere it is deployed in

China and elsewhere. Parents in New York and throughout America cannot be allowed to block the progress of G88's complete success and, more importantly, the march toward our organization's worldwide goals, simply because of their small-minded concerns. As team leader and a key liaison of our organization with the New Day owners, it is my duty to solve the question of why some children are not reacting as expected to our product, as well as the varying reactions of all students who seem to be benefitting from it. We must start to think "outside the box," as the Americans say, if we are to bring glory to our country and to the Party. We cannot be hindered by the Americans' arbitrary concerns and rules.

We must have access to those children so that our team can fulfill its task of analyzing the progress of G88. DNA samples are absolutely necessary for us to study so that we can measure the results of our product. One child had made an science exhibit which could provide effective samples. He had many of his classmates submit toothbrushes they had used for one week and in those toothbrushes are food particles containing their DNA. His purpose was to compare how the classmates brush their teeth from day to day. Obtaining this exhibit would be very useful to our analytical efforts. However, the school Principal would not let us take the exhibit because she said it must be returned to the child in its complete condition. Ms. Lundy did nothing to assist us in this regard.

Today was also the first time we heard that New Day sold our invention in America merely as an "air purification" product. It appears the Ministries did not fully appreciate the obstructions we might face in the U.S.A. if the American public were to discover that this so-called "air purification" product is actually a chemical tool for delivery of our system of DNA manipulation through our unique super-computer genetic algorithmic programming. It is much to the Party's advantage that we have no such worries about public opinion or claims about personal legal rights to people's bodies and minds and DNA in our home market. The skillful maneuvering by the Party's propaganda outlets in all of the relevant Ministries transformed the public's and academia's worries over the ethics of genetic engineering into a nationalistic mission forward. What we are creating will improve the populace beyond what they could have ever imagined. Mankind's progress cannot be impeded by its inherent shortcomings and the painfully slow speed of natural evolution. As recognized by the Party, Earth simply has not got the time for such slowness. A wise government, run by our omniscient Party, will create a boundless future for our people. When everyone throughout the world realizes the power of salvation through our products, the human race will be on course to achieve its fullest potential for peace, happiness and prosperity.

In those early days, so many years ago, I was consumed with ambition and vanity. If I had only known then the result my exertions would have in reshaping the world of my ancestors beyond anything that would have made sense to them, I should have resolved to seek a life of humility in the service of higher divine powers, and fled from the sight of the Party.

 **JOSH**

Man, I killed it last week! I mean, I'm The Shit!

I thought I was in big trouble when, just before lunchtime, GWQ received a telephone call and told me I was wanted in the Assistant Principal's office. Figured it was about the snowball fight I had with a bunch of kids in the yard that morning and that I was in deep doo-doo once again.

Check it out—Mrs. M is standing up in front of her desk, with Mr. Rugani right next to her. Both have on their serious faces, like I'm about to be marched out, stood against a wall, and offed. An envelope was in her hand. My heart stopped before my jaw dropped and I thought, "Ah, shit, how am I going to explain this to Mom? My ass is grass." I immediately envisioned ripping up the letter before I got home, you know, destroying the evidence. For sure it was a letter from the school about my lousy grades, my getting into trouble, my dishonoring the good name of the school, et cetera, et cetera, et cetera. Wouldn't have been the first time in my crappy life at I.S. 406.

So, she opened the envelope, and then they both broke into big smiles and she said, "Joshua, we're *so proud* of you. Your science project won Best Project for the seventh grade! This is our school's Certificate of Merit for Best Project. Please ask Mom to get it framed for you and place it right over your desk at home!"

I stood there dumbfounded. I looked at Mrs. M for about

five seconds, then looked at Mr. Rugani, then back and forth. They must have made some mix-up. Who would give Certificate of Merit for Best Project to a disgusting, gooky toothbrush exhibit? Made no fucking sense.

Finally, after at least a minute of my lost-in-space stares and their faces beaming ear-to-ear congratulatory smiles at me, I said, "Do you mean me? Josh Lee?" with a look of bewilderment on my mug.

Mr. Rugani leaned over, put a hand on my shoulder and said, "Josh, that project knocked it out of the park, let me tell you. It was original, it was detailed, it was downright bizarre. But, somehow, you made it work. On a day-by-day basis, student-by-student, you identified patterns of brushing, you deduced what foods had been eaten each day by the refuse in the bristles, you examined bristle direction, and you listed other indicators. It was totally your own idea and you made it work. That's what the scientific approach is all about."

"Good job, Joshua," Mrs. M said, extending her chunky hand to me for a shake.

And, as if it was orchestrated, the substantial bulk of Mrs. Dorsey crashed onto the scene. "Joshua, let me shake your hand too, young man. You have made I.S. 406 *proud*! We've had visitors from inside and outside our school system attend the school's science exhibition in the gym, as you may have noticed. Many observers were impressed with your project." She smiled widely, pointed her finger at me and said encouragingly, "Now, you keep up the good work, you hear me, young man?" And with that, she stretched her pudgy, age-spotted hand to me, and I reluctantly shook it. What else could I do? I was still in shock and not thinking, just reacting. "That's a *nice firm* grip!" she chirped. "You'll go far. We have confidence in you, young man. Now stay on track. Yes?"

I nodded my head up and down quickly. I was speechless. This must be what shell shock did to soldiers. My head was reeling, my vision was blurred, my ears buzzed, and I was lost. But, like zipping between moving cars on my skateboard, I felt so alive in that all-consuming moment.

"May I go now?" was all I could get out of my mouth as I stared up at them. They beneficently indicated that my few minutes of glory had concluded and that I was free to go to lunch.

Returning upstairs by leaps of two's and three's at a time, I felt light as a feather. Entering my classroom, it was devoid of kids who had all gone to lunch, but remaining on her throne was Her Majesty, GWQ. She was delicately chomping on celery sticks when her feline eyes looked up from the middle of some thick book to notice me open the door.

"Joshua," she teased with her annoyingly all-knowing Cheshire Cat grin, "I see you have something in your hand."

I approached and held it out. "They said I won Best Project for the seventh grade," I informed her, somewhat excitedly, but trying to curb my enthusiasm and act cool.

She eyed me for a few seconds, then said, "It seems you are a man of many surprises, Joshua Lee. I suppose when you are dedicated to a goal that you decide is worthwhile, you make a thorough job of it. I wish you felt that way about your homework every day and made greater achievement in your tests. But, in your case, I'll take whatever I can get." That last sentence was spoken with an air of resigned disappointment that still held out some small degree of hope on the fringes. "Let's hope this award is a turning point for you." Then she smiled at me as she had never smiled before. It felt genuine. "Go have a good lunch now. See you in an hour. Take your coat and hat. It's awfully cold in the schoolyard."

I put the Certificate away and slipped on my coat. Could it be she wasn't so bad as I'd thought? No, I couldn't let myself go soft. I'd been in this class since early September and now it was already the first week of March. I knew her game and I wouldn't be fooled so easily. Never let your guard down. It's an invitation to disaster.

"Say, Mrs. Hardy," I called out before leaving the room for lunch, "can I bring my exhibit home today?" I knew Harry had told Jenny at the lab what idea he had come up with for getting DNA off the kids, so we needed all those brushes back.

"Oh, goodness, I should say so!" She shuddered. "I think

we'll all rest easier once those hideous toothbrushes have made their exit from here," she chuckled.

That worked for me. Right on track, baby.

34

The following Saturday morning, Mom took a ride with Harry and me to the lab, not out of any interest in DNA exploration, but because she wanted Harry to drop her and me off at the Brooklyn Museum in the early afternoon. She must have heard about the museum from some other Chinese moms, because I knew museums were not her thing. It was "Mom and Josh bonding day," I guess. Fine with me. I needed a break from making believe I was studying anyway. A factory-issue tub of the blue ooze and a few hundred gross toothbrushes reposing in baggies lay in the trunk of the car but she hadn't seen them yet. So far, she hadn't taken any interest in any of what was going on. She trusted Harry to be my education guru just as she trusted him to be a good lawyer for the clients she pulled in, so she never asked him many questions of substance. Harry got off easy. Me, not so easy.

Harry was speeding along the highway, the radio playing U2's "Beautiful Day" and he and I singing along to it. I got off on music and Harry taught me a lot about 1960's rock. Fillmore East and Fillmore West. New York versus San Francisco. The British Invasion. It all formed a cosmic thread winding throughout his time on Earth. Mom couldn't understand a single lyric and talked to her friends on WeChat and told us irrelevant and weird information she found on it, like the report of some snake in China that died of a broken heart after the family that used to live in the hut that the snake occasionally inhabited, moved away and left it bereft of affection for the baby in the family's cradle. How the hell anybody would even know how the snake felt was beyond me, but Mom got off on such crazy tales that she found touching or strange.

It was sunny but blustery down on the Brooklyn side of the New York Bay where Jenny's lab operated. March was coming in like a lion. The wind off the water flayed the flesh off you if you weren't dressed for it. I could say, if you weren't *used* to it, but who gets *used* to a flaying?

Harry parked on the street and opened the trunk. Everything was inside a couple of large brown paper shopping bags. He carried one bag and I carried the other. Mom hugged herself tightly inside her full-length sheepskin coat with her oversized scarf wrapping her head like a mummy. For a woman raised in China's frozen Northeast, she didn't seem like she had ever gotten used to taking a flaying.

We were soon inside the building and upstairs standing outside the lab, with Harry repeatedly rapping on the heavy steel door that gave a flat and solid, not hollow, response to his increasingly sore knuckles. Allan answered, admitted us into this sanctuary of scientific discovery and brought us to the conference room. He served coffee for Harry and Mom, and hot cocoa for me. Jenny joined us a minute later, and I introduced them to Mom, who was looking with fascination at all the marvelous equipment around this bastion of wonder, but also wrinkling her nose at the assortment of chemical smells pervading the office atmosphere.

"Ms. Zhang, it's a pleasure to meet you," Jenny said. "You have a very intelligent son," she told Mom with an ingratiating smile.

Mom, never the shy one, came back quickly with "That's very kind of you to say, Jenny, and I hope Josh will grow up with very deep influence from you and Allan. We all hope he will study hard and become a great doctor." Mom was in her element with brainy, diligent, successful people to set up as examples for me to emulate. I'd heard her routine many times before. Unfortunately for me, she was dead serious each time.

"Well," said Allan, coming to my rescue, "from what we know of Josh so far, I think he'll have a bright future no matter what field he enters, and he'll make you proud." Nice of him to say, but for me, it was all just another 'yeah, whatever, let's just get on with it' moment that I hoped would pass even more quickly than it had come.

"So, Harry, are these the goodies you told us about?" asked Jenny, looking with unbridled anticipation at the two big shopping bags. Allan's eyes were practically bugging out of his head.

"Sure are," he replied. "Josh, you want to do the honors?"

I was sort of pleased about this. "Okay" was my curt retort. Turning to Jenny and Allan, I said, "First, here's the container of blue ooze you wanted." I lifted it from the first bag and set it on the table. We looked at it for a moment as it sat there like an enticing Pandora's Box. Then Allan picked it up for inspection.

"Harry," Mom commented with a curious look, "isn't that what was up on your shelf? Why did you want to bring it here?"

Mom's query caused an awkward silence for about five seconds. "Jane," Harry started in English so that Allan and Jenny could follow, "this is what Josh and I have been telling you about over the past few months. This is what his school has been exposing the children and teachers to, what they have all been breathing in each day. I think this is what's causing certain changes in the children in Queens."

Jenny picked up on the situation and jumped in. "Ms. Zhang, from what Harry and Josh have told us, this compound may contain chemicals that are having strange effects on the children. Harry asked us to analyze the compound and we're anxious to do it. Allan and I already have preliminary suspicions about it, and we need to conduct more tests before establishing findings with a reasonable degree of scientific certainty about its properties and propensities."

Mom looked with surprise from Jenny to Allan, then to Harry, to me, and then back to Jenny, as if the four of us were gang members planning a heist. "Do you mean that you actually believe what Josh said about the children breathing blue air in school?" Well, at least she had understood *that* much. I knew she had no idea what Jenny's second sentence meant.

Jenny and Allan peered back at her with grave faces. "At this early point, we have no strong reasons to doubt him, Ms. Zhang. And now that we have a sufficient quantity of this material, we can proceed with the various analyses."

"Where did this stuff come from, Josh?" Mom asked me, turning her body completely toward me and narrowing her eyes at me in an accusatory way. She was oblivious to everyone else in the room.

Harry dove right in to save me. "Now look, Jane, don't start blaming Josh. This is all on me," he said in a firm voice, attempting to mollify Mom's rising displeasure with me.

Now she directed her death ray at Harry and turned it on full force. "What's going on? Huh!!? Where did this stuff come from? Tell me!" But I had the sinking feeling that she knew perfectly well where it had come from, and how we had obtained it. The woman had a third eye that perceived too much.

Harry swallowed audibly, and I saw his Adam's apple moving up and down his throat. I guess you could call it justifiable fear. It was the old-fashioned "Shit, I really wish I wasn't here" kind of fear.

"Okay…well…it's…from I.S. 406. We needed…" but he never got to finish the sentence.

"You needed *what*? You needed to *steal* it, *right*!!??" Mom thundered. This was only going from bad to worse. Her face contorted, her lips pursed together so tightly you couldn't tell where her lower lip ended and the upper lip started. Her nostrils flared out like a horse running for its life at the Kentucky Derby. Her eyes were thin, dark brown flamethrowers, and we were getting scorched.

"Mom, chill out, *please*?" I raised my pleading voice to her. Her outbursts were embarrassing me, more for her than for myself.

She rotated from Harry to me, and next thing I knew, she slapped my left shoulder very hard and shouted into my left ear a deafening, "*YOU* chill out!!!!" The shout was so loud it reverberated from the walls and throughout my ear canal.

"*Owww*," I howled and twisted rightwards as she whacked me. That trick slug rocked me for a moment. I sat up very straight, a little shaken, but not shocked. Mom could have these moments when provoked, and I suppose learning that her son had stolen from his school could justify provocation. But my reason for stealing it was also not entirely wrong, or indefensible anyway. Harry and two scientists had sanctioned the theft. Hell, it was for science! It couldn't be that wrong. I mean, look what Dr. Frankenstein had to do to make his monster, and it was damned worth it, too.

Jenny and Allan sat shell-shocked, looking like they wanted to be anywhere else in New York but this room with this wacko lady.

And then—if this doesn't beat all—Mom just sat down, bent her head down, closed her eyes, took a deep breath, and after about five seconds, raised her head and slowly breathed out. The rest of us in the room sat still and speechless, staring at her in all her meditative grandeur. For all intents and purposes, Mom had just absorbed all the oxygen in the room and we were left with only the carbon dioxide.

"I feel better now," she said in a soft, creepy voice. "Not happy with you two at all," glaring at Harry and me, "but," she said calmly, shifting her attention to Jenny, "tell me what this stuff is." The woman could change moods faster than I could blink my eyes.

"Mom," I bravely—I suppose rudely—interjected, daring to risk her ire but proceeding nonetheless, "I'm telling you the truth. The school has been transforming this stuff into gas that they shoot into our rooms everyday around two o'clock. Like I told you before, it lasts about five minutes, and nobody moves. They all close their eyes and do their robot routine, see? Even the teachers. Then it's over, and they snap out of it and it's like it never happened. But the stuff is really affecting their behavior. And maybe their brains too. I don't know, but that's why I took the stuff, so Jenny and Allan can tell us what's in it."

JOSH

Harry had a very solemn appearance when Mom slowly turned to look at his reaction to what I had just said. "Jane," Harry said in a serious tone that foreshadowed an attempt at persuasion, and then spoke to her in Mandarin. "I've told you for several months now that the children in North Queens are acting unusual. There's no lightness and joviality to them anymore. Josh has noticed this too. He also told me that some of the children are experiencing physical problems that they didn't have before breathing the gas."

Jane looked down at her folded hands on the table and slowly shook her head, not in disagreement so much as in disbelief. "But Josh said it didn't hurt him. And the parents I talked are very happy their kids are doing much better in school now."

"That doesn't make it *right*, Jane. And who knows what might happen to their kids later on? As for Josh, I can't explain it either, but maybe Jenny and Allan can find out why, here in their laboratory. That's the reason we took this tub of the stuff."

"Ms. Zhang," Jenny interrupted, "I know how upset you are, suddenly learning about all of this, about Josh taking the material, but Allan and I are also to blame. We told him and Harry we needed it to conduct our scientific analyses."

Mom sighed and grunted in acknowledgment. "What's done is done. What are you going to do now?" Mom asked.

"The tub of blue material is one part of the puzzle. Another part of the puzzle is still inside the shopping bags, correct, Harry?" asked Allan.

"Yes." Harry stood to remove the plastic bags. Hundreds of toothbrushes with varying amounts of yuk in them. They looked like refugees from the garbage dump. Mom just sat and stared with a look of disapproval on her downturned mouth. Her entire upper body shook in revulsion and she uttered a guttural "*Oouugghhh!*" as if she'd caught a strong whiff of rotted fish.

"So your science project was just an excuse to bring all these disgusting toothbrushes here? Yes?" she asked, already knowing the answer.

Harry, Jenny, Allan and I observed a moment of silence in unison. Better not to respond too quickly. Better not to respond *at all.*

After a suitable period of quiet, Jenny addressed the question. "We told Harry that, ideally, we needed DNA samples from children at the school so that we could analyze the chemical components and determine whether there was a link, or, I should say more properly, whether we could identify a potential link, between this G88 material and the kids' DNA. We might be able to detect certain signposts which are vital indicators of alteration of DNA."

Harry translated for Mom. She digested it, directed a piercing glance at me, then turned back to Jenny, nodded and said politely but curtly in English, "Okay, good luck." Then, turning to Harry, she said in Mandarin, "I want to leave." She abruptly stood up and we all got the message that the unofficial chairlady had ended today's conference.

"I'll be in touch, Uncle Harry. Dad sends you his best regards," Jenny said.

Harry gave Jenny a peck on the cheek and shook hands with Allan, and I shook their hands. We then all turned to leave. At the front door, Allan opened it for us. Mom stood still, looked at him and Jenny, shrugged and allowed herself a half-hearted smile. "I guess if you can help the children, then that's the most important work. Thank you." She extended her hand and shook their hands. The volcano had erupted but the sky was clearing again, as it habitually did.

My shoulder still ached. The woman still packed a wallop. It never paid to get on her bad side, but I couldn't live my life afraid of doing so, come what may. Shoulders recover quickly anyway.

 # 35

I did not like what I had learned in that laboratory. I did not like the fact that my son and my boss were involved in trying to expose what those chemicals were and who was spreading them. If what they suspected was true, they had no idea how powerful the people behind this plot must be. And they had no idea that their so-called investigation would likely get us all into terrible trouble.

I had seen enough misery for one lifetime. I had seen the shattered bodies and souls of innocent—and guilty—people who had been caught up in China's political struggles. People of every generation. The accused and the accusers alike. I had seen the evil that people do. People very close to me. People I loved and trusted. People sucked along into a system that preached lofty ideals but practiced duplicity, prevarication and betrayal to satisfy their avarice and pride. Often such evil ways were the only way to survive in the face of the political insanity that ripped China apart for decades. Families were torn asunder by children devilishly lured into informing the authorities about parents who spoke openly at home about anything that could be deemed antithetical to the Party.

For reward money paid by the State, for satisfying old feuds, and sometimes for making themselves feel they were actually helping the nation, neighbors informed on neighbors who were pregnant with forbidden second children or children out-of-wedlock, and those women were subjected to forced abortions and, if they were repeat offenders, were punished with sterilizations, not to mention crushing fines, loss of jobs and even the demolition of their homes and confiscation of their property and livestock. As a result, for over three decades, myriad millions of women went into hiding at relatives' distant homes to safeguard their fetuses until delivery, and yet after delivery, those newborns were not legally recognized as people by the government and not entitled to any of the legal rights of citizens. I, too, had suffered for the illegal act of trying to bring a new soul into the world.

Neighbors informed on Christian or Muslim or other devout neighbors who were praying in family-style churches and mosques and groups not officially registered with the government, and innocent people were accused of belonging to "evil sects." Any religious group that acted outside of the government's total and exclusive control was branded an evil sect.

Workers informed on co-workers who dared to comment about government corruption, and accused them of defaming the Party and its loyal cadres. People who dared to file letters complaining about official corruption with bureaus throughout the country that, in fact, were tasked with investigating corruption, ironically often found themselves as the cruel victims of the very cadres whom they had reported. Public security organs detained, interrogated, beat and fined countless unfortunate victims of all sorts alleged wrongdoing, and even after release, the persecution did not end. The police and community cadres would continue to monitor the victims' every movement and communication, sometimes doing it themselves and sometimes paying thugs and hooligans to harass their hapless targets. Victims were often labeled as either willing or innocent dupes of "Western forces," yet victims they nonetheless became.

Journalists who strove to investigate and report on sensitive issues in society, business, politics, entertainment—you name it—along with all the lawyers who were committed to helping the victims of the Party machine, could be seized and imprisoned on trumped-up charges of stirring up trouble, disturbing the social order, subverting the Party and Government, spying for foreign entities, and a host of arbitrarily Party-sanctioned paranoic reasons that were nonsensical but were considered as challenges to the State's totalitarian order. The slightest whisper of opposition to the Party and its officials and its policies could end one's career, social standing, and even physical well-being. The various and competing security organs had vast and nebulous powers that they exercised in the nominal protection of public order and social harmony. All sorts of people—the rich and poor alike—were "disappeared" and placed in long-term detention in "black jails" or other detention centers, sometimes close to home, sometimes hundreds of miles from home. Elimination of the benefits of citizenship could be stripped from one's entire family, for the long arm of the Party grasped the aged and the youth alike in its merciless, steel grip, and everyone in the family could be tainted by the victim's bad record.

And yet, this was nothing new. Feudalism had morphed into toxic totalitarianism. It was our Chinese tradition, thousands of years old, enmeshed in our cultural DNA, unchanged and unlikely to change. I had hoped never to face it again.

Just when I was becoming confident in my new American life of safety and hope for a good future based on my own hard work, after escaping from the chaos and amorality of the past, my son and Harry had to upset everything. I had a sinking feeling that this problem they had chosen to delve into would engulf us in a tsunami of trouble.

36   AGATHA LUNDY

Early March in New York City with the wind whipping through the canyons of skyscrapers lining the narrow streets is chilling, but it can't compare with a frosty March on the Nebraska prairie with our horrific snowstorms or tornadoes that threaten man and beast alike with sudden death. People at home still talk about the Easter tornadoes of 1913 in whispers, afraid of the bad luck that arises when you speak too loudly of those murderous events. Yet my heart aches for the old days of my youth, sweet memories, when I could smell the hard earth beneath me, when the hot breath and body heat from the cows provided warmth against the bitter cold in the breezy barn between whose planks of chipped and weather-beaten, black walnut and red oak walls, the winds hissed and groaned. These city folks don't know what it is to rise at four in the morning and tend to livestock before dawn in freezing weather. It wasn't fun, but I did it to show my folks that anything my brothers could do, I could do as well or better.

"Hey, Aggie," said Walter Cranston, in his Missourian drawl, coffee cup in hand, stopping by my office that Monday morning to fill me in the agenda for our upcoming trip to Beijing, "I'm ready if you are." My Deputy Director at New Day, in charge of strategic planning, Walt had worked with me for five years. As President and Managing Director, I had hired Walt from a major university in the Midwest where he was the biochemistry department head. How strange, I mused—here we were, bent on retooling the entire human race in order to save it—not nonsense like changing babies' eye colors because parents wanted blue instead of brown, but reaching for earth-shattering evolutionary changes—and yet he and I probably worked so well together because of our common upbringing in a common location that resulted in a common mindset and common way of relating to each other and to problem-solving. We even had twangs in our pronunciation common to rural Midwesterners. Damned provincial, but we humans clicked with each other in the oddest, most tribalistic ways. That old tribalism would soon, I hoped, be replaced with a global universalism that eliminated, or at least vastly reduced, such subconscious compartmentalization.

"Have a seat, Walt." I waved him over to the small round glass table at the far end of my cavernous office. His leather-soled shoes made crackling sounds over the bare wooden floor. There were no carpets in the New Day offices. I detested carpeting in offices because it slowed people down and gave them an unnecessarily bouncy, comfortable feeling. I wanted shiny hardwood floors only, bare and businesslike, and that's what they got. But there were green plants throughout the place: fig trees, rhododendron, rubber plants, creeping ivy—you name it, we had it. Green plants, wooden floors. Natural and down-to-earth, stripped down, unapologetic.

"Here's a draft agenda of meetings for days one, two and three. Day four is still open for discussion," he said, passing me a two-page printout containing names and their respective titles, locations and specific topics. I knew many of the names from my last eight years as founder of New Day.

I smiled. "Good. I'm trying to get the Ministry of Science and Technology lined up, but no go yet. In any event, we're starting at the Ministry of Education with the Vice Minister who will set the tone for the day. Ahh...I see Madame Lu will be leading the discussions in the afternoon. She's a tough cookie but she's been a big supporter of ours. *Very* supportive, in fact." Madame Lu, formerly called Comrade Lu before the Chinese government decided to lighten up on the old Communist lingo, was a bit younger than I. Despite her toned-down, yet highly stylish, assortment of office clothing, she had shown me her private stash of luxury dresses, gowns and accessories that made my complete wardrobe look shabby in comparison. How government bigwigs could afford such things was well known to me. In some circles, it was called corruption. In other circles, it was called "the way things are done." It was not for me to moralize or set ethical standards in China. As long as New Day took no part in it, we were clear of the Foreign Corrupt Practices Act, United States federal legislation that had exposed in gruesomely embarrassing detail all sorts of bribery schemes, and laid plenty of American corporations low and cost them countless millions of dollars in penalties. New Day didn't need the hassles. The Chinese needed New Day's cooperation more than we needed them – or so I tried to convince them.

"To save time," Walt continued, "on Monday night, we'll take the overnight train down to the high tech park outside Shanghai where G88 is currently being produced, for all-day Tuesday meetings. On Wednesday, we meet with researchers at three sites in that area who will brief us on upcoming generations of G88. Thursday is open to whatever might come up. We fly back on Friday morning."

"All right. Flight and hotel arrangements?" I asked.

"As usual. Economy class. No glitzy five-star hotels. Clean, reputable four-star hotels and no fancy suites."

"Good. The less attention we draw to ourselves, the better. I want it low-key and I know those officials do too. There's no need for anyone to take notice. I need to call Washington to bring them up to date."

Besides Walt, our team included Sam Altman and Sue Whittlesey, geneticists with some facility in speaking and reading Chinese, and Charles Mao, an American-born Chinese physicist who was New Day's Chief Information Officer and a very extroverted former National Institute of Health official, spoke fluent Mandarin, and was particularly well-connected with science and technology policymakers in the federal government. Our team was uniformly immune to any inappropriate Chinese overtures that could taint us—so far. I was reasonably confident none of the team members would sell out, accept bribes or compromise our mission in any way, and I kept watchful surveillance over all their telephone records and emails as insurance against a leak.

Along with us, but not someone I could call part of our team, was Celeste Murillo-Soto, a federal official who was my contact person, my portal and my handler *vis-à-vis* the federal agency that constituted the United States government's eyes on monitoring the specific activities of New Day. Celeste was tight-lipped about her personal background, and the private agents I contracted to investigate her uncovered very little beyond the details on her CV. Whether she even deeply understood genetics was something she never let on. She was amiable but guarded in conversation and never gave me a warm, fuzzy feeling. She was all business. Not necessarily the enemy, but not an obvious and openly-committed friend. Celeste and her back-room assistants were trying to keep their fingers on the pulse of New Day and our supporters, or should I say, our array of passive and some not-so-passive enablers. My task was to make her a believer and help New Day lower administrative hurdles and promote our vision within the American political power structure, with the ultimate goal being the widespread institutionalization of the New Day concepts.

We knew the American government was unwilling to sanction our work outright because of the seriously conflicting and competing interests in our society. Religious, ethical, social and political considerations abounded to make our work dangerously controversial in the minds of many. Unpublicized support for New Day came from a growing number of visionary technocrats and policymakers in the American federal, state and local governments, people who saw the logic and promise in our goals. They knew that solutions appear when they are most needed, and now the need was great. They were making covert contributions to the Chinese effort by trying to introduce G88 and the underlying rationale for it to US educational institutions. At the moment, that was the best I could hope for from the American side, but I was aware of an ever-growing attraction, if not universal commitment, to our aims throughout the United States.

37   AGATHA LUNDY

T hree days later, on a pitch black, biting cold, rainy Sunday night, we landed at Beijing International Airport. A skeletal welcoming party of darkly-dressed men from the Ministry was present with oversized black umbrellas to whisk us into equally black waiting limousines and deliver us to our hotel. Exhausted and showered, I fell into a sleep more akin to a drunken stupor than a normal night's rest. Seven hours later, our team assembled for a quick breakfast in the hotel dining room. I drank orange juice, black coffee and ate an allegedly "New York-style bagel" that looked more akin to a Chinese mooncake, but the fruit jams were out-of-this-world delectable when spread on that pastry. Mark, Sue and Charles, old hands from all the time they had spent in East Asia, eagerly dug into the local hotel fare including a thick porridge of steaming hot rice congee, spicy sautéed clams, delicately sliced-and-diced pickled vegetables, and long, deep-fried crullers, not to mention items that only they could identify. Walt and Celeste opted for American cereal with milk, toast with butter and jam, and plates of fruit. By nine, we were again whisked by our Ministry minders into black limos driven by more silent, dark-suited men wearing mirror-reflective sunglasses. Beijing was no warmer than New York had been, and we were bundled up for the sunless, bleak late winter of that smog-choked megalopolis.

Thirty minutes later, we arrived at the Ministry of Education's new building. It was a massive monument to the success of China's 21st Century economic domination. Once inside the vast grey-and-green brindle marble-floored, marble-walled lobby, after passing through security points guarded by uniformed, hard-faced, blank-staring, expressionless men and women, some armed, some wearing facial-recognition glasses, our minders deposited us in an immense meeting room on the second floor. Our group of six was left standing there, facing massive floor-to-ceiling windows on the far side of the room, through which we gazed out at a manicured garden of faded brown shrubbery. In several minutes, our hosts made their grand entrance.

The Vice Minister of Education, Wu Zhibin, entered at the head of the entourage of eight persons. He was a tried-and-true bureaucrat in his late sixties, the scarred but triumphant survivor of a lifetime of political struggles in the Central and Provincial governmental arenas. Serving now as Vice Minister, he had been Minister of Education for seven years and so instrumental to the development of new educational policies that, as he approached the usual retirement age, the State Council insisted, that he to stay on as Vice Minister to steward the new Minister, a younger man of fifty who was the fair-haired favorite chosen to blossom under Vice Minister Wu's tutelage. So trusted was Vice Minister Wu to ensure the smooth prosecution of the policies he had spearheaded, that the new Minister was told in no uncertain terms by the State Council, we learned, that he had better get along with Vice Minister Wu or his tenure as Minister would be short. Vice Minister Wu was low-key and self-effacing, with a disarmingly charming smile, and very well-connected within the intricate web of personal relationships that constituted the State Council and its numerous executive officials who established policy, drafted laws, and supervised the administrative functions of the People's Republic of China. Yet underneath the smooth exterior resided a hardened, iron-willed warrior of vision who had somehow persevered through the political winds that intermittently—some would say, continuously—shifted and blew fiery violent, driving victims mad with the injustice of official arbitrariness. He had risen to a dizzying height in this society where one poorly-placed utterance about another person or a political policy could result in one's complete devastation of spirit and body and could tarnish the family reputation, effectively casting them into the underworld of denied legal guarantees of ordinary citizenship. Such was the precariousness of the official life that he had negotiated with uncommon grace and self-assuredness.

Vice Minister Wu was followed by Madame Lu Peimei, better known to us as Pamela. She was thought by many to be the brains, beauty and organizational brawn behind the government's long-term plan for G88. In her mid-forties but sleek as any well-toned 35-year-old, the statuesque Madame Lu cut a striking figure in a flower-pattern dress and high heels, her glossy black hair spreading down over her left shoulder, her smiling brown eyes failing to mask their laser-like sharpness. She spoke fluent English and had spent several years at Columbia University where she completed undergraduate work and then a Master's Degree at Teachers College; she had begun doctoral studies there, only to be recalled by the Ministry of Education, her employer and sponsor for the advanced degrees, to begin implementation of Vice Minister Wu's far-reaching policies.

The six cadres who obsequiously filed in behind Vice Minister Wu and Madame Lu appeared relatively young, although I was unskilled at determining their ages and had often thought people in China looked younger than their chronological ages. Except for Madame Lu, they all wore black or navy blue suits, men and women alike, and differentiated themselves solely by their choice of white and pale blue shirts and striped and paisley ties. Black shoes were *de rigueur*, even for Madame Lu, although, among the women, only she wore them with three-inch heels. Everyone except the Vice Minister carried a regulation notebook and pen in hand.

The morning meeting was formal, with both sides seated around a massive, rectangular table of blindingly-polished wood, and name cards set at each seat for the Chinese hosts and American guests. Pens and pads had been placed at each setting for my team. Large, cylindrical, porcelain teacups with matching porcelain caps sat in precisely the identical position at every setting around the table; as the morning progressed, uniformed women circled the table and refilled the cups at regular intervals. Vice Minister Wu began with a prepared speech about the lengthy historical friendship between our two nations, the need for a continuing mutual understanding of our differences and even greater appreciation of our common aspirations as the key principle behind cooperation, et cetera, et cetera, et cetera. It was a canned speech written for easy repetition no matter who the foreign guests were—just switch out country's names for a one-size-fits-all speech—sitting across from his hand-picked cadres who looked like they'd been borrowed from displays at a wax museum and dusted off for today's session. Vice Minister Wu then ceded the floor to me, as Managing Director of New Day, and I delivered a slightly less wooden rendition of the same speech, with the appropriate Americanisms, a few of which stumped the Ministry's crack interpreter, and when even Madame Lu couldn't pitch in, our Charles was nimbly able to translate. The Ministry's cadres were all well-scrubbed and sat ramrod straight with identical, rigidly attentive, unexpressive visages throughout both sides' initial sets of remarks. However, their minds were clearly racing, for each cadre was taking copious notes as the Minister and I spoke, and all heads nodded at the appropriate, designated times.

At that point, Vice Minister Wu suggested that each person around the table make an introduction. Madame Lu began, referring to herself as the Ministry's liaison with "foreign friends" in matters of explaining China's educational policies and goals, and coordinating cooperative efforts around the world. She was purposely vague and that suited me fine. I really didn't want Celeste Murillo-Soto learning too much too soon, and I preferred that I be the one to explain things to her on a need-to-know basis. Her presence, however, was useful because it boosted the Ministry's opinion of New Day by thinking that the U.S. government took more than a passing interest in New Day's efforts. It also added a certain degree of affirmation to the Vice Minister's own estimation of his government's policies, imagining that Celeste would report them favorably to the Ministry's American counterpart. The Ministry's cooperation with New Day had grown more substantial over the last couple of years and we saw no reason to doubt an increasing confluence of interests. Additionally, I was receiving reports from disparate sources in American public and private sectors that Chinese soft power was making its efforts in this novel sphere of endeavor known to targets that were also New Day's contacts and potential customers—but also to potential competitors—and I hoped this could further legitimize my guiding vision behind the project.

I had never been totally sure about Celeste's feelings on the subject, as she played her cards very close to the vest. I was, however, keenly cognizant of her assignment to monitor the Chinese attitudes and approaches and to report back to the relevant persons in her agency and affiliated agencies, her impressions of what she had observed and the direction of the developments being formulated by the Ministry of Education. She would also be evaluating New Day's relationship with the Ministry and how that should affect the U.S. government's consideration of eventually working with, or against, New Day. Disregarding New Day, however, was not a possibility. The stakes were too high.

After a few minutes of light, trivial conversation around the table, Vice Minister Wu announced that although he could not join us for lunch and the afternoon session, Madame Lu would host us at a luncheon in the Ministry's upstairs private dining room for VIPs. We adjourned for the luncheon which, thankfully, was a more casual affair. The rigid face muscles of the younger cadres relaxed as they ate and chatted with us in surprisingly good English. A few had attended college in America, Europe, Japan and Australia, and reminisced about their happy years there, surprising experiences, and so forth, and through skillful training, none of their comments was deeply substantive or critical. Likewise, they gladly exercised Sue's, Mark's and Charles' Mandarin. The courses of scrumptious food kept coming, the Qingdao beer flowed, and after one hour, we had become more comfortable, or maybe less overtly guarded, with each other.

The afternoon session was held in the same conference room as the morning session, with the late winter gloom hovering over us after that filling noontime meal. Coffee, tea, soft drinks and Chinese pastries had been set out for us on a sideboard. Madame Lu had prepared numerous materials concerning the Ministry's short-term plans for educating the masses, or certain sectors of them at any rate, for the optimal benefit of the country's needs according to upcoming five-year, ten-year and twenty-year goals.

"It's our great honor to have you all in China once again," Pamela said, scanning her eyes over my team. "This morning was devoted to all the pleasantries of our leader, Vice Minister Wu. He is a man of great vision. It is so important to him that you understand our goals, and it is his great hope that you will share our goals. These are not just Chinese goals. These are goals for the betterment of all humanity."

I had heard this speech before, but this was the first time for Celeste. Because Celeste had been invited by New Day to make this trip, I had asked Pamela to turn on the juice. It was important to make a positive impression on Celeste so that she would become a devotee and be highly motivated to garner the attention and interest of the right people in the halls of power in Washington to our cause.

"What is the purpose of education?" Pamela asked rhetorically. "It is to bring people to a state of better understanding of who they are and why they exist. It is to bring people to a state of comprehending their place in our respective societies all around the globe. It may begin with teaching them the rudiments of how to read, how to add and subtract numbers, but that is not the true goal of education. Everything that is taught is geared toward the ultimate efficient functioning of our world. At the same time, another mission of education is to develop their innate need for self-realization."

"For too long, Chinese education focused only on the skills necessary to equip the populace to perform in society. We became masters at teaching those skills, and our people became quick and thorough learners. However, what was left out of the equation was the need to bring moral purpose to students' lives. And why was that important? So many decades after our Revolution to liberate the hundreds of millions of Chinese molded and trapped by thousands of years of feudalistic persecution, and after the terrible large-scale wastage and mistakes committed by Party feuding and in-fighting during the second half of the 20th Century, and after the material successes brought about after entering the world's markets, and after taking our own place as a leading voice during the early 21st Century, it became apparent to our national leadership that our youth were bogged down by their constant struggle to obtain material security and comfort, but increasingly bereft of the noble ideals of self-sacrifice and communal dedication that had given rise to the Revolution. The blame could not solely be pinned on our youth in isolation from the rest of society. Leadership at local, provincial and even national levels had failed to put the valiant Revolutionary creeds at the fore and elevate such ideals to their proper place in the people's hearts. Given the natural condition of man, selfishness, sloth, greed and corruption were rampant."

"Life is struggle. It is as true today as it was when our Revolution's original founders asserted the reality of it, before the liberation of China from the feudalistic forces that had shaped—and restrained—the national character for thousands of years. Every individual struggles for survival. He struggles to eat, be warm and stay healthy. He struggles against other individuals because competition is necessary in society where resources are insufficient and too many mouths contest with each other for a limited amount of those resources. He struggles because employment is not plentiful and the limited number of jobs at various levels in the society requires one to take on the challenge of besting others. He struggles against his own needs and desires for greater self-esteem and vain enjoyments, and against his fears of inadequacy in his private life and work life. In so struggling, he is required to accept—most often unwillingly—a balance between what he wants and what he needs. And, generally, the balance is not what he seeks but rather what is his lot in life by default."

"In the realization that our single nation," and here she raised her forefinger in emphasis, "comprised almost a quarter of mankind and that our growing population was evolving in ways not fully consistent with our founding Revolutionary socialist ideals, the very highest level of the Party leadership understood that education of a new sort was the key to changing the consciousness of the youth, so as to promote those grand ideals throughout the society. Not only had the destructive days of rabble-rousing to motivate one class against the other been required to end, but the destructive selfishness of modern material success also had to be tempered and ultimately eliminated."

"In searching for the core concept necessary to moderate and gradually abrogate the increasingly self-centered, materialistic lack of soul in the youth that stood in opposition to our Party's original tenets, our leaders came to understand that only compassion for the human condition could rekindle in the heart of the youth that spark of selflessness required to regain our communal harmony. Yes—compassion. In the West, your Judeo-Christian texts describe compassion and your religious ministers stress compassion. In the East, our spiritual and philosophical wise men of old, from Confucius to the Buddhist masters, also taught that empathy must lie at the root of human intercourse. In our national pursuit for material survival and betterment, the idea of empathy for our fellow man was given short shrift."

"Understandable—although not totally forgivable—as this dearth of compassion might once have been, given the need to raise a billion lives out of desperate starvation and disease and poverty as quickly as possible, especially after the ravages of the Western powers on China, the savage war against Japan, then our devastating civil war to bring the Party to fulfill its destiny of resurrecting our nation, followed by mistakes of the 1950's and then the decade-long Great Cultural Revolution, it has now become clear that solely the improvement of the material standard of life for our fourteen hundred million citizens, without an accompanying transformation of moral character, must be rectified."

"And so, it became the mission of the Ministry of Education to study this issue and consider specific methodologies to engender mutual compassion in our youth in order that our country's political ideals also become its economic, social and moral ideals. The Ministry was tasked with developing tangible policies and programs to effectuate this mission."

Pamela Lu stopped speaking, looked around the room to see that all eyes were on her, rested her voice, then poured from a special teapot before her and sipped her favorite Taiwanese *dong ding oolong* tea from the tall porcelain cup bearing the name "Pamela" in cursive script. This ten-second break had a theatrical effect that allowed the audience to ruminate on her message. She had no notes from which she was speaking. She lived and breathed this topic and it was obvious that her energy arose from her deep-seated faith in the Ministry's mission.

I was watching Celeste's face during the presentation. She had looked like an impartial observer until the word "compassion" was mentioned. At that point, she arched her eyebrows and seemed to latch onto the word, as if surprised by not having expected to hear it in this sector of the world.

"Madame Lu," Celeste raised her hand slightly to signal a polite interjection, "when you speak of compassion, can you be a little more specific?"

"Yes. Please call me Pamela. May I call you Celeste?" There flashed that winning smile of confidence that bridges gaps with the infidels. One envisions St. Paul looking at the unwashed downtrodden 2,000 years ago, spreading his message with the same angelic smile that assuaged their doubts and won their loyalty to a brave and defiant new faith.

"By all means."

Pamela took a deep, contemplative breath, then slowly exhaled, all the while holding eye contact with Celeste. Gravitas had been established. "Celeste, when I was studying in America, I sensed from friends whose children were small and in nursery schools and elementary schools, even older children in high schools, that morality among students was stressed by the teachers and administrators, along with academic skills. It wasn't exactly a spiritual religion-based type of morality, at least as I thought I understood religion, but, well, a common decency of 'do unto others as you would have them do unto you.' Children were constantly reminded to be nice to one another, to hold hands, to share, to think of the safety and well-being of their classmates as being just as important as their own happiness. I was deeply impressed. And I felt, and many of us in the Ministry, especially the older officials, also felt that with China's relentless march forward from her recent past, we had lost—or perhaps failed to stress—some of our own traditional concepts of morality. In our rush to rebuild our country, to modernize, to feed and clothe and shelter over one billion people, to bring a better life to this nation, and even to reach out to the rest of the world, we had lost valuable traditional precepts that our ancient culture had held dear. We came to see those ideas reflected in Western systems of education, and we realized we had to introduce them here."

Clever lady, Pamela, finding value in the American situation so that Celeste would feel she came from a background in which the Chinese saw some merit. Pamela was building the comfort-through-praise factor. I could sense in Celeste some "good vibrations" slowly warming.

"Does the Ministry propose to promote compassion along Western lines, Pamela?"

"I'm not sure what 'Western lines' are, because compassion should be a universal emotion. No?" Turning a response into a question put the ball back in Celeste's court without giving away much.

"I would think so," Celeste replied.

"It will take time, and we are considering an array of approaches to this issue," Pamela stated. "Because our historical background and evolution is so different from that of the West, we may need to do it taking into account our own Chinese characteristics." Finally, the key buzzwords were uttered.

"I suppose so," said Celeste with circumspection. "That may be sensible."

Pamela smiled outwardly, but inwardly her dislike of Celeste simmered. Who was this American to judge her Ministry's foresight and approach as "sensible"? In this matter, she felt strongly that China would alone provide the world with the optimal paradigm for the survival of the human race. China would assume leadership where the West was clearly faltering, back-sliding with self-doubt and retreating into its own shell, country by country, little isolationist scared rabbits running back into their warrens.

The next two hours were spent in further conversation about the current state of Chinese education, American education and the relative benefits of international exchanges of students. Bland, dry statistics comparing academic performance among cities and provinces, urban and rural areas, income classes, and so forth, were reviewed. By 4:00 p.m., we were growing weary from the jet lag, and as had been prearranged, we broke for the day so that my team could retire to the hotel and ready ourselves for the overnight trip to the Shanghai area.

As program host that afternoon, Pamela concluded with the usual tactful niceties. We all rose to shake hands with the Ministry attendees, and Pamela blithely asked Celeste, "Will we have the pleasure of your company tomorrow?" knowing full well Celeste would not make the trip.

"I'm afraid my schedule doesn't permit, Pamela. But likely we'll meet again to discuss these important topics," she said smilingly but in a tepid, noncommittal tone.

"Soon, I hope," Pamela responded, wishing quite the opposite, at least until the Ministry and its agencies had perfected the next stage of the blue ooze, and beyond.

38

It was mid-March when I was in Harry's office one afternoon and he told me he'd received a telephone call from Jenny Spangler.

"Ohhhh...Josh, Old Boy," he said in his lilting, chummy way, which meant a demand to cooperate and obey was coming up next, "it seems Jenny and Allan have made their initial research findings on the toothbrushes and ooze, and they want to fill us in on it this Saturday. Are you free?"

I was ambivalent about this. Yes, I wanted to say, for I was excited to know what they had found. No, I felt like saying, because I wished I had never become involved in this predicament. Mom was giving me hell on an occasional basis, those being the occasions she felt like yelling at me for having dabbled in what she termed "Harry's troublemaking." In my defense, I told her each time about problems some of my classmates were having, how some were showing negative reactions to the daily blue gas treatments despite their improved marks in school. It wasn't so much that she didn't believe me. It was more the head shaking, finger wagging, the "But why did you have to be the one to take this on?" nagging.

Harry had gotten it even worse. Mom made his life a living hell in the office, but Harry stood his ground. Most of the time, he remained silent and let it go in one ear and out the other. But when she really got his goat, he let her have what for. I'd overheard them arguing the day before.

"Stop being so damned *simple-minded*, Jane. We can't turn our backs on this problem. It's a huge problem, can't you see? I'm sorry Josh is involved, but that's just the way it is. He's brave for taking the lead in this. We've got to get to the bottom of who's behind this brain-washing poison." She reluctantly reconciled herself to Harry's reasoning since she knew she couldn't dissuade him. I maintained silence a safe distance away during that exchange and escaped unscathed.

I just wanted to disappear, run away, join the circus, live on Mars, be any fucking place but here. But Fate wouldn't let me. Destiny had chosen me for this job and I was going to follow it through. My health and my friends' health depended on it.

I felt the heat of Harry's heavy stare as he waited for my answer. I shook my head wearily. "Whatever you say, pal," I kicked in half-heartedly.

"Good, then that's settled!" Harry retorted with his typical definitiveness. "Pick you up at home on Saturday afternoon after your violin lesson. Mom can come along again if she likes."

"She doesn't *like*. *Like* is the wrong word and you damned well know it, Harry. But you can ask her. *I'm* not stupid enough to ask her," I shot back. Harry chuckled to himself and said nothing more about it that afternoon. He was enjoying this, the sadistic rat.

Come Saturday afternoon and, lo and behold, Mom *had* decided to join us. It seemed like she had lost a bit of confidence in Harry over this whole mess and, being Mom-the-Boss–of–Everybody, she wanted to know exactly what the hell was really going on. The only upside of the day to that point was that it was sunny and getting warmer, so the woman didn't insist I wear fourteen layers of clothing. Otherwise, my stomach had butterflies and I kept to myself in his car. She was like a 120-lb. iceberg sitting in Harry's front seat during the ride—frigid and immobile, eyes staring out straight ahead—but that brain was churning hot enough to melt iron. I could feel the alpha and beta waves beaming from her skull. The woman was a volatile force of nature.

When we arrived at the lab, Jenny and Allan greeted us.

The same conference room, this time with cans of soda. Good start so far. Mom was polite but not her rarely effervescent self. I stayed to her left side since she was a righty and I didn't need that right hand lashing out again at me if my luck changed for the worse. I knew from experience that her left jab was pretty awkward and weak, although she could still throw a wicked back-hand that, in the past, had drawn blood from my lips.

"Really good of all of you to come back," Jenny began. "Allan and I and the staff did a fair amount of work on the tub of material and the toothbrushes, and we made some startling discoveries."

Mom leaned on Harry to translate. Then her eyebrows rose and she looked pensively at Jenny and Allan.

"First," Jenny announced, "let me tell you that nobody outside our lab knows about this yet. Harry, I haven't even told my dad. So, it's purely between all of us only. Allan, do you want to start explaining about the toothbrushes?"

"Well, first let me say that Josh did an amazing job orchestrating all this evidence," Allan said, gesturing in my direction and smiling at me. "Jane, you should be very proud of him."

For the record: Mom did *not* look proud of me. Her face was stone-cold blank. This was way too early in the discussion for her to feel anything but ticked off. The iceberg was far from defrosting.

"I won't bore you with the details of how we did the analyses, more than to say that we began with each student's seven-day set of brushes, and worked on day one, then day two, *ad seriatim*, and recorded the observed changes in DNA structure. And let me tell you, there *were* slight changes over the seven-day sample sets. Certain DNA and RNA chemical components appeared to alter minutely over the seven-day stretch. What this appears to indicate is that there was some sort of genetic modification being processed within the sample set."

"I knew it!" exclaimed Harry excitedly, practically jumping out of his chair. Mom just glared icily at him. I felt so fucking embarrassed.

Jenny continued where Allan left off. "The genetic modification is a huge thing. We're still working on the nature of the modifications and hope to report more about that in a few weeks. But let's talk now about the source of the modifications: the blue compound, G88, that is being aerated through the school's air ducts."

"We analyzed the chemical components of the ooze. It is heavily composed of hydrogen, carbon, nitrogen, oxygen and phosphorus, building blocks of DNA and RNA which are the very basis of what constitutes living entities. There are enzymes and acids essential to the genetic process. Other elements were also observed as binders to facilitate absorption and assimilation."

"It's apparent that this substance has been engineered in order to enter the human bloodstream through inhalation and also absorption through the pores of the skin. Upon entering the bloodstream, the chemicals in the gas apparently bond with existing DNA, RNA, and other chemicals occurring naturally in the host's body. We need more time to determine exactly how and why that bonding process is leading to the specific changes that you have observed in the children."

"We had pondered the possibility of the compound itself having been designed and manufactured such that the physical substance itself will have the desired effects on the DNA and RNA which, as you've seen, manifest themselves in different behaviors, much like any conventional medication."

"However, there are certain ingredients in the compound that are not found in conventional medication. Such ingredients may be serving as chemical conductors, much as certain elements and chemical compounds act as conductors in circuit boards and computer chips. If this is what is going on, then—hard as it may be to imagine—we suspect there may even be an external trigger that controls the operation of the bonding process by sending instructional signals to the compound's elements once they are bonding inside the host's body."

Harry looked captivated and was speechless. So was I. This was hard to swallow. Somebody feeding chemicals into kids and then manipulating their bodies and minds?

Mom hadn't a clue as to what Jenny and Allan had said. After about ten seconds, Harry returned to us from his own thoughts and translated as best he could for Mom, which was far better than I could. Mom's first reaction was typical for her. She said in pure, unadulterated English, "This is *nonsense!*" and pushed her chair back as she stood and made ready to storm out.

"Jane…please…this is not nonsense," Jenny calmly said, placing her hands before her on the tabletop. "I know it sounds very strange. Please sit down with us."

Mom huffed, stood in place for a moment as she composed herself, then took her seat. "How can I believe this? It's like from a silly movie. You want me to believe that somebody is controlling how our children are growing? Making them into… into…," she stammered, not so much searching for the right word as stricken by the word itself, "…robots?!"

"Not exactly *robots*, Jane. Let me explain. As you know, food crops like corn and rice and wheat nowadays are commonly genetically modified to change aspects of their nature so that the crops can grow differently from the way they had been accustomed to growing naturally in the wild. Even before the introduction of chemicals, people were experimenting for many hundreds of years to modify fruits and vegetables and grains. Modifications can help them withstand the cold weather better. Or they can reproduce faster. Or they can develop other characteristics that make them more palatable to humans and less palatable to animals. The genetic makeup of animals is sometimes also altered so that they develop sooner, grow fatter, or have other characteristics that they have not yet naturally developed and might never otherwise naturally develop, or which might take countless generations to evolve to such point. But they are still food crops and animals. That doesn't change."

Mom took in Harry's translation more considerately this time and remained in her seat. Her attention remained fixed on Jenny. Her face had visibly softened.

"What we're saying is that there is a possibility—how remote, we don't know yet—that the natural development of the children's mental, and likely physical, growth is being manipulated by some outside source who is utilizing this compound to accomplish it. The scientific probability of this possibility does exist. At this point, however, more testing needs to be done to establish the linkages in order to prove our hypothesis."

After another translation, Mom was silent. She turned to look at me, still silent. Turning to Jenny and Allan, she said, "Yes. This seems very serious. Thank you for your hard work. And you too, Harry. If you hadn't taken this problem so seriously, we would never know about this now."

She was clearly moved and became teary. Harry said with a warm and caring seriousness, "Jane, I know this is a difficult situation for you. Thanks for listening today and understanding. Jenny and Allan will help us. But we also have more work to do outside this lab in order to figure out who is really behind this diabolical plot. There's no way a few people at I.S. 406 could have done this alone. There must be bigger players involved behind the scenes."

"Harry, you're the lawyer, not us. Ball's in your court," said Allan.

"Might be time for me to talk to your dad again, Jenny," Harry wondered aloud. "This is some heady stuff."

Then Mom pulled a shocker. "Harry, I want you to keep Josh working on this with you. Since he's in the school every day, he can tell us everything that he observes happening to the children." Turning her lasers on me, she growled, "Josh, do you understand me?" and I knew my fate was sealed.

 **JOSH**

As I lay in bed Sunday morning, the day after our meeting with Jenny and Allen, with the scent of a brisk New York springtime seeping in through the slightly-opened window filled my nostrils, and me lolling warm under the comforter, all was right with the world. I could smell breakfast that Grandma was already cooking. I supposed it would be steamed buns, corn soup, and hopefully her signature ox-tail soup.

Now that Mom was onboard with investigating the problem of blue fog zapping everybody in class, I felt pretty relaxed about it, like there was nothing to hide anymore. Her approval confirmed my faith in Harry's decision to do what we had done so far, and although you could say I stole from the school and conned the kids into giving me their DNA samples, it was for a good cause. Maybe for a very important cause. Maybe I'd get into trouble, but having Mom and Harry, and even Jenny and Allen, in my corner, was a large comfort. It sure didn't hurt to be on the right team for once, and I figured the few dirty tricks would ultimately pay off big and be forgiven by the Big Man Upstairs.

I went to church with Mom and Grandma that morning, and Sister, back from college, joined us. I peeled off from them to attend the kids' Sunday School class. Some of the other kids were from I.S. 406 and others were from other public schools and private schools. The I.S. 406 kids were head-and-shoulders above the other kids in intelligence and seriousness about studying the Bible, just as they were so focused on schoolwork. It was kind of scary. They couldn't seem to loosen up and just be kids. Real nerds, thanks to the ooze. I enjoyed Sunday School anyway. Some interesting stories from the Bible made me think a lot, like how that Samson dude really got played by Delilah, who was really out to mess him up big-time. Maybe there really was something to Harry's advice that it's more important to be with a good girl instead of a hot-looking troublemaker. Sometimes we played jokes on the teachers, like putting Superglue on all the pens in their trays so that they struggled to lift them. Stupid shit like that was still good for lots of laughs. When the teachers weren't looking, we shot spitballs through straws at each other. Fun place.

That afternoon, I skateboarded over to the park in Bayside to play ball. It was just the kind of sunny day with crisp fresh air that let you know baseball season had arrived. New York may have changed a lot since Harry was a kid, as he always complained, but we still had stickball. I had telephoned Mary's brother, Johnny, and a bunch of the kids from our school whom we knew from the schoolyard who were also unaffected by the blue gas. I wanted to give them the dope on what the lab had found. I brought my old baseball glove which I'd kept oiled and tied with a hardball inside, my Grandma's long mop stick that I took the mophead off, and a pocket-full of pink Spaldings, and the other guys came with their gear. I also called a few of the girls who were in our circle of kids unaffected by the gas to come to the game.

"Yo, Johnny, how's it goin'?" I asked him that afternoon. He was the first kid to show up and was sipping a dripping-wet, cold Yoo-hoo on the park bench.

"Good, man. You?"

"Same ol' same ol', man. After the game, let's huddle with the kids. Yesterday was intense. Really weird stuff goin' on with that voodoo gunk."

"Yeah?? So you really went back to that laboratory?"

"Of course! I told you that we weren't foolin' around with that shit, dude. Hey, it's already the third time I was there. We all need to get on the same page about this."

Johnny looked impressed. "Wowww…you really went," he murmured, more to himself than talking to me.

"Yeah, my mom's boss took us. You know, that old guy you always think is my gramps. He's cool."

"Guess so."

By two o'clock, all the kids showed and we got up a game. After two hours, we called it quits. It had been good exercise after a full week of GWQ and the blue-outs every day. We all snagged sodas, hot dogs and pretzels off the hot dog cart, took seats in a circle on the grass and chilled.

"So, guys, I need to talk to you about the ooze. Everything we say stays between us, right? No ratting to parents or other kids, right?" Everyone nodded. Serious faces all around. We were all on the same wavelength. We had all been cool about it in school, not trying to show we were much different from all the space cadets sniffing that junk. That was part of our deal. These kids were okay with my taking the lead, and now that I had my family on my side, I felt righteous.

"So, it's like this, see? I took all those gross toothbrushes to the lab, like I told you about. I also copped a whole tub of the ooze for them to examine." A few pairs of eyebrows raised but I couldn't get hung up over the morals of this.

"Wha'd they say? Wha'd they say?" asked Phil Chapin, all nervous.

"Dude, relax, okay?! I'm getting to it," I said with a slight degree of exasperation. Phil was always a jumpy kid. Why the blue gas hadn't gotten to him, I had no idea. In his case, it might have been a good thing. He needed to zone out.

"So—and this is heavy, guys—they think this ooze has chemicals in it that can become part of our DNA and genes and then, maybe, someone is even *programming* the stuff to change how our bodies and brains work. That's why most of the kids in school are getting all fuckin' goody-goody on us now. I guess we're the ones who are immune to it, at least, so far. Say, have any of your teachers asked you about how you're feeling? Like, whether you're feeling a change?"

They looked at each other. "Miss Carlucci sometimes

talks to me when we have quiet time, when the other kids are reading. She asks me how I'm doing and why I think my test marks aren't even higher now than at the beginning of the school year. She told me not to worry, that the school was working on a way to help me do better, but she never explained what she meant," said Sarah Abramowitz.

Nicky Lin said, "My parents said they had a couple of telephone conversations with Mr. Ronkowski, because he was concerned I wasn't up to speed like the other kids in the class. He told my parents the school is using a new approach to teaching and it's '*benefitting*' all the kids in class except me, and he wondered whether there's something wrong with me that the school doctor should examine." I chuckled when he said benefitting in a long, low, sarcastic voice.

"So wha'd your parents do? Wha'd they do?" Phil piped up. Valid question, I thought. All right, Phil, give you a pass this time, but you're really a fuckin' weirdo.

"My parents told me about it, but they said they didn't want some strange school doctor examining me. Then they also asked me how come it seemed like all the kids were doing so well in school this year, and I just shrugged. I mean, I just didn't want to get into it with them, ya' know? Afraid they'd say I was making up bullshit again as an excuse for being a lazy little fuck and not studying." Nicky looked unhappy. He tried to hide the black-and-blue bruises from whacks his parents gave him for not getting high marks, but the rest of us were hip to it and never mentioned it to him. He was a good kid under too much pressure. Truth of the matter was he was a pretty straight B+ student, but that didn't cut it in the Lin family. I guess I was lucky in comparison. Mom whacked me plenty for lying and stupid shit like that, which I guess I shouldn't have been doing in the first place, but never for getting low grades.

"Don't feel so down, Nicky," Johnny said, putting his arm around Nicky's shoulder. "You're not the only one. We're all in the same boat. I mean, this crap is hurting my sister, I'm sure of it. She complains more and more about her feet."

Eddie Cho spoke up. "Yeah, I hear ya, man. Some of my

friends in class are having new problems. Becky Upton said she's getting bad headaches, Jimmy Kline is always rubbing his back because of pains he said he never had last year, and two other kids had to get new glasses because they said their eyesight is changing so fast."

"Look, guys," I said, "we all know kids who are gettin' hurt by this stuff, since except for the few of us here and some others, most of the kids in school are Blue Breathers, so we're gonna have to make a stand, whether our parents like it or not," I said. Most of them nodded approvingly. "My mom's boss is gonna talk to some of his lawyer friends and put their heads together so we can see where we're goin' next on this. We have to figure out why the school is doin' this to us. Maybe other schools are doin' it too, I dunno," I shrugged. "But it'd be *cool* to blow this thing wide open, wouldn't it, guys?" I smirked mischievously. They all nodded, some more excitedly than others, and everybody seemed to want to chug ahead. "Okay, I'll keep everybody informed about what I find out. In the meantime, guys, everybody just stay cool like you been doin'. We're all in this together, right?"

"Right!!" they exclaimed in chorus. "You betcha, man!"

"And we're in this till the wheels fall off, right?"

"Fuckin' right, dude!!"

"Then we need a name for our group. Any suggestions?" I asked and searched their faces.

"I got it!" shouted Phil. "We're the 'Untouchables!' Just like the FBI Untouchables who took down the Mafia! We can't be touched by the blue gas, we can't be changed. And we'll take down whoever is doing this at school!" Whoa! The kid was on fire.

Everyone's face lit up. Cries of "Yeah!" and "That's sick, Phil!" and "Yo! We're the Untouchables!" filled our ears.

I looked around, laughed and agreed. "Then that's it," I said with an air of authority. "We're hereby the Untouchables. When we get done with them, they'll know they've been busted!"

After another few minutes of excited banter, we agreed to keep each other informed about whatever we saw and heard in school, then we broke up and made our separate ways home.

688

This Untouchable still had homework to slosh through.

We were kids playing with fire, and, like most kids, didn't have the sense to know it. Now, years later, we ARE the fire.

40 HARRY

"Mel, it's Harry, how are you?" I asked him. I had neglected him for months since he'd put me in touch with Jenny.

"Not too bad, Harry," he replied with a sleepy lilt in his voice, suppressing a yawn, probably glad that someone—anyone—had telephoned him. He had passed his legal practice to his son and other daughter, and I'd learned from Jenny that they were busier than one-armed paper hangers.

"I hear from Jenny—no details, of course—that she's been involved in something *interesting* with you," Mel continued. The tone of his voice betrayed a latent desire to know just what all the fuss was about, but he was a professional and knew confidences were not to be laid aside just because we were friends.

Except for this time. I had a purpose in calling him to lay it all out.

"Look, Mel, we're into some very heavy things here. Could be conspiracy. Could be international. Could be governments or private groups behind it. We haven't a clue yet."
Silence. Long pregnant silence. Mel didn't jump. He was calmly waiting for me to show my cards. I did.

"Mel, so what are you doing with yourself every day?" I pried.

"Aaah, ya' know, Harry, it's retirement." His New York accent and attitude were still thick enough to slice with a knife.

"A little golf in the good weather, reading, taking the wife out shopping. I drive, she sits next to me and snoozes until we arrive, then she's awake and raring to go while I'm bored and patient and…well…you get the picture."

"Miss the *action*? The cases?"

I could hear him sigh. "I suppose so," Mel uttered reluctantly. Then he giggled and said wistfully, "It was a lot of fun for a lot of years. Really got the adrenaline going. So many challenges. There wasn't a boring day."

He had that right. We all lived for the game, for the fight.

"Mel, ya' want to get back into it? After what Jenny and her people have been finding, I need a partner to brainstorm with. You and I could have a lot of fun with this. It's very important."

"Any money in it, Harry?"

"Money?" I shrugged to myself. "Hard to say. But I can tell you this: we might be on the edge of cracking a big story that needs huge exposure. After we meet and I fill you in on everything I know, I think you'll appreciate the chance to be working *with* me, not *against* me, this time."

"How about I'll fly to New York in a few days and we can chat? And it'll give me an excuse for time off from Eliza to see Jenny and her new lab, and I can go over to the old shop to see Reggie and Kate."

"Sounds perfect, Mel. Send me your itinerary after you know when you're coming."

Mel was just the guy I needed in my corner. And he'd get a kick out of Josh. A couple of wiseguys, the both of them. But gutsy wiseguys could be very effective in a tight spot. I started sketching out a strategy.

41   HARRY

A bout one week later, Mel came to see me in Flushing. He loved Chinese food, so we had lunch at a Sichuan hotpot joint a few blocks away. It was amusing watching him mop the sweat off his balding head as he consumed mouthfuls of tantalizing red-hot spicy soup filled with meats, fish balls, chopped green cabbage, water chestnuts, three varieties of mushrooms, two varieties of bean curd, and a few items, including congealed pig's blood, that I wouldn't reveal to him for fear he'd have left the restaurant. It's amazing what a person will eat—and crave more of—when he's blissfully ignorant. But my aim in bringing Mel into our mystery was to bring I.S. 406's plot to light and end the blissful ignorance of hundreds of parents about what their children—the little Blue Breathers, as Josh called them— were being doused with daily.

By the time we got back to my office, Josh was already there. I introduced him to Mel and they shook hands like equals. "Nice to meet you, Mr. Spangler," he beamed. The boy had poise, I had to give it to him.

"Have a seat, gentlemen," I said facetiously, watching Josh place himself in one of the chairs facing my desk, while Mel smirked, grunted his amusement and plopped down alongside Josh.

"Josh," Mel began, "Jenny's told me about the experiments she's been doing in her laboratory, and how you've been so instrumental throughout all of this. Why don't you tell me all about what you've been experiencing in school? You're our key witness, you see, so I'd like to know, from the beginning, about this blue material and how it's been affecting everyone you know."

Josh ran enthusiastically with the ball. He was quite informative, detailed, eloquent, and even entertaining in his descriptions of what had been occurring over the last seven months. Many of the details were even news to me. I imagined that if he were to apply the same degree of attentiveness and thoroughness to his schoolwork as he invested in our investigation, he'd be a straight-A student, even without the benefit—if it truly was a benefit at all—of the blue ooze.

Mel was a patient listener, and after about 10 minutes of focusing on Josh's explanation, Mel raised his eyebrows, impressed with the strangeness of the tale, looked from Josh to me and back at Josh, and cried, "I don't think I've ever heard anything as unusual as this. It's *incredible*."

"Incredible in terms of bizarre, yes. Incredible in terms of not capable of being believed by others, maybe also yes. That's why we have to dig deeper into who's behind this, how far into the Board of Education it goes, and whether it even goes beyond them," I said. "Mel, Jenny has briefed you on all her findings and you know how thorough she is." I shook my head, hardly believing the gravity of what she had uncovered. "Her scientific findings make clear that Josh's school is determined to alter the children's genetic structure. There's no other logical explanation, given the material that's being used and the scope of results we've seen."

The three of us were silent for about 10 seconds, a slice of eternity in a meeting in a law office.

Turning to Josh, Mel said, "Josh, you're quite a young man. I'm glad you're on our team," and patted him on the shoulder. "Or, maybe it's the other way around. I'm glad to be on *your* team! Say, Harry, why don't we let Josh get started on his homework, and you and I get to work on some ideas."

"Capital idea," I said to Mel. Turning to Josh, I said,

"Josh, talk to you a little later and fill you in on what Mel and I come up with."

HARRY

Josh rose from his seat, visibly pleased that he had contributed so much to our conversation and was part of this ongoing project, and headed for the door to exit my room.

"Oh, Josh," I called out, and he turned back. I winked at him and said, "Tell Mom I said you're good for a soda now."

"Yeah, right," he grinned and then quipped sardonically, "like what we say matters to her? She thinks *she's* my boss." Then he harrumphed loudly and his head rocked.

"Not just *yours*, buddy," I chuckled.

42   AGATHA LUNDY

After our Monday meeting at the Ministry, we bade Celeste a safe journey pursuing the rest of her itinerary in Asia and assured her that we would resume contact back in the United States. Our team was shuttled to the high-speed railway where we boarded the overnight train down to Shanghai, catching forty winks while the train sped along tracks laid over slumbering fields and rice paddies and through soot-black dingy factory towns, under a heavy, overcast sky that forebode more dirty weather. Pamela Lu and a small team from the Ministry were separately making their own way down.

After checking in at our respective hotels and freshening up, her group picked us up Tuesday morning in a large, unmarked, industrial turquoise van and we drove about 20 miles outside Shanghai to a top-security laboratory complex, a hulking, dull gray affair under the strict eye of the Party. Despite the bland appearance of facility, there was no doubt the minds pioneering G88 were anything but bland, for they were uncommonly knowledgeable, inspired, diligent and determined. Personal reputations counted as much here as in the United States, and careers could be catapulted far ahead if G88 succeeded. This was not the single Party system preaching liberty, equality and fraternity that had replaced the *ancien regime*. This was the single Party system of dog-eat-dog and scrambling to make it to the top, with all the wonderful material benefits available at the apex. The top was a tenuous spot, and one clawed in desperation to stay at the top, because there was always someone brighter or better connected on the way up. China had become the modernistic totalitarian version of "money talks, bullshit walks." There were no erudite mandarins with wispy flowing beards floating through the bamboo groves reciting beguiling poetry. There was no discernable charm at all, ancient or modern.

G88 was the Party's daring scientific gamble at softening this Marxist-Leninist stronghold's rough edges, realigning human priorities on a grand scale, and fast-forwarding what God would have taken His own sweet time at.

We once again met the inimitable Dr. Wang, one of the most incisive minds involved in G88. Dressed in his white lab coat with plastic pocket protector crammed full of a half-dozen multicolored pens and a tiny notebook, he caught a glimpse of us through suspicious eyes behind round wire-rimmed glasses, straightened his posture and approached, hand outstretched, and vigorously shook each of ours. "Welcome to China, Ms. Lundy."

"Good to see you again, Dr. Wang, and on your own turf," I replied, although I immediately thought better of using slang expressions that might throw him off balance. He didn't seem fazed, however, but maintained that distant, placid, waxen stare that so many scientists, no matter where, seem to sport, their minds preoccupied with experiments and formulae and notions that mere mortals could never perceive except when watching a sci-fi movie, but which scientists hope can alter for the better the lives of those mere mortals—or satisfy their hunger for power—solely due to their brilliance and tireless efforts. That universally borderless nobility of purpose, the flip side of megalomania, was never lost on me.

Dr. Wang trained his sights on Pamela and said, "Madame Lu, everything is prepared for our discussions today. Would you like to begin now?"

Showing no emotion but imperiousness, Pamela nodded. She uttered not a sound. Dr. Wang took his cue and led us through the research facility, accompanied by the two lab-coated scientists who had shadowed him on their recent U.S. trip. It was clear

that although Dr. Wang was the head of this groundbreaking genetic research facility, the leadership in Beijing promulgated all
policy decisions regarding the direction of his institute's work,
and Pamela was key to its execution. They called the shots and
he was their instrument for executing their decisions. The pecking order was clear to all in attendance: it was duly respected and
feared by those directly subject to its political whims.

Everyone went into an antechamber—males and females
into their respective "bio-mudrooms," as Walt flippantly referred
to them—where they stripped to underwear and donned cutting-
edge bio-sterile suits that encapsulated the entire human body. In
the next chamber, the suits were then sprayed with an aerosol-
generated solution that was designed to kill any bacteria and
viruses that might have been on the wearers' hands while they
were handling them; faces were protected by visors, nose flaps
and mouth flaps that could be further manipulated as necessary.
On their backs were oxygen supplies for the breathing apparatus.
Flashing lights from numerous meters were on the walls and du-
plicated on the arms of these moon suits as a failsafe device.

Everyone proceeded into the next area which was a large
state-of-the-art laboratory, on whose walls were displayed several
lines of Chinese characters in luminous fire-engine red. Walt was
particularly curious about this and asked Dr. Wang the meaning
of the characters. Pamela overheard the question and before Dr.
Wang could reply, she interjected loudly, "These are words of encouragement and inspiration from Vice Minister Wu. They say:
> 'What you create here will propel our Nation
> forward into the brightest future for the next
> 10,000 years. Your fellow countrymen for the
> next 1,000 generations will owe their successful
> and happy lives to your brave and relentless
> struggles. Long live our loyal scientists!
> Long may they honorably serve our Party,
> our Nation, our People!'
It is the greatest honor to serve one's nation and people, Walter.
And now, you and your team at New Day are sharing in this
honor for your own country." She beamed with pride and spoke

every word, every syllable of every word, with a tug of commitment that rose from somewhere deep within her psyche. Walter, to his credit, smiled and kept silent, for New Day's personnel were instructed to give a wide berth to these nationalistic and Party rants.

We moved deeper into the laboratory and observed whiteboards filled with rows of handwritten algebraic formulae, atomic microscopes of the strongest intensity, numerous testing and monitoring stations and computer stations operated by women and men in special uniforms who paid us no heed because they were thoroughly immersed in their tasks. There were several hundred such operators. It was a dizzying hive of single-minded activity that was conducted in a range of sound that never exceeded a soft buzz of intermittent whispers.

"These workers are developing the genetic algorithmic sequences for the genome manipulation control codes," said Dr. Wang. "They are brilliant young graduates of our best colleges and universities, and also returnees—we call them our 'sea turtles'—from universities in North America, Japan, Europe and Australia. They go through rigorous technical training when they enter our institute and we provide continuing education as an integral part of their work experience here. Additionally, the Political Office of our institute ensures that all employees are clear about our Ministry's mission and are completely devoted to our mission. *Our* mission is *their* mission."

I was curious about what happened to employees who didn't cut the mustard, but kept that thought to myself.

"We are changing the course of human evolution, Agatha, and solving…no, we are actually working so that humans can avoid…the problems they would otherwise face through unaltered natural selection," Pamela said to us. She spoke with all the single-minded force of an unquestioning cult devotee.

"Yesterday, I spoke of our children and young people needing compassion in their lives. This is where that compassion is being developed!" Pamela exclaimed, both arms extended out and apart, palms upward and ten fingers outstretched toward the entire laboratory in a majestic, sweeping arc.

Dr. Wang nodded enthusiastically. "G88 is the great chemical conductor that bonds with the existing DNA and RNA in our subjects' bodies. And it is these algorithmic sequences that are remotely communicated to the G88 with the commands that will accomplish the physiological and neurological changes in the subjects."

My team at New Day had been selected after I, on behalf of the Ministry, had made myriad inquiries at universities throughout the United States, quietly interviewing genetics professors and researchers whose scientific expertise was already known to me, about their personal positions on the ethics of genetically engineering human subjects. The Ministry knew the papers I had authored on the subject and found we were sympatico. What the Chinese were trying to accomplish was being done against the backdrop of their societal needs. As a totalitarian regime, their government could institute monumental programs by decreeing their necessity, and that command had clearly been given by officials at the acme of the pyramid of power in the Party. The Great Wall, the Grand Canal, and numerous other massive public projects throughout Chinese history had come to fruition when the Emperor and his ministers gave the command, and the Party was now effectively the replacement imperial control panel. The Party led the government, and the government had the power to mandate the genetic alteration and acceleration of its youth's mental and physical capabilities, and was now experimenting with more spiritual characteristics. The effective management of 1.4 billion humans, roughly one quarter of the Earth's humanity, on an arable land mass too small to accommodate all their needs for food, water, raw materials, housing and so forth, required the most intricate—and, hopefully, enlightened—control in order to sustain the lives of so many people, maintain social harmony, and provide a peaceful homeland for future generations.

Although America had a population of less than one-quarter of China's and land to spare, with natural resources which were being managed surgically after years of careful sci-

entific study and the application of numerous legal protections to ensure wise administration of those limited resources, Americans nonetheless faced a similar need for a secure world for future generations to enjoy. Because American education levels in most academic subject areas fell well below those of other industrial nations in Europe and Asia, it was imperative that we reverse that trend. Simply understanding the reasons for the decline was not enough. It seemed to some of us in the scientific community that the American system of laws, regulations, statutes—indeed, the entire system of checks-and-balances on political power—was restraining, if not choking, American progress. The American national psyche, born of four hundred years of struggle, conquest and exploitation of a vast continent, with its accompanying absorption of peoples with widely distinctive cultural backgrounds from Europe, Africa and Asia, had created a self-perpetuating and continuous give-and-take of discussion, debate, acrimony, dislike and disrespect, but out of which was idealistically hoped a synthesis of 'right thinking.' After World War II, America's hegemony in political and economic and cultural spheres, with the resulting spiral in economic costs that led to the offshoring of the means of production—theoretically unavoidable, to be sure, given our freewheeling capitalist model— had resulted in a population no longer creating goods on a massive scale but rather 'servicing' each other's needs. Virile men who would otherwise have found outlet for their energy in farming or factory work now found little outlet except military service, the alternative to which was flipping hamburgers or brewing overpriced cups of coffee, or working in big-box stores and racing through gigantic warehouses filling shipping orders. Women, thankfully, were achieving more than they had ever been permitted in the past, but they too were falling prey to the mind-numbing ease of modern electronic conveniences made possible by inexorable advances in technology. The entire population was becoming more selfish, more self-satisfied, more contentious, more fragmented, more insecure. Racism, with its scourge of tribalism and senseless hatreds, was unshaken. The recent pandemics had made that fact all the more obvious.

And now terrible new and far-reaching challenges faced all of us, Chinese and American alike, and the entire population on Earth, in the form of climate change. The scientific reasons for it could be debated, but it was painfully apparent that the change in planetary climatic conditions had become irreversible. All we could hope for the discovery of ways to cope; whether we could harness the climatic change to our benefit would be a task better left to the next generation. The titanic alteration called 'global warming' was certain to cause convulsions the world over; scarcer resources of fresh water and food would become the objects of violent contest within and between nations. Seasons were becoming more extreme as winters became colder and summers became unbearably hotter. Record temperatures were already being recorded. Vast wildfires were now commonplace. Once-arable lands that had fed widespread populations would become barren, and the Sahara and other deserts and dried-up seas were proof enough that it had already happened long ago. Cities along coastlines around the globe would become endangered by rising tides to the point where entire existing urban infrastructures that had coalesced two and three millennia ago, due to their proximity to rivers and seas and oceans as sources of transportation and means of communication, would have to be protected where possible and abandoned where no alternative was feasible. Hundreds of millions around the world would be uprooted. Diseases would rage throughout the nations and decimate populations. This catastrophe would effectively alter how humans conceive of life in relation to their environment on a scale that, in psychohistorical terms, would equal or surpass the Great Flood in the Bible and which most likely occurred some 7,000 years ago, resulting in the sudden, cataclysmic expansion of the Black Sea. Humans would forever after mark their past as irretrievable, and just as we today studied civilizations of the past, so would our descendants in the future look back at the 21st Century world as an inconceivable combination of relics, mistakes and lost opportunities.

But as we faced these cataclysms of nature, a non-natural cataclysm was also reshaping our planet. With the predictions, both extreme and troubling, of how American society, indeed all societies, would change in currently unimaginable ways as artificial intelligence gained greater and more widespread traction in the decades to come, I was among those who believed that the need to reshape the human mind to accept and adapt to such inevitable challenges was urgent. The AI revolution would streamline the entire working world in ways we could not foresee with any degree of specificity, but experts had formed a general consensus that the world—especially the industrialized countries— would soon contain an abundance of humans with little or no utilitarian function in society. This situation would create even greater instability as too many humans competed for too few jobs that paid living wages. Never before had mankind faced such a traumatic psychosocial development of its own making that moved forward at a relentless pace.

Life on the planet was transforming at breakneck speed, yet the unaided human mind could not objectively perceive of its danger within this whirlwind. I held no illusion as to how disastrously this great transformation would shake out if left unmanaged by the few of us with the vision and courage to take drastic steps to reshape our species.

We knew DNA was not a static substance, for it changed not just with the introduction of new DNA from a sexual mate to create a new person, but was also affected by the environment outside the body and by the experiences to which people were subjected. Animals in arctic regions had mutated in accordance with their environment so that bears, wolves, foxes, rabbits and other creatures similarly had white fur; fish, insects, birds and reptiles all evolved in response to their particular environments and their experiences within those environments. The rapid digitalization of the electronic lives of people everywhere was similarly working barely detectable but nonetheless real changes in our DNA, but we needed to control and direct such changes to accommodate the conflicting needs for the survival of our species.

And so, we resolved that genetic manipulation of humans' physical, mental and spiritual qualities would be critical in surmounting these unprecedented problems.

G88

The goal of the Ministry of Education had become New Day's goal, for I was a true believer. Our aim was to create a harmonious world where people and AI coexisted without contradiction. That harmonious world would also be crucial for the species to survive the unavoidable physical changes in the world's ecosystems. To achieve our purpose, we had to mold a new human psyche. We were not aiming to create a race of sheep, but of people who employed their heightened senses of community, common sense and compassion to survive and carry the species forward. Enlightened genetic engineering would save the human race from self-destruction. We feared we had an ever-shortening window of opportunity to avoid that eventuality.

"Dr. Lundy," Dr. Wang called out, bringing me back from my momentary reverie, "I now want to introduce out latest improvement in G88, which is still in the developmental stage. We call it 'G99.' With the full support of the Ministry of Education," nodding with an acknowledging smile to Pamela, then returning his attention to me, "this new substance is more powerfully bonding the genetic algorithms of optimization of programming to the human genome in order to...what is the word you use in English? *Tweak*...yes...*tweak* the genes so that they evolve at an ever-increasing rate in accordance with the instructions communicated to them through our programming."

Pamela interrupted at this point. "You see, as you all know from our earlier discussions, artificial intelligence will also require a new set of offsetting responses from humans. Our government is taking the leading role among the nations of the world in forging a new vision for all humanity. We are confident that, like you at New Day, your government will soon also see the logic to this momentous historic endeavor. This is not a political or economic or military competition for superiority. We will all need to work together to bring mankind into a new relationship with....," she paused, looking from me to Walt, Sue, Charles and Mark, as if to maximize the effect of her thought, and continued, "...with *itself.*"

43 HARRY

During the next week of balmy rainstorms and gleaming rainbows that arched majestically across New York's clear blue sky, Mel and I brainstormed about how to approach dealing with the school's heinous experiment on the children in I.S. 406. We thought about finding an enterprising journalist to investigate and then publish the results. We thought about a frontal assault of confronting the Principal of the school. We thought along various avenues that all led back to the same starting point—we had to take the bull by the horns and not delegate this task.

We decided that the two of us should be the ones to make initial contact with the Board of Education's Legal Department to address our concerns. We would be the fulcrum at the center of what might become a multi-branched situational chart of the Board of Education, I.S. 406, the children at the school, and who-knew-how-many-other actors who might surface in this mystery that all the hallmarks of a nefarious scheme. We knew not where it all began and we certainly had no way of knowing where it would all end.

Knowing that I might become a fact witness in this puzzle, I realized I couldn't use my own law firm's name to go forward with this inquiry. Mel agreed and suggested we speak to his son, Reggie, and other daughter, Kate, about getting their law firm involved. I liked that idea, keeping it all in the family. It would facilitate ease of communication with their sister, Jenny, so that the legal and scientific resources on our side would make common cause.

Josh, of course, had to be onboard. He was our inside man at I.S. 406. Mel and I ran the idea past him over pizza one afternoon after school and he was receptive.

"Harry," Mel guffawed gruffly while Josh used the bathroom in the pizza parlor, "This kid is a piece of work. Here we are, two old buzzards, and this kid is holding his own with us. Talks like a little mensch, doesn't he? And we're clearing *our* plans through *him*." He chuckled again and shook his head in disbelief. "The world is changing, old friend," he lamented. "It's certainly changing. Bloody upside-down," he said wistfully, staring unfocused out the shop's window at what I imagined were silhouettes from the past 60 years of his memory.

"That's just the way it is, Mel." I swallowed hard, then said, "This kid's pretty precocious, his lousy school grades notwithstanding. He's savvy and has guts. Not exactly Teflon-coated, but he rolls with the punches pretty well. He's been garnering support among the other kids in school who've also not been affected by the two o'clock gassings. He'll be crucial in this."

"Ummm," Mel grunted in guttural agreement, head bobbing slowly, trying to make his way back to the present.

The next day was a Friday, no homework due until Monday, so after school let out, Jane let us take Josh to the Manhattan law office of Spangler & Spangler, Esqs. Fancy digs. Madison Avenue, 32nd Floor, beautiful wallpaper above and painted wainscoting below the chair-rails lining the walls in every conference room, embroidered draperies on the windows, glass walls cordoning off each room from the central area, striking artwork adorning the hallways, exquisite carpeting underfoot, and Redweld file folders everywhere. The air had a floral scent to it, no, several scents depending on where in the office you stood: lavender here, sandalwood there, citrus coming from the library. Gone were the odors that permeated the law firms of my youth: musty, leathery books, and thick smoke from the pipes, cigars and cigarettes that lawyers and clients smoked without refrain; more signs of a changing world. The buzz of activity raised my blood pressure as I saw a flurry of lawyers dressed in their finery, their leather soles creaking authoritatively with each step, talking with each other and on cellphones as they sped down brightly-painted hallways. The high energy level transported me back to the first thirty years of practice on Wall Street when I lived for the fight, every day and night. If I couldn't be a prizefighter in the ring, litigating other people's problems in court was a decent runner-up.

Josh was in wide-eyed awe, head turning 270° to take in all the new sights of this polished office. "Hey, this place is *slick*," he said to Mel and me. "Harry, how come your office doesn't look like this?" Josh asked, wishing he could spend his after-school hours romping in such formalistic professional splendor. Mel chuckled.

"Harry's old office looked more distinguished than this glitzy place, Josh," Mel recollected. "It was already 135 years old, one of the most famous old-line law firms in America, when Harry and I battled each other down in Foley Square. In its heyday, his firm was mighty. It put judges on the federal bench and at least one novel was written about it and its powerhouse partners. But times change and firms close down."

"And people move on...like it or not," I said wearily. I didn't like talking about the old place because I had never wanted to leave it. Instead, it left me. It was a sort of psychological rupture I preferred not to think about. Redirecting the conversation, I said, looking around the place, "You laid a fabulous foundation for Reggie and Kate, Mel. They owe you a great deal."

Mel grinned. "I suppose so. But the two of them have a vision I never had. I was just concerned about winning cases and providing for my family and trying to enjoy my family in the little bit of spare time I could give them. These two kids seem to live for this, like there's nothing else." Then remembering Josh's comment, Mel looked at him and said, "Son, no matter what you do in school, and in life, put your passion into it. Life is nothing but the hours strung together and they don't stop. They only move forward and the ones that came before are lost in the void. Put all your effort into what you do *now*. It's the '*now*' that counts. The '*now*' will lead to the 'later.' Without your strong 'now,' you can't count on having a strong 'later.' You need both and you need to live, I mean really *live*, for both. You understand?"

Josh heard the advice and assumed a ruminating stance. "You sound like Harry," said Josh, his voice not dismissive, but not totally accepting.

Mel smirked. "That's what people said about us in high school too."

Josh stared at him. "You mean you went to that Stuyvesant place *too*, huh?" he questioned rhetorically. "No wonder," he muttered.

After another few minutes, Reggie entered the conference room to greet us. He hugged his father for they had always been close. There was a deep mutual respect between them that I had watched develop over many years. "Uncle Harry, great to see you!" and he hugged me too. "You're looking as snazzy as always. How are your kids, Uncle Harry? I haven't talked to them in such a long time. Seems we've all become so busy that we lose touch, doesn't it?" he mused. More minutes of catching up and then we sat down to talk turkey.

"Harry, I've talked to Dad about this situation, and Jenny has told me about your meetings and her chemical analyses." Turning to Josh, Reggie said, "And you're the man who's behind all this, right, Josh?"

Josh was in his element, once again a central actor in this adventure. "Yeah, well, it's been pretty weird, Mr. Spangler."

"Reggie, Josh, just Reggie." He extended his hand and Josh clasped it in a firm grip and shook. I had taught him that people expect a firm handshake as the mark of sincerity when meeting and he'd taken that lesson to heart.

After a few minutes of Josh relaying his observations of what was transpiring at I.S. 406, I said, "Reggie, Mel and I have been thinking that since he's retired and I'm running my own solo practice, it might be most efficacious if he and I did a lot of the work in this matter, and your firm take on the official legal representation of Josh and other kids who join, either by name or as John and Jane Does. We're thinking initially of a letter to the Board of Ed. and then see where that leads. If there's no useful result from a meeting with the Board of Ed., then consider a lawsuit to stop the school from further using that blue sludge."

"Dad had mentioned your ideas and I agree that's the way to start. He also said you two have already hammered out a draft letter to the Board of Ed."

I took a folded two-page letter from my blue blazer's inside pocket and passed it to him. "This is it. Have a look, mull it over, and if we can finalize it sometime next week, that would be ideal."

"Will do, Harry," Reggie said cooperatively. "And I'm glad to see you've gotten the old man out of retirement," gesturing with a casual jolt of his head toward Mel.

Mel took a deep breath and exhaled quickly. "That makes two of us, kid, or," he paused, and jerking his head at me, "at least three! I could only read so many newspapers and books, watch so many movies, and fish and swim. It seems like a noble ambition when you're not retired, but when that time arrives and you've done it awhile, time weighs on you and just getting up from the recliner to take out the garbage is an adventurous break in the day. Plus, this way, I get some time off for good behavior from the warden."

Mel, Josh and I left Spangler & Spangler feeling good. A self-congratulatory trip to a nearby dessert place for coffee and, for Josh, a brownie heaped high with vanilla ice cream and hot, molten fudge running down the sides of the culinary volcano, was well-deserved.

44 HARRY

After some fine-tuning of our draft, Reggie finalized the letter seeking a meeting and mailed it to the Chancellor of the Board of Education. About one week later, Reggie's telephone rang. The Chancellor's Office was concerned about our inquiry and wished to have a sit-down. A date was set for the following week. The weather was predicted to be the kind of stunning sun-drenched spring day that New Yorkers remember in the deep recesses of their collective subconscious, when the cool air that follows the showers of April is the harbinger of lustrous yellow daffodils and rainbow-displays of tulips that blossom in the city parks and you wish you were a kid again with a bag of peanuts or a hot pretzel at the Central Park Zoo. It was a good omen.

Mel and I accompanied Reggie to the Chancellor's executive office in the old Boss Tweed Courthouse building on Chambers Street in Manhattan, a magnificent and daunting century-and-a-half old edifice that had been designed to reflect the dominating mercantile power of New York City just after the Civil War. Nowadays, however, it was a tired structure, badly neglected and in need of a full restoration to its original glory and deserved awe-inspiring forcefulness. Nonetheless, its imposing stone-block visage with thick, fluted colonnades and an expansive set of steps leading from the sidewalk up to the soaring, thick wooden front doors communicated the continuity and gravitas of the government that administered the city from behind these cold, scarred walls.

We were directed up a flight of winding, white marble stairs to a long, narrow reception hall for guests. The ceiling must have been 15 feet high, and the crown moldings were exquisitely crafted, if one overlooked the peeling gold-leaf paint from decades past. All the walls were marble of green-gray brindle and crying out for refacing. The upholstered oxblood-color leather chairs into which we sank down were similarly well-aged, showing signs of crinkling and cracking, and badly in need of long-overdue oiling.

A few minutes later, in strode with aplomb a pair of smartly dressed servants of the people. They introduced themselves as Martin Chisholm and Dorothy Romski, Vice Chancellor and Chief of Information Operations, respectively.

"I'm Reginald Spangler," Reggie said, shaking hands. "With me today are Melvin Spangler and Harry Epstein, both Of Counsel to my firm." We likewise shook with the typical formality that indicated neither like nor dislike. It was an archaic habit of politeness and phony comraderie that rarely relayed any warmth and more often transmitted germs. We resumed our seats.

Chisholm studied us and, politely grinning, said to Reggie, "I certainly see the likeness. I assume Mr. Spangler is your father?"

"Indeed, he is. And I inherited more than just my good looks from him." With that, the ice was broken and we were all slightly more at ease. It was a false ease, however, and I could feel the nervous vibrations of Chisholm's and Romski's pulsing brainwaves. They looked into each of our faces for what seemed like an awkward eternity before speaking.

"Well, gentlemen," Chisholm said hesitantly, finally breaking the silence, "we've looked into the queries raised in your letter," Chisholm nodded toward me, putting on a serious face, his voice dropping in pitch to assume a tone of solemnity and sincerity. "We take such inquiries very, very seriously." Romski sat looking attentive but moved not a muscle. It was obvious that she and Chisholm had rehearsed what they would say, who would say what, and even how they would stress which syllables and inflect their voices.

Chisholm slowly continued. "Initially, we've been able to determine that the only substance that approaches the pungent-smelling odor that you describe is an air freshener that the school has been using as a hygienic disinfectant. We've confirmed that the air freshener complies with health regulations established by the Federal Food and Drug Administration and our own New York State requirements, as applicable to schools." He looked at the Reggie, Mel and me, smiling empathetically. Ms. Romski's smile was now absolutely angelic. Two smiles that were intended to dispel all our worries and send us on our merry way with our faith in the Board of Education's goodness and righteousness reaffirmed. It didn't work.

"Mr. Chisholm, I hear what you're saying," Reggie responded coolly and firmly, "but there are children in I.S. 406 who believe that significant changes are occurring in most of their classmates, and those changes seem to be affecting them physically and mentally. We have been retained to look into their very serious claims."

Chisholm looked to Romski, who then responded to Reggie, saying, "Mr. Spangler, we can well understand their concerns, and we have already begun looking into the claims made in your letter. Our initial examination of the situation does not indicate any reports from parents or students of health concerns that vary from the norm. In fact, to the contrary, we understand that I.S. 406 is quite a pleasant environment and is outpacing not only its district, and not only the Borough of Queens, but actually most of the other junior high schools in the City, both public and private. At the Board of Ed., we are exceedingly proud of the school's achievement. Nonetheless, as Mr. Chisholm told you, we are truly dedicated to the students' well-being. No stone will go unturned in the attention we'll keep paying to the points raised in your letter. May I suggest we continue this discussion when Mr. Chisholm and I have had additional time to review further facts and information about the situation?"

Reggie looked at Mel and me in a tacit request for input,

and Mel spoke up. "Ms. Romski, we appreciate that you will be devoting more time and effort to investigating this situation. That the school is performing at such a high level is certainly admirable. My own children and Mr. Epstein's are all the products of our public school system, as are he and I. But, in this case, the children who came to us are quite worried, and frankly, Mr. Epstein and I have noticed a rather *altered*," and here he paused for effect, "attitude prevalent among many of the children in the north Queens area around I.S. 406. In fact, it may be that children attending other schools in the surrounding neighborhoods have been similarly affected. We just don't know at this point. For that reason, your prompt cooperation is really needed so we can all get a handle on this."

"Of course, Mr. Spangler, of course. The children's welfare is our primary goal. Always. There can be no question about that," Chisholm said with all the unctuousness he could gather to placate us. He then rose from his seat to tower over us at what must have been a full six-and-one-half feet of officialdom, signaling that our audience with these two luminaries of the Board of Education had just ended.

"Ms. Romski and I truly appreciate you spending precious time to come down today to meet with us and alert us to the students' concerns. Please assure them that we are totally invested in providing safe environments for them to study and learn in, and that we always view their needs and welfare as our first priority. Why don't you give us, say, another two weeks, and by that time, we should be able to meet with you again to report on our additional findings."

Reggie looked at Mel and me. I winked at him, giving my approval. Mel was silent. We three rose to stand. Reggie turned to Chisholm and replied, "That would be fine, Mr. Chisholm. Feel free to email or telephone me as soon as you can, so we can arrange a time to talk about what you've found."

Chisholm seemed relieved that this had been a spectacularly short and argument-free meeting. Sort of a "meet and greet" before the storm. For myself, this was exactly the way I always began inquiries into messy matters with opponents. No need to be unpleasant and start a pissing match right off the bat. Get in close and feel out the enemy. As Sun Zi says in *The Art of War*, know yourself and know the enemy, then you can fight one hundred times and win one hundred times. Chisholm and Romski knew this issue would not evaporate. This was only Day One in what might become a protracted war lasting who-knew-how-long. Today, the two of them and the three of us were merely envoys meeting in the middle of the battlefield to eyeball each other.

"Absolutely. We'll be in touch very soon," he said with all the ingenuous conviction of a used car salesman centered on making his sale of a worthless jalopy that he can't unload fast enough. We shook hands, exchanged a few more niceties, bantered about how we thought the Yankees and Mets would fare this season in yet another sham show of good-fellowship, and turned to leave.

As we approached the door to the reception room to leave, I turned for a last look at the contest that awaited us. When I saw Chisholm and Romski facing each other and poorly hiding muted but stern looks of dismay, I knew we had successfully lobbed the first cannonball against the castle wall. I also knew the defenders would not sit idly by.

What we didn't realize was that we had just kicked a hornets' nest that would change our lives in ways that nobody that moment could imagine in his wildest dreams—or nightmares.

45 JOSH

"Hey, Josh, do you want me to help you with today's homework? You looked so confused in class this morning," Mary Jackson said to me during our lunch recess. It was coincidentally the same day Harry and his friends were to have their meeting at the Board of Ed. and I had been distracted with thoughts of how it might have gone.

"Sure, that'd be good, Mary. I can't understand what she was teaching about those algebraic formulas and how to apply them to the word problems. I'll text you tonight after I try to do them, okay?" I asked.

She looked at me with those soft brown eyes and smiled. I melted every time.

"Say, Mary," I asked hesitantly, "how do you feel nowadays? I mean, sometimes you seem kind of tired. You okay?" I prodded her for a reaction.

She shrugged. "I guess so." She paused, eyes lingering on mine for a couple of seconds, and said, "My feet feel strange, sometimes, like a tingling and numbing." She looked down at them and then looked up, meeting my eyes with a curious squint. "Does that ever happen to you?"

How to reply to her baffled me. How far should I go to tell her what I knew was happening in the class and in the school? Would she believe me if I told her? Had she and her brother, Johnny, ever discussed this, I wondered?

"Nah, I don't think so," I answered. Then I took the jump. "Mary, do you ever talk to Johnny about it?"

"I did. He's been carrying heavy things for me at home, and when we come to school and go home again."

"Did he have any problems like you have?"

"No, he never said anything about his feet or anything else bothering him."

"Mary, do you ever think about why your feet hurt you?"

"Yeah, but I really don't know. I only know they started hurting a few months ago. It's funny, that's around the same time I started feeling good about school. It's like my brain got vitamins or something to make me enjoy reading and doing homework. Isn't that weird? A lot of the kids said they feel good like that, too." She looked around at the kids in the cafeteria. "Seems like most everybody is trying to do really well nowadays, huh?"

"Johnny, too?"

She giggled. "Johnny just likes to play ball, videogames, as usual. He's my big brother, but I'm the one helping him with his homework! That's funny, huh?!" she exclaimed.

No, that wasn't funny to me. But I'd softened her up, so I figured now was as good a time as any to pounce.

"Mary, you ever see, like, *blue gas* in the air in the class-room?"

I held my breath for the answer, which came like a shock out of hell.

She turned to look at me as if I had three heads. She scrunched up her face in total disbelief and let out a long, "*Whaaaaattt*??" as though I had asked something totally ridiculous, way beyond ridiculous.

"I mean," shaking my head as I eased into the question, "do you ever smell the beach every afternoon around, like, two o'clock? Do you ever close your eyes and just breathe deeply for a while?"

"The beach!? Close my eyes at two o'clock!? I don't know what you're talking about, Josh Lee!" she said reproachfully and then brusquely turned her face away from me as if I hadn't bathed for two weeks.

JOSH

"Mary! Listen to me!" I put my hand on her arm. "They're trying to *brainwash* us!" I said emphatically, but in a low enough voice to avoid other kids overhearing. "The school is pumping *blue gas* into the classroom every afternoon. That's how they do it!"

"Oh my God, Josh, you're *crazy*!" She shot up from her chair and looked at me in horrified amazement. "My mom told me I should be careful about you, that you're a bad influence on other kids in class and you don't appreciate Mrs. Hardy. You've been like this for all the years I've known you, Josh! You have a reputation, do you know that, Josh? Even the parents all know. But I told my mom 'No,' that you were just sort of silly and liked to mess around, but now I think she was really right!"

Mary stood up, took her lunch tray in hand, looked down at me with sincere disappointment in those gorgeous peepers and said sternly, "Josh, you need to stop always making bizarre things up. Why do you think you don't have a lot of friends? Huh? They think you're *weird*. That's why. We've all tried to be so nice to you this year, but listen to yourself!! Blue gas!! Brainwashing!! You're a teenager now and still talking nonsense. Now I know where Johnny got that from, because he asked me that too, the other day. Have you been filling his imagination with this nonsense too? You geeks need to get real! Okay?!"

And then, just like a puff of smoke, Mary was gone. My head ached. What the hell! I was the only one with his head screwed on straight in this crazy place. This was going to be a real "us against them" thing. And why the fuck did I even need this hassle?! I was only thirteen and here I was in the middle of the wackiest situation of my life.

Well, at least Mom believed me now, so I had *that* powerhouse behind me. Harry, too.

Small consolation.

My life still sucked.

46

I saw Harry in the office a couple of days after he had his un-eventful meeting with the Board of Education people. At least, it seemed uneventful to me, although he called it a "strategic meeting." *Some* strategy, all right. Seemed to me they were just stringing us along, but what did I know? I was just a kid, right?

"So, Old Timer, those people didn't tell you the truth about what my school has been doing to us? I didn't think they would. Who'd be stupid enough to admit they were twisting our DNA into something new, huh? Making us mutants? Shit, I sure wouldn't if I were those people."

Harry looked at me with a lackluster stare. "You're a reg-ular genius, aren't you?" he said in that flat tone he used when he was sarcastic.

"Yeah, I'd say I'm pretty smart."

"Oh, really? Well, at least that makes one of us." That kind of hurt my feelings, but then he broke into a big grin and he chuckled. "Only goofing on you, Josh. You had it pegged right. Of course they wouldn't admit it outright. Who would?! That's why Mel and I aren't going to sit on our hands until two weeks or longer pass us by. For all we know, they'll never get back to us. They thought they could kiss us off with that air freshener jazz? Forget it."

"So, what's your plan?"

"I'm happy you asked, Little Man. We're going into court on this. And guess who's the star witness?"

Just what I needed. Not. "Oh, man, now what am I going to have to do, Harry?" I could see my life going down the drain already. The Principal, the Assistant Principal…damn! Every teacher and worker in that building would be gunning for me. The Blue Breathers in orbit in La La Land would find out about this and hate my guts. Their parents would see me every day at dismissal and curse me. Dammit!

"Josh, you're turning very pale," he said, noticing my angst. "Are you feeling all right?" Harry soothingly asked. He rose from his seat, laid a hand on my shoulder.

"Can I please have a very cold soda?" My head was in both my hands, face down to the floor.

Harry came back with a Coke. I popped the tab, and five gulps later the can was empty. I started to feel better, restored by the holy waters of whatever was in there these days.

"Harry, ya know, this is gonna totally fuck me over in that school."

He looked at me with deep empathy, his forehead furrowed and eyebrows coming together. He inhaled long and blew it out even more slowly. "I know. I know." He nodded slowly in his heavy, introspective way, recognizing my predicament. "But who else is going to stand up for those kids, Josh? Who else has been through as much as you, together with me, on this? Who else is going to step forward to take down these criminals, Josh? And you know they're *criminals*, don't you?"

I looked away from his eyes down to the floor. I needed to focus. I said nothing for a long time. Neither did he. I'll bet five minutes went by. I could feel the air moving around me. I could hear every car in the street and differentiate each one's size and speed by how its engine roared or purred. I could pick up snippets of conversations from the main part of the office, all the different Chinese accents from various parts of China that I knew existed but that I might never live through this situation to hear again. I could hear the second hand ticking on the clock hanging on the wall near Mom's desk. I thought of Mary, how she had shamed me in the lunchroom. I thought of all those kids who were changing over all these months. They weren't the same kids I had known for a few years. Mary was so pleased with herself nowadays. Sure, she felt pain that she had never had before, and so did some other kids, but what right did I have to start banging the drums and become a rabble-rouser to upset all those Blue Breathers' satisfaction with how well they were doing in school, how good they felt about themselves, how much they were pleasing their folks. For a lot of them, it was the very first time their parents felt their kids were finally making headway in school. I wasn't affected by the gas, so why not just mind my own damned business?

But I had also made myself out to be a big shot among the kids who were like me, who weren't affected by the blue ooze. They were depending on me to lead this charge. I had repeatedly told them we were on to something humongous.

"What happens if I don't help you on this one, Harry?" I asked, not really wanting to hear what came next, because I knew Harry was for real and didn't pull punches.

"If you duck out of this one, Josh, then Mel and I might not be able to pull it off. It's *that* simple, see? There has to be at least one plaintiff bringing the case against the Board of Ed. Let's face it, *you* are the boy in class every day. *You* are the boy who sees the gas get pumped in every day, *you* are the boy who sees everyone in the room go into trances, and *you* are the boy who sees how everyone performs as a result of inhaling those daily doses. And, in any event, the court doesn't do anything without evidence, right? So where are we going to get evidence without live witnesses to say what they saw?" Harry paused. "You get my drift, amigo?" and he raised his eyebrows and just gawked at me hood-eyed, to indicate that there was no reasonable alternative and that I was the only viable option.

"Did you talk to Mom about this yet?"

"No, but after you understand the situation, I will."

I was cornered. Cornered by him, cornered by my friends whom I'd promised I would help, probably cornered by Mom who would be gung-ho to push this, and cornered by my own realization that I had to do what was best for all the Blue Breathers, no matter whether they hated me for it.

"After I *understand* it? You mean, after I *cave*." I shrugged in surrender and sighed the sigh of realizing I had no alternative. "Yeah, fine. Whatever. What would I need to do?"

"You're doing the right thing, Josh," Harry said, patting me on the shoulder again. "You know that, I'm sure. We've worked hard on this for the last few months. You won't regret it. Now, what I want you to do is write an essay about what you've been experiencing in school. Write down everything you know about that blue gas and how it's been affecting people. I'll correct the grammar, don't worry. Do you think you can talk to other kids to write about it too?"

"A few of them are pretty angry about it, so, sure, I think I can get them to write about what they've seen."

"Excellent. Don't talk much about it in school. Maybe just one or two other students need to cooperate. We don't want to advertise what we're doing, not just yet."

"I got it," I said in a voice of grudging complicity.

I could feel the quicksand pulling me in by both legs.

47   AGATHA LUNDY

On a breezy afternoon in mid-April, an unobstructed sun clearing the skies after a long, dismal drizzle, my telephone rang with a number I recognized and to which I had not assigned a name on my frayed Post-It list of contacts. Our company rule was "no names." If you weren't bright enough to memorize every essential telephone number, you weren't New Day material.

"Aggie, it's Denise." Denise Romski blurted the words at a fast, choppy clip. There was an anxious but controlled urgency in her voice.

"Denise," I said casually to calm her, "nice to hear from you." I had to dominate the mood of the conversation to steer it into unemotional territory.

"Aggie, Marty asked me to call you. There's been a bit of a problem."

"Really?" I asked easily and teasingly. Problems were always to be expected. The skill was in solving them.

"Yes. We had a short meeting with a few lawyers from uptown who claim they represent some children at I.S. 406 in Bayside."

"And?" I asked, my voice inflected upward in a slow, rolling way, inviting her response.

"They claim some children have told them *something strange* is happening in the school. They're talking about blue-colored gas in classrooms. They're claiming it's affecting the students' health. They want an explanation."

In the same gently playful tone, I said, "I see. No problem, I'll help you deal with it." Then, addressing what I believed was a more important issue, I said smoothly, making it sound like an innocent afterthought, "By the way, Denise, I thought we had agreed that in the event you received correspondence containing inquiries, you'd pass it along to New Day before taking any action? In the future, please follow our protocol. Be a dear and send me what you have. We'll chat after I've reviewed it."

Denise proceeded to email me the Spangler law firm letter and then relate the details of the meeting. There were several large domestic obstacles to the promotion of our goals: the media, the government and the legal community. (Parents constituted our smallest concern, since they were almost uniformly ecstatic about their children's improved behavior, focus and higher school grades. What parents want to investigate the causes behind their child's newfound success?) Negotiating our way around the real obstacles was a never-ending challenge that could make or break New Day.

Equally crucial were the international implications for New Day, since the power behind us lay—at least for the present—in China. We had to work hand-in-glove with the Chinese Ministry of Education and Ministry of Science and Technology to develop the G88 product modifications specific to the U.S. gene pool, which was extremely heterogeneous and thoroughly unlike China's relatively homogenous gene pool of ethnic Han people who formed the vast majority of the population and represented China past, present and future; the minorities could be kept in line by cajoling or by force, as the Party would choose and as it had demonstrated in Xinjiang, although even there, G88 was working wonders at mollifying the locals and diluting the differences.

Then we had to arrange ocean and air shipments for importing G88 as "air freshener," as we were compelled to disguise its true nature and purpose until the time was ripe to alter that description. The product went into specially-designated, secure warehouses in nondescript locations around the United States so as not to draw attention. We had daily correspondence with the Chinese side on all aspects of coordination. Any stumbles we made along the way in America could have major global repercussions for the overall mission, not to mention international relations between the two countries.

There was, obviously, no shortage of ethical issues surrounding our work. Despite New Day's internal and uniform resolution of those ethical issues as irrelevant and, indeed, counterproductive to our mission, we faced professional ostracization and extermination as geneticists and biochemists, not to mention potential criminal and civil liability, if we took a single misstep.

"For now," I instructed Denise in closing, "stay in contact with Mr. Spangler but delay giving any details until further notice from me. Let me know as soon as he contacts your office again."

Next, I telephoned Claudine Dorsey at I.S. 406.

"Hello, Agatha," she heartily greeted. "I was just planning to call you about the wonderful test results on the Statewide."

She'd have breathlessly continued her victory lap had I not brusquely cut her off with a note of congratulation, and redirected her attention. "Honey, it seems a midtown firm wrote to the Board Chancellor claiming to represent students at 406, and they're demanding an investigation of the situation at the school. Denise Romski and Martin Chisholm over there will keep me informed, and they are to do nothing before I am informed. Likewise, I am requesting the same from you," I told her.

We discussed the matter for another few minutes until she sounded rushed by several people who had entered her office, and she rapidly spouted, "Of course, Agatha. I'm sure it will blow over," and hung up. I was less sure and wasn't about to sit around and wait for trouble.

I debated whether to bring this up with the Chinese Ministry of Education or even Celeste. Each was crucial in the implementation of my vision for America. I decided to sleep on it.

Looking back on it now, I could never have foreseen what would come to pass. Even had I had the gift of clairvoyance at that time, the boy still would have eluded me. But that was then, and because we always live in the "now," it is useless "now" to look back and ask, "what if...?"

48 AGATHA LUNDY

I t had been a very tense two weeks. After Denise Romski informed me of the visit by the lawyers, I notified Pamela Lu by encrypted message on the cellphone with sim cards furnished by the Ministry solely for our communications. "We have an inquiry here, Pamela." "Inquiry" was our codeword that meant trouble from third parties.

"Send information," was the icy response.

After a telephone conversation with Denise and Martin to learn the full particulars, I sent a follow-up encrypted message to Pamela, and received her reply two hours later. "Inquiry ascending ladder. Will revert after completion of climb."

It was three days afterward when the climb had apparently come to rest at the appropriate rung. A decision had been made. "Are considering proper protocol and will revert. Please identify all possible sources of inquiry."

My comeback was, "Will attend."

Who could be the source? The possible complainants could be anyone within the school's purview: teachers, workers, students, parents. To have hired some lawyers to look into the school's use of G88 demonstrated someone's, or some group's, determination to uncover details of our program. Very inconvenient.

I called Claudine Dorsey to arrange a quiet meeting at a coffee shop near I.S. 406 but far enough away from familiar eyes.

"Of course, I am concerned about this, Agatha. But there

are limits on our end as to what we can do to identify the persons who hired those lawyers. Denise Romski mentioned that they only said that some students and parents had retained them," Claudine said defensively.

"I understand that, Claudine, but we need to narrow the field of focus. Have any children or parents come into your office to complain? I've not received reports of any."

"That's because there have been none at all. On the other hand, we've had numerous parents come in to thank us for their children's improved performance."

"Please make lists of students who have not shown any improvement and students who are borderline. Maybe their parents are our malcontents. You know the type: envious of classmates' success and dissatisfaction with their own mediocre results. Can you think of any likely candidates for stirring up this trouble?"

"Frankly, we've noted only a dozen or so children throughout the school who have had sub-optimal experience with G88. But there's been no feedback from those parents. It's all the parents whose children are suddenly doing so well who are giving us rave reviews."

Then, her gaze following her finger which traced the rim of her coffee cup, she mused slowly, "You know, it's funny, but we were all rather taken by surprise by that Joshua Lee creating such a well thought-out and executed science project. It's been the only bright light in his otherwise continually dismal career this year in school, so maybe G88 is working on him too, albeit slowly. Do you recall that toothbrush project analyzing food residue?"

"I do, indeed." Where was Claudine going with this? Why go off on a tangent?

"Isn't it ironic, Agatha, that that Chinese professor who led his team to visit us at that time, actually wanted DNA samples from our students, and yet, here *this* little boy comes up with a project that probably contained *all sorts* of DNA in the filth?" She snickered and shook her head as if perplexed, but what was her point?

"Yes. Ironic," I said curtly. But I wasn't snickering or shaking my head, and certainly wasn't interested in Claudine's mental meandering over toothbrushes. I was considering how messy and troublesome this lawyer problem might get and how to secure a quick solution to it.

Three days later, Pamela contacted me from Beijing. "Agatha, it has been decided that Dr. Wang and I will fly in two days to New York. We must meet face-to-face to discuss this development. This is becoming a very sensitive subject here at the Ministry and we need to monitor the inquiry more closely on site." The Chinese government was swinging into damage control mode, and when it "monitored" a problem, it was often heavy-handed. This was the last thing New Day needed, and I had the ominous feeling this situation would become worse before it became better.

49

I had no problem convincing Jane to serve as plaintiff in the lawsuit that Mel and I were drafting. She now had all the verve of a new convert and gave her full support to exposing I.S. 406's DNA–altering schemes.

Josh prepared a three-page essay which fleshed out everything he had experienced over the last half-year in school that involved G88 and his classmates' changes due to inhalation of it—all the good, the bad and the ugly of it. I wanted it in his own handwriting to add flavor to the authenticity of a young student's impressions. It began:

"Dear Judge:

My name is Joshua Lee and I am a 13-year-old student in I.S. 406 in Bayside, Queens. I am writing this because there are very strange things happening in my school which I need your help to stop. These things are hurting the health of all the students. Before you read this, I want to let you know that it is all true. I am not making any of this up.

Every day at 2:00 p.m., my school releases blue gas through the air ducts into my classroom and every other classroom. When that happens, everybody except a few people, like me, goes into a trance. They close their eyes and breathe the gas very deeply. Nobody talks. Everybody is in another world. At 2:05 p.m., the gas stops and everybody opens eyes, like nothing at all happened. Nobody remembers anything about it. I've seen this happening for about six or seven months already.

This gas has not affected me, at least I do not think so. There are a few other kids like me who are still the way they used to be, and they also want to investigate why the school is doing this to us. But most of the other children feel very good from it. They act very peacefully and they study much harder. Now my school brags that this year it is one of the best schools in New York. I believe it is all because of this gas which is making the children's brains change.

The essay went on to detail a dozen instances of children who had been poor or average students now suddenly doing unusually well on tests and homework, and children who complained of recent physical ailments that had come on unexpectedly and for which their family doctors had no explanations and could make no certain diagnoses. It ended:

Judge, I know this seems like an incredible story but it is real. I'm only a teenager, so my mother is also in this case as my parent, because my lawyer friend told me I cannot sue anybody in my own name until I'm older. My mother also believes this is real. I also got a few of my friends from school to write to you. I'm including their reports here for you to read. Thank you for all your help.

Joshua Lee

We then put it into affidavit format and notarized his signature. Exhibit No. 1 was ready. Josh was also trying to convince his friends who were similarly unaffected by G88 to include their essays. One week later he gave me unsigned reports written by John Jackson, Philip Chapin and Nicholas Lin that confirmed the facts in Josh's affidavit, and told me they and their parents would come to my office on the upcoming Saturday to discuss adding their names to the Complaint and then the boys would sign their essays in front of me before I notarized them.

I decided not to attach Jenny's lab report yet. Better to keep an ace up my sleeve until the right time, in order to maximize the effect. Besides, there might be questions about how the blue ooze had come into the lab's possession and I wasn't ready to deal with that issue until a judge was already on our side and convinced that something smelled rotten in I.S. 406.

While Mel was in my office on one of those afternoons, Josh came in from school, grabbed a Coke from the refrigerator when his mother was preoccupied with a client and unable to notice that he was breaking yet another of her countless rules, and came into my room. "Harry, I need to talk to you. I need Mel to hear this too." He looked slightly agitated.

"Sure, kid, what's the matter?"

"Can you just get Mel in here, then I'll tell you both?" It wasn't a request. Thirteen years old and he was giving directions, just like his mother. The apple doesn't fall far from the tree. This kid would go far in life if he didn't get the stuffing kicked out of him first.

I asked Mel to come into my office, and what Josh told us made us realize we had a tiger of a case by the tail.

In time, Josh did get the stuffing kicked out of him, more than once, and it made him stronger. How far in life he went is a continuing matter of substantial discussion in particular rarified circles around the world.

50   JOSH

It's funny how sometimes a day can begin one way and take all sorts of unexpected turns, all during the same day. Grandma used to tell me that good health and a good attitude are the two most important assets a person can have, because if you have those two strong benefits on your side, then no matter what happens, you can deal with anything. The older I got, the more I realized that old lady made a lot of sense. That day in school proved Grandma right.

I was in the schoolyard playing catch with a few kids before the whistle blew for us to line up with our classes. Sunny out, not much breeze, real comfortable spring morning. Dalton Wu, Ronny Sanchez, Phil Chapin and I enjoyed fifteen minutes before I had to see Green Witch Queen Hardy and sit through another day of sheer boredom. Even though Dalton and Ronny were all goody-goody from their daily 2:00 p.m. zap treatment, they were actually fun to play with now, because they didn't act like stupid asses anymore like trying to hit me and each other in the nuts when they threw the ball. Last year I was once doubled over on the ground in pain and those shitheads were laughing hysterically. Kind of glad that those pranks are over with now.

Anyway, Dalton called out to me after one of my catches, saying that GWQ was with some Asian-looking man some distance away from us, in the corner of the yard, and she was pointing at us. He was dressed in a funky blue suit that looked like it was made for somebody skinnier, because it was so tight he couldn't button it on his best day 10 years ago. He was wearing geek glasses and has super short hair. I didn't pay him or her any mind and neither did the other guys, and we just kept playing until the whistle blew and then we dragged ourselves up to class.

Around 10:30—I remember seeing the clock in the front of the room because I was usually so bored I kept counting down the time until lunch—GWQ got a call on the school telephone, and she looked over at me. She spoke a few words, hung up, walked over to me and said, in her ice-cold flat-liner voice, "Joshua, please go down to the Principal's office now."

I stared at her and didn't move. "What for? I didn't *do* anything," I said defensively. Maybe I had gotten a little too huffy with her, because next thing I knew, instead of getting an explanation from her about why the Principal was calling for me, she fucking grabbed me under an armpit and lifted me clear out of my seat with one hand like I was a feather pillow, and she held me suspended in air so my feet couldn't even touch the floor! Like fucking Superwoman.

"You will obey." She didn't even raise her low-pitch voice. Her green eyes flashed her furious yet flat command, and for the first time, I actually felt concerned. She then lowered me to the floor. I wasn't afraid, see, but I knew this was getting weird. Just as bizarre was that none of the kids in class even registered any surprise at this freak show.

"Yeah…fine…whatever. Chill, okay? I'm going. I'm going." I straightened out my shirt from where she had mussed it up and walked slowly to the door. "Jerk," I whispered angrily under my breath, just loud enough for her to think she might have heard me say it, but not be sure. I'd be lying if I said I wasn't a little bit shaken up, but no way would I let that witch have the pleasure of knowing it.

I took my time going downstairs. Not for nothing, I wondered whether the Principal somehow had gotten wind of what Harry and Mel were planning, and whether any of the kids who'd given me written stories for the judge, had turned yellow and ratted us out to their parents. But I couldn't let those worries show.

I stopped at every water fountain for a sip, peeked into some of the classrooms along the way and had a gander at different classes' exhibits posted to the walls in the hallways. Some pretty creative artwork, especially the paintings of the Avengers. I had always wondered what it would feel like to be the Hulk, you know, get crazy angry and turn green and huge, my clothes bursting apart. I never understood, though, how the Hulk's pants still stayed on him, and that's when I figured he couldn't be real, or at least, that Stan Lee hadn't gotten that part right.

I walked into the Main Office and stood at the counter for a few minutes until one of those lazy ladies who make believe they're busy, looked up and asked what I wanted and why I wasn't in class. "Mrs. Hardy said Mrs. Dorsey wants to see me."

Looking thoroughly bored and uninterested, she said, "Okay, come this way," and led me toward Mrs. Dorsey's office. "Wait here," she motioned to me, like telling a dog, "Stay, boy." She went into the office and came directly out. "Mrs. Dorsey will see you now," and she prodded me with a hand on my shoulder into the office.

Mrs. Dorsey was seated behind her grand wooden desk, surrounded by photographs and diplomas on the walls. She had that old lady, school Principal yukky-perfume smell, not at all like Mom's expensive perfumes that say "Chanel" and which I knew I'd probably have to buy for my first real girlfriend.

There were two armchairs in front of her desk and she said, "Joshua, come over and take a seat, please." At that moment, I noticed that someone was already sitting in the chair farther from the door. It was that Asian guy who had been in the yard this morning.

I sat down and looked at her, then looked down to my hands folded in my lap. I didn't have a clue what I was in for.

"Joshua, this is Dr. Wang. He's a friend of mine. He happened to be here a month ago and saw your wonderful science project. We were all very proud of you. You know that, don't you?" She was speaking in a gentle, encouraging tone. I looked up and saw her smiling weakly at me. I gave a slow nod. This was all going somewhere, and although I had no idea where it was headed, I wasn't getting a warm and fuzzy feeling.

Dr. Wang was a fidgety character. I didn't look directly at him, but I could sense he was looking at me, then at Mrs. Dorsey, back and forth. He was nervous and moving around in his chair even more than a kid holding it because some sadistic teacher wouldn't let him go to the bathroom. The geek was freaking me out.

"Dr. Wang would like to ask you some questions about your project," she said. I really thought he should go to the bathroom first before we got into a discussion, the way he was squirming.

"Hello, Joshua," he said with a typically heavy accent like a bunch of my relatives when they try to speak English. But they dress much better and don't act edgy like this goof. This dude must have been right off the boat.

"Hello," I said, turning my head just enough to qualify as being polite without having to make eye contact. "Nice to meet you," I lied.

So much for the irrelevant and insincere pleasantries, as Harry called them. Dr. Wang wasted no time on any more of those.

"I am from China. Have you ever been there?" he asked in a blandly amiable way.

"Yeah, a few times." I wasn't interested in making small talk with this geek at 9:45 in the morning. He was eyeing me very strangely, like I was a lab rat for him to observe and then dissect. You wouldn't be wrong if you thought I felt creeped out, especially because he and Mrs. Dorsey were both quiet for about a minute. I just sat there looking at my hands. Totally awkward.

"You did a fascinating project, and I was wondering whether I could take it back to China to show my daughter?"

Holy mackerel, was this shit bizarre or what?! Show his daughter? In China? Did he think I was born yesterday? It was exactly my project which Jenny had needed so she could study the DNA of my classmates, and it was the reason Harry and Mel and I were working to see what the Board of Education knew about the ooze, and now...bingo! This doctor or whatever he was, said he wanted to take it back to China to show his kid?! I wasn't having any of it but I couldn't let them see my real face.

"Oh, I'm real sorry, Dr. Wang," I shrugged, "I threw it away after the exhibition ended. Mom said we had nowhere to keep it at home." I glanced at him, then at Mrs. Dorsey. I shrugged again to show my innocent disappointment that I couldn't help them.

Mrs. Dorsey looked perturbed and said, "Joshua, it was my understanding that your teacher specifically told all her students, as each teacher did, that all students must retain their full exhibits until the end of the semester. Do you recall Mrs. Hardy telling you that?"

Man, this old lady was really trying to put me on the spot, and this squirmy Dr. Wang character was breathing his stinky breakfast of garlic through the fabric of his tight suit. "Look, I'm sorry, but our apartment is really small, and I guess my Mom tossed it. She's the boss, you know what I mean? So…" I had nothing to say after that and shrugged again and faked a demure smiley face.

Mrs. Dorsey clenched her teeth and stared at me. Her eyes revealed nothing, her jaw was set tight, and I could tell she was thinking about her next step. "I see. All right, Joshua, you can go now."

"Say, Dr. Wang," I began, just trying to have a little fun at his expense, "why don't you just tell your daughter to follow the way I did my experiment, with her own classmates in China? I'll bet she'd really enjoy that. It's very educational, ya' know?" He stared straight ahead, refusing to turn to look at me, let alone answer me. He was seething with anger and I could feel the heat rising in his reddening face.

Seeing that he ignored me, I stood up, looked at Mrs. Dorsey and shrugged again. "Oh, well, it's been nice chatting with you. Tell your daughter 'hi' from me." I didn't wait for a response, which was smart, because the two of them looked downright morose, and I knew I had been the reason.

I left Mrs. Dorsey's office and she closed her door behind me. I walked out through the Main Office and into the school hallway, then back past her other door that opens onto the hallway. Nobody was in the hallway, so I put my ear to the door crack and could hear them speaking.

In an angry tone, Dr. Wang said loudly and in no uncertain terms, "This is not good at all. As soon as Mrs. Lundy found out that lawyers were looking into our work, she called the Ministry of Education and we held a crucial meeting. Do you know that?! The Vice Minister of Education wants us to deal with this situation immediately! Do you realize that? This boy might be connected with those lawyers. What if they have his project and try to use it against us? We must get it back."

Mrs. Dorsey replied apologetically, "If I had known where this might lead, I would have taken the project away after the exhibition in the school."

"That does not help us now," he complained. "We need to know more about this boy. Who are his friends?"

"Dr. Wang, I cannot agree to your interference in this child's life. We are educators, not police and detectives."

"You have no choice anymore, Mrs. Dorsey! We will hold you responsible."

"*We*?" she raised her voice. "And who is '*we*'? Now let me tell you something, Doctor. I'm over 70 and I'm not afraid of you people. But if you try to make mischief, this could create a big incident, do you understand? Against my better judgment, I permitted Mrs. Lundy to let you come here today to meet Joshua Lee. If he says he threw out his project, then that's the end of it. It's over!"

"It is over when *we* say it is over, not *you*!" he hissed loudly.

Man, this was *some* argument and it was all about me and my project. My stomach was starting to churn but I was frozen against the door. It was getting intense in there.

"How *dare* you talk to me that way! Leave my office *now*, Dr. Wang," Mrs. Dorsey commanded.

Silence. Silence for five seconds. Then I heard her office door slam shut, and I figured he'd come out any moment, so I scurried along the hallway and ducked into the stairwell but peeked back out into the hallway, just in time to see Dr. Wang walking in the opposite direction toward the school's exit. I ran over to a window in the stairwell facing the street and saw him storm out of the school and across the street to a fancy black Benz, bend down to speak through the open back window on the driver's side, to two people sitting in the back seat, then walk around it to get into the front passenger seat. I could see two women in the back seat; looked like a white one and an Asian one. As the car pulled away, I noticed the license plate read NEWDAY1.

As I sipped some water at the fountain to calm down, I kept remembering what Mrs. Dorsey had told that Dr. Wang guy about not interfering in my life, and then he almost yelling that it's only over when "*we*" say it's over. Who the hell was "we"?

I was getting scared. One thing was for sure—Grandma knew what she was talking about. It was only around ten o'clock in the morning and already my day had started to tank big time.

51 AGATHA LUNDY

After an unpleasantly frosty ride back to my office during which only a few words in Chinese were spoken between Dr. Wang and Pamela, and the tension between them was uncomfortably palpable, Pamela said in her definitive voice, in English, "We must talk about this in your office now." We ascended the skyscraper's elevator to New Day and took seats around my conference table. The good doctor was breathing heavily and his face was blank. Pamela simply looked stern with a simmering determination.

"Let me call Walter and Charles to join us," I suggested, as I reached for the interoffice telephone, "so that we can all…"

"No," interrupted Pamela, "we must first discuss this among ourselves without them. Agatha, you are the only person at New Day who can know about this problem for the time being. Yes?" It was not a question but an order barked to elicit my prompt compliance.

"I see. Yes…for now," my voice trailed off. I could not let Pamela assume I was their puppet, but I would let her sense I'd play along for the moment.

Dr. Wang recounted the substance of his meetings that morning with Claudine Dorsey, before, while and after the boy, Joshua Lee, had been in Claudine's office with them. The scientist was in a very animated state. He was not having a good day. None of us were.

"I'm informed by Claudine Dorsey's text messages just now that you were rather curt with the boy and then quite impolite to Mrs. Dorsey, Dr. Wang. Is that so?" I asked the question in a calm but purposely patronizing way so that he and Pamela would know I was displeased with his heavy-handed approach.

Dr. Wang refused to answer my question. In fact, he refused to look at me, staring intensely from his pained, waxen face, like a petulant schoolboy, at some imaginary point on the table about 12 inches from the edge.

Pamela did her best to control her mood but it was apparent that this trip to New York had not been her idea. "A g a t h a, this is the first time our Ministry has faced any kind of determined inquiry about G88 in any country. There is a lot of pressure on us. Do you understand the implications? The Vice Minister is extremely interested in how this plays out. *All* of us will be impacted," she emphasized, making it sound more like a threat than an observation.

I had no doubt about that. In Pamela's and Dr. Wang's cases, however, a public embarrassment to the Ministry could, in the extreme, result in their detention and internment in a "re-education" facility in some near or distant, and certainly inhospitable, location of China for the better part of a year, to atone for events in America that they had neither sparked nor exacerbated. But the Ministry would find scapegoats and these two would make convenient candidates; Pamela, especially, as she could be accused of having foreign leanings due to her years of study here and her various friends and acquaintances in the United States. Trumped up charges might be leveled against them, and their public and private lives could be ruined.

In the case of New Day, we had allies in the United States who saw merit to our surreptitious endeavor, and I was confident my organization would survive, with or without assistance from the Chinese. If the Chinese cut us loose, I had alternate avenues to manufacture a G88-like alternative, but the start-up time would be significant and, as the Chinese were generously underwriting the various costs of our current importation of the product, I'd need to look high and low to find dark financing. The Chinese, however, had too much invested and too much to lose from abandoning the project here, and New Day was their key foothold in the USA.

"Pamela, I'm sure we'll be able to manage this incident. If you'll leave this in New Day's capable hands, we'll see it through to a peaceful and uneventful conclusion."

Her eyes were on me and I could tell her mind was working in overdrive. "It is the Ministry's wish that Dr. Wang remain in New York at New Day until this matter is resolved."

"Really?" I asked noncommittally. I looked at Dr. Wang, who was sitting silently attentive. It was obvious he was following the script that Pamela had set, and she was executing the Ministry's directive.

"Yes. Really," she stated flatly as she trained her eyes on me to drive home the decision that Dr. Wang would become a fixture in my office.

"This is highly unusual and I don't think it will work. For example," I began, but I never got to finish the sentence.

"Make it work!" Pamela growled in her coldest, lowest voice. After a few seconds of struggling to regain her composure, she said, "Dr. Wang and I are leaving now for meetings elsewhere. He will return here tomorrow. You and I will keep in touch in the usual manner." She rose, and taking his cue, so did he. She approached me and took my hand. Her hand was warm and her grasp was sincere. "Agatha, I am sorry but we have no choice," she consoled in her apologetic attempt at personal frankness, before turning on her stiletto-sharp heels and leaving New Day's offices.

I smelled trouble coming. It was clear that the Ministry was employing its own tactics to deal with this "American problem," but whether the problem would be alleviated or worsened was anybody's guess. If the problem worsened because of the Ministry's activities, New Day had an exit strategy.

52 HARRY

I stared in silence at Josh after he told us what had occurred in school. Mel could only slouch back in his chair and say, "Man, oh, man!"

"Harry, you can't tell Mom yet. Okay?" Josh implored me. "She'll be really upset."

"Yeah, I know." But I also knew I couldn't keep it from her for too long. Things were moving fast now. It was apparent that Josh was in for some hard times unless our next moves forestalled them. My own guilt complex was kicking in, because I was largely responsible for putting him in the middle of this mess.

"Mel, we need to get this into court as soon as possible. Let's start the legal proceeding now and seek an immediate Order to Show Cause for a court order to protect Josh from any retribution by his school and the Board of Education," I said.

"Good idea, Harry," Mel agreed. Looking at Josh, Mel said, "Josh, you're going to be fine, understand?" He put a comforting hand on Josh's shoulder. "I know you're worried, but you have Harry and me and Reggie, and soon you'll have a judge in court, too, to look out for you."

Josh was about three shades paler than usual. He was looking at me with eyebrows knitted in deep worry. "Shit, I never expected *this*. I mean..." he thought aloud, "...I'm only a kid. Why is this happening to me?"

HARRY

"Look," I said, trying to calm him and reason with him, "it happened and we just have to deal with it. Okay? You just go back to school tomorrow and stay alert. And, by the way, please do your schoolwork well and keep a low profile. Got it?"

"Got it. I want to leave now. I have a headache."

For the next two days, Mel and I cranked out legal documents, including an updated draft affidavit for Josh to revise in his own words and then sign, summarizing the events of that strange morning in the Principal's office that he had witnessed while sitting in there and also what he had overheard through the door. I was concerned for his safety and I wanted to put it all on paper now. No holding back or tiptoeing around the facts.

And that's when the unexpected occurred.

Looking back on it all these years later, perhaps it was to be expected. We were challenging a behemoth on a world-scale ideological tear.

53

O n the balmy Friday morning a couple of days after being called down to Mrs. Dorsey's office to meet that creepy doctor, I was skateboarding to school when a car slowed down near me. I thought nothing of it since plenty of parents drove their kids to I.S. 406 and generally drove slowly as they approached, or maybe one of their little darlings told Mommy Dearest to slow down so he could yell "Hey Josh" to me out the window.

Suddenly, the car pulled up a couple of yards from me and slowed to keep pace. The front passenger window rolled down and an Asian man I'd never seen before extended his hand, waving me over. No way, buster. This was New York and I wasn't stupid. I ignored him and skated faster ahead. Then he called out in Mandarin, "Hey, Xiao Lee, come over here."

Holy shit! He knew my *name*! He was calling me "Little Lee," in the Chinese style when you speak in a familiar way to someone younger than you. This was too freaky. Even though I skateboarded more quickly toward the school building, the car sped up alongside me.

"You'd better behave," the guy yelled at me, pointing an accusatory finger. "Stop making trouble with lawyers. You hear? Otherwise, next time we won't be so polite to you. You understand?"

I thought about my options: give him the middle finger

and shout back in Mandarin, "Mind your own business, you turtle egg!" which was a pretty bad curse to Chinese people; skate faster to school and then report him; ignore him and hope it was just a hallucination; or lose it completely and pee in my pants from fear.

I decided on another option: to slow down and even move closer to the car. I looked intently at him, studying his face and trying to memorize his features. He had unkempt thick black hair, dirty brownish-orange teeth and a scar down his right cheek. I could smell the chokingly pungent odor of cigarettes on his breath. I looked carefully but quickly at the car's details so I could later recall its make and color, and most importantly, the license plate number.

"We can make trouble for your whole family. You better be smart and stop talking to people. You hear, Xiao Lee?" Then the car sped off down a side street.

I was plenty scared. Who were these people? Who'd sent them? I knew my problems had just risen to a whole new level. My family and I were being threatened.

That was when I made a decision.

The wrong one.

I entered the school and went into the Main Office where I found Mrs. Moskowitz. She had always been nice to me so I thought she would be a safe choice. "Mrs. Moskowitz, we have to talk." I told her what had just happened on my way to school. She looked genuinely worried for me. She told me she would speak to Mrs. Dorsey and I should go along to class. I asked her to speak to Mrs. Dorsey right now, otherwise I'd be unable to focus on my schoolwork all day. She thanked me for coming to her and then went into Mrs. Dorsey's office. I hurried outside of the Main Office and, as I'd done two days ago after leaving Mrs. Dorsey's office, I walked around to the hallway side of Mrs. Dorsey's door.

I could hear the two women talking about what I had just experienced. It was a very brief conversation and I heard Mrs. Dorsey say, "I see. All right. I'll deal with it." I heard Mrs. Dorsey's door shut, and the next thing I heard was Mrs. Dorsey's voice saying, "Agatha? Yes, it's the boy, Joshua Lee, for sure." There was silence for a few seconds and then I heard her say, "I agree. They'll need to focus on this today. Cannot delay any longer. The situation needs to be neutralized."

Neutralized! I knew that word from video games where a risk is to be neutralized. That meant exterminated. Killed. Finito. Hasta la vista, baby!

I did an about-face in controlled panic mode and, with a ramrod-straight back, walked toward the front door of the school. I walked fast, eyes straight. Thank goodness for the chaos of the early morning. I mixed in with the parents and kids entering the building and avoided the gaze of the school guard. I slipped out of the school building and skateboarded home like my life depended on it. It did!

Shit!! Not even 8:00 a.m. yet and I was already a marked man.

54 JOSH

I never stopped skateboarding except when I was out of breath or my leg muscles hurt, and even then, I forced myself onward. When I arrived at the house, I rang the bell. No answer. I rang again and again. Finally, Grandma answered the intercom in a raspy voice, "Who is it?"

"Me!" I shouted in Mandarin.

"*Aiii yaaahh*!!! Just open the door for me!" No fucking patience for her silly questions. My heart was thumping 150 miles per hour.

I got upstairs into the apartment and Grandma looked shocked. "What did you forget now?" she asked. I had a reputation for neglecting to pack lunch bags and schoolbooks in my backpack so she thought it was just more of the same. But then she saw how worried I looked. I was standing in the center of the living room, eyes wide and staring into nothingness, shifting my gaze from left to right and in all four directions of the compass, struggling to control my breathing.

"You look terrible," she consoled me. "Sit down. Have some juice." She started for the kitchen.

"No, Grandma. We have to get to Mom's office. Now! I need to talk to her. I need to see Harry!" I said as I ran to the bathroom to release my bladder. I had been so worked up and flying through the streets so urgently to get home that, once in the bathroom, it took me almost a full minute to feel "evacuation complete." Now I understood why old men walked out of bathrooms looking so relieved.

Grandma was as flabbergasted as an old lady can get at about 8:10 in the morning, still sleepy and thrown into irrational turmoil by her ridiculous grandson. "What are you talking about?" she asked in confusion. "You look like you saw a ghost. What exactly is going on with you now?" There were mixed notes of concern and consternation in her voice. I couldn't blame her, but I was in no mood to start being all sensitive to her, at least not after what I'd just been through.

I sighed like I'd just lost my best friend, sat down on the couch, bent forward rocking my forehead in my hands for a while, then looked up and said, "Grandma, I know you think I'm acting crazy now, but something just happened on the street and then I heard something terrible in school and I have to tell Mom. It's very urgent."

"Are you okay? Did a car hit you?"

"No, nothing like that. Don't ask me more questions. I'll explain it later. Can we just *go*, please?"

She mumbled to herself about what a lot of trouble I was, that this was all because my mother wasn't strict enough with me, because I had no father at home, how no children were ever like me when she was growing up in China, and plenty of other crap. Tired bullshit I'd heard a thousand times. But I wasn't about to pick a fight with her. She got out her drab blue lightweight spring coat and grabbed her purse.

"I want to take a taxi. We don't have time for some slow bus," I urged.

She also wasn't in the mood to argue. "Fine, fine," she replied testily. She called a local Chinese car service and in less than ten minutes there was a funky sedan with horses painted on the doors, waiting outside. We hopped in and I gave the driver the address. No conversation. At least not from me. Grandma alternated between mumbling to herself and telling the driver how I was a strange boy, how I suddenly appeared back home this morning, how I rushed her to take the ride, blah, blah, blah. Good thing she couldn't speak English, otherwise Americans would have thought she was nuts; right now, only the Chinese driver thought that. Come to think of it, his own grandmother couldn't have been much different from Grandma; from what I'd seen, they're all pretty much alike at that age.

During the whole ride, the events of the past hour kept flashing through my mind, replaying themselves over and over. I could see that guy's piercing eyes, his angry curled lips, his threats, even the car itself as the instrument of my destruction. I could hear the menace in his voice, how he spit his words out at me, demanding my obedience or else. The streets and traffic whizzed by but my eyes registered nothing.

Despite it being the tail end of the morning rush hour, I sensed that we had made good time in arriving at the office. Or maybe I was so preoccupied with the drama that I had no aware-ness of time passing. Grandma paid the man and, next thing I knew, I was already outside holding the car door open for her. She was working on dragging herself out of the car while making her departing remarks to the driver.

"Come on, Granny, let's go, let's go. Say good bye and good luck!" I urged her in English and Chinese, not that she could understand English, but I was too nervous to be selective in my linguistics. Damn, but she was one slow old lady. "Chop chop! You hear me!" I hurriedly barked at her in English, only to be reprimanded in her thick Northeastern farmer's accent. I remem-ber looking left and right, and across the street, scared I would see that automobile from hell with the brown-teeth puke-breath man stalking me. Boy, oh boy, that image wouldn't disappear anytime soon, that was for sure.

In the back of my mind, I kept thinking that I was only a kid. A big 13. I needed this hassle like a fucking hole in the head. Why was this happening to me? But I wasn't about to address this question to my family or else I'd get their typically philo-sophical answer like in the Chinese kung fu movies: "We don't choose our fates, Joshua. They choose us," or some such bullshit. Hell of a day so far. It had nowhere to go but downhill. Bad mornings were becoming a pattern in my life.

Grandma finally sidled herself out of the car, stepped on

to the sidewalk and toward the office building, all the time muttering about the trouble I had put her to. I slammed the car door hard, faced the building, and over my shoulder heard the driver shout back something impolite at me before he drove off.

After we got upstairs into the office, Mom saw me and freaked out. "What happened?!" she exclaimed as she popped up from her seat behind her desk and crossed the room briskly to us. "Why aren't you in school now?"

"Mom, this is crazy," I exclaimed, rife with all the excitement pulsing through me. "Let me tell you what happened to me this morning on the way to school." Meanwhile, Grandma trailed behind me, still muttering, but louder than before, so that Mom would feel sorry for the inconvenience I had caused the old lady. But that shit wasn't catching any traction and Grandma knew it.

"Where's Harry?" I looked around as I asked.

"He'll be here soon. I want to hear about what happened, so start talking."

We all sat down in the conference room and I related the tale. Mom was taking this very seriously. Grandma was mostly silent but she still couldn't help herself from mumbling, despite our ignoring her. About 15 minutes later, Harry came into the office, briefcase in hand. As he walked toward his own office and past the conference room, he noticed us, looked very surprised and marched right in.

"What's *this* all about?" he asked, sounding quite concerned, and sat down without taking off his coat. I told him the whole story again. Grandma still spluttered until Mom finally told her to stop complaining because this was a serious matter; the old lady looked annoyed but at least she kept quiet.

"Interesting. So…they knew your name. Hmmm…," Harry mused, grinning as if this were funny. "And today is only two days after you met that Chinese doctor in Mrs. Dorsey's office." He slowly drummed the table with his fingers, over and over, his head cocked to one side, staring into space. I could see him getting very Zen about this, letting the entire situation swirl in his mind before gelling into a plan or a variety of alternative plans.

"What are we going to do about this?" Mom demanded to know. "Now my son is being threatened, and I and my mother and daughter too. All because of this blue smoke!!"

"It's not smoke, Mom, it's ooze that gasifies so kids can breathe it in," I pedantically corrected her.

"*Don't* correct me!! I'm your *mother*!" she snarled.

I wasn't going to touch that one. I had tried plenty of times before and always lost. I just hung my head to avoid meeting her eyes, cleared my throat and muttered under my breath, "Yeah, whatever."

"Be *polite*!" she shouted. Grandma was jolted in her seat by Mom's cannon blast even though she couldn't understand a word of English. That only set the old lady to talking to herself again in Chinese. The whole thing was a hilarious sight, and I had all to do to suppress my giggling.

"Jane, please calm down," Harry said to defuse her fury. "I know this is very upsetting. But you two getting on each other won't help. What we need to focus on is how to protect all of you while we expose this school's DNA gas and whoever is behind it."

"And how are we supposed to protect ourselves? Get guns? Hire bodyguards? Go hide somewhere?" Mom asked peevishly.

"Josh, for now, let Grandma take you back to school. Let me think about how to deal with this, and I'll discuss it with Mom and Mel."

Mom held her tongue, which was not her strong suit, and simply fumed.

I shook my drooping head. "This is one fucking mess we're in," I sighed in frustration.

"We'll work it out, Josh," Harry said with an air of assuredness. I always appreciated his confident tone even when it was just a bluff. It made me feel we'd get through all right. "I'll see you at school at dismissal. Here," he said, reaching for a piece of paper and jotting down something short, "is a note to give the Main Office when you get back there. A sick note for why you're late. Jane, sign it here," he commanded, pointing to a spot at the bottom of the note. She obeyed, probably the first time I could remember her just obeying without first asserting herself.

I took the note and spoke to Grandma in Mandarin to explain that we were going back to school. She looked like the perfect picture of someone being royally jerked around at the pleasure of others. She stood up, glanced icily at Jane and Harry, and blurted out to me in clipped Mandarin, "Go," sort of a combination of an order plus her own resignation of any authority to her daughter, grandson and Harry.

 **JOSH**

We arrived at school about an hour before lunch break. The rule was kids coming in this late had to be accompanied by an adult, so Grandma walked in with me. I handed in the note at the counter in the Main Office and the Office Lady who took it nodded politely at Grandma, but gave me anything but a smile. "Thank you, Josh. Feeling better, I hope?" she asked with a doubtful squint.

"Just *peachy*. See ya," I called out while turning to leave the Office. Fucking murderous bastards asking me how I felt! I had had my share of run-ins with them and I could hear them whispering about me each time I'd been hauled down to Mrs. Moskowitz's office. I said goodbye to Grandma and she left to walk home. I didn't feel bad for the old girl anyway, since the weather was warm and she needed the exercise. Hell, I did her a favor getting her out of the apartment on such a nice day. She could moan and groan all she wanted. Made no difference. Sometimes people just don't want to look on the bright side of things. Although, that day, there was no bright side at all for me yet. But I figured my karma would turn it around.

I got up to class and sauntered over to my desk. Mrs. Hardy was in front of the room talking about the American Revolution, pointing to a map of the American colonies. She stopped and watched as I crossed the room. So did 26 other pairs of my classmates' eyes and that creepy helper-teacher's bug-eyed peepers. I looked up at her after sitting down and forced a weak smile. She peered at me for a few seconds as if she knew something, but I didn't make anything of it because she was always giving me the evil eye. She resumed her lecture and the kids busily took notes. They acted like everything she said was a pearl of wisdom. It had been like that for months since the blue gas treatment began. At this point, I wouldn't have expected anything else.

The lunch bell rang and, in a few minutes, I was in line at the cafeteria, tray in hand for a hot lunch. After sitting with Mary and a few other friends to wolf down the slop they passed off as food, I headed out the door to the yard to unwind. Fidgety Phil Chapin came skipping over to me and said hurriedly, "Hey, Josh, you okay? Heard you were sick."

"Bad morning but I'm fine now. You?"

"I'm good, but Nicky Lin had a rough time this morning, man. Mrs. Dorsey called him down to her office and when he came back to class, he looked scared."

"Where's he now?" I asked, scanning the school yard to locate him.

"He told the teacher he wanted to go home, so they called his mother to come and get him."

"I wonder what Dorsey said to him. You have any idea?"

"Not exactly, but he told me on the way down from class that some strange Chinese or Korean guy, some 'Doctor Wang,' was there too, asking him all sorts of questions about how he's been doing in school, and if he knows other kids who have not been improving their schoolwork this year. That's pretty weird, right?"

That was another "holy shit!" moment. My eyes opened to double their normal size and I gasped. This day was only getting worse. "Phil, I have to tell you something. That Dr. Wang guy talked to me two days ago in Dorsey's office too. Then, today, on my way to school, some stalkers in a car called out my name and threatened me that I better shut up about the ooze."

Phil, ordinarily a nervous kid, suddenly couldn't move or find any words. He just stood paralyzed and stared at me like he'd seen a ghost.

"Phil, you okay?" I asked him. He looked genuinely terrified. "Snap out of it, man, you're freakin' me out." I shook him by the arm.

"Oh, shit, dude, that means they might come after me too, right?! I mean, you, Nicky, me and the other kids who all know about this stuff but are, like, immune to it? We're all in trouble?" he asked in a very shaky voice. I thought he'd start the waterworks any minute now, either from up top by crying or down below by wetting his pants. I couldn't deal with that crap now. I had enough to do to hold my own shit together.

I usually kept my cool under fire, and since I didn't want to make Phil more nervous, I took a deep breath, raised my eyebrows, forced myself to grin confidently at him, put my arm around his shoulders, and said, "Look, man, it'll be okay. But we just have to chill and hang together on this, like we agreed in the park. Got it?" I shifted my arm around his neck, gently pulled him forward and playfully mussed up his hair to relax him. It was a losing battle.

"I don't want to see this Dr. Wang guy, Josh!" Phil cried out. "I'm afraid!" He was practically gasping for air. "What if he asks me what I know about all of us? Huh? What do I say?" Phil pleaded, looking to me for guidance. Me! Like suddenly I had all the answers!

"Look, Phil, your parents already know about this because you wrote your paper for our lawyer, Harry Epstein, and your folks agreed. So they're on your side. Right? That should make you feel good. If all our parents know about this, like my Mom knows, like your parents know, it'll be easier to handle. We're The Untouchables, dude! *Remember*? *Okay*?!?" I kept my arm draped over his shoulder like a security blanket for the kid.

He shook his head. "I know my parents agreed, but they've also been on my case for my grades being so low in the class this year. They've seen how all the Blue Breathers are doing, and the teacher tells them that I've disappointed her. It's just so damned confusing, you know what I mean?"

"Man, that's just the way it is, Phil," I snapped impatiently at him. Then I looked around to make sure nobody overheard us. I looked back at him at said, sighed and said gently, "Look it, Phil, did anybody *ask* you to get low grades?! No. That's on *you*, bro. Okay? Just like I screw around and do lousy. I'll get my act together someday, and so will you. So, just get over it and get a hold of yourself."

Phil seemed to calm down a bit, and I said, "Look, man, something heavy is going on. We just have to hunker down. We can't stop this Dr. Wang asshole from showing up here, and we can't stop Mrs. Dorsey from letting him ask his questions, and, sure, they've got people following us who know who we are. But parents have to be told. We need them on our side even more now. You hear me?" I said to him with some urgency in my voice, trying to keep his attention focused on the message instead of his own fear. I wasn't scared now, but I didn't need a nervous jackass like Phil on my conscience either. "Anyway, you wrote that paper for Harry Epstein to use in the court. But he can't use it unless your parents come over to his office to sign something, since you're only a kid, so you need to get on that, okay?"

Phil's face was regaining some color and his breathing sounded regular again, but who could tell with him?

"Look it, man, today is Friday, Phil. Tell all the kids in our group that we have to meet again at the park on Sunday afternoon. I'll also tell them today. And talk to your mom or dad about going to Harry Epstein's office over the next few days. I'll email you his address again later. Now scoot over there and let's play some catch before it's time to go in. It'll help ya focus."

He nodded and quickly walked about 50 paces away, turned and caught the pink Spaulding I threw in a high arc. I had to keep this guy engaged otherwise he'd skid off the tracks.

Never a dull moment, I thought to myself. Where this was all going was anybody's guess.

I called Mel on Friday morning to come over to help me complete the court papers. When he arrived, he was flabbergasted to hear about Josh being threatened from a passing car of thugs obviously dispatched by Dr. Wang or affiliated with him, and he agreed that, for the court case, this latest development was the sweetener. If this didn't convince a judge of the urgent necessity to crack down on this scheme, nothing would. Based on what Josh had told me in the morning, I prepared a short draft of an affidavit for him to review, change if he wanted to include anything else, and then sign, so we could include it with the statements he and his classmates had already given us. We still needed those classmates' parents to permit the use of their children's statements. I knew Josh was campaigning with his Untouchables to get this done. If by Monday we couldn't obtain their authorizations, we'd proceed with Josh's evidence alone. Time was of the essence.

Then I had an idea to bounce off Mel. "Say, how about this? We aim to finalize everything for Monday, but before going into court, you, Reggie and I pay a visit to those characters at the Board of Education to show them the papers and gauge their reaction. They're right down the block from the courthouse anyway. What do we have to lose? Right?"

"Sounds fine to me, Harry. After all, in this situation, there's really no advantage in springing a surprise court order on them. If they were savvy, they should have been waiting for one since our first meeting with them. I'll call Reggie to keep Monday afternoon open for us."

Jane popped her head in to ask Mel and I what we wanted for lunch and then phoned a Cantonese restaurant for delivery of a *dim sum* meal of more than a half-dozen different items. I always drank beer with lunch on Fridays. It was sort of a tradition to celebrate having made it through another week, fighting the good fight. Mel and Jane joined with bottles I kept in the refrigerator.

"Harry, I'm really worried about what happened this morning to Josh," Jane said during lunch. "Do you think the judge can truly stop these people?"

Before I could respond, Mel said with an air of complete and contagious self-confidence, "Jane, Harry and I aren't going to let these people get away with this, I guarantee you. We may be old but we've been through a lot together, and we'll see this through to the end of the line. Right, Harry?"

"You *said* it, pal," I responded, but in my heart of hearts, I didn't know where the end of the line would find us.

"I trust you two. Please. My son's life in your hands. Maybe my whole family's too. And not just here in New York. If these people know about Josh and me, then they might find our family in China too," Jane explained, her voice emphatic. "Harry, you *know* how they operate."

Her fear was real and she had good reason to fear. Chinese history had been a series of turbulent struggles for as long as history had been recorded. People were pawns to be manipulated and sacrificed as necessary. When I had visited old friends in China a few years after the Cultural Revolution, they raised glasses to toast each other over their remarkably lucky fortune in surviving those horrific times. They related stories of the murders, robberies and rapes that purposely went unsolved. They recalled the sufferings and suicides of innumerable hopeless people who had been wronged simply because of who their ancestors had been and which earned them the damning humiliation and dishonor of being officially listed as one of the "Five Black

Types" of persons branded by the regime as bad elements and re-actionaries, and which demeaned them as second-class citizens in every sense and manner. Even before the Cultural Revolution, there had been the unnecessary deaths of tens of millions throughout China from starvation and disease, all the result of political turmoil and blind, ideological decisions. Collective and individual memories of such chaos never fade. If the government was behind this, then relatives there could be strong-armed to persuade Jane to drop whatever it was we were going to do here. Or else.

I patted Jane's hand. "You know we'll do everything we can, Jane," I said in my most reassuring tone. "Don't make your-self more upset."

By 2:15 p.m. I left the office and drove to pick up Josh from school. I parked and waited across the street from where most parents gathered. The weather was good and I was relishing a bowl of a strong Virginia and Perique blend in a sandblasted Canadian carved in Vermont by one of my pipe-making friends. Everything seemed normal until I noticed a car pull up about 25 feet away, drop off two Asian men, then pull off. The car didn't fit the description of the one Josh indicated this morning, so, at first, I didn't make anything too unusual of it. One man was tall and thin, the other short and stocky. They were both dressed in fancy casual clothes and didn't look particularly incongruous. Fathers waiting for their kids? Likely so. The tall one took out a pack of cigarettes and each man lit up. They paid no attention to me, as I probably appeared to them to be somebody's grandfather waiting for his grandchild to be dismissed.

After about ten minutes, as the school doors started open-ing and kids filed out, I heard the stocky man near me say in South China-accented Mandarin, "Quickly, here they come. Start filming." They each produced state-of-the-art cellphones, tossed their cigarettes in the gutter, and intently captured every move-ment from every door. "Dr. Wang said to watch especially for kids who act rough, loud, who run instead of walk, like that," said the stocky man to the tall fellow. "Got it," said the tall one in clear, North China-accented Mandarin, moving the cellphone away from his eye so he could survey the entire scene before choosing more targets. "Also, don't forget, look for Xiao Lee and anybody he talks too, and whoever picks him up."

My mind was now racing at full speed because I knew these guys were the real deal. They knew who Josh was and what he looked like. They may have been the same ones who had threatened him earlier in the morning on his way to school. In China, it was a common *modus operandi* for thugs—real thugs, not the Serpico kind of undercover cops—to be dispatched by the authorities to harass targets, and it looked like they were employing that tactic here too. I took out my cell phone and fiddled with it while trying to be nonchalant and film these two characters. They never noticed me next to them recording them, because their attention was riveted on the activity across the street. I walked slowly nearer to them, capturing the details of their appearances as clearly as possible. I knew I was making myself a fact-witness, which could technically interfere with my legal representation of Josh, but I'd worry about that detail later.

Although I was more focused on them than the children being dismissed, my ears perked up when the stocky fellow exclaimed, "Xiao Lee just came out! See him over there?!" He took the cellphone away from his eye and elbowed the tall fellow's arm. "I see, I see," the tall one retorted, shifting position to train his phone on Josh.

Decision time. Make a move?

No.

I let Josh stand on the sidewalk as he panned the crowd, searching for me. After a minute or two of not seeing me, during which he chatted with classmates, he went back inside the building. I didn't want to reveal myself to these two agents yet and certainly could not allow them to see my car and license plate. I had to rely on Josh to wait inside the school, so that I could continue to monitor the actions of these watchers for as long as practicable.

I overheard the tall man say, "Strange, nobody came for him. How long do we have to wait here?" The stocky fellow said, "Let's wait until 3:30. No telling when he'll come out. Otherwise, we'll get him again on Monday, unless Dr. Wang can find us the kid's home address." I slipped my cell phone into my pocket, knocked out the ashes of my pipe, ran a pipe cleaner through it and then refilled it.

I walked down the block and puffed the pipe as the clock ticked on, doing my best to seem uninterested in the street action while still keeping an eye on those two, all the time trying to look like an inconspicuous, bored old man who been given permission by his wife to go out for a stroll and smoke. By 3:30, it was apparent that they were giving up, made a call, and soon boarded the same car that had earlier dropped them off. I allowed another 10 minutes to pass just to make sure they weren't circling. Then I crossed the street and entered the school to retrieve Josh.

"Harry!" he exclaimed, very dismayed. "What the hell happened to you, huh? I've been waiting more than a half-hour. I called Mom and she said you were supposed to be here at dismissal."

"Relax, Shorty," I said in my slow, low-pitched, calm-inducing voice. "I was here. But so were two goons. They were across the street, waiting for you and waiting to see who came to pick you up. They're gone now. Just hurry up to the car and let's get out of here."

Josh regained focus. "Fine with me." He shouldered his backpack and we walked briskly. Outside the school, there was still no sign of those two men or the car they had left in.

57 HARRY

Back at the office, I told Mel and Jane about the two watchers across from the school. "These people are serious, Harry," warned Mel, shaking his head to himself. "First, this morning, they're following Josh and shouting threats and warnings. Now they're hanging out at school to wait for him. This is something new for me. We have to put a stop to this. It's out of control. Harassment, pure and simple. It's criminal behavior."

"We'll get this under control on Monday for sure, Mel," I replied. "How are the court papers coming?"

"Good. Just about finished with all the drafts. Let's go over them together."

We spent another hour, then broke for dinner. It was Friday evening and my habit was to attend synagogue for Friday night Shabbat services. Mel and I had a good dinner at a Shanghai-style restaurant and, although he was neither Jewish nor religious, he accompanied me to attend services. As kids, we had attended each other's church and synagogue for all sorts of religious holidays and it was always a given that no matter what religious denomination our families were, we enjoyed participating in each other's events. After all, it was how New Yorkers related to each other. James Cagney, the great tough guy of film and another Stuyvesant High boy, was a Roman Catholic Irish-American who spoke pretty decent Yiddish because of all his Jewish friends and neighbors when he was a kid. This was our New

York, the real melting pot. Now we were sharing it with increasing numbers of immigrants from other countries and their children born here, and it was wonderful to see all these people joining our American club—the club of the American spirit.

We left the synagogue around 9:30 p.m. and planned to meet back at the office Sunday to finalize and assemble all the court papers.

"I have a feeling we're going to flabbergast some judge with this case on Monday, Harry," Mel said with verve in his voice. "I'm *excited*! I can't tell you how grateful I am to you for having gotten me off my duff and back into action." He gripped my shoulder tightly and shook it. His face beamed with eagerness.

"Mel, old friend, I can't think of anybody I'd rather have next to me in this fight. We'll do right by Josh and these kids, I just *know* it," I responded, with sincerity and deep purpose in every word. "Now, get home safely and see you on Sunday afternoon around two to finalize the papers."

Little could I imagine, on that Friday evening, how Monday was going to be unlike anything we had planned.

58   AGATHA LUNDY

It was Sunday afternoon and I was in New Day's office, and not by choice. Pamela had remained in New York since the prior week's trip here and, that morning, had abruptly called a meeting from which I had no excuse to bow out.

I heard her from my desk in the rear of the office as she strode in directly from our front door into the conference room, those high heels making their unmistakable chipping and poking sound on our wood floor. Dr. Wang had come with her, slowly following behind at his customary several paces. They walked through the office as if they owned it, which always irked me; it shouldn't have, since they paid the rent and had keys to the entrance. I sat down in the presence of their deadly serious eyes as Walt ambled in to participate. I wanted him there as my witness, Sunday notwithstanding.

"Agatha," Pamela fired away in a chilly tone, "I want your suggestions about how to make the boy cooperate with us and make his lawyers stop investigating us." She never beat around the bush. No friendly chit-chat. Dr. Wang sat silently, the very image of an exhausted, overworked scientist.

"The 'boy'?" I coyly asked. "I assume you are referring to young Joshua Lee who did the toothbrush project that you can't get your hands on?" I suggested.

Without answering my no-need-to-answer question, her drop-dead gorgeous, long-lashed, phoenix eyes bore into me, cold as a raptor's eyes locked on to its prey, as she patiently awaited a serious response. I took a deep breath. This was going to be an unpleasant afternoon.

"Pamela," I began, knowing that I was heading at an un-safe speed into a brick wall, "you lived here long enough to know that we can't *force* the boy to do anything. We can't *barge* into his home to *search* for the toothbrushes. We can't *grab* him off the street to make him confess to the whereabouts of the tooth-brushes. We can't *threaten* him into stopping whatever he and his friends have started in regard to investigating G88. Agreed?"

Pamela sat as a veritable iceberg, hard and unforgiving. Her impatience was tangible. Dr. Wang was so agitated he could hardly control himself. "We cannot let them do this to us!" Dr. Wang barked.

Now it was my turn to stare. After many long, silent seconds, I asked, "Why not?" I knew this dare would only further infuriate him. The question sent him into a fit. He jerked his head to look at Pamela, Walt, then me. Speechless. He was fuming.

"Dr. Wang," I said slowly, "Do you believe that G88, and your improvements to G88, will revolutionize the world?"

"Yes, but..."

"Then you must have faith." I refused to say more.

Dr. Wang looked at me in astonishment. Still speechless despite his twitching lips. Pamela thawed out, turned to look at Walt who sat quietly, peering down at the coffee cup in his hands, just taking it all in. She then rose and said, "Fine. We'll handle this ourselves, Agatha. This has been a most unproductive meet-ing. I don't think the Vice Minister will be very pleased with my report." Dr. Wang stood on cue to follow Pamela out of the con-ference room.

They didn't get far before I called out, "Oh, Pamela," in a slightly fetching tone. "Do come back now." I felt like a cat toying with a mouse under its paw: hold it, let it go, pounce again.

She stopped, looked up at the ceiling as if deciding, then turned and said with an equal tone of amused boredom purposed to match mine, as if to bait me, "Do you have any ideas?" The mouse as cat.

"Yes. But they will stay right here in this room. Switch off your cell phones and place them on my assistant's desk, then come back here and close the door behind you." It was a good feeling to let this little *parvenu* know who had control on my turf, their money be damned.

They did so and returned to their seats. I stood and poured coffee for myself. "Feel free, everyone. Cookies are in the closet next to the coffee pot. I'm afraid there's no tea left." Despite the fact that I thrived on good Chinese tea, and Dr. Wang never touched coffee, I needed to make a point.

"Dr. Wang, have you attempted to contact the boy after the other day's meeting with him and Mrs. Dorsey?" Although I knew nothing, I knew something about how things worked in China and I was concerned they might pull a similar stunt here. He looked at Pamela, who gave an ever-so-slight nod that authorized him to speak. "Yes. Two of our agents tried to make contact with him."

"Two agents? What kind of agents, exactly?"

"Local people we know. Reliable."

"Oh, really?" I asked softly, nonchalantly. "Tell me what happened, please."

"They found him going to school on Friday morning and told him to stop bothering about this case."

I was astounded. Walt looked like his head couldn't contain his eyeballs inside it. He looked from Dr. Wang to me, his baby blues still bulging from disbelief.

"Pamela, were you aware of this?" I asked gently, searchingly, like a parent calmly interrogating her errant child. Self-control is everything.

She straightened in her seat. Mouth closed, her tongue ran over her teeth, back and forth several times, distorting her face. She chose not to look at me but instead at the table. After a long pause of some five seconds that ticked far longer around the table, she responded with a reluctant but defiant "Yes."

I rested my hands, fingers intertwined, on the table, nodded slowly and grinned at them. "Did you think that was *clever*?"

"It was decided that we should proceed in such manner,"

the pasty-faced Dr. Wang woodenly announced.

"Without consulting me first, I see," I replied, equally matter-of-factly. "Sending your gangsters to scare children? Was your next step in that plan to send the gangsters after the lawyers?"

After a few seconds of silence around the table, I shook my head and said, "Now, this is how we're going to handle things. Pamela, you'll please get on the phone with the Vice Minister or whomever you need to, after I tell you how I want to proceed, at least for the initial step, otherwise New Day is out of the picture from now on and you folks are back to Square One in the United States."

"I'm listening," Pamela replied with an uncharacteristic hint at tentative compromise. She set her mouth tightly and I saw her jaw muscles flexing under the skin as her nostrils flared.

"Pamela, Dr. Wang," looking at each one in turn, "let me schedule a meeting with these lawyers and see where we stand with them. We need to know as much as we can about what they know or suspect. Then we can move forward. New Day needs to know their intentions and so does the Ministry. You won't lose more than a few days on whatever you had been planning anyway. Agreed?"

Dr. Wang looked sullen and remained silent, deferring to Pamela. "Fine, you deal with them," she replied with reluctance. "It seems we can't easily hide from this. If you can work out an arrangement, I'll do my best to convince the Ministry to support it. If you can't, then a new direction will be determined."

I spent the rest of the afternoon with them laying plans that might lead to a positive outcome from a meeting with the lawyers. In the back of my mind, I was also considering the potential steps New Day would take if we could not come to terms with the lawyers. In any event, I couldn't allow these rough-riding cowboys from China to ruin all the work I had devoted the past few years to achieve. The careers of a lot of people at New Day were on the line.

59   AGATHA LUNDY

T he Chinese wanted action and I decided that I'd give them the show they asked for. Just a few minutes after nine o'-clock on Monday morning, I telephoned the Spangler & Spangler firm whose letter to the Board of Education had been forwarded to me by Denise Romski. Reginald Spangler was not yet available and my call was directed to his voicemail.

"Hello, Reginald Spangler, my name is Agatha Lundy. You have been waiting for a response from the Board of Education about what your clients feel may be happening at I.S. 406. I'm the appropriate person to deal with. Let's meet today at 11:00 a.m. to discuss the matter. I think I can put your mind to rest." I left my contact information.

Fifteen minutes later, I received a text message agreeing to meet, but no earlier than 1:30 p.m., as he was occupied until then. I texted back my agreement.

At 1:45 p.m., three gentlemen appeared in the lobby of New Day. From my interoffice camera, I noticed a man about 40 years old, dressed very dapperly in a charcoal gray chalk-stripe suit, spread collar shirt with bright paisley tie, and dark brown wingtip shoes. With him were two older men, one of whom bore a striking resemblance to the younger man and wore a brash plaid sport jacket, open-necked shirt, khaki slacks and light brown Gucci loafers with tassels. The other man wore a navy blue suit, white shirt, regimental striped tie, and black cap-toe shoes. A motley group of lawyers, old school and new school. This would be quite a meeting.

"Walt, they're here. I want it all recorded for us to edit before we send the session to Pamela. Please set up in the conference room and make sure Curtis arranged the afternoon dessert spread." Cakes and cookies would provide sugar to please their dopamine receptors, and hopefully encourage a more positive reaction to what I was about to tell them. Until we could serve up G88 in edibles, fattening desserts would have to do the trick.

"Oh, Walt, also make sure to tell them to leave their cellphones turned off and placed in a tray that Curtis keeps inside his desk."

A few minutes later, my administrative assistant, Curtis, brought the three lawyers into the conference room. "Ms. Lundy will be right with you, gentlemen," he said. "Please help yourselves to the refreshments on the credenza." I was watching them on the interoffice camera at my desk to gauge their reactions and eavesdrop on their comments to each other. They seemed quite at ease. But with lawyers, nobody could tell what they might do after our meeting. I couldn't worry about that now. I stood up, straightened my dress, looked into the mirror, winked and uttered, "Showtime," to myself.

They were chatting amiably with Walt, who could charm anyone, when I entered. As they all stood to greet me, I beamed my executive smile. "Gentlemen, I'm only the president of New Day, not the judge entering the courtroom. Please don't be so formal." This elicited grins as each man sat and I took my place at the head of the table. We made introductions and the usual pleasantries. So far, no blatant hostility by anyone.

"I invited you to New Day today because I know where you are headed with your investigation. I've seen Mr. Spangler's letter to the Board of Ed. I'm not a lawyer and have little patience for them myself, but you fellows look like a very reasonable group."

Harry Epstein, who looked like a Richard Dreyfuss caricature, interrupted my initial statement by gesturing with his hand that he wished to say something. Polite, didn't just blurt out his comments. I stopped and said, "Yes, Mr. Epstein?"

"Harry, Agatha. Harry." He spoke softly and pleasantly, but with conviction. "Let's all get to the point so we don't waste your time." He then reached into a worn, brown leather briefcase with his initials etched in gold filigree and pulled out a mason jar.

My heart stopped for a moment. Breathe, I told myself. Breathe. Keep the poker face on. Keep that plastic smile pasted on straight.

It was G88. How the hell did they obtain it? These were resourceful people and I was going to have to up my game now. This revelation did not change my intention to discuss the matter with them, but it did alter the sequence of facts I had wanted to present in making my case. I would have to accelerate the discussion and get to the point. Less room for fluff and filler.

"Agatha, it was good of you to invite us here. I believe this blue compound is related to New Day somehow, isn't it? Otherwise, you wouldn't have telephoned Reggie." He asked this as a plain vanilla question, no attitude.

"Yes, Harry, it is," I confessed. I had no interest in denials. New Day had a pioneering mission and was not a charlatan peddling snake oil. We were world-class geneticists and proud of it. I looked around the table at each of the Spanglers. They had apparently agreed in advance to allow Harry to take the lead and now I was getting a feel for the reason. Walt's face had lost its amiable, boyish grin as the hard-edged reality of our confronters hit him square on.

I didn't want to yield the momentum to Harry, so I said, "You are holding a jar of the future, Harry. I think you know it, don't you?" He and the Spanglers were about to speak when I quickly continued. "What you are holding is a chemical compound that will change our world for the better. Vastly better."

Harry spoke now. "Agatha, we've already had this tested and are aware it's somehow bonding with the subjects' DNA. Isn't that so?" he asked in an emotionless, inquisitorial way.

"Correct. Are you going to ask me why?"

"It *would* be interesting to hear your reasons. We know it's already changing the kids. They are calmer, more focused, less rambunctious, and so on. There are also reports of kids experiencing physical ailments they didn't have before. And the ethical and medical and legal ramifications of you doing something like this are..."

I looked around the table at Harry and the Spanglers and nodded as he spoke. Then I briskly interrupted his pedantic sentence. "This is not a quick-fix chemical, gentlemen. It's not intended as a cure for Attention Deficit Disorder or ADHD or any of those sorts of conditions."

They exchanged glances with each other, and Mel Spangler asked, "Then what is the purpose of this?"

I signaled to Walt to continue the discussion. "Gentlemen," he said, "technology has and continues to alter life on Earth in ways that are both good and, well, not so good. Wouldn't you agree?"

"Please get to the point, Walt," urged Reggie.

Walt was unruffled. With his usual poise, he continued. "I will, Reggie, I will. Have you seen the canister from which that blue compound comes?"

"Yes," replied Harry. "There's no writing on it except Chinese characters and 'G88'."

"Then you know where it comes from."

"And I know that Chinese thumb-breakers have been threatening children here. I can't believe..." Harry blurted, losing his cool.

"That will not happen anymore, Harry," I interjected. "That was not orchestrated by us at New Day."

"Then...?" He quizzically uttered just that one word.

I sighed. "That was the ill-advised idea of people affiliated with the makers of G88. It won't happen again. Please accept my apologies on their behalf," I offered.

"*Just what the hell is going on? Who's responsible for this? It has to stop!*" erupted Mel, slapping the table in a fit of pique.

Walt stepped in again, this time more forcefully. "Well, Mel, lemme tell you, '*just what the hell is going on*' is that life on Earth is no longer proceeding in a 'business as usual' manner, if you hadn't already noticed." This was Walt in a sarcastic mode

I'd never experienced in all the years of knowing him. I liked it.

"Mel, the world is too damned large now. It's spinning faster and faster, and I'm not referring to rotation around its axis, but technologically, climatically, politically, culturally. It was less noticeable and, frankly, very manageable, two hundred years ago. In the twentieth century, the whole ball of yarn began unraveling. For whatever reasons—and I don't want to get into all that here and now—we're at eight billion people and counting, and the you-know-what is starting to hit the fan. The climate is out of control, out of whack. According to all current analyses by the best brains in the field, it's not coming back anytime soon to where it used to be; at least no time soon that will do any of our descendants any good for hundreds of years. Water levels will rise within our children's lifetimes, and your own grandchildren, come thirty or forty years from now, will likely be at wit's end wondering how they and *their* children will ever survive the famines and diseases that disruption to the weather patterns will have caused. Politically, the world is in the worst shape it's been since World War II. Every nation is rent apart with internal dissent unlike anything any of us has lived through since the War. I'm talking a ticking timebomb. Am I saying anything that sounds vaguely familiar, Mel?"

Mel looked consternated by Walt's sardonic lecture. He rose from his chair and erupted once again. "Look, we're here because this stuff is being pumped into classrooms filled with kids. Somebody has to answer for that! And I'll be goddamned if I'm gonna let you trumped up jackasses play God with everyone's life!!"

Reggie tugged at Mel's jacket sleeve. "Dad, sit down, please," he said, respectfully but with an air of command. "This is getting interesting."

"Interesting?! *Interesting*?!" cried Mel, raising his voice, looking down at Reggie. "I didn't come here for a goddamned chat about world affairs! Do you have any idea what these people are trying to do?!" His face was quickly reddening.

Harry sat pensively, observing it all. I could almost hear the wheels in his head spinning. He was behind all this, I felt sure, pulling the legalistic strings. Claudine Dorsey had informed me of his close relationship with the Lee boy.

"Mr. Spangler," I said soothingly, "Please sit down. Try to relax. I can assure you that we want to resolve this situation just as much as you do, and to the benefit of everyone." I turned to Harry, gave him a strained smile and said in a tone of voice filled with familiarity, "Quite a situation you and Joshua Lee stumbled on to, isn't it, Harry?"

He returned my grin and chuckled. Eyebrows raised, he sighed and said, "Agatha, Walt, I know where you're going with this. Unlike New Day, however, we're lawyers with clients. We're not at liberty to give advice based on the big picture, as you present it, and tell them to just chalk it up to the destiny of the planet. The clients came to us with an immediate problem and asked us for a reliable and fair solution to their current dilemma. So, you tell me, how are we going to strike that kind of a balance today?" Touche, Harry, you hit the ball back to my side of the net.

"Harry. Mel. Reggie," I addressed each one in turn, "I suppose you could file a lawsuit to try to stop New Day from promoting G88, but I have a feeling it would be like having filed a lawsuit in the 1980s and 90s against developers of smartphones. Would that have stopped Andy Rubin and the Android system? Steve Jobs and Apple's iPhone? And the many thousands of other bright young people bent on pushing society—pushing mankind—forward in order to give us these new and amazing devices that serve us?" I shrugged and knitted my eyebrows as I narrowed my eyes and shook my head quickly. "Temporary roadblocks. Nothing more than momentary inconveniences. You know that. There's a natural evolution of technological developments—seems like an oxymoron, doesn't it? Natural evolution and technological development, all in one breath? You're probably thinking it should be 'unnatural' since these are technological changes brought about by humans and not possible of occurring on their own—at least, not yet, that is—but it's actually quite *natural*. The changes arise from man's needs. To evolve is part of our nature. It's part of every living organism's internal clockwork."

"Last year, my teenage son spent a fair amount of his summer break from college on his stomach after having an operation to remove a perianal cyst. The medical specialist says it was most likely caused when his constant bike-riding triggered an infection of the hair underneath the skin on his 'tailbone.' That 'hair' is really the vestigial tail that we humans have as a result of having evolved over a couple of million years from our simian ancestors. Likewise, five-fingered creatures and five-fingered humans have *that* in common, no? Did it ever strike you that evolution is a rather inexorable process that boggles the imagination, since we really can only perceive of it through study and hypotheses, but cannot sufficiently experience it within ourselves—at least not with any keen awareness—in a single lifetime?"

"G88 is another—and only the latest in a never-ending series—another technological boost to mankind's needs. What needs? I'm glad you asked, even though you didn't. Mankind must do what we can, everything we can, to meet the coming crises. Make no mistake, these crises won't be solved with band-aid solutions. They will be solved only when we adapt the necessary technology to address the problems. And that means we must adapt ourselves to become the solution."

"And you think G88 is going to solve all those problems?" asked Reggie.

"It's not 'THE' solution, but it *is* the key to helping mankind help itself. And do you know why it's the key?"

Before I could answer my own question, Harry responded with the same words I would have used, albeit in a slightly mocking voice. "Because G88 is going to jumpstart human evolution. Isn't that your plan, Agatha?"

"I knew I should keep my eye on you, Harry Epstein," I retorted light-heartedly. "You hit the nail on the head."

"This is way out of control, Agatha, not to mention totally illegal," interjected Reggie sarcastically. "There's a plethora of legal problems surrounding this. First, you've got what is likely an unregistered, illegal substance. Second, you're introducing it into spaces owned and operated by public institutions. Third, you have no right exposing people—*children*—to it without probably years of testing and then FDA and other agency approvals. Fourth, and probably just as important if not more so, you don't even notify parents and legal guardians in advance and give them a fair opportunity to voice their opinions, to object or—Heaven forbid this stuff is ever officially approved—a chance to opt out. You've somehow convinced I.S. 406 to make the G88 treatments a part of the daily routine of school, for God's sake." Reggie was a toned-down emotional version of his father, but there was no mistaking the lineage. The old man was already scarlet red with dismay and at a loss for words.

"So, Agatha," Harry sighed and said in his world-wise, world-weary way, the sum of thousands of years of collective consciousness, who knew this mission of New Day's wasn't going away easily, "we have a dilemma here, don't we?"

"Goddamned right there's a dilemma here!" barked Mel. His son and Harry ignored his outburst.

"Gentlemen," Agatha coolly replied, "you might be able to delay New Day for a while, but we have contacts in such high places as will astound you. History is on our side, not yours. There really is no stopping this. However, I am authorized to make you a special offer. For negotiation and settlement purposes only. Want to listen?"

They looked at each other and I observed eyebrows raised, foreheads wrinkled in doubt, shrugs, and finally curious replies of "Sure" and "What do we have to lose?".

"For you to go away quietly and maintain silence and confidentiality, two million dollars for each of the three of you. Sign the nondisclosure agreement and general release that my counsel has prepared and three cashier's checks can be handed to you by 4:00 p.m. today."

As I expected, three jaws dropped in unison. Silence reigned for about 60 seconds as shock set in. It was a thing of wonder to watch.

I stood to pour myself a cup of tea. After more than a minute, I asked, "Any takers?"

"We have clients," Reggie said sheepishly, his mind sifting through the barriers to taking what was essentially a bribe to go away and forget about it all. "We do have certain ethical responsibilities to them, you know."

I sensed that he was caught on my hook and wasn't easily wriggling off. "I realize it could be a problem for you. But I'm confident you'll be able to work that out for yourselves," I said sympathetically.

Mel and Harry had remained silent, thoughtful. Harry said, "Can you give us some time alone, Agatha? We'll discuss your offer."

"That's reasonable. Just stick your head outside the conference room when you're finished and ask Curtis for me." I left the room, struggling to contain my Cheshire Cat grin and proceeded to my office, locked the door and watched them on my videocam talking quietly amongst themselves. About 20 minutes later, I saw Reggie asking Curtis to contact me.

Back in the conference room, Reggie did the talking for them. "Well, it's like this, Agatha. You are asking a tremendous thing from us. In order for us to do the right thing by our clients, we would need to..." I didn't allow him to finish. I raised a hand to wave off his sentence.

"Reggie, I'm not a great businessperson, so I'll just do the wrong thing and cut to the chase. You'll tell your clients that for personal reasons, you cannot continue representing them. You're not selling them out. You're simply bowing out, leaving them to decide what they want to do next. We're not stopping *them*. We're taking *you three* out of the picture. Call it for what is: New Day's stop-gap measure."

Turning my attention to Harry, I said, "In your case, my dear Mr. Epstein, there's something a bit more we're requesting. You haven't told me how you obtained that jar of G88—which, by the way, I'd like you to leave here on your way out—but I have a sneaking suspicion you are a man of many methods. No matter. That's your business and not mine, although I am trying hard to suppress my curiosity about how that jar came into your possession. Therefore, as part of your particular settlement, it must stay 'your business' forever, no mention of it to anyone. You would not even testify 'under legal compulsion,' were you somehow to get drawn into some similar mess, and you would actively place yourself outside the jurisdiction in order to avoid being subpoenaed for testimony."

"That's really asking a lot, Agatha."

"I would imagine that two million dollars would help you comply with my requests. After all, it will come in handy to pay off your gambling debts in Flushing, no?" I asked rhetorically, knowing from my sources that Harry was an inveterate card player who lost more often than he won and had insufficient disposable income to clear up his obligations. I also had learned that the people he played with in the Chinese community were a tough bunch who had lost patience and were making their own self-help plans to collect, or else Harry might become a statistic.

Harry laughed heartily as he said, "It certainly would." He looked down at his hands spread on the table and then said, "Seems you've done your homework." I pursed my lips, stared back with mildly compassionate air, and said nothing.

Reggie spoke next. "Agatha, given the circumstances, frankly speaking, two million won't do the trick. Five million for each of us is more like it."

I wasn't surprised. I had greater authority than only two million dollars per man, but starting low was my instruction. I didn't know whether he was being serious or just testing the waters as an exercise in haggling. "Reggie," I tried to sound surprised, "that's huge money! With all due respect, gentlemen, I think you're seriously overestimating the value of your importance and your case."

"More likely we'd have a field day with this case. First the courts, then—or maybe simultaneously—the press conferences. This could break New Day, Agatha, and could involve a lot of people who would otherwise prefer to remain in the shadows."

I nodded in mock agreement. "Maybe so. But did you ever consider that bringing G88 into the light might create the opposite uproar? People clamoring for it? Parents demanding it for every child? Children demanding it for the almost guaranteed success it could bring them? And then the anxiousness of awaiting permutations of G88 to increase physical or mental abilities?

To render medical cures? The list of potential benefits could go on and on. You might find yourselves shoveling sand against the tide."

"But Agatha," Harry said, "we already suspect that it's not G88 alone that's causing your miraculous changes in the kids at I.S. 406. G88 is only the conductor. It may be the hardware of your system, but there's powerful software streaming through it, isn't there? The ooze is like the musical instrument for the brain, but the bigger issue is who's composing the symphony? And what happens when the maestro wishes to change the composition, write a new one, delete the old one, and so on. Will the kids be millions upon millions of little puppets, with G88 as the network of strings attached to them, with some grand wizard behind the curtain?"

"Harry, Harry, Harry," I shook my head slowly. "Where will all these questions get us? Is that what you'll argue in court? Have you ever considered what the court of public opinion will conclude? Have all the studies that indicate the potential dangers of using cell phones stopped anyone from using them? When the benefits outweigh the costs by such a gigantic margin, is there even a contest?" I shrugged with total confidence.

Mel had been reticent during this part of the discussion, but his confusion had been percolating and was palpable, and he now piped up. "This has been one very odd meeting. I don't see how we can possibly arrive at a decision this afternoon. Too much to consider," shaking his head.

"You're right, Mel," I said agreeably. "Let's meet back here tomorrow at 10:00 a.m. I think we have a good momentum going. Don't you? But if we're to keep this negotiation alive, I need your good faith commitment that no court proceeding gets filed in the meantime, no contact with the media or other busybody third parties."

Quick looks back and forth, steady nods, and Reggie said, "Agreed."

"Well, at least it looks like we're making some progress," I said. "I'll see you fellows back here tomorrow at ten. Hot coffee and pastries, so don't eat breakfast," I promised with a wink.

After a few more pleasantries, I showed them to the elevator. As they were about to enter, I lowered the boom and called out, "Oh, and Harry…please be sure to bring the entire toothbrush display, and I want to see Joshua Lee here too. That's a must. Have a good evening." I showered them with my signature smile as the elevator door closed, their three pairs of eyes widening with mystification.

Returning to my office, I forwarded to Pamela the recording of the afternoon's session. That evening, over two pots of hot sake and plates of sashimi and sushi at my favorite Japanese restaurant around the corner from the office, the two of us did a post-mortem on the session for a long time to analyze the many angles of what had been said and what hadn't, and tried to anticipate how the next morning would play out. I didn't have a particularly good sleep that night, but it was what it was and I'd roll with it. No matter how things went, New Day would survive. That was my first priority.

60

W e walked back in a daze to Reggie's office, only a few blocks away from New Day's place, to discuss the incredible meeting. It's not every day a lawyer is offered five million bucks just to tell his clients he's off the case. The professional ethics problem was a killer. Dropping representation of clients for a profit, courtesy of the opposition, is like throwing a ballgame or taking a dive in a boxing match. Moreover, Agatha's last-minute demands were deeply disconcerting. What ethically defensible reasons could we find for turning over the toothbrushes? Each set of toothbrushes and the DNA embedded in them belonged to a readily-identifiable child. We knew why New Day wanted those toothbrushes, or more specifically, the DNA in them. Jenny had supposed the geneticists in China would analyze each child's DNA to examine the effectiveness of G88 and, presumably the algorithmic programming which was delivered through the gasified ooze, over a week's progression, on a racially heterogeneous sample of children in the American context. Turning over this material would be tantamount to knowingly and intentionally violating every child's right to privacy, which legally only a parent could do, and even then, only under strict and informed conditions. Much worse, however, was the fact that we were being bribed to deny each of those children and the parents the information that there even existed such a system of chemically-assisted DNA alteration, thereby making us complicit in the New Day project.

We all agreed that our legal exposure to the risk of violating various federal, state and local laws was huge. Our reputations were more valuable than even the huge cash payday by New Day. And we didn't even know if it was truly New Day's money that was being tendered. Maybe the Chinese government was buying us off. Maybe the US government. Maybe even some other unknown organization behind New Day was involved, as Agatha had alluded to New Day's wide net of contacts and influence. It was all so nebulous that I knew I'd lose too much sleep regretting I'd compromised my professional ethical duty and sold out my clients and maybe their mental and physical health too, and always fearing what repercussions would result, and never knowing when the moment of revelation of my wrongdoing would befall me. At my age, I didn't need the *tsuris*. Indeed, at no age would I have betrayed my sacred duty to my clients, and I'd be damned if I would start now.

I was perplexed about what possible motivation lay behind Agatha's demand to see Josh. Of what use could his presence be at a settlement meeting? And how could I justify to his mother that her son was being summoned to the offices of the organization that had spent the last eight or nine months trying— unsuccessfully so far—to change her son's DNA?

Although the three of us agreed there was no way we would accept Agatha's monetary offer or comply with her last two demands, we decided to regroup at her office the next morning to tell her so. In the meantime, I returned to my office, called Jane into my room, closed the door so Josh, who was doing homework in the conference room, would not hear the exchange, and explained the situation.

"You must be joking!!" were the first words of Jane's heated response that she hurled at me like rotten fish. "They think I would let them see my son? No way!" She followed with some rather crude curses in Chinese not fit for Josh's ears, although I had no doubt he'd heard them all before. "If they paid me $10 million, I still wouldn't let them near my child! Do you understand?!"

"Okay, Jane. Relax, for heaven's sake. All right?" I barked back in my feeble attempt to calm the woman down. "My gosh! I was just telling you what went on at the meeting. I wasn't suggesting that Josh attend. I already explained to you the legal and ethical reasons why the deal is inappropriate and unfeasible."

After another few minutes of trying to cap the fire on this human oil wellhead blowout, my ears ached from the high-pitched objections and I was glad when she finally stormed out of the room. I washed down two aspirin with an icy can of Coke and closed my eyes for about five minutes to contemplate what else could go wrong at the next meeting with New Day and how we would need to handle it. During the evening, I drank several cups of tea while smoking a few bowls of a Balkan blend I mixed from over a half-dozen types of Virginia, Perique, Yenidje, Xanthi and highly sought after Syrian Latakia leaves. This was quite a three-pipe problem requiring my deep concentration to envision all the permutations of how the next morning and its aftermath might unfold.

The next day, Mel and Reggie met me at Reggie's Manhattan office about an hour earlier than the appointment. We had already agreed to reject the entire proposal and demand an immediate cessation of all New Day activities in I.S. 406 and anywhere else in the United States.

Before we left Reggie's office, his paralegal, Nick Milano, downloaded from the tiny recording device Reggie had kept in his pocket, the recording of the meeting the day before. "Transfer it to a thumb drive and tell Kate to lock it inside our office safe," Reggie instructed Nick. We had all expected that New Day would insist cellphones be left outside any conference area, and we had suspected they would take us at our word and not pat us down for other devices, so Reggie brought along his little silent toy to record the proceedings.

What we were most curious about was the algorithmic programming that was encoding the genetic messages through G88. We knew that only through court orders would we have any realistic hope of discovering such sensitive and crucial information. We also considered contacting the Manhattan District Attorney's Office and the U.S. Attorney's Office for the Southern District of New York to press them to pursue criminal actions.

When we arrived at New Day's offices, we were directly escorted into the conference room by Curtis, where a lavish continental breakfast was spread across the credenza. Agatha made her entrance in grand style some ten minutes later while I was eating my second croissant. Reggie was nibbling a cookie and sipping tea and stood immediately to greet her. Mel was too nervous to eat anything, for he was chomping at the bit to have a go at Agatha. He hadn't changed his habits in the nearly six decades I knew him, still wiry and unable to keep food down as his stomach growled in anticipation, no matter whether facing a trigonometry test or a product liability trial. I put down what was left of my pastry, wiped off, leapt to attention, and we all shook hands.

Agatha was a handsome, statuesque woman whom I took to be in her late 40s, always athlete-erect, dressed for this late spring day in a floral-pattern dress and white low-heel pumps, a diamond pendant on a thin silver or platinum chain around her neck, hair pulled back in a pony-tail that gave her a serious appearance. She smiled as her brown eyes, crow's feet prematurely developing to mark middle age, canvassed the room in obvious search of Josh and a large bag or box containing the several hundred toothbrushes. Her expression altered ever so slightly from a general lightness to a gradual retrenchment and then a knowing smirk as she comprehended that her last two requirements had gone unsatisfied. Those clever eyes belied the mental gymnastics she was instinctively performing about her chances for success in her proposal and how to play the ensuing moves. No matter what happened, I believed, she would react spontaneously to maintain equilibrium, a veritable feline landing on her feet.

"Well, gentlemen, I see our young friend is not attending today's gathering. And, I suppose his toothbrushes were *trashed*?" she sarcastically quipped.

"I thought he already informed the mysterious Dr. Wang, who so very wanted to show them to his daughter in China. I would have thought Dr. Wang had shared that tidbit with you?" I retorted, parrying her blow.

Agatha mock giggled. "I had hoped for a miraculous recovery of Joshua's exhibit from the depths of the alleged garbage bin. It would have been so useful…" and her voice trailed off. She gave me a knowing glance that indicated she did not believe for a moment Josh's excuse to Dr. Wang that his mother had thrown away the offending exhibit. Let her believe as she wished. In fact, the whole passel of toothbrushes in their separate plastic baggies were under lock-and-key in Jenny Spangler's lab.

"So, what's your excuse for why young Mr. Joshua could not join us today for this momentous occasion?" she asked, not letting the matter rest.

"Let's get something straight, Agatha. We're not the ones who need to make excuses here. We're not the ones exposing our children to chemicals from *The Island of Dr. Moreau* in order to create a new species, or whatever you and your friends in China are trying to achieve," said Reggie in the sarcastic voice of righteous indignation.

Agatha glowered at Reggie, then turned her accusing stare on Mel and me. "So that's the way it is today? Is there any interest, or even any point, in discussing my offer of yesterday?"

"We have huge interest, Agatha," Mel said, "but it's not happening. For a number of reasons. All non-negotiable."

She wasn't surprised. She grinned, shrugged and said, "I thought it was a long shot, but worth trying. So where are you going with this now?"

"We're considering all options at this point," answered Reggie.

"None of which will be very palatable to me, I'm sure. Do you wish to communicate with my legal counsel?"

"That will likely come soon enough. However, you need to be very clear that it would be illegal to dispose of any written records, computer records, and physical evidence relating to G88 and New Day's affairs."

"Thank you, *counselor*," Agatha replied, her tone turned icy. "I'm sure you know the way out." She settled her final stare on me and it rested there uncomfortably for about five very long seconds. It was anything but a warm and fuzzy feeling she left me with. She knew we had just declared war and she fully intended to fend off our attacks.

She straight away turned and departed from the conference room, leaving the three of us alone. "Well," I commented to Mel and Reggie, "we know what we have to do, but this has certainly been an interesting two days. Before we leave, anyone want another croissant?"

We looked at each other, chuckled, and Mel said, "Sure, what the hell. The visit shouldn't be a total waste," and grabbed another before we departed.

61 HARRY

It was a little after 1:00 p.m. by the time I returned to the office from that undelightful breakfast meeting at New Day and quick follow-up at Reggie's office to bestow our blessing on the papers we planned to file in court the next day. I was looking forward to lunch and a slow afternoon. Upon entering the office, however, Jane told me that a young American lady was waiting in my room to speak with me. She had told Jane she knew me from a project we had worked on in the past and she had an urgent matter to discuss with me. My sense of surprise was much aroused as I had very few American clients, because nowadays I had a mainly Chinese practice, and I could not imagine what project the woman was referring to.

With aplomb, I strolled into my office and a sharply-dressed, stern-looking young woman rose from her chair and extended to me a long arm, at the end of which was a beautifully-manicured hand. I felt her warm and firm grip, and was certain I had never met her before and, since she had lied in order to seek a meeting, my antennae were up and I was wary of whatever would ensue. Under such peculiar circumstances, as well as my sensitivity to the current atmosphere of possible harassment accusations that could be made when talks were conducted in private, I left my door open. The lady immediately resumed her seat and, although I hadn't the slightest idea who she was, I was nevertheless polite and walked around to my side of the desk and remained standing. She appeared extremely self-assured as she looked directly into my eyes and her fulsome scarlet-painted lips began to speak.

"Mr. Epstein, you and I do not know each other, and I apologize for having told your assistant otherwise, but it could not be avoided. My name is Marie Cristobal and I need a few minutes of your time."

I was fatigued from the morning and this was rather bothersome. I chalked it up to yet another self-centered person who thought that whatever her legal problem was at the moment, it took priority to anything else I might have to do.

"I'm awfully busy, Ms. Cristobal, and I wish you had telephoned ahead to make an appointment. Now, if you like, we can set a time, say, this Friday morning, at the earliest."

She appeared not in the least perturbed and, with perfect composure, announced with finality, "No, Mr. Epstein, *now* will be just fine. What I have to say cannot be postponed."

Still standing, I returned her steady gaze with a sigh of petulant resignation. I was in no mood to argue and assumed she would stop at nothing to tell me her tale of woe, so I asked with genuine curiosity, "Ms. Cristobal, how did you learn of my name? My clientele is almost exclusively Asian, and…"

"Please close the door, Mr. Epstein," she said in a commanding tone.

"Now, *listen* here," I began testily. "In *my* office, I'll…"

"You'll kindly do as I ask or otherwise the United States government will have to make more formal *requests* of you and your associates in this matter."

"What the *hell* are you talking about?" I demanded in an angry tone, raising my voice. Now I was really losing patience with this stranger.

She was unflustered. "You came from a meeting today with Agatha Lundy at New Day. You don't have to confirm or deny. We know these things. I am not with New Day. But I am aware of what they are working on. You are to keep hands off. We will handle it."

"Who the *hell* are *we*? And for that matter, who the hell

are *you*?!" I blurted out loud, almost shouting.

"Please don't make this more difficult than it needs to be, Mr. Epstein. If you and your associates at Spangler & Spangler interfere any further, the consequences for all of you could be dire. The federal government is dealing with this New Day situation. It must be handled very delicately and not by private counsel in court."

I sat down, squinted at her and remained silent as I tried to absorb all this. I hadn't had lunch yet, I was tired from running around New York all morning, and my head was starting to throb. In an effort to control myself and stay centered, I looked to my side, through the window, to the busy street with people hurrying about in the early afternoon sunshine. Ms. Cristobal said nothing and waited for my reaction. Swiveling my chair around to face her again, I said, "Show me some identification. Who are you with?"

"Suffice it to say I am affiliated with the Feds. Here is my telephone number." She reached for the pad on my desk and jotted down her number. "We can stay in touch this way. We appreciate your concern in this matter, but you must believe that we have the matter in hand now. Do we understand each other?" she asked, a phony power smile creasing her unfriendly face.

"You're going to have to give me more to go on, Ms. Cristobal. Since you seem to know my business, let me tell you that I have clients who are being affected in a Queens public school in ways we will have no possible idea about until, Heaven forbid, disaster strikes them. Children are being exposed every day to some sort of foreign, very possibly toxic, substance. Parents are complaining. There's no transparency about this situation at all from the school. Nobody was alerted to it in advance and no prior consent was obtained from the parents. New Day spins a yarn that they are trying to change the world, and suddenly here you are, telling me the U.S. government is aware of what's going on…and I'm supposed to stand down?" I said, shaking my head with disgust. "This won't do, young lady. It won't do at all."

The woman remained as unruffled and stolid as the Rock of Gibraltar. She slowly rose from her chair and said authoritatively, "Mr. Epstein, your government is telling you to stand down. Don't make things difficult for yourself and everyone involved."

"Are you *threatening* me?" I challenged her.

"Mr. Epstein, we never threaten anyone. But we do keep our promises," she said in a placid voice. She extended her hand, and with a lukewarm smile, said, "We're all on the same side. Thank you for taking the time to speak with me this afternoon. I will leave you now."

"I wish I could say it was a pleasure, but I'm not in the habit of lying," I retorted. When she realized I was not about to shake her hand, Ms. Cristobal turned, opened my door, walked through the office and, I hoped, out of my life.

It was not even 1:20 on a Tuesday afternoon and I had already had two unpleasant confrontations today. I poured a cup of coffee and asked Jane to order lunch for me. I had not only a lunch but also this latest warning to chew on and digest. As it was Tuesday, this was Josh's chess club afternoon at school and he would not need to be picked up until five o'clock. I used the time to meditate on this latest shock-and-awe presentation and confer with Mel and Reggie.

After explaining to them what had occurred, we agreed to hold off filing court papers for another day, and instead to meet on Wednesday morning to discuss the latest developments. By four o'clock, Jane was occupied with intake for a new client and I knew she'd be tied up at least another hour, so I drove up to I.S. 406. I parked nearby and filled my pipe for a smoke before getting Josh. So far, so good—no goons waiting outside to scope out the school and report to New Day and whomever else. Reading between the lines of what the mysterious Ms. Cristobal had said, I assumed New Day and the Chinese makers of G88 were thick as thieves and that the U.S. government was working on a bust. Perhaps it would be better to stay in the background until the entire picture became clearer? My mind raced along a decision tree, trying to assign names and scenarios to each of the branches.

When Josh exited with his buddies around five o'clock, one of the kids said, "Hey, Josh, your grandfather's here for you."

Josh guffawed and replied, "Nah, man, he's my mom's boss," and skateboarded over to me.

"Yo, Harry, guess what?"

"I can't guess. I'm old and tired. Just tell me."

"No blue gas today at two o'clock! First time in over seven months!"

I perked up. Could this sudden break in the daily pattern merely be coincidental with today's odd meeting with Ms. Cristobal and the morning meeting with Agatha, or could it somehow be related? Or had the school simply run out of G88? My mind began speculating wildly on the possibilities.

"Any idea why?" I asked Josh.

"Beats me," he replied. "When two o'clock rolled by, I didn't even notice, because I was so used to the whole rigmarole that it wasn't even freaky to me anymore. But by about two-fifteen, it struck me that I didn't smell that special fragrance and the kids hadn't gone into trances."

"Something's going on, Josh, and I think we might be the reason, but I can't be positive," I mused. "Mel and Reggie and I had meetings yesterday and today with New Day. I think they're the ones who brought in that Dr. Wang to the school to talk to you. But then just this afternoon, some lady came to my office to warn us to lay off New Day and this entire situation. She said she was from the U.S. government, but wouldn't say more."

"Do you believe her?" Josh queried, his voice rising in disbelief.

I shrugged my shoulders and raised my eyebrows in uncertainty. I raised my pipe to my lips and lit it again. After a few puffs, I turned to Josh and exclaimed, "It's been a confusing day, no question about it."

"Something else, Harry," Josh added. "Just before dismissal, an announcement was made over the loudspeaker that school's closed tomorrow. No classes."

I stopped dead in my tracks. I felt like ice water had been thrown on my face and my breathing had stopped for a few seconds as my mind grappled with the problematic timing of this latest development. "But…tomorrow is not a holiday," I said with a nervous lilt. "Did they give a reason?"

"Nope. Mrs. Hardy just said she'd see all of us on Thursday, and that was that. No reasons, no discussion, no nothing. It was like it had just happened out of nowhere," Josh observed.

I felt like I was standing on shifting sands as the tide ran out. My instincts told me something was brewing. Something not good.

62

On Tuesday evening, I got in touch with the Untouchables. Since Wednesday was predicted to be a gorgeous spring day and nobody had expected to have the day off, we all agreed to meet in the park around two o'clock to talk about the latest developments. For sure, everyone in our group was commenting about how the fact there had been no release of blue gas that afternoon, combined with the announcement right after that about school closure on Wednesday, might be a big deal. Everybody had a different guess as to what that big deal might be. To say we were all anxious would be an understatement.

We gathered at our usual spot in a meadow and sat in a circle. "So," I began, in my role as ringleader and Exposer-of-the-Blue-Ooze, "I guess we all know something must be going on at 406, but what it is, who knows? You guys all remember Harry, my mom's boss, right? Some of your parents have met him too, to sign the papers we need for court. Well, on Monday and Tuesday, he and his lawyer buddies went to see the people at New Day. New Day owns the car that drove that Dr. Wang guy away from 406 the other day, after he gave me that line of bullshit about wanting my toothbrush exhibit to show his daughter in China. Who the hell brings some American kid's science exhibit back to another country to show his daughter? What does he think, we're all fucking stupid or something?" Lots of giggles and heads bobbing in agreement.

"So, anyway, after Harry's other lawyer, Reggie, wrote the complaint letter to the Board of Ed., I guess they showed it to New Day, and New Day telephoned Reggie that they wanted to discuss this directly with him and to leave the Board of Ed. out of it for now. So, Harry and Reggie and his old man, named Mel, all went up to New Day on Monday, and again yesterday morning. Seems New Day wanted to make some sort of deal, but they wanted me to go to their offices, and they wouldn't say why. They wanted all the toothbrushes too. My mom said, 'Hell, no,' so that was the end of *that* idea. And the lawyers said 'no' to the deal New Day was proposing. From what Harry said, New Day wanted to pay them off bigtime to shut up and forget everything. So that was yesterday morning, like I said. Then—Bingo!—no gas attack yesterday afternoon and school gets closed right after that!" I looked around the circle. Some eyes on me, some eyes on the ground, but all eyes focused wherever in deep concentration. "What do *you* guys think?" I probed.

"Could be they just ran out of the blue gunk, man. Might be on again tomorrow, same as usual," said Nicky Lin.

"Nah," shaking her head, "I bet they're up to something," opined Sarah Abramowitz, eyes gazing into the distance, then zeroing back in on the kids. "The timing is too close for this to be some random accident." Sarah was smart. She was always an "A-" student and the blue ooze wouldn't have improved her brain at all, despite what her teacher had told her about expecting even better marks. She was always helping her friends with homework and she still found time to be on the girls' soccer team and play piano at all the school events. I sort of liked her but she thought—or at least used to think—I was a dork, not that she ever said so, but I could tell from the way she used to throw her eyes to the sky when I'd just be me.

"So, what's Harry going to *do* now, Josh? *Huh*?" asked fidgety Phil Chapin.

"Well, that's the crazy part, guys. He was all set to file the papers in court to stop 406 from pumping in the blue gas, and then—oh, yeah—this is *big*, I forgot to tell you guys—so yesterday afternoon, probably right around the time the school shut off the gas—okay, maybe they ran short of it, but I think Sarah's right—some lady shows up at Harry's office to threaten him not to do anything else about New Day and the gas! Says she's from the government—like, Washington, see?—and he's to knock it off, and that she'll deal with it."

That had all the kids buzzing. "Man, this is getting really bizarre," said Johnny Jackson. "Was Harry scared?"

"I don't think so. But it really confused him. He said this must be hot stuff if the government is getting involved and warning him to stop. But he still wants to file the papers in court."

A chorus of "Good" and "Yeah, let's get these guys" reassured me that these kids wanted to go all the way. I'd let Harry know he still had everyone's support to roast those fuckers.

 **JOSH**

On Thursday, I woke up at the usual time, ate the usual breakfast of orange juice and toast with honey, dressed in the usual clothes for a warm late spring day, laced up my usual sneakers, gave Mom the usual kiss and waved goodbye in the usual way to Grandma, bounced my usual basketball along the sidewalk, and skateboarded through and around all the pedestrians along my usual route to school. I saw kids I knew from other classes, some I knew by name but most only by sight, and almost all of them had fallen under the influence of the blue ooze. They were bright-eyed and bushy-tailed, looking like model junior citizens, wholesome and cheery and like they had just leapt off ancient *Boys' Life* and *Girl Scouts* magazine covers into real life, ready to take on the world, although in the mellow, orderly way they'd become adjusted to over the last few months. They weren't of the 21st Century, but seemed more like from 100 years ago. There was a lot of life to them but not the high-amp electric neutron-charged bristling kind that used to run through them.

I went to the schoolyard as usual, found Johnny, Ronny and few of the guys and shot b-ball for a while until line-up and the Green Witch Queen led us upstairs. Once seated, an announcement by a strange, new voice came across the squeaky muddle-toned loudspeakers in class. The voice definitely didn't have the thick New York accent most of the people running the school had, and like all us kids had.

"Ladies and gentlemen of I.S. 406: Mrs. Dorsey, Mrs. Moskowitz and Mr. Rugani have been temporarily reassigned to new positions outside of I.S. 406 and have asked me to let you all know how much they will miss you, and how very proud they are to have taught you. They express their deep gratitude to the Board of Education and to your families for the many years they were able to contribute to your education and cultivation as responsible young people."

The voice went on to announce a new Principal, Assistant Principal and head of the Science Committee and asked us to give them our full cooperation in making them feel welcome at 'our happy community.' The new Principal, Mr. Deakins, had previously served as Principal at various schools in the "Great State of Arkansas," the voice intoned; his Assistant Principal, Ms. Schulmeister, had been affiliated with schools in the "Great State of Utah," and the new head of the Science Committee was Dr. Wang, a scientist from China who had been so impressed with our school that he had made a special request to be allowed to serve as head of the Science Committee of our school.

What the fuck! Dr. Wang! Could this be *the same*…?

All around me, my classmates writhed with excitement. The room was filled with sounds of restrained glee, comments like "how wonderful," and other ridiculous murmurings from these pitiful wimps.

The thought of Dr. Wang being a regular fixture in school suddenly made me feel nauseous. I raised my hand. "Yes, Mr. Lee?" asked Mrs. Hardy in her haughty way.

"I don't feel so well, Mrs. Hardy. May I call my mother to take me home?" I asked with a face calculated—naturally and effortlessly, in this case, since I was far from pretending—to evince extreme discomfort. I felt like I was turning green. "I need some cool air. I need a drink of water," I pleaded.

I endured her condescending stare for what seemed like an eternity until she finally relented with a laconic, "Fine. Go to the Main Office. Tell them to telephone me after they've sorted you out."

Sure, whatever the hell that meant.

JOSH

I had to get air, I had to get to my feet and walk and think. I plodded down the hallway, very confused about what had happened in the school. Was this all a coincidence? No blue gas on Tuesday, no school on Wednesday, then new top administrators on Thursday...something was happening fast. Was the blue ooze out and were we going back to normal, or at least what I thought used to be normal at the beginning of the school year, before this wackiness had begun, this massive takeover by the goody-goodies? Did this mean no more goons cruising outside the school and threatening me and my family? Maybe Harry and Mel and Reggie had scared them all away, like the tough lawyers I hoped they were?

I schlurped down mouthfuls of water from the hallway fountain while I pondered what to do next. Should I wait until dismissal and then report this to Harry and Mom in the afternoon? I decided to hang in, took a few deep breaths, reversed course and plodded back to class.

Lunchtime came, same old routine. Took the basketball with me, wolfed down a hot lunch and OJ, and made for the yard. Started shooting hoops with a few of the guys. The weather was really fine. The girls were milling around watching us dribble, pass, bob and weave, shoot. I liked having an audience.

As the ball left my hand, arching up toward the hoop, from behind me in a heavily-accented voice that was vaguely familiar, came words into my ear in a very soft, almost caressing tone, "Very nice, Mr. Lee. And I still want your 'toothbrush exhibit.'"

What I felt at that moment is hard to describe. It's not pleasant to recollect. It was a voice from a nightmare. It was cold eyes stinging the nape of my neck. It was a shock of electricity traveling up my spine. It was my throat constricting and my mouth going dry and metallic with the taste of fear. It was my eyes staring straight ahead and too frightened to look away from the hoop. I never saw where the ball hit or landed. There was no ball. There was only my beating heart.

When I finally gained the nerve to turn around, I saw nobody.

"Yo! Josh! What's the *deal*, man?!" Ronny sounded peeved for the first time in many months, since he was a Blue

Breather. "You shoot and then just stand there like a mannequin?"

"Yeah, kind of *weird*, dude," echoed a couple of others.

I looked from face to face all around me. "Did you guys see somebody behind me talk to me while I shot?"

They looked at each other with an assortment of frowns and down-turned mouths, like I had just asked the stupidest question in the world. "You loony, Josh? Maybe you should have gone home instead of coming back to class this morning. The teacher told you to go the Office, right? You go?"

"Nah, I…I felt better after walking around a little, and there's nothing to do at home anyway, so…."

They shook their heads. "You better sit down, man. You don't look so good," said Mickey.

I sat out the next little while until the whistle blew. Johnny Jackson came over to me and said, "Dude, you look like you just saw a ghost. You're sweating. What happened?"

I was afraid he'd think I was whack, but here it went anyway. "Johnny, I could have sworn I heard a Chinese guy's voice behind me calling my name and saying, 'I want your toothbrush exhibit.'"

"What the *hell*, man!" Johnny said aloud, so loudly that several other kids turned to stare at us. In a lower voice, he said, "What the hell are you *talking* about?"

I shook my head, must have been at least 20 times, as I responded, "I dunno, man, but it's so bizarre, I could swear that Dr. Wang guy from a week or two ago…the one who had come to see me in Mrs. Dorsey's office…that he was right in back of me saying that to me as I was shooting the hoop. It was so real. That's why I froze."

"You need to *relax*, dude. Okay? Mrs. Dorsey and the others are gone, and maybe the gas is, too. It's gonna be cool now," he said confidently as he patted me on the shoulder.

I tried to chill, but it wasn't easy. "Hell, Johnny, only us Untouchables will even realize there's no gas anymore, if it really stops at all. The Blue Breathers never even knew it was there, never remembered anything about it after they came out of their trances every day. I just hope it's over." I shook my head as if trying to rattle a nightmare out of my memory.

The whistle blew and we parted ways to head upstairs to our classes. Afternoon was nothing out of the ordinary, and when two o'clock came…nothing. So now it was three days in a row with no blue gas treatment. Maybe this really was the beginning of the end, I told myself. I started to have a good feeling, like cresting a hill on the skateboard and hoping it was all downhill from there, no more steep climbs.

I had Music Club after dismissal and spent the next two hours in there, doing homework, snacking and strumming a guitar while kids played other instruments and jammed to old arrangements and new ones they'd cooked up. By five o'clock, the sun still shining brightly outside, we knocked off and I walked through the school's front lobby toward the main exit door to leave, expecting Mom or Harry or someone to give me a lift back.

Just as my hand reached for the door to the street, I heard the same accented voice from a short distance behind, calling out to me, and not soft at all this time, but firm and commanding, "Good night, Mr. Lee, and bring me the toothbrush exhibit tomorrow so we won't have any trouble."

64

I turned and there he was! Standing on the other side of the lobby, in his crumpled white shirt with funky purple tie and goofy tight suit, was Dr. Wang!

Holy shit!

I swallowed like never before and just about choked on it while my chest constricted. My eyes practically popped out of their sockets. The skin on my skull stretched so tight that my ears even stiffened. I spun around quickly to get away, practically pushing the door off its hinges, and ran for dear life out of the school. Harry was outside waiting for me.

"Whoa, hold your horses there, Big Guy!" he cried as I came galloping at him. He looked serious. "You okay?"

"Fuck *no*! I'm *not* okay! Not by a long shot! We gotta *move*!" I gasped for breath.

What was even more odd was that Harry didn't look surprised, just very cautious. It was almost as if he expected something "not okay." I grabbed his sleeve and pulled him along as I walked fast.

"Are *you* okay, Harry?" I probed, watching his facial expression darken.

"Let's get to the car," he said.

Once inside and driving back to the office, he said, "Something big is going down, Josh. Katie Spangler, Mel's daughter, called me today to say the Reggie and Mel haven't been heard from all day. She's been calling their cell phones, but no answer. She's very nervous and if she doesn't hear from them by tonight, she's calling the police. I'm very worried for them."

"Is Mom okay?" I blurted. Funny, I usually never thought much in terms of her safety. She was always so strong and determined, but she was the first person to jump to mind and worry about.

"Yeah, she's fine, she's in the office waiting for you."

"And Grandma and Sister?"

"All fine, last I heard," he assured me.

"You're never gonna believe this, Harry, but that mad scientist guy, Dr. Asshole Wang, who I told you about, is now working in my school! And he just fucking threatened me on my way out!" I told Harry all about it, and also about the mysterious experience in the schoolyard, of sensing Dr. Wang whispering in my ear the same sick command: "Bring me the toothbrushes."

Harry was deep in thought as he drove, but I knew he was listening to me because he was murmuring "hmmm" and "um-hum," and nodding his head. It's the type of thing he often did in the office while reading, writing and thinking to himself. Sometimes he even talked to himself, not loud, but you knew there was a conversation going on between Harry and Harry. Must be an old person thing.

"We know Dr. Wang is somehow connected with New Day, because you saw him get into their car not long after you had met with him and then he argued with Mrs. Dorsey and left her office. And now, immediately after we met with New Day on Monday and Tuesday, the Principal and Assistant Principal and the science guy are all pulled—no idea to where—and these hicks from the middle of nowhere that you told me about on Tuesday, plus Dr. Wang, all show up to take over the school. I'm wondering—actually, I'm assuming now—that New Day has clout in very, very high places, Josh. This is intense."

"No shit, Sherlock!" I said sarcastically, if rudely.

"People in lofty places in the Board of Ed. must have thought Mrs. Dorsey wasn't gung-ho enough. Or maybe it was New Day that dictated its demands to the Board of Ed.…." His voice trailed off as it became more apparent to him, and me, that New Day must have been calling the plays.

"But how did they get those characters from fucking Hooterville in here? That's what I don't understand," I asked.

"Josh, this reaches higher and farther than we know. We've got to get into court on this quickly before it snowballs out of control."

I just stared out the window while he drove. Too many inexplicable events were occurring in a super short period.

"I'll keep in touch with Katie tonight, and first thing tomorrow, I'm heading back to the Board of Ed. to speak with those two big shots whom we spoke with recently. I need to confront them on all of these changes at 406. Then I'll deal with that Agatha in short order. And to hell with the U.S. government telling me to stay out of it."

When we arrived at the office, Mom was working with a client and assembling documents Harry needed for the client's upcoming hearing. When the client left a half-hour later, she asked Harry whether there was any further word from Katie or Jenny.

"Not yet."

She looked very upset. "I don't like this. I'm worried about our safety! Harry, you don't understand what can happen. I know how much damage those people in China with so much power can do. They will use their power to hurt us too if we interfere with their plans."

"Jane, you knew this situation a few months ago when we had our meetings at Jenny Spangler's lab. We're already committed to exposing them. I realize there may be some risk, but I don't think we're in danger here."

"What are you saying? Some *risk* but no *danger*?" Mom said with increasing frustration. "What's the *difference*? They already threatened my family! You heard what Josh told us the other day. And you stood near them when they were watching kids coming out of school. These people don't play *games*, Harry. And now *nobody* knows where Reggie and Mel are!"

Mom certainly had a point, although there was no use in

freaking out now. We would just have to ride out the rest of the evening and hope tomorrow showed improvement. I didn't dare to tell her about Dr. Wang now working in 406 because that would have sent her over the edge. Harry and I looked at each other with that kind of conspiratorial glance that said, "Let's keep a lid on this."

65

O n Thursday evening, Katie and Jenny told me they still hadn't heard from Reggie or Mel. I told them to call the police and file missing persons reports, and then make notes on the last time they and anyone else had heard from son and father. We'd be able to piece together a timeline and geographic scenario for each man leading up to the moments they had disappeared.

Before going to sleep, I checked in with Jane. Everything was copasetic over there, with doors double-locked and windows latched tight. At least I knew they'd make it through to Friday morning unharmed.

Came Friday morning and Jane said she'd taken no chances, for she'd accompanied Josh to school to ensure he arrived there without a hitch. Her daughter was at college in New England and safely outside New York. Granny was doing her usual thing, which wasn't much of anything, even at the best of times.

I left Jane in charge of the office around 10:00 a.m. and drove to Manhattan unannounced to see Martin Chisholm and Dorothy Romski. There'd been too many coincidences for the last few days' harrowing activities to have been random occurrences, and I felt certain those two were in on this. I'd turn them upside down and shake the facts out of them, if need be. I was angry, pumped for action, and anticipating a confrontation.

The result was anti-climactic.

HARRY

There were no Martin Chisholm and Dorothy Romski to shake upside down.

The receptionist at the Board of Ed. said they were not in their offices. Refusing to take that for a final answer, I demanded to see each one's Administrative Assistant, next-in-command, whomever. They all said they had had no word from Chisholm or Romski that morning. No calls in to say they were busy at home or sick. Simply no contact at all. Telephone calls to their respective homes and cell phones, text messages and emails had gone unanswered.

My initial anger now gave way to bafflement. First Reggie and Mel, now these two luminaries of the Board of Education, unaccounted for. I left my business card with the missing executives' lieutenants and reckoned that if anyone had answers, it was Agatha.

I left the car parked downtown near City Hall, descended into the nearby subway station and chewed some thick and sugary pink bubble gum to exercise my nerves while I waited for the No. 4 express train up Lexington Avenue. Still had the comic inside the gum wrapper. Nice to see at least something hadn't changed in over 60 years.

About 20 minutes later I resurfaced a few miles uptown and walked to the building that housed New Day. Busy midtown office tower, swanky suits and dresses galore as far as the eye could see. Up elevator. The usual make-believe-nobody-is-in-the-elevator silence all the way up while I impatiently ascended to my destination. Out at the fifty-fifth floor. A steady pace as I proceeded left, then down a long hallway, then turned right to face New Day's entrance.

Only, there was no "New Day" stenciled on the beautiful glass double doors.

I looked through the doors. To the right, there was no furniture. To the left, there was no furniture. The place looked naked. What the hell?

I shook my head in confusion, but it was more likely self-doubt that I was trying to shake off. The wrong floor? I made the journey back to the bank of elevators, this time with a little less vigor in my step. I had to be careful not to slip into a blue funk that would wear me down. Not now, I told myself. Must figure this out.

I found the computerized building directory tucked in a corner of the lobby and typed in the company's name. Expecting to find a different floor number for New Day, I found instead… no New Day.

This made no bloody sense. I might have been mistaken about the floor number, but I knew this was the building.

Last option: find the building manager's office and inquire what had happened.

"Damnedest thing, Mr. Epstein," a Mr. Marston working in the manager's office told me after I'd introduced myself and explained the situation. "They were here yesterday, but suddenly moved everything out over the evening. They hadn't given any notice. They weren't late on rent payments. They still had over three prepaid months left on the lease." He was frowning and scratching his head with the same puzzlement I felt, although his frustration was limited to dollars and cents, whereas I had lost dear friends and, now, the most likely key to locating them.

My heart was sinking and I had to sit down. Marston brought me a cold bottle of water and I sipped slowly. I was breathing heavily and he eyed me with concern.

"If I hear anything, Mr. Epstein, I'll definitely call you," he tried to mollify me.

Words failed me. I was sighing repeatedly and had no voice. After a couple of minutes, I rose, thanked him for the water, left my business card, offered him a dispirited nod of the head and departed.

None of this made any sense, yet I was sure it was all connected. And it was becoming more nefarious.

Back to the garage, I was as quiet and withdrawn as the day my mother had died. My world was slipping out from under me and I was facing it all alone. I was fighting that miserable feeling of being in existential freefall.

Once back in the office, Jane could tell from my face that something was badly amiss. "Harry," she said in Mandarin, "what's wrong with you? Your face is so pale."

I explained to her what my morning had been like. It was not my first preference to tell her all the truth about this—not that I usually withheld the truth from her, but during the drive back to Flushing, I had thought about how I might avoid telling her the cold facts without lying about them, so as to spare her further grief—but finally I had opted for the easiest way out, that is, just spew out the details. It was therapeutic for me to talk it all out, but her reaction was anything but therapeutic for either of us. She started crying, and not the therapeutic type of crying. Hysterical crying. It took me and another member of the staff a long time to bring her back down to somewhere near manageable, but nowhere near normal.

"Harry, people in China disappear this way for a reason! Please get up to Josh's school as soon as you can! I'm afraid for him!"

"Jane, I know this is bizarre," I said, trying my ineffectual best to sound rational and calm her nerves. "I'm calling the cops now. And the Manhattan District Attorney and Queens District Attorney." That only stimulated more waterworks by accentuating the extremity of the dilemma.

I made the calls and left detailed messages, as nobody in authority at any location was available. I gobbled half a sandwich and an ale to ease my nerves. By that time, it was already two o'clock in the afternoon and Jane insisted I drive to pick up Josh because she was too shaken to drive. I got up to 406 around two-thirty, parked a couple of blocks from the school and walked over. I was still quite shaken up from the morning and would only be able to rest a little easier once Josh was in the car and we were safely back in my office. At this point, I thought all I could do was to take it day-by-day, try to make sure Jane and her family stayed safe, keep my own wits about me and push the police and county DAs to investigate. We needed answers pronto.

By 2:45 p.m. Mrs. Hardy was visible from where I stood waiting, and the kids were coming out in dribs and drabs. I recognized a few of the faces. No Josh. I waited another few minutes in the expectation that he'd gone to the bathroom or gone back upstairs to retrieve a textbook he'd forgotten to pack or was chatting with another kid. I kept an eye on my wristwatch. Three minutes. Five minutes. After ten minutes had passed and he still hadn't come out, my antennae started itching and I grew too impatient to keep standing on the sidewalk like a lamppost.

The school's front doors were open because kids were still streaming out and the familiar school guard who stood nearby smiled and asked, "How ya doin' today? Lookin' for Josh?"

I grinned back at her and said slowly, "I sure am. Getting tired of hanging around outside while he dawdles. Mind if I see whether he's in the Main Office?"

She waved me ahead and I entered the Office and asked the nearest seated assistant whether he could help me locate Josh. He responded with a knowing crease of the forehead and said, "I think he's in with the Principal, Mr. Deakins, right now. I'll let them know you are here to pick him up." I thanked the fellow and waited at the counter, drumming my fingers lightly as my mind raced.

Out of the Principal's office stepped spritely a tall, crisply-dressed, bespectacled man who looked to be in his late fifties. He walked over, smiled broadly, extended his hand which I took, then felt him pump it vigorously up and down as he introduced himself as Mr. Deakins. "I'm awfully glad to meet you, Mr....Epstein, isn't it?" His cheery Southern drawl was so pronounced that it seemed awfully incongruous in this Queens, New York school where probably some 60% of the students were New York-born Asian kids and almost all the teachers were native New Yorkers. This must be the Arkansan whom Josh had told me replaced his former Principal, Mrs. Dorsey. I had met Mrs. Dorsey in the past and was impressed with her dedication to the children's education as a holistic exercise in their upbringing—at least, until G88 became employed as part of the educational program. I wondered whether this new chap was part of the apparent new solution in eliminating Mrs. Dorsey and ending the blue gas treatment.

"Yes, Mr. Deakins, I am," I responded with equal, if forced, good humor in my voice. "I've come to pick Josh up."

"Of course, of course. He and I have just been having a

pleasant conversation in my office. It seems he had a tussle with another classmate during the afternoon and Mrs. Hardy thought it advisable if Josh met with me to discuss the problem. His guidance counselor is out today and the Assistant Principal is busy with other things." Mr. Deakins' manner was straight-forward and folksy, and he had mastered the method of getting on the inside and putting people at ease. His appointment as Principal might well be an positive change for the school, I pondered.

"Say, why don't you come with Josh and me downstairs to the school library where we can sit more comfortably to chat? If you're not in a great hurry, that is."

This was the first friendly reception I had had all day, and if it could help smooth things over for Josh in school, all the better. "Sounds like a nice idea, Mr. Deakins. I'd be pleased to," I replied with new-found vim in my voice.

Mr. Deakins brought Josh out of his office, mentioned to him what he'd just said to me, and the three of us walked down to the school library in the basement. Josh had a disgusted look on his face the whole way and kept muttering beneath his breath, "Fuckin' bullshit, all the time, here." We took seats around a rectangular table, Josh and I facing the windows that were built into the upper part of the wall, and Mr. Deakins facing us.

"Oh my, I almost forgot my manners," he exclaimed. "Let me get a bottle of water for each of you. It's so warm today." He jumped up from his seat, and left the room.

"What a polite fellow, eh, Josh?" I remarked.

"I'd rather be outside playing ball than sitting here with you two. No offense, Harry."

"None taken. We'll just chat for a few minutes and then leave," I assured him.

From behind me I suddenly heard, "I don't think so," in that same Southern drawl, only this time neither folksy nor comforting, but firm and threatening.

Someone had grabbed my forehead from behind and was covering my nose and mouth with a thick cloth. It was wet and had a vinegary, almost alcoholic reek to it. I noticed from my peripheral vision that someone had Josh in the same hold with a cloth to his face.

"Mr. Epstein," came a slow growl out of Deakins' mouth, as he sidled around the table to face me, "you have been a major, I mean, *major*, pain in the ass. There are forces at work here that you and your friends are diddling with that are way above your pay grade."

If there ever was an evil eye, he was giving it to me now. But my vision was growing dimmer.

"Now, we don't know why this kid hasn't been responding to the special formula, the way almost all the students here have been, but we aim to find out. And our Dr. Wang here has some ideas about how to figure it out."

A middle-aged Asian man walked over to join Deakins and glare at Josh and me. Josh had been squirming like a madman, but when Dr. Wang stood next to Deakins in front of us, Josh's arms and legs began lashing out. I had been trying to dislodge the grip around my head and face, but I felt a second set of arms restrain my hands.

Our attempts at freedom did neither of us any good. Over the next minute or longer, they stood there watching us, cold and expressionless, nodding to the people behind us and saying, "Continue."

My vision became blurrier and I felt an uncontrollable urge to sleep. I sensed that Josh had also stopped waving his arms and kicking out his legs and was slipping away.

And then I entered oblivion.

EPILOGUE

When Josh and Harry failed to return to the office that afternoon, Jane was frantic. She called numerous parents, none of whom could remember having seen either the boy or the older man at the school. She grabbed a taxi to the school, but it was already closed for the weekend. She grabbed another taxi to the police station nearest the school and reported them as missing persons. The police were patient with her, took down all the particulars and promised to open a file and investigate immediately. A policewoman, Officer Grant, accompanied Jane home and made sure she got settled for the evening, and left her telephone number so that Jane could call her at any time to follow up on the investigation. It would be a long and sleepless night for Jane.

"She's home now," said Officer Grant into her cellphone, back in the squad car. "I planted the bug under a table when she wasn't looking."

"Good," responded Agatha Lundy's voice on the other end. "We'll handle everything from here on."

ABOUT THE AUTHOR

Todd L. Platek has lived and worked in Taiwan and Mainland China at various times since 1975. Formerly a partner in the New York admiralty firms of Kirlin, Campbell & Keating, and DeOrchis & Partners, he has practiced maritime and commercial litigation throughout the United States since 1986. He divides his time between Athens, Georgia, and New York City, with his Labrador retriever, Selkie.

www.ingramcontent.com/pod-product-compliance
Lightning Source LLC
Chambersburg PA
CBHW021307250626

47155CB00002B/421